THE WITCHES
OF SERNA

Also by Morgan Spring-Glace:

The War of the Mountains
> The Witches of Serna
>
> Unseen Wrath
>
> Winter Fever (Autumn 2026)
>
> The All-Consuming Flame (Autumn 2027)

www.morganspringglace.com

https://www.instagram.com/morgan_springglace/

MORGAN_SPRINGGLACE

https://linktr.ee/morgan.springglace

THE WITCHES OF SERNA

Book I of the
War of the Mountains

Morgan Spring-Glace

ISBN 979-8-9914481-1-6 (paperback)
ISBN 979-8-9914481-0-9 (e-book)

Cover Design: Sam Kipp and Morgan Spring-Glace
Formatting: Morgan Spring-Glace
Editing: Sam Kipp and Morgan Spring-Glace
Maps by: Luke Bauer and Morgan Spring-Glace
Illustrations: Dale Cordes and Morgan Spring-Glace
Calligraphy by Esther Wong

www.morganspringglace.com

Acknowledgements

In this second printing, I am grateful to the seed of the idea to write, but I could not have started writing in the first place without Amanda Hemmingsen, who took a chance on me and gave me some much-needed encouragement.

To my editor, Sam Kipp, who also took a plunge with me on this.

To Jade, one of my test readers, for such enthusiasm and detailed feedback. Jade nearly made me cry when she started producing what I would consider my first fan art. Jade has produced some of the illustrations for the appendix on humans in the back.

To Tom, another one of my test readers, who has given me the honor of reading this story and providing a wealth of constructive feedback.

To Melissa, who has been crucial in proof reading and been a joy with whom to explore this world.

To Luke Bauer, who has helped me bring these many maps to life.

To Dale Cordes, who was the original cover artist for the first printing, who's masterful work is now an internal illustration

To my Mother, Sandra Spring, who has been incredibly supportive and has helped to inspire me to try making some of my own drawings, and for being a model of an artist.

To gamer developers, writers, story-tellers, musicians, historians, reenactors, and the internet at large for making such a breadth of information available.

And to you, the reader, for taking a chance with me…

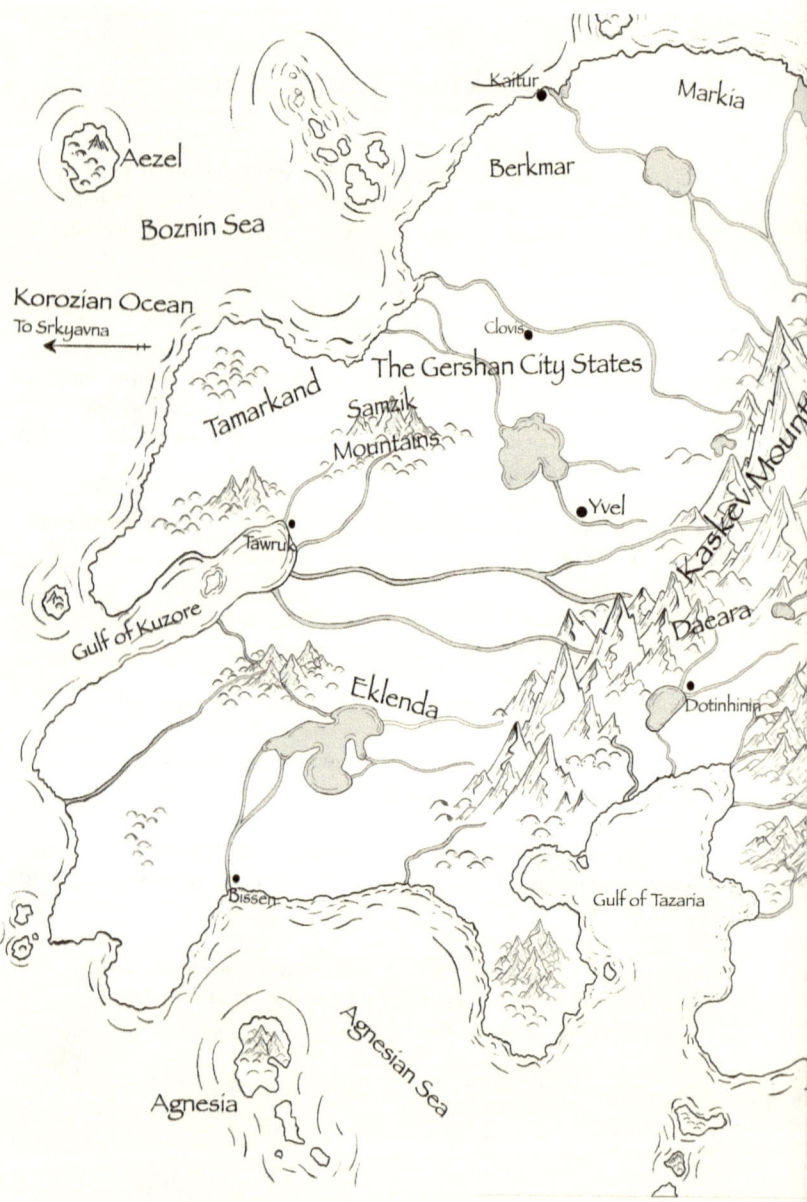

Figure 1: Map of the continent of Paeta

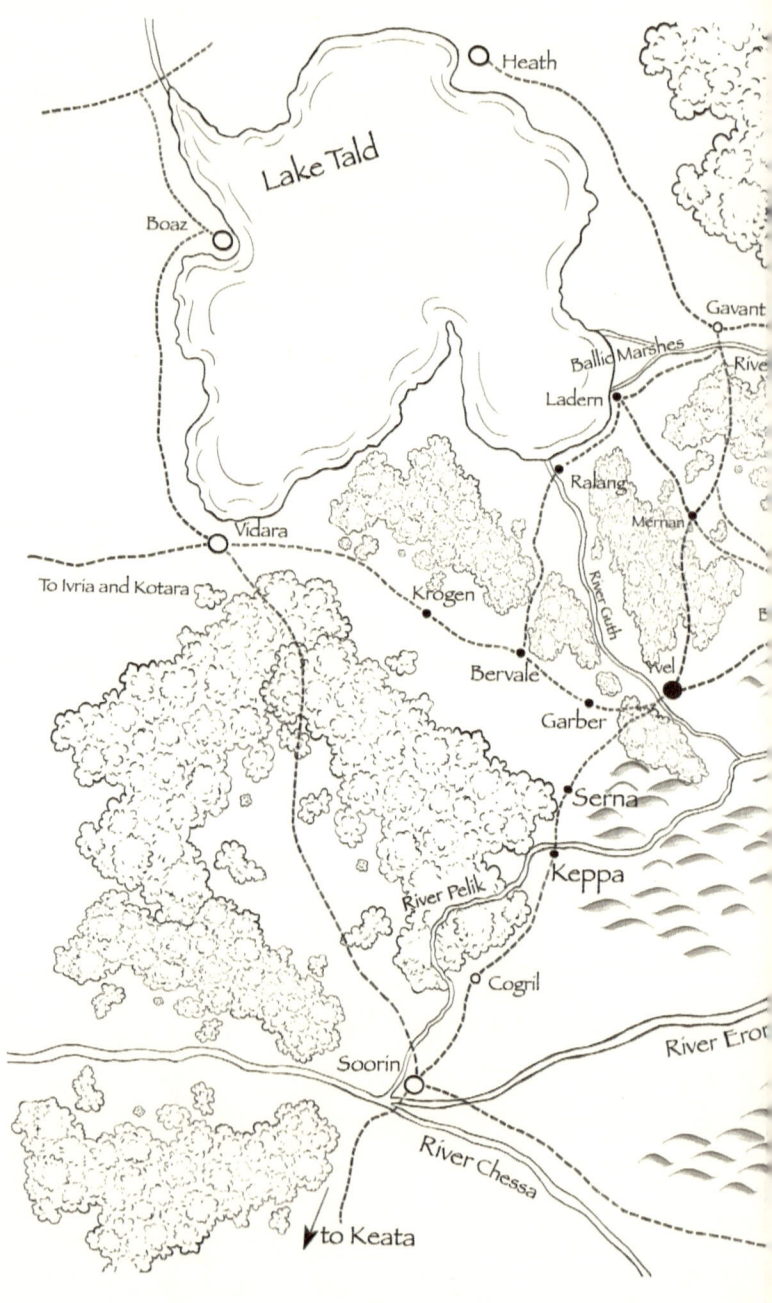

Heath

Lake Tald

Boaz

Gavant

Ballic Marshes

Ladern

River

Vidara

Ralang

Mernan

To Ivria and Kotara

Krogen

River Guth

Wel

Bervale

Garber

Serna

Keppa

River Pelik

Cogril

River Eron

Soorin

River Chessa

to Keata

Figure 2: Map of Yvel Principality and nearby vassal towns

To Versinth

Versingt

Karkev Mountains

Ardara

Legend
- ● Yvel
- • Yvel vassal towns
- ○ Other Princely cities
- ○ Other Princely city vassal towns

Contents

List of Figures and Tables

Prologue

Training yards, Rykooth Castle (Stone of Rykooth, to its current inhabitants).
Nestled in the heights of the Kaskev Mountains.
By the Elven Calendar, seventy-eighth day of Spring, 18028.
By the Goblin Calendar, eighteenth day of the Sixth Moon Cycle, 3113.
By the Human Calendar, Fryday (eighth day of the week), second week of Aiz (third month of the year), 792.
A sunny, late spring morning.

Oygariyet wiped the sweat from his dust-covered brow as he unconcernedly dropped his spiked mace to the dirt of the courtyard. He peeled back his dark blue lips into a toothy, jagged grin. The sunlight streamed over the walls and into the crowded courtyard, casting light and shadow onto the audience of the trial.

The towering hobgoblin unsheathed his skinning knife as he slowly strode towards Arkiban's writhing form. Lying on his left side with his left leg bent unnaturally from his crushed knee, Arkiban shuddered, his ribs crushed from Oygaritet's mace and his chest grotesquely heaving in its effort to draw breath. He looked up at Oygariyet with large, golden eyes set back over pock-marked, blue-skinned cheeks. Even in death, he must face his foe.

Oygariyet, aware of the kindnesses he could extend and the benefits he could reap, considered his options. The two hobgoblins wordlessly communicated. *A moderate path, then,* Oygariyet decided. He reached down, grasped his foe by a pointed ear, and hoisted his purple-skinned head up, twisting his beaten figure so that both figures, victor and vanquished, faced the largest part of the audience.

"By Leriyet's holy rules, I take this head and this tribe!" Oygariyet barked in the angular tones of his Goblin dialect, slitting the strap holding a ring of overlapping scales protecting Arkiban's neck. "This clan shall keep its name and serve me!" The crowd murmured in surprise, and Arkiban's battered body sagged in relief that his tribe's name would live on. Oygariyet jerked his wrist, and deftly pulled his long knife across Arkiban's neck. Crimson blood rushed out over the blade and Oygariyet's hand. Oygariyet worked and pulled, the skin and sinews of the fallen great one's neck parting and snapping. He wrenched the large ear with added force, drew his knife arm back, and freed the head from the bone with a sharp chop.

Oygariyet wiped the blade on Arkiban's cheek before sheathing it. He gripped both earrings on the Arkiban's other ear between two knuckles and yanked them free. Holding the head aloft, he strode towards the audience. Oygariyet, on an impulse, decided to grant one last kindness. He stuck one of his knuckles into his mouth and cleaned Arkiban's blood off of the knuckle.

"And I add his strength to my own and let the weakness drain away," he heralded. "I take his slaves as my due. You," he said, pointing to a purple-skinned hobgoblin woman that looked to be Arkiban's Second, "will lead this tribe in my name. I name you Indariyet." Oygariyet thrust the head at Indariyet, who fumbled to accept it in her surprise. "Present this to me and you shall earn your name." Oygariyet pocketed the earrings.

The crowd murmured as the two tribes, those of Oygariyet and of Arkiban–no, Indariyet–resumed their work. Oygariyet brusquely motioned to his Third. The Third, Oygariyet knew, would see to the quartering needs of Indariyet's immediate household of bonded slaves and retainers, if she had any of her own, or other chosen tribals who traveled with her. The Third would also make provisions for the smith to assist Indariyet in preparing Arkiban's head.

Oygariyet strode across the courtyard and seized the chain leashes of his four new slaves: two hobgoblin females, a goblin male, and an orc male missing two fingers from his right hand, with a wooden peg for his right leg below the knee. The orc was a typical greenskin with small tusks set in a large jaw, a broad nose, beady and almost-animal stupid eyes, and small, pointed ears. Though most orcs had black hair, some had grey, red, or green, like this one. His wiry, swampy-hued hair was shaved down to stubble, and his ears were pointed, *though his were those pitiful, small ears with mild points. Even in consideration of the ears, even goblins were superior to orcs*, Oygariyet thought to himself, tinged with contempt. The orc would have towered over Oygariyet by a full hand but for his peg leg. Oygariyet also noted he was missing two fingers from his right hand. *Why would Arkiban keep this one? It's a burden,* he puzzled.

The goblin was full grown, just past Oygariyet's waist, his skin turned dark blue, like Oygariyet's own, meaning that he was from the Liberator Side of the Mountains and that he had spent much time in the sun. He had all of his fingers, which meant he was either lucky or useful.

Ah now, here's a prize. Between the two hobgoblin females, one was a light-skinned grey, meaning she stayed indoors or in tents during most daylight, and was from far to the left side of the Mountains. She had a coarse mane of jet hair with finely pointed ears jutting perpendicular to her head. The other was quite the exotic, with her dark red skin. *She had to come from the other side of the Mountains or far to the right side*, he mused. Her hair was shaved short and had lost its intensity of color, but Oygariyet could tell that it would grow in with time. *There is more to her*, he mused more before shaking himself out of his daydreaming. He had things to do, after all. He bade the goblin in a manner deceivingly nonchalant, "Get my mace."

***

The next day brought fresh snow to Rykooth. Oygariyet's attendants sealed the windows and heaped more wood on the fires. High in the central mountains, the castle was nestled into the side of a rock face on a small plateau. The keep was built into the mountain itself, embedded walls and turrets creating a courtyard. A cramped settlement of crafters, herders, and farmers consumed the remaining space.

Oygariyet entered his hall. The hall had within it his throne as the Master of Rykooth, a map table, and a long feasting table, all situated around a large firepit which was used routinely for roasting meats, and when the occasion arose, celebrations. Lit torches mounted on the walls sustained a comfortable warmth in the space.

The time of celebrating the addition of Indariyet's Okaramine tribal banner under Oygariyet's own Zirn tribal banner had passed, so the fire was low. Oygariyet's Second, Third, and Fourth congregated around the feasting table, as were Indariyet and her newly promoted Second. Oygariyet's throne was set upon a dais, opposite the main entrance to the hall, with six of his personal slaves positioned on either side of his throne in various states of standing, kneeling, or sitting on the stone floor.

Oygariyet strode past the fire, up the two steps of the dais to three kneeling hobgoblin slave women staring at the floor. He placed a hand on the cheek of the blueskin. She looked up at his face as he moved his thumb over her mouth. His favorite. She had been with him for six winters now, since he had become the Master of Rykooth. The greyskin knelt and looked up obediently when touched, but the other one, the redskin taken from Arkiban, did not look up when he touched her cheek with his other hand. In mild irritation, his hand slid up and grabbed her ear, forcing her to tilt her face up, but she did not wince.

He smiled at them both. *Perhaps Arkiban had just taken her. She is completely untrained.* He knew he would have to oversee the training of the new additions, and knew that he could depend on his favorite for most of it. He would have to see his Third about getting her the herbs to help this one's hair grow to a desirable length and luster.

Turning, he strode toward the feasting table where the others waited silently. Indariyet stepped aside to reveal Arkiban's head, cast in bronze and polished to a dull shine, reflecting the flickering of the low, hissing flames of the central firepit.

"I offer you this trophy, Oygariyet, Great One of Zirn, Surent, Ablar, Kilindiban, and Master of the Stone of Rykooth. May it please you to add the banner of Okaramine to yours," uttered

Indariyet plaintively.

Oygariyet examined the head. This would be Oygariyet's sixth trophy of this type and he was deeply familiar with the process of crafting them. The small dimples from the sand-mold casting were mostly smoothed away, and it was completely unnoticeable where Arkiban's skin had been blemished and cratered. Arkiban's stern expression had been preserved, and would illustrate how the strength of the Okaramine would add to Oygariyet's own Zirn tribe.

"I accept. Lead them well or I shall pour out your weakness," said Oygariyet as he reached into his pocket and offered the two earrings. Indariyet took them, clenched her purple fists and joined them together in front of her, bowing to Oygariyet.

"Our strength united," intoned Indariyet.

"Let us take this feast, then," offered Oygariyet dutifully.

It was customary that the great one of a hosting tribe or stone would hold a nightly feast with any other tribal great ones sharing the space. Oygariyet, weary of ceremony, did not want another extravagant feast to welcome Indariyet and her Okaramine. This small observance was merely a formality, as he had immediately selected her after defeating Arkiban's challenge for mastery of Rykooth Castle.

"Great One, I have something to ask you. It is my own matter," began Indariyet.

"What is it?"

"The orc slave you took from the former head of Okaramine. I want to buy it," she said.

"Oh?" replied Oygariyet bemusedly, "I can only think of a few things you could use him for." Oygariyet chortled.

"Your price?" Indariyet insisted. She was not overstepping herself. Newly appointed or not, any great one was still a great one, and was allowed to boldly approach any other great one among the tribes–for any matter.

5

Oygariyet sighed. "For this? Ten mountains," he said finally.

"Done." Coins jingled as she immediately produced ten bronze coins, stamped silhouettes of mountains minted upon them.

The group ate contentedly in relative silence and adjourned to the map table. As the group settled around the central fire, Oygariyet noted that one of the slaves must have put more wood on the pit.

"I prepared a new map with your Second, showing the joined lands and our two mines," began Indariyet. The flames flickered brighter for a moment. Oygariyet glanced in irritation to see which slave had fed the fire. None were near the pit.

He turned back to the map. "There are wolves in those woods." Oygariyet indicated a forest nestled in a valley, near one of the mines. "I want you to be able to put two full fists of wolf riders in battle, and we need to discuss how you organize your fists. No more than six hundred warriors in a fist."

"We don't have enough houndmasters," explained Indariyet.

Light flared behind them as the fire in the central pit suddenly roared. The flames swirled in a column, as if trapped in a glass tube. Blades rasped from their scabbards as everyone whirled to the threat, Oygariyet gripping his long-hafted spiked mace with both hands.

"Magick!" exclaimed Oygariyet's Fourth.

"I COMMAND THE MASTER OF THESE TRIBES AND THESE CLANS," boomed a voice from the flames.

"Who dares!?" demanded Oygariyet's Second.

Jagged lightning coursed from the pillar of flame and struck the Second, sending him soaring backwards. Slamming forcefully into the wall, leaving his leather boots torn and smoking on the floor where he had stood, his blade clattered to the ground, arcing with blue bolts and sparks. The flames subsided with a hiss, leaving a glowing silhouette.

"IT IS I," boomed the silhouette, striding towards the assembly of witnesses from the pit, "WRITER OF THE HOLY RULES." The glow of the silhouette faded revealing a hobgoblin wearing a fine coat of mail, an axe, a mace, a sword, and a dagger across its belt. A bow and a shield were slung upon its back.

"GREATEST OF OUR KIND," it continued. The face was unmistakable. Oygariyet and the others jolted in shock. "I AM LERIYET. I COME TO CHARGE YOU, MASTER OF THESE PEOPLE."

"YOU WILL UNITE ALL OF THE TRIBES, ALL OF THE CLANS, AND YOU SHALL UNITE THE LESSERS UNDER YOU. THE GOBLINS, THE ORCS, THE BUGBEARS, THE OGRES, THE GNOLLS, ALL THAT YOU MUST. YOU WILL GO FORTH AND TAKE THE LOWLANDS FROM THE HUMANS. YOU WILL RIGHTFULLY EXTERMINATE THE ELVES. YOU WILL CEASE THIS SLOTH AS YOU CONTENT YOURSELF WITH PETTY HOLDINGS AND PITHY CONQUESTS. YOU SHALL MAKE YOUR NAME ACROSS ALL OF THE LANDS."

"I COMMAND YOU, LEST I PUKE WITH DISCONTENT. YOU ARE THE GREATEST AMONG OUR LIVING KIND AND THIS IS ALL YOU ARE? I COMMAND YOU TO THIRST FOR GLORY AND CONQUEST AND NEVER BE QUENCHED! WHAT SAY YOU?"

Oygariyet trembled and dropped to his knees. "Yes, Greatest One. I shall make my name across this land. By your holy blessing, I will unite all."

"DO NOT DISAPPOINT." Leriyet stepped back into the burning pit. "TAKE THE BLADE OF YOUR SECOND. I HAVE RIPPED HIS SOUL FROM HIM AND PUT IT IN THE BLADE. HE WAS STRONG AND THE BLADE IS STRONGER NOW. USE IT WELL."

Leriyet began to glow from his center until he became a shining silhouette again. Flames roared into a pillar and, in an instant, he had vanished.

The room turned eerily quiet. Oygariyet stared at the pit in disbelief for a moment. Getting back to his feet, he slammed his open palm on the table. Everyone startled, shaken from their dazes.

"Messengers. I need messengers to the other tribes. Send word to your outlying friends. Send to Garsiyet and Jolaban at Kogylar," he commanded Indariyet. Then to his Third, "You are my Second now. Make messages to the rest of our tribe and vassals. Levy the goblin tribes–they will come if we send a fist to make it clear who they answer to."

He turned to Indariyet, "We will need to bring back the practice of clans among our own kind, like in the Greatest One's times. Great effort will be needed to bring the orc tribes to heel, but we will need their numbers and our own tribes leading them."

"I hear they have a Place, a city, in the Mountains further north. If we can seize the city and force the prominent tribes there to our side, we will have an easier time bringing the Mountain tribes under our banner. I trust you have some contacts in this city? What did they call the place? Place-called-Baan?"

***

Leriyet, the greatest hobgoblin that ever lived, immortalized by the collective belief of all goblinkind, written or spoken, and the legends of the number of souls he drank, stepped down from the summoning circle and cast aside the sword he had just switched with a transposition spell. Candle-sized flames flickered from the sands in the summoning circle, the glow of the runes subsiding. He strode down the stairs and looked down upon the Dark Elf maiden reclining on a settee in his laboratory. Her jet-black, supple form was covered in thin, draping and overlapping layers of deep blue and rich dark purple in the finest mushroom-fiber cloth. Only her hands, feet, neck, and face were exposed.

She had discarded her slippers to recline on the couch. *She is a very odd princess*, Leriyet observed. Her eyes were totally white, which meant she had undergone some of the rites and rituals, and her tiara glittered through the curtain of hair that spilled over the side of the divan. He had to stop his mind from wandering. He could not let himself desire her. Pairing with her in any way would bring an awful price.

"*Leriyet the Great*. You make it look so easy, Seros," she teased admiringly. Her eyes twinkled with a mirth and mischief that belied the danger she wielded to those that knew her.

The image rippled before fading away altogether. Where Leriyet stood was now a dark elf, like her, but plainly dressed and more drab-looking. Where her fine cloth and jewelry designated her of a high station, his plain garb of undyed browns and greys, ornamented with the occasional chemical stain from labor in a room like this, clearly painted him as a working wizard, lacking any affiliation to a strong house.

"You are too kind to me, My Princess," Seros replied with a small bow. "I am your humble servant for the duration of my contract."

"Your modesty is boring, Seros." Her voice grew coy, "What if we made this a more permanent arrangement?"

I prefer my soul and my long lifespan, thank you, Seros mentally answered. "My Lady, I do know I am quite good with illusions and charms, make no mistake. Nonetheless, I shall discharge this contract and you shall have the effect you desire. I find permanent affiliations with anyone... unhealthy," replied Seros as he moved over to a table laden with open books, diagrams on paper, and sealed bottles of variously colored sands and powders.

"Oh, that is boring, too," she said in her lilting Elven voice. There was a characteristically different tonal pattern to the cadence of an aristocratic Dark Elf and low-born one, like himself. "Do not make it too easy for them, though. It would be a chore if they actually win."

Seros looked up in mild surprise, "Oh?"

"Oh, yes, of course!" she explained. "They will not get what they want. But I will get what I want. I always do." She looked at him predatorily.

Somewhat flustered, he stammered, "Of course, My Lady. That makes this contract considerably simpler, and I will have to refund some of the fee." *Debts to you are unhealthy*, he worried. "There is much less to manage if you do not wish me to ensure their success."

"Oh, you *are* boring!" she accused. "I suppose you can have your boring, safe life, then!" She huffed in exasperation. "Keep the extra fee and show me your *boring* list of other *boring* services. This is not the only little project, you know. We will not get what we want from this endeavor alone."

"At once, My Lady." Seros shuffled a stack of papers before producing three lists of various services. "Far be it from me to question, My Lady."

"Hmm," she studied the lists and pointed towards the scribbles. "I think these three. What do you think, Risiar?" The other Dark Elf in the room who had been silently sipping his tea and watching set aside his cup, rose from his seat on the other side of Seros' table, and leaned over to see the items the Princess indicated.

"That one, too," Risiar, who had been silent up to this point, said flatly.

"There now," she said to Seros, "I can always trust Lord Risiar to catch that last thing."

"Very good, My Lady," Seros said deferentially.

"Any issues with the sword?" Risiar asked Seros.

"No, Excellency. They did not notice the switch," Seros said.

"You are certain that they will not notice? It would go poorly if they suspected any tampering."

"By the Ways, I took much care in copying every detail from the swords of Oygariyet and his close associates. They have the soul-infused blade, and I possess the original, here, along with the other infused doubles," Seros said calmly.

"Good. How soon can hobgoblins be ready, Master Seros?" Risiar looked up from the list at Seros, his gaze boring into Seros.

His eyes still had their pupils and purple irises. Risiar had not undergone any of the rituals. *Those eyes.* Seros immediately dropped his gaze to the floor. *Do not let him think you would be a challenge.*

***

"You are a poor host," accused the dwarf in his own coarse language.

Risiar smiled placidly, having already lowered himself to speak in this dialect of Dwarvish, its sounds so disparate from that of the superfluously elegant Elven. "So harsh, Lord Garitan. I have provided richly for you and your entourage. Let us address this matter with measured perspective."

"Do not hide behind this lavish bundle of falsehoods," replied Garitan. "Feasts and

entertainment are all fine, but you send for me just to insult me? You would have me return to

my king with *this*?" Garitan swept an arm wide in an exaggerated show of outrage.

"Lord Garitan, please be reasonable. We have been cultivating this business relationship for the last seventeen flood seasons, and have agreed that we would buy minerals, ores, materials, and such exclusively from his majesty, the King Nerim. We have an increased need over the next five flood seasons, and this is our new need." Risiar indicated towards the ledger in front of Garitan as he patiently explained.

Garitan rolled his eyes. "Yes, yes, I know that. You know that. I know you know that. You know I know that. Get to it and stop dancing around the point. You know the king's mines cannot maintain this quota," replied Garitan irritably.

"Oh?" Risiar feigned surprise. "The king's mines cannot keep the quota."

"DON'T YOU CONDESCEND TO ME!" roared Garitan. "This is exactly the insult I mean!" *That should do it*, thought Risiar. The incense should be taking its effect. He just needed to provoke Garitan to an agitated state and have him inhale deeply. Seros, his presence concealed by an ornate screen, would be monitoring the developments, maintaining a ward against the fumes so they would not affect Risiar or his staff. Risiar changed tactics at the cue.

"Tell me, dear Garitan–" Risiar began.

"*Lord* Garitan," Garitan corrected.

"*Lord* Garitan, excuse me," Risiar continued. "How is it that the great nation of Drenia, ruled by the Iron Crown, which rests upon the noble brow of Nerim, son of Neril, with all of its industrious dwarves, makers of the world as they are, cannot produce as stories have told of them producing?" Risiar gently needled.

Garitan blinked blearily.

"Are you well, Lord Garitan?"

"Yes… " replied Garitan, blinking again and focusing on Risiar. Risiar paused. The dose

should have been strong enough for a dwarf, even one with such a mature health as Garitan. Risiar had used most of the scentless powder from Seros.

"Yes... your question... yes, because Drenia used to be larger. You would know this, I think, Risiar. Drenia lost several wars against Dranomar, Medria, and Aedon and lost some territory to the orcs around Ikria," explained Garitan.

Risiar knew the opportunity for suggestion was very brief. There were other ways to make a suggestion to one such as Garitan, but they were easier to detect by the subject and others.

"So, I should tell Princess Erisa that she should seek additional contracts with Dranomar,

Medria, and Aedon, and that we cannot rely on the storied capacity of Drenia so far that we must

establish contact with even those lowly creatures that infest Ikria?" Risiar broached.

"What? No!" Snapped Garitan.

"Then, what to do? Are you telling me that Drenia shall endeavor to reclaim what is rightly its own?"

"What is rightfully ours... " Garitan mused under the influence of the incense.

"No need for us to decide right now, Lord Garitan. I appreciate the effort you have made to journey here. Perhaps you can convene with your king and his advisors on the best method of addressing the situation—best for Drenia, that is," suggested Risiar. *That should put the seed in, firmly. To leave this unresolved and lingering with him. His only way of resolving it is through his king.*

"Yes... the king and his advisors... "

"And take this." Risiar presented a brass bottle that he took from a waiting servant. "A gift that you would have bought for your king. You know how your good King Nerim enjoys a stout spirit, and this is as stout as we can make them."

Risiar offering the bottle was the signal for Seros to adjust the ward from the next room, dispersing the rest of the fumes from the incense. A gentle breeze blew from the door as a servant retreated with the finished meals.

"Yes… a gift that I got for… " mumbled Garitan.

The window of suggestion closed and Garitan slipped back into predictably curt and irritable conversation, in which he informed and frequently reminded Risiar of the inconvenience that had been imposed upon him to journey all of the way to Urrissio, the city of elves exiled in the darkness, merely to return to convene with his king, with nary to show but a paltry souvenir.

That was the confirmation that Risiar needed; confident that the suggestion had taken hold, he was assured that Garitan thought of the endeavor as his own idea. More importantly, the drug in the root liquor was quite challenging to detect, and should pass most of the drug and poison tests that Risiar and Seros knew the dwarves to possess. The sole matter left to uncontrolled chance was the assumption that Garitan would discuss the endeavor of reconquering historic Drenia over the bottle of root liquor, making Nerim vulnerable to suggestion and Garitan as the agent. If it failed, Garitan would fully believe that he procured the root liquor independently, and would bear the guilt if he was accused.

Garitan shook his head irritably and glared at his wine cup. "Empty." He eyed the room until a servant came forward to fill his cup. "I cannot as such return to my king with only this," he said, knocking the bottle of root liquor. "I shall make to the market and find another gift. I expect some recommendations for a good jeweler or some such. Surely your kind makes your version of precious metalwork, eh?"

The afternoon, if it could be considered to be such this far underground, progressed and Garitan left to investigate some of Risiar's recommendations before retiring to his guest apartment. The princess and Seros arrived separately in the evening, joining Risiar in his quarters.

"Oh, you are a dastardly one, Risiar!" Erisa accused

playfully.

Risiar's eyes moved to look up from a book before smiling without replying. He took his glass of wine as he rose to greet her. "Tricking poor Garitan like that," she mocked. "You should feel some–" she laughed, unable to stifle her amusement.

Risiar beheld her for a moment with a very small smile, though it was not one of shared mirth. "My Princess, if I were to regret anything in this endeavor, it would be the length to which Nerim will go to attain what we suggest to him and his subjects. While they are the best agents to keep the other dwarves from interfering with what Seros has set in motion, I fear–no, anticipate– that perhaps they will do something that we have not fully anticipated. Not that we cannot deal with whatever mess they make, but it can prove to be an awful chore."

Risiar turned and strode to the railing. The three were on the balcony of Risiar's manor on the outskirts of Urrissio, the great city of dark elves set in a series of connected caverns. The buildings dotted the floor of the caverns and lined the sides of stony spikes rising from the floor, some connecting to the ceiling of the cavern. It would take hours of travel to reach the other side, perhaps an entire waking cycle. Small lights marked each and every building, for the city never slept.

"Oh, Risiar, how you do worry," Erisa admonished. She stared wistfully at the view. "Still, you are the one that measures the risks. I never considered how much fun it would be to get things we want."

"We *will* get what we want, My Princess. We have paid the price, and it has been a long time coming." Risiar paused, taking in the view of the city that sparkled in its unending, sleepless night. Turning abruptly, he spoke to Seros, "I will have another task for you towards the end of the flooding season. I would make use of your canny skill for impersonation, but this one I say will be a challenge."

"A challenge, My Lord? More than impersonating the greatest hobgoblin that ever lived and convincing that entire race to descend the mountains and wage war on the rest of the lands?" Seros asked with subtle irony.

"Yes, I believe so. I would have you masquerade as someone known to another, demonstrate a skill, and like we did with Garitan, convince the person you impersonated that it was their own idea after you have taught them how to do it," explained Risiar.

Seros paused and considered. "Those will be several additional fees, Lord Risiar."

***

Nicholas absently brushed a strand of his otherwise neatly combed black hair out of his face as he finished studying the final ledger of the plan and tossed it atop yet another map scrawled with figures and icons of the Prince's Army. He reclined in his simply carved wooden chair, finishing his tea and setting the teacup down on a small stack of books, copies of *The History of the Ancient Kings of Gersh*, *The Life of Achadar*, and *The Life of Berin the Great* perched at the top.

"It'll work, my friend. It will all fall into place," the Blue-Eyed Man, putting his feet up and contentedly lacing his fingers over his belly, his well-dressed lazing contrasting with his lean and powerful form.

"It's terribly ambitious," cautioned Nicholas. "Besides, the Prince would never go along with it."

"Oh, truly," replied the Blue-Eyed Man, patiently. "Truly. We'll just have to wait for the Prince to be out of the way."

"That could be quite some time and we could be quite old by then. I'd be ready to be a

pensioner myself before he knocked off," said Nicholas, somewhat dismissively.

"It could be... but it doesn't hurt to be ready. You know, just in case." The Blue-Eyed Man brightened as a servant approached with a tray and placed a saucer and cup in front of him. The servant filled the cup with coffee that looked to be scarlet as the light shone through, but appeared black in the cup. The Blue-Eyed Man waved off sugar and cream, but accepted two small rings of fried dough.

The Blue-Eyed Man was rapt in savoring the first sip of his coffee, inhaling deeply with his eyes closed and leaning back in his own chair, the front legs rising off the floor.

Nicholas chuckled. "Surely, my friend," he remarked, picking up an almanac of crop yields from Marin Gersh from beneath a ledger of criminals, thieves, bandits, deserters and the like who were being held in the Yvelian prisons.

Finishing the second ring of fried dough, the Blue-Eyed Man rose to his feet, coffee in his hand. "Let me know what else you find. Since we don't know how much time we have, we can assume we have the luxury of continuing to plan."

Nicholas shook his head. "You never change."

The Blue-Eyed Man swallowed another sip of coffee before speaking. "Of course not," he said finally. "In this world of power, strength, weakness, uncertainty... cruelty and opportunity... you have to be able to depend on something, right?"

Chapter 1

Third Tower Library, Elven city of Ebariel, Elven Lands.
By the Elven Calendar, sixteenth day of Autumn, 18029.
By the Human Calendar, Sortingday (sixth day of the week), second week
of Banreni (seventh month of the year), 792.
A clear, breezy mid-autumn evening.

ingers gripped and drove the pen tip across the page, bleeding words in flowing Elven script. Lifting the pen tip with finality, the fingers grasped a jar of sand and shook some out on the page to aid the drying ink. The fingers wasted no time, immediately threading a needle and stitching the already finished pages together in gatherings of twenty. By the time that the hands had finished stitching the first four gatherings of twenty pages, the ink was dry on the last pages. The hands shook the pages and brushed off the sand before stitching the last seventeen pages together and setting the five gatherings aside. The hands moved forward on the desk and pulled a wooden block with a parallel arm extending over it and four cords stretched taut between the block and the parallel arm. The hands placed the gatherings against the cords, threaded a different needle and proceeded to sew the gatherings together. As the shadows shifted quietly, the last stitch holding the gatherings together was completed.

Pushing the block back to the edge of the desk, the hands reached under the work desk and into an open drawer, pulling out a prepared leather rectangle, a small jar, and a brush. Fingers dipped the brush into the jar and painted the stitching of the gatherings with glue and placed strips of cloth at the top and bottom of the spine of the gatherings. Once in place, fingers applied more glue and another strip of cloth that ran the length of the spine before adding the last application of adhesive and placing the gatherings in the center of the leather rectangle before folding the cover over the newly bound book. Hands wrapped the rest of the cover around the book and tied it shut with leather cord before placing it on the block again. Hands began to stitch the edge of the binding when the shadows shifted suddenly and covered the hands.

"Your pardon, but my light is being blocked," stated Tyrnimar. He shook his head tightly to shake unruly silvery locks of hair out of his eyes to view the unwanted guest, only to jostle his desk. His blue robes shuffled to catch the toppling glue jar and tipped it in the other direction. The visitor averted disaster by catching the jar and pinning it into place with the deft movement of a single finger.

"Oh," replied the intruder. "I came to deliver this summons."

Tyrnimar put down the needle and looked up in mild irritation. He pushed back the book sewing block. "A summons?" Tyrnimar examined the messenger's dusty clothing. The messenger was either a Sylvan Elf or a High Elf, judging by the brown hair and the bright green eyes. The messenger's complexion indicated a High Elf by its lightness, but her build told of long hours on the road and long nights in the rain, indicating the life of a Sylvan.

"Yes, from the Council of Guardians."

Tyrnimar's eyebrows raised a little in slight surprise. "The Guardian Council? A summons was brought here to Ebariel from Juin?"

"You are Tyrnimar Iquarren, studying under Under-Provost Isriaden?" she asked.

"Yes. It is really her that needs to be seen with a summons such as this," Tyrnimar insisted.

"I have seen her. She appointed you to answer this," she answered, producing the summons and a letter of appointment from a scroll tube at her belt.

Scanning the documents, Tyrnimar said at last, "Here, no rudeness is meant. The road must have been long. Dinner and a clean lodge can be provided. How are you called?" Tyrnimar rose, shouldered a leather bag stuffed to the brim with small books and stacks of notes loosely bound with cord, and collected his project.

"Eevarel Mazurnine of the Western Wood."

An hour later, Tyrnimar was serving a dinner of roasted vegetables and herbed hen with eggs from his pan over the fireplace. "Did the Under-Provost say why I am to go?" asked Tyrnimar.

"She did not, but the summons requires an aura reader," Eevarel answered.

"An aura reader? Why would an aura reader be needed?" Tyrnimar asked, "Are there no others?" he muttered to himself as he finished serving her portion.

"I cannot say really. Some requirement for the journey, I suppose," she shrugged.

"Journey?" Tyrnimar looked up with surprise, then realization flashed in his mind, "Oh…" he groaned quietly.

Eevarel paused. "Did you not read the summons?"

Tyrnimar hastily snatched up the summons and scanned the text again. His eyes reached lower and lower in the document, eyebrows pressing together in concentration until they slackened in annoyance. "This part did not get read earlier. These lands have not been left by me before."

"The Under-Provost said that, too. Worry not, this will be a very healthy group of Travelers," she assured bemusedly.

"A horse has not been ridden for fifty years, nor has a bow or sword been practiced!" Tyrnimar fretted.

"Hmm. Sounds neglectful." Eevarel tried teasing.

Tyrnimar, too caught up in his worries, failed to notice and stared at his food for a moment. "The memory must be regained by me," he resolved.

"I suppose so," sighed Eevarel, anticipating her company on the trip ahead. She tasted the roasted hen. "What did you do to this!?" she exclaimed in alarm.

"What is meant?" he asked, taken aback by her sudden remark.

"The taste! I watched you take the hen. You didn't rub it with any herbs, you barely cooked it. You barely had time to slaughter it! How is it that it tastes like this?" she accused.

"Oh." Tyrnimar exhaled. "Some herbal and saline charms were used," he said, adding, "and some cantrips for the slaughter."

She stared at him for a moment. "You used magic to cook?" she asked incredulously after a while.

"Why would I not?" he asked quizzically. "A tool is there. It should be used to the fullest where there is good to be had."

"Do you not think that is a little bit improper?" she asked.

"No," Tyrnimar simply answered, finishing his portion and still not comprehending Eevarel's objection. He picked up his book binding project and began to stitch the border.

"Why do not you use magic for that?" she asked.

"The charm is elusive," he answered and then sighed, "and there is no point in learning it before the trip."

"Why not?" she asked.

"The humans, of course. Magic must remain an unreachable legend for them," he explained.

"Yes, yes, I know," she answered impatiently, "but we will not be around humans all of the time."

"Still, safer to not be in the habit of using magic so as not to slip when near humans."

"Do you always talk like this?" she asked.

"Is this way always spoken by you?" he asked in return.

***

Tyrnimar and Eevarel departed Ebariel two days later to Juin and rode for nine days. *It really has been a long time,* Tyrnimar thought, adjusting his seating, feeling the soreness of each day in the saddle stack upon the soreness of the previous day in the saddle. *She seems quite accustomed to it,* he grumbled.

Besides riding for the first time in a very, very long time, Eevarel insisted on imparting refreshers in the wielding of the sword and bow, stating that he would need them on the journey. Tyrnimar had to use Eevarel's sword and bow during practice while she made do with a stick or her dagger for pacing his sword forms or sparring. But the practices were brief, and they spent most of the days traveling at a brisk pace.

"At least try to enjoy yourself," Eevarel suggested.

Tyrnimar shifted uncomfortably in his saddle. "Effort is being made," he muttered, as evenly as he could manage.

"I can tell." She chuckled.

Are you amused? He thought irritably. *One more day until Juin is reached.*

Eevarel explained what she knew of the journey, which to Tyrnimar's quiet chagrin, he learned that he would have Eevarel snickering at him for the entire journey to wherever they were going and back, along with a small company of twelve other travelers.

Tyrnimar had never left the Elven Lands before. He viewed himself a simple and humble Grey Elf, not wanting to be involved in the affairs of state or concerns of the Guardian Council. He was very content remaining in the Under-Provost's tower, reading and writing books, and studying magic. Tyrnimar was resigned that this journey would delay his studies for over a year. This journey was a significant inconvenience as it already was. Still, reluctant as he was to be involved in matters like these, he would not shirk the call of his people. He was glad that he was just finishing writing his project when he met Eevarel.

"I have been meaning to ask you," Eevarel began, as if she had been reading his mind, "what was that book about, the one you were writing when I so rudely blocked your light?" She easily guided her horse with her knees while drinking from her waterskin.

"My light? Oh." Tyrnimar recalled their meeting. "A small handbook. For healing incantations, herbal invocations, contracts with dryads to remove disease and infections. Things alike to that," he explained.

"May I read a bit of it?" she asked.

He hesitated. "It would be my pleasure." *What will be under scrutiny now?* he pondered morosely. They stopped by the side of the road where he dismounted and produced the small book from a saddle bag nearly bursting with other similar books.

"You brought *all* of those?" she asked incredulously. "You know, we are going to be on the road quite a bit. There will be perils. That's why we have a larger company."

"Yes, that has been anticipated," he replied. "That is the reason these books are needed. Is it expected to be talking and conversing the whole time?"

She gave him a skeptical look as she opened the book before finally glancing down at the beginning.

"Have you ever met a dryad?" she asked.

She has that tone again. "No," he admitted.

***

Tyrnimar had not been to Juin in nearly thirty years and had to stop to admire it as soon as it came into view. The great trees of Juin, trees hundreds of paces around and probably a thousand paces tall, guided the road through the city lined with stone buildings nestled into the trunks of the tree.

Juin rested on the River Beros, as the elves called it, with multiple stone and wooden bridges arcing gracefully over it. The horseshoes clopping on the wooden planks of the bridge were mostly drowned out by the babbling of the river, its waters still cold from their origin in the mountains to the west. As they entered the city, Tyrnimar ignored Eevarel's smirks.

"What are you looking at up there? You're going to ride your horse into the river if you don't watch where you're going."

Tyrnimar looked at the apartments set in the trunks of the great trees where the wood warped into hollows large enough for families to live with openings for windows and doors. Tyrnimar knew that stairways were warped into and through the trunk, so that elves could live high up in the tree while the tree continued to thrive. "Wood magic for making the houses and apartments in the great trees has always been interesting. Never have I studied it," he explained as soon as he could break enough attention away from the sight.

"I have to thank you," she said.

"For what?" He pulled his attention from the splendor of the blurred boundary between the order of nature and Elven civilization.

"I have never eaten so well on the road. I remember you saying that you wanted to stop using magic on the trip. It was very nice, the flavors you added to the bread and dried meat."

"Oh. Well… there was no trouble to it," he said sheepishly. *I mean no ingratitude, but the dried meat was bland and the same taste of the bread every day became boring.*

Eevarel led Tyrnimar to a large, graceful stone building which served as the hall of the Guardian Council. They dismounted and were admitted by a pink-haired attendant wearing the purple and silver ten-pointed star livery of the Guardian Council and an amused expression. The hall was a functional building of stone, but for elves, function and beauty flowed together. Scrollwork carved into the stone gave an intuitive sense of where visitors were meant to walk or wait, or which way the library or administrative offices were. There was a sense of security about the place. A sense that the council in this building were aware of concerns in far-off places, and that everything was well in hand. *Except that I will be part of that hand that holds everything*, Tyrnimar thought anxiously.

"The council is ready for you," the attendant announced. Eevarel arched a playful eyebrow at him as they passed.

Tyrnimar took a deep breath as he entered, led by the attendant and flanked by Eevarel. The audience chamber was an oval, and its members sat behind a long bench that curved around the opposite wall. There were only seven council members present. Each of them was a distinguished scholar, magician, statesman, diplomat, or warrior; usually a mixture of two or more.

Tyrnimar hesitated. "The summons of this council is answered by Magus Tyrnimar Iquarren of the Blue Order," he announced with a bow.

"Thank you, Magus Tyrnimar, for your hasty answer to this summons. I am Guardian Iriaden Olari, also of the Blue Order," replied one of the light blue-haired female councilors with a light, pleasant smile, dressed in robes of silver and blue. "You are summoned here for your specific skills to perform the duties of a Traveler. There are a variety of survey requirements for the human territories west of the Kaskevs. This council has chosen to group several survey missions together, so you will have a large group of Travelers with many requirements."

25

The other side of the Kaskevs!? fretted Tyrnimar momentarily. Tyrnimar felt the anxiety of his curiosity overwhelm his anxiety at being examined by the Guardian Council. *Call it a summons, call it a request, call it duty; I am being examined and this will make a mark on my record!* shot a bitter voice in Tyrnimar's head before he blurted out, "Requirements of what sort and which of the territories?"

"All of them, good magus," answered a red-haired male councilor with a long, impatient face. Tyrnimar recognized this one. He was Akriun Ydren, a long-serving diplomat who had written extensively on the bloodlines of human royalty and nobility, particularly west of the Kaskev Mountains. Tyrnimar remembered him from a lecture of his that he had attended fifteen or twenty years ago. "It is the beginning of a new cycle for a variety of survey requirements, and the requirements are quite far-reaching. We require updated information on their economic capabilities, political sensitivities, and the like. Of course, we need what you can provide. Under-Provost Kasriel tells us that you are the most talented of her aura readers." Councilor Ydren explained.

Most talented when there are only three in the order is hardly high acclaim, Tyrnimar mentally observed.

"... And to that end, especially for what you can provide to this mission, we would need surveys from the foothills in the broken lands to the Tamark coast. That type of survey has not been performed in that area for quite some time, nearly eighty years," Councilor Ydren finished.

As the audience with the Council continued, Tyrnimar felt mixed dread at the prospect of being on the road for over a year–among humans, no less–warring with the excitement of performing such a broad scope of research. Tyrnimar asked questions, gradually becoming slightly more comfortable. In addition to Eevarel, Tyrnimar learned about the other twelve companions he would have on the journey. Trinien Orsir, the attendant that had admitted Tyrnimar and Eevarel would be one of their companions. *A coloring charm must be used on his hair before travel is begun by us. It should be something unremarkable to humans, like brown or yellow hair*, Tyrnimar noted, eyeing the pink locks. *Perhaps a coloring charm has already been used upon his hair...*

Of his future companions, only one of them was familiar to him, Irduin Usrani of the Order of the Sword. Tyrnimar had heard of her because she was one of the few swordbearers that wrote books. Her specialty seemed to be herbs, roots, and fungi found in forests, though she had written quite a few books regarding swordcraft, sword techniques, wars, and battles, and other militaristic topics. Tyrnimar had used some of her books on the former as research materials.

"Who will the Lead Traveler be?" Tyrnimar finally asked.

"Holbrin Arozrien of the Sword, bringing the total of you to fourteen," answered Councilor Olari.

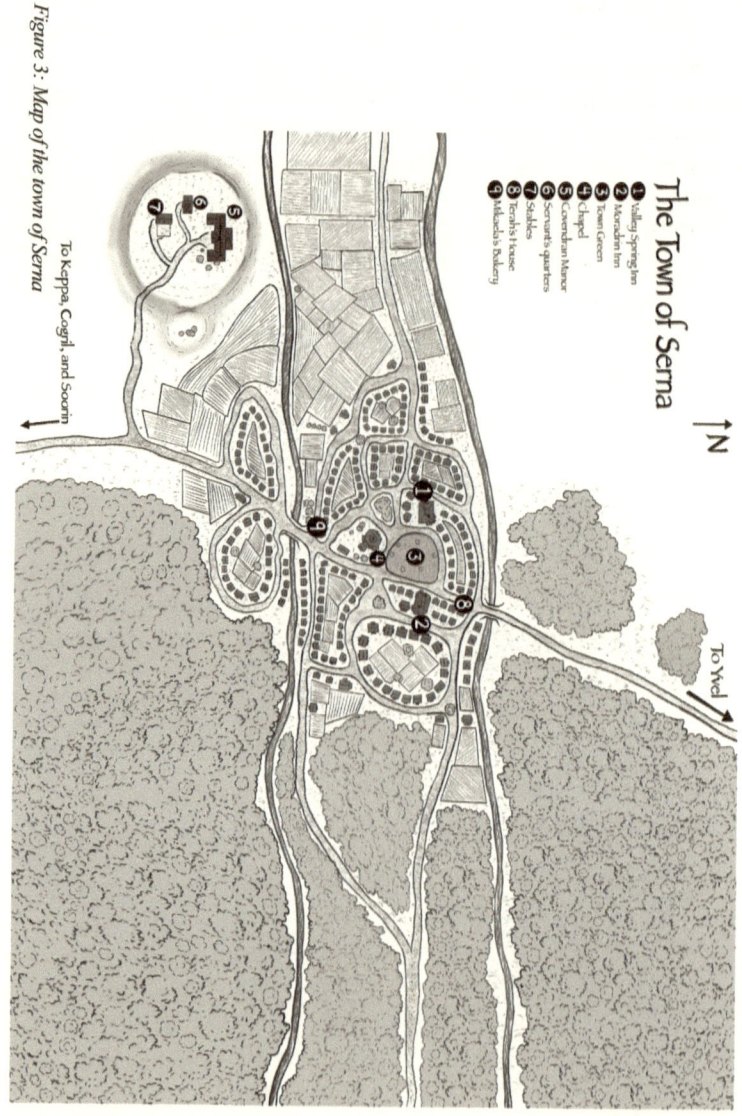

The Town of Serna

1. Valleg Spring Inn
2. Moradim Inn
3. Town Green
4. Chapel
5. Greenthan Manor
6. Servant's quarters
7. Stables
8. Teoah's house
9. Miluda's bakery

To Ved

To Keppa, Cogyl, and Soum

Figure 3: Map of the town of Serna

Chapter 2

Northern edge of the town of Serna, Yvel Principality.
By the Human Calendar, Fryday, second week of Talinochis (twelfth month of the year), 793.
Sunny midday, melting snow, late winter.

"Excuse me, master child," the elf said to Ziek.

Ziek looked up with trepidation from the spiced meat pie that he had just stolen. "Huh?"

He was being addressed by a very tall man with long brown hair falling over pointed ears. He looked young, but he seemed... old... like Ziek's grandfather. Calm. He was leading a strong, brown horse, and wore brown trousers with a blue shirt and a white cape, but Ziek could not help but stare at the ears. "Huh?" Ziek repeated after realizing the man was talking to him.

"I said, could you please direct me to the nearest inn? My companions are weary from the road," the man said again in a voice that sounded like he never ever lost his patience or temper. Ziek noticed the man's companions behind him standing in the late winter's midday sunlight. They all had pointed ears like him, or their hair covered their ears. They were also leading their horses or riding them. Ziek had never seen so many horses at once.

"Oh, uh... I dunno. I guess, um. Here! Let me show you." Ziek struggled with words at the strangeness of these people. Ziek stashed the pie under a hand cart, prompting a raised eyebrow from the man. "It's, uh, to keep it safe." Ziek explained.

"Indeed," said the man with pointed ears.

"This way," Ziek offered as he set out for the center of the village. Ziek took them to the village green in the center, passing rows of one- and two-story buildings painted various colors with tiled roofs.

"This place is called Serna, master child?" asked the man.

"Yeah, sir." answered Ziek. "That's the Moradran Inn, and

that's the Valley Spring Inn." Ziek pointed at the two inns on the edge of the green, both three-floor buildings.

"Thank you," the elf said. Ziek stood in front of the group expectantly.

The strange man looked at Ziek for a moment. "Tell me good master child, where can I find the lord of your town?"

"Lord Koval? He lives in that house over there." Ziek pointed to a three-floor manor on a snowy hill overlooking the town. "You don' wanna meet him, though. He's scary." Ziek continued to bar the way of the strange man and his companions.

A moment passed awkwardly as Holbrin waited for the man-child to leave. He didn't, so Holbrin decided to speak. "One more thing, master child."

"Ya?" Ziek shot back.

"There was a man watching us from the woods as we came into town. Who was he?"

"I dunno. Some people are hunters here, so it mighta bin one o' them," Ziek answered.

After a moment passed, the man looking at Ziek and Ziek looking at the man, the elf broke the silence. "Is there something else?"

"You're supposed to pay me for my trouble, sir."

"Oh? Your trouble master child?" replied the man. He sounded almost amused.

"Yeah, I was just about to eat my hard-earned pie when I had to help you and your lost and wandering friends."

"Indeed," he replied, and reached into his pocket and pressed a coin into Ziek's eagerly waiting hand. Ziek looked down and looked again in surprise that the man had given him a silver mark! *Wait. There's no crown. There was supposed to be a crown! Instead, there was some bird on one side and a creepy eye on the other.* It was a foreign coin, maybe from Markia.

When Ziek came back to his senses, he called after the man and his companions. "Hey, sir."

The man looked back from leading his horse towards the Valley Spring Inn. "Yes?"

"What kind of person are you with your weird ears? Are you like the Seven Lady?"

"One of their tales of the fae, of the Lady of Seven," explained one of the other elves.

"No, sir. It's a fairy tale about the Seven Lady. Are you like that?" Ziek asked.

"…No, master child. We are not fae. Fairies, as you would say," the elf replied.

"Oh. Well, are you from Markia, then?"

"No, we are not from Markia, we just traveled through there a short while ago. We are elves from the other side of the mountains."

"Really!? From the other side?"

"Yes, truly, master child."

"Why do you call me that?" Ziek asked as they made to walk away.

"Is that not how I should call you respectfully?" answered the tall elf.

"I dunno." Ziek replied. Then he grinned and left to find his now-cold pie.

***

Holbrin Arozrien watched the human child go, unsure of whether he had earned or stolen the meat pie before chuckling to himself and thought, *he is a bold one*. Holbrin motioned for his companions to follow. Holbrin and Trinien left the reins of their horses with their companions and entered the Valley Spring Inn.

It was a blocky building, a red-painted wooden rectangle with two smaller additions, a clay tile roof like most other buildings in Serna, and a stone chimney. The interior vaguely reminded Holbrin of Dwarven architecture. The common room was flanked by two fireplaces on either end. It was still winter, so both fires were pouring heat into the room. The rest of the room was lit by sunlight from the windows, though the wall was lined with sconces for the evenings. Wooden tables dotted the room with three or four chairs each and a bar counter dominated the room from the other side. *Cleaner than most places we see*, Holbrin thought as he made arrangements with the barkeep.

"One more thing, Master Clay." said Holbrin in the Marin tongue.

"Yeah?" replied the barkeep.

"You say that people here speak both this language and the Eklendan language?" Holbrin asked politely.

"Yeah, sort of. Most speak one or the other, but a lot of folk speak both. Lot of mixed blood in this area and we get a lot of travel between Yvel and Soorin," answered Clay, growing curious about Holbrin's interest.

"And so, Lord Covendran speaks Eklendan? That is an Eklendan name, is it not?" inquired Holbrin.

Clay was growing skeptical of Holbrin's questions. "Sure, what's it to you?"

"I was hoping to meet him and want to pay him the proper respect," answered Holbrin.

"Huh," said Clay. "Well, he'd be taking his tea this time of day. He takes most of his audiences around this time."

Holbrin thanked the barkeep after finishing the arrangements for lodging his companions and the horses. He left the others to put the horses up in the stables and take their midday meal, bringing only Tyrnimar and Trinien to Covendran Manor. They were admitted by a plump maid, bustling at encountering elves for the first time, who showed them to a sitting room where a middle-aged man was already seated.

This was Koval Covendran, Lord of Serna, his black hair barely tinged with hairs of grey at his temples and lines of care etching the skin around his eyes, starting to crawl down the cheeks of his narrow face. He wore a carefully trimmed beard, also barely touched with a few whiskers of grey. He seemed a bit nervous at receiving such exotic guests, and was doing a poor job of hiding it.

"You my house blue welcome greetings!" said Koval in broken, badly accented Elvish while rising to greet them with an overly welcoming smile. He was taller than most humans Holbrin had met on this trip, meeting Holbrin eye to eye.

Holbrin put on a small, gracious smile and replied to his host in Eklendan. "Thank you, Lord Serna, you honor us. As we are humble guests in your town, please let us pay you the honor and speak in your language."

"Well... if you insist," replied Koval, returning to his seat and failing to hide his relief at further struggles in a language he did not know. "Tell me, what brings you and your fine company along this way? Fourteen in total, yes?"

"We are merely passing through. It is customary among our people to travel the lands and see how the cities and peoples have changed. We merely meant to pay respect to you on our way through," Holbrin explained patiently, the small pleasant smile pinned in place, as he and his two companions seated themselves on a nearby couch. The maid returned with a tray of steaming cups of tea, which Tyrnimar and Trinien took.

"Well, I cannot have such grand travelers pass through without me showing anything short of the best hospitality. The new year is upon us. We shall have the new year's feast a bit early! There shall be music." Koval gave his staff a pointed glare which sent them into a flush of bows and curtsies before scurrying off to prepare for the evening's feast.

A younger man bearing a resemblance to Koval entered the room. He was a bit taller than Koval Covendran and had the narrow jaw and brown eyes of his father. "Please, meet my son, Dareum." Dareum Covendran was clean-shaven, red-haired man of his very early twenties, by Holbrin's estimate, with the look of someone who spent much of his time riding or hunting. Holbrin guessed Dareum's age from what he knew of humans, whereas Koval seemed past forty years but not quite yet to fifty.

Holbrin took a cup of tea from the maid, as did Dareum as he sat with his father and the travelers as the other family members joined. Lady Serna, Mariss Covendran, seemed about the same age as her husband, with those same brown eyes and black hair, but the similarities stopped there. Where Koval's whole face was narrower and his skin fair, Mariss' jaw was the only part of her face that narrowed and her skin was more olive. Trinien had told Holbrin that these were more common characteristics for humans with Eklendan blood. Holbrin thought it odd that the Koval looked more Marin, yet he had an Eklendan name. *Must be as the barkeep said. The blood is so intermixed that there are no clear boundaries here between them.* Their daughter, Judane, black-haired like her parents and who looked to be only a little younger than Dareum, also joined them.

Holbrin and his companions maintained polite conversation with Lord and Lady Serna, as well as the two scions while finishing their tea. Holbrin found himself unable to graciously decline an invitation for a hunt with Dareum Covendran before the tea service was finished. After departing, Holbrin and his two companions walked down the muddy path towards the rest of town.

"Your manners are improving. I hardly noticed you squinting," Trinien said in Elvish, smirking with a sidelong look at Tyrnimar.

"Concentration must be achieved to see the aura," Tyrnimar replied while looking at the ground.

Holbrin walked ahead of them by a few paces, calm-faced. *Calm on the outside.* "What did you see?" he prompted Tyrnimar.

"There is no doubt. The older Covendran is a Fearmonger, the younger is a Warmonger. The older is surely awakened. Sureness of the younger man cannot be made by me. The Lady Serna is a Charmer. The aura of the daughter has not been seen by me. She is not awoken. Not yet, but the barrier is thin," Tyrnimar replied with trepidation.

"It makes sense. The Covendran line goes back to just before the time between the Imperial Secession War and the Western Secession Wars. It is a wonder that Serna was not included in the last three surveys." Trinien observed.

"Yes, good work, Tyrnimar. We would have missed this place if not for your diligence," Holbrin said over his shoulder, his face calm as morning to hide his rising alarm.

"There is more," Tyrnimar continued. "The aura of a Firebrand, a Healer and, perhaps, a Stormbearer or an Invisible Hand have been seen here, and a few others that are mysterious to me."

Such a concentration! Holbrin fretted internally. "How

many are active?"

"It cannot be determined," answered Tyrnimar, "except for the older Covendrans. They are active as was said earlier, though they do not seem aware of what they do. A thorough survey of this town and the surrounding villages is needed."

"We will make time for that. This evening is an excellent opportunity to expand the information you have already collected," Holbrin said to Tyrnimar with a look that meant Tyrnimar was going to go to the feast.

"Do not worry about the crowds, friend Tyrnimar. Eevarel will keep them away from you," said Trinien, his smirk returning.

Tyrnimar looked up from the ground at Trinien, perplexed. "What is meant by that?"

***

Word spread through the town quickly and the town was quietly bustling with the preparations. The manor staff sent orders for musicians, wine, mead, additional staff, and a boar to roast. Young couriers delivered the invitations, which would be otherwise considered rudely short notice except that the recipients surely knew of the opportunity that the Lord Serna sensed and dared not deprive him of it.

Serna's modest elite of merchants, inn owners, craftsmen, and Elder Ereman Dum'ail from the chapel turned out for the festivities. As Buin was excitedly babbling about how he was going to earn fifteen tin pennies for helping in the kitchen, Ziek did his best to manage his smile and make it look like he was excited for his friend.

But what Ziek truly looked forward to was *opportunity*. Sunset came early this time of year, so it would already be getting dark with the beginning of the festivities. However, Ziek knew that the boar would take forever to roast through and the party would be eating and drinking late.

He cheerily helped his friends with their chores and bided his time, careful to avoid being seen in any one place for too long.

He waited until he was sure that everyone that was going to the feast had already left before moving again and looked down the road to the manor and across the green. He saw a few shopkeepers cleaning up for the fuss of providing for the event at the manor. Ziek walked across the road in a way that was perfectly natural for someone that was doing exactly what they were supposed to be doing. Reaching the other side, he nonchalantly turned right along the front of the inn.

When he arrived at the corner, he turned left with his hands stuffed into the pockets of his breeches. He strolled up the alley on the side of the inn and turned left again to approach the back door. Deftly, he gripped the door handle with both hands and pushed the door up in the frame slightly to reduce the squeak when he opened it. Noiselessly, he slipped in and let the door close with only a small thud of the door meeting the frame.

Peering around the corner into the common room, Ziek saw the aisle from the kitchen past the bar into the sitting area of the common room. To his right, past the bar, was the hallway and stairway to the guest rooms. In his way was Selonikah the serving maid minding the bar in case any patrons came in, though most of the guests and staff were attending the celebration. *She's strict! She beat me three times before she handed me over to mama last time…*

Ziek crept low as he moved out of the kitchen behind the bar, silently behind and past Selonikah. Rounding the corner, he kept to the left side of the stairs–he knew that the center and the right side squeaked, so steered clear. He reached the top of the stairs and darted down the hall. Ziek was glad that Buin had told him that the elf travelers were taking all of the rooms on the second floor.

He was just reaching into his pocket when he heard voices emerging from behind one of the doors. His feet padded to a table in the hall under which he crawled to hide, the long shadows of the winter evening creating a cloak for him under the table. He could very clearly hear what the voices–two Elven men–were saying, though he had no idea what the words meant. Some words were repeated several times, but he had trouble even remembering how they were pronounced. The shadows lengthened before the two elf men opened the door. They closed and locked it before striding down the hall and squeaking down the stairs.

As the sound of their footsteps faded and he heard the creak of the front door to the common room, Ziek crawled out from under the table and moved towards the door from which the two men had exited. Again, he reached into his pocket and pulled out a nail as long as his finger and several thick pieces of wire bent at different angles and patterns. Ziek was squinting while just inserting the nail into the lock when he heard the stairs creak. *Did they forget something?* Putting the nail back into his pocket, he shrouded himself in the darkness under the table against the wall and waited.

Selonikah's face emerged from the ground floor as she topped the stairs and moved into the hall. Ziek held his breath as her footsteps came nearer. She stopped right in front of the table and paused before rising on the toes of her shoes. It seemed a very long time to Ziek before candlelight blossomed into the hall. Ziek almost let out a sigh of relief. Selonikah moved to the end of another hall where she lit another candle sconce on the wall and turned around. Ziek froze again, but Selonikah did not see him. She walked past and up the stairs to the third floor.

Ziek let out his breath quietly when she was out of sight, but he waited for her to come back down from lighting the sconces on the third floor and go back to the bar before he once again emerged from concealment under the table and began fumbling with the lock and ironically glad that Selonikah had made it easier to see. The lock gave a relenting dull clunk and Ziek eased the door open just enough to slip inside.

There were two beds in the room, with two trunks at the foot of each. A window looked out onto the town green, and a coat rack by the door held two dusty travel cloaks. Next to both trunks were a pair of saddle bags. Ziek unbuckled the steel clasp and pulled back the leather flap. *Books?* Ziek picked one up and opened it. Ziek's eyebrows scrunched down as his eyes tried to find anything familiar among the flowing script that seemed more like scrollwork than writing.

Ziek did not know letters, but this was too strange to him. He flipped through a few pages and stopped to look at a diagram of a tree and a woman superimposed over it with a hexagon drawn around them and notes in that same flowing, enigmatic script at each of the points. Ziek was staring so hard at the diagram that he jumped from being startled at the roar and screams outside.

Chapter 3

The town of Serna, Yvel Principality.
By the Human Calendar, Fryday, second week of Talinochis, 793.
A clear, briskly cold late winter night.

Mkaela peered towards the sky, her wavy brown hair falling away from her face as her confused eyes looked above. *Why is the sky orange?*

BECAUSE I HAVE BROUGHT YOU HERE, replied a presence.

Mkaela turned around, looking in every direction, casting about her gaze. This was her town, there was the chapel, the green lined by shops and the two inns, the tannery behind it–*Wait. There's no smell.* Mkaela couldn't smell anything. This was her town, but no people. The rows of houses, Covendran Manor on the hill, the edge of the forest close to the edge of town, everything was here. *Except the snow. No snow on the hill, no snow on the trees. No mud in the streets.* There. A shadow moved by the chapel.

How was there a shadow there? There are no shadows on that side of the building, she puzzled. She approached the building tentatively. There was a diffuse light everywhere, like it was dawn, midday, and dusk at the same time. The light cast no shadows, yet it was faint. As she drew near the chapel, the shadow poured out from the wall of the chapel and took form, towering over her, eating the faint light.

She recoiled. "What do you want?"

FEAR NOT, it replied. I HAVE COME WITH A WARNING.

"A warning?"

TRULY, TRULY I SAY. LOOK. It did not move as far as she could tell, yet she felt as if it directed her to look to her right, to the east.

The rows of houses and forest shrank and receded from

vision as she felt pulled, or was it pushed, and the ground blurred under her as the Kaskev Mountains appeared in the distance. She knew they were too far to see at all from the town, yet they loomed and grew in size. The ground continued to speed beneath her and the mountains grew large. Several of them spat green fire with white cyclones forming a bridge of air between the mountains and the orange sky. Jagged bolts of black lightning crackled from the cyclones.

"Why are you showing me this? What does it mean?" she asked, surprised by her calm as she stared at the crackling cyclone.

A WARNING. THIS PLACE, THINGS APPEAR AS THEY ARE AND YET AS THEY ARE NOT. THERE IS A SORROW IN THE MOUNTAINS AND IT POURS OUT ONTO THE LAND.

"What am I supposed to do about this?" she repeated in the same even tone.

NOTHING. YOU CANNOT STOP THIS. BUT THE SORROW OF THE MOUNTAINS WILL POUR ONTO THE LAND.

"What do you mean?" she asked, looking back from the cyclone. The shadow grew darker, drinking the light, threatening to erase everything in her field of view, yet it felt warm. It was the only thing here that felt like anything. The ground blurred under her again. They were back in Serna, but instead of the forest, the mountains stormed and loomed in the distance. The shadow stood by the chapel again. "What does that have to do with here? The mountains are too far away."

LOOK AGAIN, instructed the shadow.

Mkaela looked back towards the mountains. A steaming river of green with sprays of flame was bursting from its eddies, rushing and coursing through the town and filling the street–but nothing burned, not even singed. The green river flowed over her feet and rose up to her knees. It was not hot, only warm. She gazed into it, not understanding, until it turned red. Red like blood from a fresh cut. She looked back at the shadow in confusion.

HELP THEM, bade the shadow. Mkaela looked at the river of blood and saw hands and noiselessly wailing faces rise to the surface of the river, reaching and silently pleading. She recognized some of the faces. But some of the faces were ugly, like monsters with huge teeth or broad heads with big eyes and large, sideways-pointing ears. She looked at the shadow. HELP THEM. I GIVE YOU THE WAY.

Mkaela started awake to the sound of screams and the glow of a large fire shining in through the window.

***

Feet beat the ground viciously in rapid succession. The feet ached and screamed with pain. The left foot viciously struck the ground, then the right. The right foot sunk into a muddy low spot in the street, snagging the leather shoe. The mud greedily engulfed the shoe and coveted it for itself, taking it from the right foot, the right forfeiting the brief struggle and abandoning the shoe in desperation.

Ziek staggered as he lost his shoe, but kept running for his life. He ducked under a wagon and scurried between the wheels, not daring to look back as he came out the other side and ran on, hearing screams of terror and howls of glee and rage behind him, Selonikah's terror still ringing in his mind from just seconds ago. Ziek panted and wheezed too hard to sound a cry that would match the tears and snot running down his face as his legs pumped and burned for all they were and ever would ever be worth.

Ziek ran past other people and clawed his way past obstacles, not really seeing them, pushing them behind him in a vain effort to propel himself even just a little faster. He cleared a corner and was straining his hips to get his legs to change direction when something thumped him in the back very hard, just below his ribs, slamming him into the mud on his side. At the same time, he felt the faintest prick above his belly and the fast spread of warmth. His legs were suddenly made of the greatest weights of lead. His arms seemed to be tied to where they were by a thousand invisible strings; he could barely move them even with the greatest effort.

Everything was suddenly slow and it was getting cold as winter. His eyes creaked down, rotating in his head. He had grown a horn of steel out of his belly, but it was off-center. *When did that happen?* He brushed his hand on it and it came away red, like the steel horn was leaking red paint. *What's this?* The warmth on his skin dripped down his stomach to the ground.

There was a bright flickering light behind him, and a shining orange light in front of him. A figure stepped into his view, the orange light shining on it. It looked tall–taller than a man, and thick. It had overlapping layers of hide wrapped around its waist and chest, up to the armpits. *Green skin?* That couldn't be right.

As it stepped closer, Ziek vaguely registered something in its hands. He tried to talk to it to ask what it was doing, what was its name. Warm copper came up in his mouth and drowned his words. The shadows became very dark and everything he could see became bright, so bright it lost its color. Ziek opened his eyes wide. He had never seen so much brightness without it hurting his eyes. Then the brightness started running away. He tried to lift his hand to catch it as he saw the figure grip the thing in both hands and raise it towards the night sky.

***

The still, cold evening air was seared by a dozen arrows streaking like angry hornets, peppering the tall orc through its hide wrappings, two ripping through its throat, and one lodging in its eye. Every one of its muscles tensed before it dropped the axe and keeled backwards. Arynn raced past the dead orc and the dying boy, closely behind Dareum Covendran, whose big lumbering strides hauled his body and his longsword gleaming in the firelight. Behind her, Tyrnimar rushed to the boy with the javelin stuck through him.

Ahead two buildings burned brightly, fully aflame, threatening to spread to others on all sides. Dareum and Arynn raced through the streets against a sparse flow of townsfolk racing towards some perceived safety. Behind them came a horde of tall, green-skinned orcs, bald or with coarse manes of hair, clad in ragged skins about the hips and shoulders, and bearing wide toothy and tusked grins, large two-handed, square-tipped falchions, and crescent-bladed axes. Some clutched spears and javelins as they laughed and howled in delight.

Dareum drew up short and Arynn knew well enough to not rush on by herself. Arynn looked over at him. *Will he run?* The air grew faintly darker around Dareum as his face curled into a veiny mask of rage and hate, made to look like wizened, gnarled tree bark in the firelight. He howled in anger from the bottom of his lungs, from a depth of his being that stopped the fleeing townsfolk in their tracks and the orcs' laughter mid-guffaw. Their gazes suddenly fixed to Dareum Covendran as if tied with strings, watching him.

He gritted his teeth. "COME ON! KILL 'EM ALL!" he cursed. Arynn felt a boiling fist of rage clench her chest, coursing her blood fast. Dareum leaped at them, longsword flashing in the orange light, batting away the first axe with a two-handed grip before whipping the tip up to rip through a green throat, severing the jawbone and tearing the mouth and nose open. The blade came away, racing past two green hands rushing up to try to hold back a flood of red and gurgling cries.

One by one, the townsfolk turned around and picked up a rock and threw it, or grabbed a pitchfork or a shovel from overturned carts. They formed into an angry mob and charged, shouting with raised weapons and hurling sticks, stones, and cookpots. Dareum's face twisted into rage and hate as he pursued the falling, broken orc, continuing to hack at it, heedless of the surrounding orcs. Arynn fought the fist of blind rage down as a cold lump of fear formed next to it. She struggled to master the two of them.

Recovering from their initial shock from facing any opposition, some of the orcs found their grins again, and plunged with their speartips, axes blades, and forward-curving swords, spraying and dripping red as the townsfolk were slaughtered on the green. Leaping in with both hands gripping the hilt of her own long-bladed, curved sword, Arynn deflected a spear coursing for Dareum's back. She crashed into him, shoving him onto another orc who had its foot on one of the servants from the feast as he was pulling his spear out of her. The three toppled over while Arynn, finally shoving both emotions down, whirled around and eviscerated the orc with the spear. It dropped its spear while falling to its knees, innards pulsing out while he desperately tried to put them back in with a panicked whine. Dareum was on his feet, kicking the head of the orc with whom he had fallen. The orc stared at the sky, its neck broken, while Dareum, lost in the berserk, stomped and kicked and raged while the woman laid on the ground, moaning in pain with the spear still stuck in her.

Two vigorous strides brought Arynn to Dareum. She slapped him across the face, "DAREUM COVENDRAN! These people need you!"

In the light of the burning buildings, the air around him seemed to ease and the haze faded from his eyes as he seemed to come back to some of his senses. Arynn internally breathed a small sigh of relief. She turned and rejoined the fray to keep the few remaining townsfolk fighting on the green from being cut down like so many others. She heard Dareum's voice calling out to the other townsfolk to fight as he rejoined the melee.

Arynn still felt the controlled rage inside her and allowed herself to use it sparingly. More townsfolk emerged from hiding, armed with chairs, sledgehammers, frypans, fire pokers, knives, cudgels, an older one with an orc sword–however he managed to get that, and whatever else they could find. But they were overmatched against the gleeful orcs, who were stronger, taller, used to handling weapons, and keenly enjoying fighting and killing. Arynn, Dareum, and the townsman with the orc sword were desperately fighting to hold back the tide of a complete slaughter.

Arynn saw Dareum slip on a puddle of blood from the corner of her eye and lose his grip on his sword. She knew she could not reach him in time, but batted aside an axe and sprinted towards him, watching in slow motion as a laughing orc raised his axe. A green fist sped into her vision from her left and slammed into her face before she could change course, sending her sprawling into the bloody mud. She rolled over, her eyes darting between the orc advancing towards her with its long, square-tipped sword and the one towering over prone Dareum, raised on its toes with its axe held high.

Time froze for an instant before the moment was broken by a hail of arrows from the direction of the firelight, riddling the front row of orcs. Arynn twisted to see her companions and a few humans with bows firing on the orcs as some humans–four of them–mounted on horses charged with swords and spears. She recognized

Koval Covendran, the lord of these parts, atop a white horse, wearing a shirt of mail and hurling a spear into the cluster of orcs.

***

Tyrnimar pulled his blade from the orc's throat, watching the others rush off in the distance. Casting it aside and silently thanking Eevarel for her insistence on training, he rushed to the bleeding child. He looked at the javelin protruding from both sides, the blood trickling out of him, and the increasing labor of shallow breath. He was already unconscious.

Tyrnimar fumbled in his pockets and produced a small book while kneeling between the child and the fighting, opening the book and frantically flipping through the pages until he found the right one. Casting with barely controlled panic, he gasped with gratitude spotting a small, winter-bare sapling growing out of the foundation of the building next to where the child fell. Searching the lines on the paper until he found the beginning of what he sought, he whispered the incantation in the Elven tongue as the sapling shined faintly green.

A bright green form emerged, elbow first, then shoulder, then head. When it was out, it was a miniature, nude, elf-like creature with green luminescent skin and darker green luminescent hair. It yawned sleepily and smiled at Tyrnimar. Overcoming his awe and fascination that it actually worked, he remembered where he was and whispered the rest of the incantation. The miniature green elf whispered something that Tyrnimar suddenly knew, but did not hear.

The figure reached towards the child and touched it with a small green glow. The blood stopped flowing from his body and his breathing eased slightly. Tyrnimar gripped the javelin and looked at the creature. It winked at Tyrnimar and he slowly drew the javelin out of the boy and marveled at the wound as it glowed green at the entry and exit. The green light diminished as the wound closed and winked out as it closed.

The skin was scarred in a strange way. A strange way for skin on humans or elves to scar, but Tyrnimar knew it was not skin anymore—at least not human skin. It was tree bark. The child breathed easily and Tyrnimar let out a gasp in relief. He looked at the creature one more time and he knew by its returning gaze that he had better remember his end of the bargain. *Accept your fate.* It disappeared back into the sapling.

Urgency is needed, he fretted as he picked up his sword while stuffing the book back into his pocket and was running off towards the fight when a soft golden glow caught his eye. It would have been easy to miss it in the bright light of the fire. Others would have seen only the faint golden glow, if they noticed it at all, and maybe dismissed it as a candle, eerily peaceful with the tangled mixture of desperation, dread, and glee a few dozen paces away.

Tyrnimar squinted and almost lost the aura sight in surprise. A golden blaze of light, that only he could see with his eyes and his aura sight, shone down from amid the roofs one street away. Down the street from the fight Tyrnimar ran, darted down an alley, and peeked through a window. He was not sure how to explain what he saw.

***

Mkaela was not sure what she was doing; it just felt right. She finished pulling Seedar Torin'ail through the door, trailing blood and grime behind him. She was not breathing and had a gaping wound between her shoulder and neck, cleaving through her collarbone, blood trickling out of it, having been furiously gushing just moments ago. Her arm dragged at an unnatural angle. Mkaela took a deep breath and placed her hand over the tear in Seedar's body.

NOW! The voice of the shadow boomed in Mkaela's head.

Now what? Who are *you?* implored Mkaela internally.

USE MY POWER! it commanded.

"How? What am I supposed to do?" Mkaela pleaded out loud.

LET IT IN, YOUR FEAR IS BLOCKING ME.

"I'm *afraid*, alright? Kostray, help me! Orneth, help me!"

Mkaela retorted. Seedar's blood was seeping through Mkaela's fingers. "You said you could help," she accused, "SO HELP!" Tears of frustration formed in her eyes as she looked at the blood, desperately wanting it to stop. Her hand glowed and she pulled it back, recoiling in fear.

THAT WAS IT, the shadow said to her.

"*What* was it?" Mkaela begged. "What happened?"

YOUR FOCUS, THE ENERGY, LIKE YOU DID JUST NOW. DO IT AGAIN.

Steeling herself, Mkaela took another deep breath and placed her bloody hand over Seedar's wound and wanted the bleeding to stop. Again, her hand began to glow. She tensed, but held her hand firmly. Everything stood still for a moment.

The trickle of blood stopped. The glow grew brighter and shone from deep inside the wound. Mkaela marveled as the flesh she could see deep inside the wound knit itself together. Like the reverse of a rope tearing, she could see strands of muscle come together and tie themselves anew. She heard a pop from Seedar's shoulder as her arm rotated and the shoulder righted itself. The collarbone joined and reknitted itself with a small grinding sound, like scraping stones together. The air was hot and smelled of iron. The glow grew brighter as the skin closed and scarred over the collarbone. Mkaela followed the impulse to 'push' and the glow grew a bit brighter against Seedar's chest as Mkaela felt her body begin to labor vigorously. Mkaela felt new blood coursing in Seedar's veins. Seedar gasped for air and the glow faded as Mkaela breathed hoarsely. Seedar breathed easily, but in a deep sleep.

Mkaela fell back, exhausted. YES. NOW, DO THAT UNTO OTHERS. YOU CALLED AND I WILL HELP YOU.

I'm so tired. Mkaela forced herself up. There was still fighting outside. She peeked out the door, unaware of the spying eyes peering above the window frame on the opposite wall, and spied Damerwyn Perndran and Amryst Veradran. *They'll burn me as a witch if they find out*, she fretted before darting out the door.

Chapter 4

The town of Serna, Yvel Principality.
By the Human Calendar, Playday (ninth day of the week), second week of
Talinochis, 793.
A sunny winter morning.

Holbrin struck Tyrnimar hard enough to knock him down to the mud. Some of the other travelers gasped at Holbrin's display of anger.

YOU FOOL! HOW COULD YOU BE SO STUPID!? Holbrin internally howled under his mask of calm, despite striking Tyrnimar.

Tyrnimar was slowly getting up while Holbrin spoke. "You know what is at risk. Why did you do something so reckless? This is so very unlike you?"

"What was meant to be done by me?" Tyrnimar asked, picking up his leather bag, wary of being struck again. "For that boy to die should be allowed by me? Is that our way?"

"Do not dare preach to me of the Ways, young one." Holbrin warned placidly, "You know of what happened the last time humans had magic from reading about it, but I was actually there and watched everything burn with my own eyes."

"Is how a child could be saved changed by that which happened all that time ago?" Tyrnimar challenged. Eyebrows raised from the other travelers at Tyrnimar's sudden brazenness.

"It does," replied Holbrin coldly. "We cannot risk humans regaining magic–not even to save a life–for the life saved will cost hundreds of other lives. Thousands. Once humans regain magic, those among them that quest for power will destroy much in that pursuit."

"There is no disagreement, but we are too late," Tyrnimar said.

"Yes, yes, you have already mentioned the latent potential and burgeoning users, we may return to take them."

"Something else is meant. A healer has been seen by me," Tyrnimar replied.

"What?" said Holbrin, surprise almost cracking his mask of calm.

The younger Grey Elf explained himself. "That is the reason for a delay by me in joining the fight."

"Explain this." Holbrin's statement was quiet, simple, and calm, yet rang to the travelers as a cold demand.

Tyrnimar shrank a little from Holbrin, but continued. "A young woman from the town, her name is not known to me, but the sight of her is familiar. Six attempts at healing were made by her on mortally wounded humans from this town. Four were saved by her, the third and the fifth person were not saved. She was taken by exhaustion after the sixth attempt and passed out."

Holbrin took a small step back and let out a breath. He was about to say something when the sound of human words spoken at him from behind tore him from the moment. The ring of travelers parted and Holbrin smoothly made the mental shift from Elven to Marin. "My apologies, good sir, could you please say that again?"

The light of dawn was just beginning to shine on the tops of the remaining buildings. To the human onlookers, they had just concluded a calm discussion about tending the horses, aside from the smears of mud on Tyrnimar's clothes.

"Uh, ya, Master Holbrin." This human was one of the ones that had fared well last night, relatively speaking. He was old for a human, with curly, ragged, wiry grey hair and a scraggly, iron beard marking his age, yet he stood with an able stature compared to most other humans his age. A forward-curving Orcish sword was at his belt, nestled in a hastily fashioned scabbard.

Fine lines of care were etched across his face. His coloring was different from most of the other townspeople; more of a coppery tone than the fair-skinned Marins or olive-skinned Eklendans. There was no way he could be as old as most of the elves, but his eyes seemed like they had seen as much as most of them; he looked exhausted, covered in ash and dried blood, with one fresh bead of sweat running from his forehead down his left cheek. "The Lord Serna wants to speak to a lot of folk here in the common room. He said that he's probably going to ask for your help."

Inside the common room of the Moradran Inn–the Valley Spring had burned down along with quite a few other buildings last night–the gentle light from the fire in its rightful place was still unnerving to the gathering of exhausted people. After they had driven the orcs off (or had they just left?), they had fought the fires for the rest of the night before trudging to the Moradran common room at their lord's summons.

There was a modest stage one step off of the floor of the common room where musicians and storytellers would spin their craft to a variably drunken audience. Koval Covendran stood atop that stage, pacing nervously, waiting for the townsfolk to enter, while Mariss Covendran sat in a chair on the stage with a grim calmness. Dareum and Judane Covendran were standing to the side.

Holbrin noted that the attendance was more than came to the previous night's abortive feast. He waited for his companions to enter the crowded common room where there was only standing space. *This must be the whole town and some of the outlying farms*, he thought, noting some dirt and stains on their clothes and well-worn gloves. More townsfolk arrived and crowded around the open windows. He pressed through the crowd to follow his companions in and the man that came to get them signaled to his liege that all were present.

Koval Covendran stopped pacing.

***

The old man who had fetched the elves, Taram, brushed his scraggly grey hair out of his eyes as he waited for the last of the elves to enter the Moradran common room before entering himself, to the low murmur of closely packed, worried people. Adjusting his newly acquired curved Orcish sword, so as not to poke anyone with the scabbard, Taram made eye contact with Koval and nodded his weather-wrinkled face to him, signaling that all were present.

The lord stopped pacing and faced the crowd. The murmur silenced as a subtle wave of anxiety gripped the crowd, hinging on what he was about to say. Taram saw the one called 'Holbrin' make eye contact with the one called 'Tyrnimar' and give him some kind of meaningful look. The one called 'Tyrnimar' looked back at the lord. Taram would have been considerably more curious had he been less tired and vengeful.

"I have no flowery speech for this day," Koval began. He looked as exhausted as everyone else. "We have a lot to do and we don't know how much time we have. We cannot accept that last night won't happen again, so we must be ready." He paused.

"First, this is clearly beyond what we are able to handle by ourselves. We will fortify, rebuild, and defend Serna, but the enemy remains at large. We shall send to Prince Gerald in Yvel for the assistance of the army. Master Panr'ail and Miss Venodran, please approach." He paused and waited for them to register that he had called them. The crowd remained silent as they muddled their way uncertainly through the crowd. They unsteadily emerged at the front of the crowd to stand by their lord. Taram could not recognize Julian Panr'ail from this distance, but he recognized Liri Venodran by the pair of Marin-style braids that she favored.

"You will escort the Lady Serna on her journey to Yvel as she entreats the Prince to aid us," he said. He handed a sealed envelope to his wife. "My own message to the Prince." She smiled grimly as she accepted the letter.

"We shall return only when we have a good answer," Mariss Covendran said to him. She spoke quietly. Most would not hear her words or make them out over the murmur, but Taram's ears could. The two townsfolk receded back into the crowd.

"Let me be clear about last night," Koval continued. "We did not drive the orcs off. They chose to leave. Yes, we killed almost twenty, but we paid for that with seventy-three dead, twenty-five taken prisoner and carried off, and nine buildings burnt to the ground. We have scant resources, but we need to at least find those taken, try to get them back, and find where the enemy is coming from so the army can deal with them. Your Lord Dareum will lead a small company of thirty to perform this task." The younger Lord Covendran nodded his acceptance to the task.

"I will remain with you," Koval said to the crowd, "to supervise the fortification of our town, standing up a militia, and repairing the damage done."

He then declared every able-bodied townsperson to be a member of the new Serna Militia with himself as the marshal. His daughter, Lady Judane, was placed as captain of another militia company guarding the town. Beren Enkr'ail, a well-fed traveling merchant with a storefront in Serna would now be the militia quartermaster. The blacksmith, Evren Jundran, would assist him by tallying the captured orc's weapons and converting tools and farm implements into weapons. Allana Hunr'ail, the local carpenter, would assist with planning the wooden palisade. Korane Lowdran would be the scoutmaster. The list went on Koval detailed the list of necessary staff to fortify the town, organize supplies, gather materials, and clear out the trees surrounding the town.

When he finished, he stepped down from the platform. The crowd wordlessly parted in front of him, forming a bubble around him, as he made his way towards the one called 'Holbrin.' Taram noted that 'Holbrin' and his fellows did not shy away from the lord as all others did.

"And so, Master Holbrin," he began, "I must ask for your assistance, too. For the sake of my people, I must ask for your help from you and your fellow travelers. Though I know you are not soldiers, you are obviously skilled fighters."

The elf inclined his head. "Of course, Your Lordship. We could not in good faith stand by and let this happen and do nothing," he placidly replied.

Chapter 5

Forested hills east of the town of Serna, Yvel Principality.
By the Human Calendar, Morningday (first day of the week), third week of
Talinochis, 793.
A cold and raw late winter afternoon.

"**W**ell?" said Dareum impatiently.

"We're getting very close, My Lord. Maybe a couple more hours," Korane said evenly, but there was an edge to her voice. One thin, white lock stood out against her otherwise raven black hair, neatly tied back. Dareum almost had to look away from her quietly burning gaze.

"They don't seem to be moving as a group," Garven, a young scruffy tracker, added.

The two trackers got up and moved ahead while Dareum remounted his horse, Creasan, a brown gelding. Dareum had led twenty-two tired townsmen and eight of their newfound Elven allies for two days following the orc raiders. The tracking was easy enough in the slush and mud, but Dareum wanted to know how many there were and to keep the patrol from being ambushed.

After the first twelve hours, some of the villagers had simply started to pass out from exhaustion, forcing a few hours' rest. Those first twelve hours had been the most painful. Some wept as they marched on, others stared blankly, merely placing one foot in front of the other as they followed the person in front of them. The elves were much more stolid, but were still tired from their travels, being awake for almost two days, and fighting a fire. There was a change after the rest with news from the trackers a few hours after the march resumed.

Korane had told Dareum that the orcs did not seem to be moving in any rush and that it would be easy to catch them. They had been resting, too. The Sernans continued on until they found the first body, blood staining the melting snow. Many recognized it as Iblar Enardran, a farmer who had made the trip into town to sell crops on the day of the feast. His body lay in a puddle of bloody mud and had been ripped open, ribs broken off, and innards taken out. The innards were nowhere in sight.

The sight of this transformed shock and grief into grim outrage. The march continued at a quicker pace. On the second day, Dareum's patrol found three more bodies, two ripped apart and one that had gotten away and hidden, but had suffered a bad wound, probably from a spear, and bled out.

It was odd being around Korane like this. She was nearly twenty years older than he was, and he had never had a reason to interact with her much, except occasionally on hunts with his father. In Dareum's younger years, he had the kind of lovestruck eyes for Korane that a young boy has for an older woman. He remembered the pangs of jealousy as he watched her marry and have a son. The memory shamed him, now.

Now, they had been on the move for two days and were near catching at least some of them. After an hour, Garven moved quietly back towards the main body, signaling to stop. Dareum passed back the message and waited.

"Just ahead, My Lord, there's four or five of them. Three are sleeping, one's eating, and one's…. with one of ours." Garven said.

Dareum's mouth set grimly and nodded. He could feel his blood heating from the steady simmer of the past two days and coming to a boil. He wheeled Creasan around and circled the patrol, drawing his sword.

"Sernans!" He spoke in a low sharp voice. The townsfolk returned his hard-eyed gaze. "They're just ahead. Follow me quietly, then charge and kill them all. We can get some of our folk back."

"Lord Dareum–" said Holbrin in a quietly urgent objection, but it was too late. Dareum was already moving, faster than the foot patrol could move quietly. He felt his anger grow. Seeing Korane's face, she pointed ahead to a small clearing. Dareum kicked Creasan into a charge, crashing through the bare brush, spraying clops of mud, barging into the clearing.

Dareum spotted one of the orcs eating the innards out

of a townswoman, hand over fist, looking up in surprise. Dareum wheeled Creasan around and slashed him across the face, severing off his left hand. It dropped and was replaced by four orcs rising from sleep. Dareum vaguely heard women sobbing as his steel met theirs. He slashed at the four of them viciously as they encroached on both sides with a sword, an axe, and two spears. He poked the one with the sword through the throat, but felt three meaty hands grab from the other side, rip him from the saddle and slam him on the ground, knocking the air from his lungs. In the corner of his view, he saw Creasan rear up and kick another orc as it punched Creasan in the face.

Two orcs stood over Dareum, grinning as Creasan fell over. One raised its spear high, but then both suddenly looked over their shoulders and turned. The villagers had caught up and were charging. Sprinting in low and in front of them was one of the elves, blade flashing, and eviscerated the two orcs. They dropped to their knees, staring at the fountain of blood pouring from their stomachs before falling to the ground. The townsfolk charged in and stabbed, hacked, and kicked the orcs in a fury. The elf leaped over Creasan, deflecting the spear, and parting a third orc's head in one clean movement.

Suddenly it was over. The wailing of the captured townsfolk being freed came to the fore as Dareum's anger subsided and his breath returned.

"Lord Covendran," said an elf, the one that seemed in charge of them. Dareum thought his name was Holbrin.

"Yeah?" said Dareum, still somewhat breathlessly. "Mkaela, go see if they can walk," he said to Mkaela as he spotted her.

"You cannot be doing that," said Holbrin firmly.

"Can't do what?" retorted Dareum.

"Charging in blindly and nearly getting yourself killed," Holbrin answered coolly.

"These are my people!" Dareum said, his temper rising again.

"Master your emotions, Lord Covendran. I am here as your ally," said Holbrin patiently. "I understand your passion, but you cannot help your people if you die in the first week."

Dareum turned away in a huff and stalked towards Mkaela, who was kneeling next to the rescued villagers. It looked like they had saved three women and a man; Aphra and Marlar Lin'ail, two sisters, Alis Benidran, who worked in the tannery, and Damarus Olid'ail, a stablehand at the Valley Spring Inn.

"How are they?" he asked Mkaela, gradually calming down. Dareum knew that Mkaela, though a baker with her family, had been apprenticing with the apothecary, and better than anyone in the patrol, would be able to judge their condition.

One of the other elves approached; the tall one that always had the blue tunic over his riding breeches. "May the Lady Mkaela be assisted, My Lord?"

Dareum glared at him for a moment before huffing and wordlessly jerking his head over in Mkaela's direction. He hurried off towards Mkaela. "Lady Mkaela, indeed," he grumbled to himself irritably. The thought of Mkaela being bowed to in a room of finery seemed ridiculous. Mkaela always seemed the type to come out of her family's bakery with flour and grease smeared on her apron or stains on her hands from grinding herbs for the apothecary. *Lady Mkaela.*

Moments later Mkaela approached Dareum, the elf was still kneeling with the rescued townsfolk. "They have no major injuries, My Lord. They can walk."

"Good. Let's get back on the move." said Dareum.

"What?" said Mkaela, hastily adding, "–My Lord."

Dareum moving towards Creasan, half turned and looked at Mkaela, silently asking if she was questioning him.

"My Lord, with what these people have been through, they're exhausted. They can't go on like this without slowing us down, and they're too tired to fight," said Mkaela.

Dareum turned towards her now, towering over her, but there was suddenly a flare of defiance in her eye and she stood before him, returning his glare. They stood there for a moment, more and more of the townsfolk-turned-militia stopped to look at them.

"My Lord," said the elf that had run in and saved him from the orcs with the spear and the axe. He looked at her. He did not remember her name. She was finishing cleaning off red orc blood from the blade with a cloth she had from her pocket. He did not miss the outstretched, feathered wing engraved along the length of the blade, and was almost distracted by the graceful curve of the wing so closely following the curve of the blade but shook himself from it. She wore brown riding breeches and a red tunic with braided knots and weaves embroidered around the collar and sleeve cuffs. Her silver hair was kept from her face by a simple leather band around her head and a cord tying it back behind her. Dareum had never seen anyone with yellow eyes before. Dareum was quite sure that she had slapped him that night during the fighting.

"What?" he said with an irritable shake.

"She is right. They will only slow us down. If we have to fight, we would have to protect them."

"Come now, they're as angry as all of us are!" Dareum insisted.

"My Lord, look at them. They have seen their fellows eaten alive. Their captors have probably been with them."

"Been with them? What do you mean!?" said Dareum incredulously.

She raised her thin eyebrows at him, producing a single crease in her forehead. Dareum started to take her meaning and shook his head looking to Mkaela, wordless demanding an answer.

Mkaela hesitated and then nodded. "Aphra and Marlar."

The tensions drained from Dareum's shoulders as he let out his breath, eyes widening in surprise. Dareum didn't know what to do. After a moment passed, "Korane."

"My Lord?" Korane approached from the trail ahead.

"Take these folk back to town."

Korane stared at him in disbelief for an instant. "But, My Lord, we're so close. We can just–"

"Now, Korane. We need to make sure they don't get lost and have something to eat for the two or three days back."

The two locked glares for another long moment before

Korane looked down. "Yes, My Lord. Hope you can manage to keep the track with Garven," she spat. Garven was her apprentice, Dareum's own age, or near enough. He was off to the side and glanced at her sidelong. He was also an able hunter and tracker, though not as experienced as Korane. Not nearly. But, he would do well enough with how obvious the trail was. Dareum knew that Korane was just spoiling for revenge and resenting Dareum for blocking her from it.

Dareum grabbed her by the arm and said to her in a low voice, "Listen, I need someone that I can rely on to get these people back without any other help. That's you. You have a very able apprentice, but he is not at your level for what I need you to do. There will be other fights. There is no way that orcs come for the first time in anyone's lifetime and only come once. These are people we can save right now. We can't bring anyone back that's already dead." Then he let her go.

After Korane and the rescued survivors left, Holbrin said to Dareum, "Some of my companions are skilled in tracking and can assist your man, if you would like." Dareum did not look back from adjusting a strap on Creasan's saddle when he nodded. Holbrin looked over at his companions. "Arynn, Turaean, help with the tracking up front."

Dareum saw a male and female elf move toward the trail of orc tracks alongside Garven. Garven watched them approach and Dareum heard them start to discuss the meaning of the signs in the tracks.

***

"Would you at least consider it?" said Holbrin.

"I dunno if we're even going to have time," said Dareum. "The whole town still has to be fortified, the militia has to be armed and drilled, and somehow everyone has to get fed and stay warm. Planting season is nearly upon us. With this whole thing, the farmers are too busy with spears to mind the farms and pull the crops during harvest."

"And you are the one and only that will make sure this

happens?" said Holbrin.

"Well..." Dareum fumbled to protest. Holbrin had been prodding Dareum on this same topic for the past two days, since their last scuffle with the orcs.

"I am certain that you can spare one or two hours a day to better learn the sword and better learn to fight from a horse," Holbrin said, briskly exploiting the small victory. *Heavens and the morning pray that you will even start to get a sense of when not to charge in*, he added to himself.

"Fine," said Dareum, relenting. "I will do as you ask, Master Holbrin."

"My Lord!" someone called.

Dareum's head whipped to the front to see Garven and the two elves, Arynn and Turaean sprinting towards them. "They're on us!"

Behind them, Dareum saw a cluster of orcs running their way. Unlike his first meeting with them, they were not hooting, howling, and laughing, although most of them were grinning. Now that they were in sight, three of them in the front roared. Dareum began to hear more of them crashing through the brush in the right to the left. Now he knew what to do.

"An ambush!" cried Holbrin, tearing his sword from its scabbard.

Dareum spurred Creasan, feeling his anger bubble and roil to the surface before setting into a blaze. The militia roared and screamed in challenging defiance behind him as Elven and militia arrows flew by him, toppling the first few orcs. Dareum slashed another one as Creasan reared up on its hind legs and kicked at two others. Spears, square-tipped swords, axes, and a few maces flowed around and past Creasan to crash into the hastily formed militia rank.

Dareum hollered and raged as he slashed and stroked at the orcs around him. Every third or fourth stroke would find a mark and he would receive a grunt or cry of pain as his blade nicked and slashed his targets. More often, he was blocked by a mass of weapons seeking him. A moment later, Creasan reared up and threw him hard. One last swing completely missed as his feet came out of the stirrups and he lost his seat. He hit the ground hard, knocking the wind–and the rage–from him. Struggling to get up, Creasan's massive body rolled over his legs, trapping him, with two spears buried past the steel into Creasan's ribs.

An orc bounding over Creasan tripped on Dareum, kicking and kneeing him in the chest, robbing him of the breath that he had regained. Gasping and struggling to pull air back into his chest, he looked around wildly. Lying on his back, trapped under Creasan's dying mass, he craned his head up to see the militia behind him, being hacked to pieces. Jorn Baydran, a farmer, and his son Garen Baydran were both down with gushing axe wounds, staring blankly at the mass of orc legs between him and his companions. He could hear Holbrin shouting orders to steady the ranks. The elf woman called Arynn slashed away an orc arm, creating a short window for Garven's bow to send an arrow into another orc bearing down on Taram. Taram finished the job, gripping his curved sword with two hands, batting aside his opponent's unsteady blade and cleaving through its neck.

Baryn took a spear deep in the stomach and tripped Bonwyn, his wife. The two fell together and another orc split Bonwyn's head. She died atop her husband. Hifen, an apprentice smith, slipped in the newly forming pool of bloody mud. Dareum saw another fall, a ruined face pouring blood onto the ground.

The din of the slaughter was pierced by a shriek. A long, sustained shriek to break glass. A shriek that said death was here. The shriek bore on as gouts of fire blossomed between the militia and the orcs, engulfing the orcs, burning them.

The burning orcs howled in pain, stumbling around, some collapsing and some cut down by the remaining militia or elves. The unburned orcs yelled in surprise and fear before running. Flames continued to spurt, uncontrolled, generally towards the orcs, but almost engulfing Urduin, the elf that had saved him the other day, or Taram who was finishing off a fleeing orc that he had tripped. Arrows and hollers chased off the remaining green-skinned orcs.

The flames died down and sputtered from Kora Orint'ail's hands. She had thrown them up instinctively to shield herself from a sword or a spear just seconds ago. She collapsed into unrestrained, hysterical sobbing. The sound of moans and weeping of the wounded began to rise to the fore as the ring of steel and twang of bowstrings faded.

***

Breaths later.

Kora Orint'ail had been a normal young woman, except for her red hair, leading a normal life, working in her family's glassblowing shop one row off of the main road through Serna. She liked red dresses, but only had brown ones. Her mother's peach pies could be smelled through the smoke and ash of the glass furnace. Over the past four days, all of that had burned and crashed down around her. Right now, she wore her mother's leather breeches that she used to work in the studio, her brother's brown tunic, and her father's leather apron in place of a gambeson. She sat on the ground, curled into a ball with her knees clutched to her chest, surrounded by charred orc bodies and the burned remains of her spear, sobbing uncontrollably. Everyone around her shouted, screamed, and moaned. Kora's sister, Ayza, rushed over to her, dropping her own spear and wrapping her arms around Kora.

"WHAT IN THE PIT WAS *THAT*!?" demanded someone. Mkaela could not see who.

"She's a witch!" accused someone else.

THIS WILL BE A TRIAL FOR YOU, said the shadow in Mkaela's mind. ACT.

Oh, Kostray help me. What am I supposed to do? she pleaded.

YOU MUST ACT. I DO NOT HAVE ANOTHER ANSWER. I CAN ONLY HAVE FAITH IN YOU. IF YOU ONLY SAVE OTHERS WHEN YOU ARE SAFE, WHAT GOOD IS THAT?

"Kill 'er before she burns all of us!" That was Arbera Rollodran, the miller's wife.

"Yeah!" cheered Amryst Veradran.

"Right, then," Mkaela heard someone else say. Orn Blar'ail, she thought, the tile layer. Mkaela saw the glint of light off of Orn's axe blade and his blue-breeched legs walking through the crowd towards Kora. Ayza clutched her sister protectively.

Mkaela forced her way through the hollering crowd with a rough hand, between an undecided, sour-faced Dyram Torin'ail and surprised Amryst. The latter stared at Mkaela skeptically, as if remembering a dream about which she did not want to ask. Mkaela moved past them all and stood between the sisters and Orn.

The crowd was divided between the ones yelling and hollering for Orn to kill the witch and the undecided ones.

"Move," said Orn.

"Don't you think there's been enough?" she said, standing firm, feet planted a little wider than her shoulders. Her hands grasped her spear in front of her, held across her chest.

"I said move," repeated Orn.

"No."

"She's a witch."

Mkaela hesitated. *What in the Pit!?* "So am I."

"What?"

"I said, so am I," she said more loudly.

"Truly? Prove it," he said coldly.

Mkaela looked around. It didn't take long before her eyes rested on Baryn Kevr'ail, bleeding to death under his dead wife and crying silently. She forcefully pushed past Orn and strode to the fallen husband and wife. She knelt and gently pulled Bonwyn's ruined body off of him.

Blood leaked out of Baryn as he looked at Mkaela, tears streaming silently. "It's alright. I'll be with her soon."

"I'm sorry. I need your help," said Mkaela, placing her hand over the deep tear in his stomach. The crowd had stopped cheering Orn on and watched to see what Mkaela would do. She willed the bleeding to stop and the wound to mend. Her hand began to glow and a few in the crowd gasped. Baryn started in surprise, eyes wide, watching the blood stop despite Mkaela pressing on the wound, listening to the sickening grinding sound as the flesh reknit beneath her hands. Finally, she pulled her hands away and wiped the blood off scarred skin.

Baryn unsteadily rose to his knees, pulled the ripped white shirt back, and looked at his stomach in disbelief. He rubbed the spot where he had just been mortally wounded and where there was now only discolored skin. After a few seconds, his disbelief crumbled to despair as he buried his face in his wife's blood-soaked dress, quietly shaking with sadness.

"Please," he sobbed, "save her, too. I can't be without her."

"I'm sorry, Baryn. I can't save someone when they're already gone." She put a hand on his shoulder as it shook in sadness.

Mkaela slowly stood and turned to face the silent crowd with Orn standing at their front, axe still in hand.

***

Eevarel saw Tyrnimar begin to move towards the humans, but Holbrin stopped him, catching him by the strap of his leather shoulder bag.

"Something must be done," Tyrnimar quietly said to Holbrin.

"Not yet," said Holbrin. "The Ways also say that you must help those worthy of it. Otherwise, you will come to regret what you saved. We must watch them to see if they, on the whole, are governed by their fear or their compassion."

Orn, the man with the axe leading the uncertain mob, took a step towards Mkaela, only to be stopped by another human male who roughly strode past him. This man, with an Orcish spear to match Mkaela's, turned to stand shoulder-to-shoulder with Mkaela. "You need to step back, Orn. There's been enough today and we have work to do," he said.

Orn looked at them and then back towards the Firecaster, who was now blocked by another man, Taram, bearing his own square-tipped Orcish blade. Orn scowled at each of them in turn.

"That's enough, Orn." The crowd turned to see an unsteady Dareum Covendran. He hobbled over to the Firebrand. The crowd parted in front of him as he knelt in front of her and Ayza. She had stopped crying, but gave a drained stare to Dareum. He idled for a moment and Eevarel wondered that these were the only two humans in Serna with red hair. Eevarel could not see his face. Something passed between them before he turned to the crowd.

"Witch or not, she saved us," he said to them. He looked around at each one of them. "If she hadn't done... whatever she did... most, or all of us, would be dead right now." He let that sink in. "We still have things to do–Taram, how many did we lose?"

"Uhm, five dead, My Lord," said Taram, shifting uncertainly. He had acquired a heavy knotted club from one of the fallen orcs to add to his sword.

Dareum looked at the ground for a moment, pursing his lips. "Who?"

"Uh, Jorn and Garen Baydran, uh, Abiah Zug'ail, Bonwyn Kevr'ail, and um, Yamis Jutzdran." said Taram.

Dareum let out a long breath after Taram finished. "Right. Dress them up and mark this location. Check with Garven to make sure we can find this place again," he said.

"My Lord?"

"We can't take them with us, we have to push on," Dareum said. "We'll have to come back for them and take them for proper rites when we get... when we get home."

"Yes, My Lord."

As the townsfolk sprung to movement, Eevarel watched Dareum's face. He was not a man trained to conceal his emotions well. Fear and conflict played across his face as he was no doubt imagining the prospect of bringing acknowledged witches back into their community.

Chapter 6

Forested hills east of the town of Serna, Yvel Principality
By the Human Calendar, Morningday, third week of Talinochis, 793.

A witch! A witch*! What am I going to do!? What will the Elder say? What will my* father *say?* Dareum worriedly stroked Creasan's mane and absently shivered off the cold. His horse's breathing was becoming labored and it began to shiver. He was trying to be with his friend in his final moments, but felt pangs of guilt at being so distracted.

"Lord Dareum."

Dareum looked up to see one of the Elven women. Most of them had red tunics, but this one had black hair that she wore in a braid. He thought she might be Sieraean. "Yes, Miss Sieraean?"

"Jovaela, My Lord."

"Right. Jovaela. Sorry." Dareum felt oddly awkward and did not say anything for a moment. Looking around briefly, he spotted Siraean and saw his mistake. They both had the same black hair, braided the same way into one thick strand that hung past the shoulders in the back, both wore a red tunic with the same silvery, embroidered knots and braids about the neck and sleeves, and both wore a curved sword at their belts. But where Sieraean seemed calm, Jovaela seemed… intense. "What is it?"

"One problem at a time," she said simply.

Dareum sharply exhaled. *One problem at time–alright!* he thought ruefully. "Right, could you send Master Holbrin to me, if he's not busy?"

"Of course," she said and turned to leave.

A moment later, Holbrin strode up to see Dareum gently stroking Creasan's mane. Creasan was lying on his side looking at Holbrin with an upward-facing eye. "Lord Dareum?"

"I'm in a great dilemma and I could use your advice," Dareum said.

"Oh?" said Holbrin.

Dareum looked at Holbrin somewhat irritably. *Don't play dumb.* "I'm not sure what to do. If I take Mkaela and Kora back and everyone finds out they're witches, they'll be burned. If I cast them off, then what does that say?" Dareum threw his hands out in front of him angrily. "I mean, they saved us. Kora saved us all and Mkaela saved Baryn. If I tell everyone not to say anything, then it's just a matter of time before someone tells the Elder." *Especially Orn or someone like him.* "The Elder... I'm not sure what the Elder will do, but he'll press my father very hard. He's the only person in town that's not afraid of my father... and I'm *afraid* of my father. What will he do...? I don't know. I don't know what to do." He paused and looked up at Holbrin after a moment. A puddle of drool was spreading under Creasan's mouth.

"Well, sir, I can't tell you what to do or what you should do," Holbrin said. Dareum's shoulders sagged, but Holbrin continued, "but I am curious about what your decision would be. Clearly, it would be a well-informed decision, based on the realities of your situation to the best of your knowledge and with full understanding of the consequences of your decision and its moral basis. That is correct, is it not?"

"Of course," Dareum said, hesitantly. *A game*, he thought bitterly.

"So, tell me, in the context of your decision, who are you?"

"What do you mean?" Dareum said.

"I mean, what is your role in this situation? In a battle, a soldier and a general both make decisions, but the decisions have different levels of reach. So, who are you? The soldier, the general, or somewhere in between?" Holbrin said.

"Somewhere in between, I suppose. I'm the son of the lord of this town, heir to the title of the town... and leader of this small company, I suppose," Dareum said.

"And what does that mean?" Holbrin prodded.

"What do you mean? I rule in my father's stead, I guess." *What's he on about?*

"And so, what are you responsible for?"

"Uh, finding our missing people," Dareum was beginning to tire of the game, "Look–are we going somewhere with this?"

"Yes, good sir, please be patient. I just want to understand the basis of your decision."

Dareum heaved a big sigh. "Alright, so what? I'm supposed to get our people back. What does that have to do with this?"

"Why are you getting your people back?"

"Because they're missing. Look, really–"

"But why does it matter that your people are missing? What is your responsibility?" Holbrin cut in.

"Oh, well," Dareum began, exasperated, raising an arm. "By Orneth! Of course, a lord has to take care of his people!"

"Ah, so you are responsible for your people's well-being. So, Miss Mkaela and Miss Kora, what did they do that brings this dilemma?"

"They used witchcraft…" Dareum said tiredly. *Damn his game.*

"And what was the effect of that witchcraft?" Holbrin continued, leading Dareum along.

"It saved us."

"So, then, the witchcraft acted towards fulfilling your responsibilities, so I have a hard time understanding how your father could have a problem with that by itself."

"Yes, right, of course. This is all what Elder Dum'ail would be having on about," Dareum sighed.

"What are Elder Dum'ail's concerns?" asked Holbrin.

"The Elder would probably go on about how witches are a threat to the faithful and the Church," answered Dareum.

"What is this church you speak of?" Holbrin asked.

Dareum looked at Holbrin sardonically. "The Church of Orneth, Holbrin. You know, with the Book of Orneth and all. You know these answers, so why do you ask?"

"I ask so that I understand the basis of your decision. I already said this," Holbrin said placidly, like the calm trickle of a stream.

"Fine." Dareum heaved another sigh.

"Is what you think Elder Dum'ail is going to say the same as what the Book of Orneth says?" Holbrin asked.

Dareum hesitated. "I mean, I don't know. It says a lot of things. I'm not an elder myself. I don't–"

"Let me ask a better question," Holbrin cut in. "Is the witchcraft that you saw today a threat to these people? Assuming these people are the 'faithful,' to whom you believe Elder Dum'ail would be referring."

"No..." Dareum began hesitantly, eyebrows furrowed before the tension in them released and he stopped squinting. "It was no threat at all. It was the opposite. They saved us."

"And does the Book of Orneth talk about helping and saving people?" Holbrin asked mildly.

"Yes," Dareum said pensively, "all the time."

"So then do you see what basis the elder could object to this witchcraft, since it saved people instead of killed them, which is the opposite of what he purports a witch to do and be, and that it acted in line with what the Book of Orneth says are good things," Holbrin said before pausing. "Right?"

"Right," Dareum said, still pensively. *Saved by a witch... by witches...*

"So, if you have that established that the witchcraft–at least *this* witchcraft–is in line with both what you are responsible for–the well-being of your people, and what the Book of Orneth professes to be a good thing–helping and saving people–what would happen if you turned them in as witches?"

"They'd be burned and I'd never forgive myself," said Dareum.

"What would happen if you tried to hide that they were witches?" Holbrin asked.

"I'd be burned with them," said Dareum.

"So, it seems that you are saying there is no point in hiding them. So what would happen if you declared that they were witches and that they helped save people–in line with what this expedition is meant to do, and in line with what the Book of Orneth says are good things to do and be?"

Dareum hesitated, "I don't know."

"But you do know how it would go otherwise, do you not?" Holbrin asked, mild as the beginning, as if they were discussing what to eat.

"Yes, I do." Dareum looked up again.

"Remind me again, good sir, who is responsible for the well-being of these people here?" Holbrin asked.

"I am," answered Dareum. "Thanks."

Holbrin smiled mildly, "What do you mean, good sir? I only wanted to understand the basis of your decision."

"Sure," Dareum said, rolling his eyes before turning to address the other townsfolk. They had finished preparations to move and were watching the exchange between Dareum and Holbrin. Some were gathered protectively around Kora and Mkaela; Taram and Dyram from the earlier confrontation with Orn, Amryst Veradran, and Kora's black-haired sister, Ayza. Apart from them, predictably, was Orn, and a thankfully smaller group of others looking upon Holbrin and the other elves with distrust, hostility, and outrage.

"Hear me," Dareum began, "when we get back to town, I will take responsibility for everything that happens here. I will explain what happened. If that means that Mkaela and Kora get burned as witches, then they'll have to go through me first. Anyone that's got a problem with that can tell the elder straight when we get back. 'Til then, we have an unfinished task."

Dareum waited for protest, but none came. He looked down at the fading Creasan. *Damned either way, I guess.* "Mkaela," Dareum said.

"Y-Yes, My Lord?" Mkaela answered.

"Can you help me with something?"

***

The glow faded as life flowed back into Creasan. He nodded his head and rolled onto his side to get up. Dareum stroked Creasan's mane again. The other townsfolk-turned-militia looked on with a mixture of awe, unease, and disapproval. Taram, Garven, and Kora were standing behind the crowd and looking back at the elves, seeming to gauge their reaction.

"Great irony is contained in that speech." Tyrnimar's Elvish words to Eevarel were wry. Jovaela reminded herself to talk to Holbrin about Eevarel later. Jovaela's eyes scanned over to Holbrin, who was exchanging another meaningful glance with Tyrnimar. They were doing that an awful lot around these particular humans over the past five days, she noted.

"Holbrin," said Jovaela in a low voice, "is it wise to let ourselves make references to such things in the open?"

Holbrin pursed his lips. "It is very unlikely that any of them speak or understand our tongue," he paused, and glanced at Tyrnimar as he squinted, "but you are correct. We should be more guarded."

"I want to parley," called out a voice in Eklendan, coarse and accented. "I do not wish to fight. May I come out?"

Dareum looked at Holbrin briefly before replying, "You may come out, but you'll be watched!"

From behind a stout-trunked pine at the opposite end of the muddy clearing, stepped out an orc unlike any of the others. Whereas the other orcs that raided Serna had worn ragged skins, this one wore a vest and pauldrons of untooled hardened leather over a padded gambeson, and breeches with leather greaves splinted with steel. The other orcs favored axes, large curved swords, and spears, but this one favored a recurved horn bow with a short sword at his belt. Much shorter than other orcs, his skin was a greyer shade than the others, but still very green. The main resemblance to the others was that he was still undoubtedly an orc, tusky teeth and all, and, like some of the others, was shaven bald.

He held his arms openly in a gesture that seemed to mean that he was not a threat. His steps crossed over his legs as he slowly made his way toward the crowd. The militia hollered and yelled threats at him as Dareum stood at their fore, seething with a hand on his sword hilt.

Holbrin strode past, briskly parting the crowd to reach Dareum directly. Placing a hand on Dareum's shoulder firmly, "Master Dareum, this is a parley. A most unusual one, at that. Perhaps we should see what he wishes to speak of."

Dareum focused on Holbrin and his breathing eased. "Right." Dareum turned back to the odd orc as the crowd quieted. "What do you want?"

"I want to know–I *must* know–how you did that?" the orc said.

"Did what?" replied Dareum.

"You know what I speak about," said the orc.

"What's that?" said Dareum.

The orc sighed and smiled. "That one," he said, pointing at Kora, "that woman, she spat fire from her hands and burned your enemies. How did you do that?" He addressed the question to Kora this time, who shrank from him behind Dyram and Taram.

"And you," he pointed at Mkaela. "That horse and that man, they were dead–*almost* dead–how did you make them live?"

"Why should I tell you *anything*?" Dareum took control of the conversation. "Who in the Pit are *you*, anyways? What do you *want*?"

"I told you before," he said. "I want to know how you did that, those things I just said."

"Why do you want to know?" Dareum said with a mix of hostility and suspicion.

The orc hesitated. "Because it is interesting to me."

"*Interesting!?*" said Dareum incredulously.

"Yes," answered the orc plainly.

"So, why should I tell you?"

The orc paused again. "Those are even words. You owe me nothing and I owe you nothing. We have no bargain. I would like to make a bargain with you."

"A bargain?" Holbrin barged in with just a hint of surprise.

The orc shifted his attention to Holbrin. "Yes, if that can be agreed to be even."

"So, who are you?" Dareum was trying again to regain control of the exchange.

The orc gave Dareum an even look. "I am called Grotis. I am a bargainer."

"A *merchant!?*" Dareum said incredulously.

"No, I am still learning more words in this language. I make bargains to do things." Grotis said.

"So, you're a mercenary?" Dareum said.

"What is 'mercenary'?" Grotis asked. Jovaela found it incredibly odd how genuinely interested Grotis seemed to be to learn a new word.

Dareum hesitated, perhaps thinking this was a joke at his expense. "Someone who fights for pay but is not part of a lord or king's army."

"Oh, no I am not a mercenary," Grotis said. "Sometimes I fight, but that is usually when things do not go as I want. Many times that I make bargains, it is to find people and places or help other people find people or places. Sometimes I hunt, sometimes I find…" Grotis paused searching for words, "… people or places or things going on at places and tell people for pay."

"I see," said Holbrin. "I presume you know who we are and what we are about?"

"What is 'presume'? No, I can think it. Yes, more or less. I know what you are about and can guess who most of you are. Though, you, elf, and your elf-friends, I did not think you would be here." Grotis seemed intrigued by it. It was uncanny for Jovaela to see an orc this thoughtful and articulate.

"So, you made a bargain with these other orcs? You're not part of them?" Dareum said.

"Part of them?" Grotis began. "No, no, no," he chuckled, shaking his head. "No, not part of them. I made a bargain with them. The bargain to help them find the places near the forest where humans live, I think you call them 'towns' and 'villages,' yes?" These were clearly new words to Grotis. "Then I make sure the remaining warriors return to a place."

"And they've already returned?" Holbrin prodded.

"Well…" Grotis looked away smirking.

Is he amused? Jovaela wondered.

"You make my bargain less big when you kill many of the warriors. The not-dead-warriors, they can find the way back," said Grotis. "So, the bargain is done. I will visit that location for my pay."

"So, you don't care about them?" Dareum ventured.

"What is 'care'?"

There is that interest again, Jovaela observed.

"That means that you want to know what happens to something or someone later and you want it to be a certain way," said Holbrin.

"That is 'care'…" Grotis said pensively. "I… have heard the word before, but have not had chance to learn its meaning."

"So, a bargain? For what?" Holbrin said, just a hint of impatience edging into his voice. Jovaela caught it, but only the travelers that had known Holbrin long would hear it.

"Yes, a bargain, I waste your time," Grotis said. "What do you want?"

Dareum hesitated. "I want to know this place that the orcs are going."

Grotis turned his head slightly and narrowed his eyes. "This is a bad bargain for you, I think. You will find this on your own and do not need my help. I think, too, that you do not want me around much," Grotis said, seeming to take note of the other townsfolk.

"Fine," Holbrin broke in. "How many orcs are there and what do they want?"

Grotis smiled approvingly. "A better bargain for you. What is my pay? How did you make fire and bring back life to those?"

"We cannot say. We do not really understand it," said Dareum.

"I know what you mean. You do not know the answer," said Grotis. He searched about in the crowd. "What about… your arrows?"

"Our arrows?" Dareum said, not understanding what value Grotis could have in arrows, "you already have plenty."

"Not your arrows, their arrows," he said, pointing at Eevarel, Siraean, and Jovaela.

"No," Holbrin said.

That *would be quite a note in the travel report*, thought Jovaela.

Grotis was clearly disappointed. "Then can I make a picture of them?"

"A picture?" Holbrin said quizzically.

Grotis slowly reached behind him, taking care to not appear as a threat, and produced a leather tube and a small pouch. Inside was parchment or paper, Jovaela could not tell which, and what appeared to be charcoal.

Who is *this orc?* Jovaela wondered.

Holbrin hesitated. "Very well." He motioned for someone to hand him an arrow.

"Are you certain of this, Master Holbrin?" Jovaela hissed in Elvish as she handed him one of her arrows.

"No, it is a risk, but I believe it to be worth it to determine the purpose of this activity and the purpose behind the purpose," said Holbrin.

"Here," said Holbrin, switching back to Eklendan.

Grotis eagerly snatched the arrow and began to produce a charcoal rubbing of the head and fletching. *He is practically giddy*, thought Jovaela. Grotis was very quick, but Jovaela noted a particular attention to detail and precision in the movement of his hands and fingers, despite the sharp finger nails, bordering on claws, that orcs had. Grotis began scribbling notes on the paper.

When Grotis began writing notes, Tyrnimar pushed the front, abandoning propriety and came to stand over Grotis, intently staring at his writing.

Grotis stopped writing after Tyrnimar stood over him and turned to say, "You are in my light."

"Sorry." Tyrnimar hastily moved over, stumbling a bit.

"Where was that learned by you?" Tyrnimar asked, clearly alarmed.

"Is this part of the bargain?"

"Well... " Tyrnimar fumbled.

"No," said Holbrin, giving a pointed look to Tyrnimar, "not if it changes what we would owe."

Turning to Tyrnimar, Grotis asked, "Is this a new bargain? Could I have some of your writing papers?"

Tyrnimar was suddenly also disappointed, "Sorry, no. That cannot be done."

Grotis looked back to his notes, wordlessly dismissing Tyrnimar. When he finished, he rolled the paper up, placing it in the leather tube, and storing it back where it was. Jovaela could now see that he carried a small bag on his back, which he could reach some parts of without removing it. Tyrnimar nervously returned to the crowd, lost in another one of his ruminations, eyes looking at the ground and darting about while nervously fingering the clasp of his leather shoulder bag.

"Right," Grotis began, in very animated spirits. He even grinned a toothy smile. "There are maybe nine hundred orc warriors in this warband."

He can count*!* Jovaela fretted. *He knows numbers...*

"And their purpose?" Holbrin said patiently.

"As I can see, they were told to be here, maybe by an orc king," Grotis said.

"A *king*?" Dareum said skeptically.

"You have those here, yes?" Grotis said.

"Yes. Well, no, not here, but there are kings–wait, an orc king?" Dareum said.

"Yes... it does happen." Grotis said.

"Why?" Holbrin said.

"Well, when the many tribes can be–" Grotis began.

"No, I mean why did the king order it?" Dareum reworded.

"I do not know myself that he did, but this is the only

way that I can think of that this would happen. The order does not make sense by itself. I believe there must be a bigger reason for this. Perhaps the king is forced to give this order by someone else. Someone even bigger and stronger."

"And what will these nine hundred orcs be doing?" Holbrin said.

"Nine hundred orc warriors," Grotis corrected, "they would be doing more of the same," said Grotis.

"Are there other groups of orcs like that coming here?" Holbrin asked.

"I do not think so, but I think there are other groups of orcs moving to other places to do the same thing," Grotis said.

He really does not care about them... Jovaela mused.

"Very well," said Holbrin. Holbrin looked over to Dareum, "Do you have any questions for our friend here?"

"Friend!?" interjected Grotis, perplexed. "I thought... oh, I understand." He fell silent, amused.

"Who made the bargain with you to show them our town?" Dareum said.

"I cannot tell this," said Grotis. "I do not tell who gives me work and, usually, not the work. This work was not hard or very..." he searched for the word, "secret. But I do tell you, go and find these nine hundred orc warriors and you will find him."

Chapter 7

Forested hills east of the town of Serna, Yvel Principality.
By the Human Calendar, Weddingday (third day of the week), third week
of Talinochis, 793.
The next morning, cold and drizzling.

"That is exactly the point being made by me!" Tyrnimar said in Elvish with exasperation.

"What are you two going on about?" asked Dareum in Eklendan.

Holbrin looked over to Dareum astride Creasan as he and Tyrnimar walked with the patrol. "An excellent question." He turned back to Tyrnimar, speaking in Eklendan. "Why not explain it again, Tyrnimar? I have lost track of your original point."

Tyrnimar exhaled vexedly. "My point is that this is very big, that the orcs would be ruled by a king."

Dareum hesitated. "That's it? I thought we already knew that. Isn't that what that odd orc told us a couple days ago?"

"Yes, he did," Holbrin said to Dareum, "but my friend is having trouble expressing the depth of his point." He turned to Tyrnimar. "At the risk of being general, based on the size of the orc incursion that you believe to be there, how far can it go? How much territory could it potentially take and hold?"

"Markia, Eklenda, and the eastern cities–Yvel included absolutely–can be taken by the attackers–"

"You mean the orcs," said Dareum, shivering off the rain.

"No," Tyrnimar said pointedly with a small smile, showing he was glad that Dareum asked the question.

"What do you mean?" Dareum asked.

"Many more than orcs. Probably hobgoblins, goblins, ogres, trolls, and some others," Tyrnimar said.

"All that? Where's this coming from?" Dareum said, alarmed.

"This is my point, my friend," Holbrin said to Tyrnimar. "You have not been tried at the debate halls like Trinien and get distracted." Speaking again to Dareum, Holbrin turned his gaze. "Tyrnimar will explain that in a moment. First, he needs to explain why he thinks that these attackers, orcs or no, can seize and hold all of that territory."

Tyrnimar paused, collecting his thoughts. "Yes, in due course. The nine hundred orc warriors were seen by us yesterday. The meaning of Grotis is now taken. By orc warriors it was meant by him to differentiate from orc non-warriors—and there are many. Among the warriors were those like the ones that attacked Serna, but also there were others. Sentries were seen by us—"

"Remind me about sentries at the end of this," Holbrin said quietly to Dareum.

"Serna was attacked by orcs that do not post sentries," said Tyrnimar.

"So what?" said Dareum.

"Cooperation between orc tribes is meant," said Tyrnimar.

"So… ?" said Dareum, still not understanding.

"This is a good point to explain something," Holbrin broke in. "What I have managed to have Tyrnimar explain to me since breakfast, among other things, is that most of you may have a concept of orcs that they roam about hunting and raiding, living off of the pillage, occasionally trading loot, captives, and such." Holbrin paused to step around a tree trunk as they walked.

"Yes, and—" Tyrnimar broke in excitedly.

Holbrin continued to speak through Tyrnimar's interruption. "Note that the orcs we have fought so far, have had only square-tipped swords, two-hander axes, and spears, maybe a few heavy clubs or maces. Any ranged weapons are thrown spears and javelins. None of them used bows or crossbows. On the other hand, the sentry patrol that we silenced yesterday all had bows, hand axes, and hide-wrapped shields."

Holbrin paused and they walked in a conspicuous silence as Holbrin eyed Tyrnimar. Tyrnimar held his peace and Holbrin continued. "If you noticed, the cut of the skins and furs that they wore was different, as well. The ones that attacked Serna had skins that were tied about them with minimal stitching. The sentry patrol orcs had clothing that displayed the skins seamed together into trousers and shirts or long tunics. They had belts, loops for their axes, slings on their shields, quivers, and the like. Such a great difference is beyond simply stature within the same greater tribe, they are from wholly different tribes."

"Yes!" Tyrnimar resumed enthusiastically. "Tribes that have no reason to cooperate!"

"The orcs that we commonly think of–the ones that live off of hunting and pillaging–certainly exist, but they exist outside of the kingdoms of orcs, roaming the mountains and hills, maybe in the underworld, and maybe a few have small villages," said Holbrin.

"Right… but that's what the odd orc said, sort of, that there was an orc king that made them cooperate. So, wait, what's the underworld?" said Dareum.

"And another thing those both are!" Tyrnimar said excitedly.

"Not yet, Tyrnimar, and keep your voice down. We do not know if we are pursued by patrols. It's hard enough as it is to hide this amount of tracks in the mud," Holbrin said to Tyrnimar, then addressed Dareum. "The orcs we fought so far in this little outing care little for stealth and are probably a rather small tribe. If they were large enough, then they would be able to hunt and pillage enough food that they would be able to dedicate a portion of their tribe to craftsmanship. Since they all wear loosely stitched, ill-treated animal skins with no metal reinforcement, they probably each made those themselves or had their slaves do it."

Tyrnimar started on another addition, but snapped his mouth shut at Holbrin's glance. Holbrin then continued. "Since they do not have better-made leather or quilted armor, let alone any mail, their weapons are probably pillaged or traded, particularly the steel ones. This particular tribe has a mix of different weapon styles. You can notice particularly in the swords: some are square-tipped and some are forward-curving. The inconsistency makes me think that they do not make their own and have to trade or pillage with other sources. I would further venture that the ones that we fought are among the youngest warriors in the tribe, eager to prove themselves to their tribe leader. Maybe thirteen or fourteen summers old,"

Holbrin said.

"Thirteen or fourteen!?" exclaimed Dareum.

"Your voice down, please," said Holbrin chidingly. "Yes. Orcs reach adult age much faster than humans. Just as humans age much faster than elves."

Tyrnimar spoke again. "That the amount of orc tribes cooperating is forced by an orc king is given–"

"*An* orc king? There's *more*?" Dareum said, keeping his voice down.

"Yes," answered Tyrnimar offhandedly, "it is given, and so, a reason for an orc king to do this for his own sake does not exist. He must be forced by another to do this. That all of the orc kings are mostly equal in power means that another orc king forcing the first to do this is not likely."

"Wait… that another…" Dareum puzzled.

"He meant that it is unlikely that one orc king is making this orc king gather these orcs," said Holbrin.

"Right," said Tyrnimar. "More likely, several orcs kings are being forced into this by another, more powerful leader. Since this leader is powerful enough to force several orc kings into this, that means it is also likely to be powerful enough that other cast-out races would be forced into doing things other than they normally would by it."

"Sorry," Dareum broke in and then paused. "Your method of speaking is difficult for me to follow."

Tyrnimar looked perplexed. "Sorry?"

Holbrin suppressed a smirk. "Tyrnimar comes from a region in our lands where they speak an Elvish dialect in this way. My friend here has learned most of the languages that he knows through studying them in books and his method of thinking and speaking echoes in the other languages that he knows, even if he cannot think in the other languages."

"Thinking in other languages can be done by me, by way of course," Tyrnimar muttered under his breath.

"Most of us have traveled more and learned languages among the people that speak them," Holbrin finished.

"None of you are from that region besides Tyrnimar?" Dareum asked.

"Irduin Usrani is from the same region, but she has traveled much more. We are getting distracted from our main topic, however," said Holbrin.

"Yeah, the cast-out races?" said Dareum.

"Yes, orcs, goblins, hobgoblins, all those listed before by me, and a few others," said Tyrnimar.

"What do you mean 'cast-out'?" asked Dareum.

Tyrnimar glanced at Holbrin for reassurance before speaking. "A few tens of thousands of years ago, the whole lands were covered by all of the different races and mixed together–not mixed together as in side by side, but on the same grassy plain or forest would be a village of humans, a clan of hobgoblins and goblins, a tribe of orcs, a village of halflings. Mostly staying in the same places were the elves, dwarves, gnomes, and dragons."

"Dragons?" Dareum said, "You're telling me those exist?"

Holbrin regarded Dareum. "Is what you have seen over the past week perfectly normal to you?" Dareum pursed his lips and looked away as Holbrin continued. "Please further suspend your skepticism that dragons exist, as well."

Doesn't that mean that they knew about magic all along? thought Garven, who had been listening to the whole conversation. *They probably can't admit it, though. Otherwise, we would be having very different conversations… I wonder if they know magic themselves… and they never answered Lord Dareum's question about the underworld.*

"Repulsive and hostile to us are the ways of the orcs, the hobgoblins, and the others of that ilk. Elves, humans, dwarves, gnomes, and halflings are meant when 'us' was said by me," said Tyrnimar. "War and conflict were bred by this hostility. The hobgoblins, orcs, and such were cast out by us, hence 'cast-out races.' A broad summary is here. Nuances and exceptions are many and there were some others–" Tyrnimar broke off at a look from Holbrin.

"My friend's point, that we seem to continually distract ourselves from," said Holbrin placidly while giving Tyrnimar a sidelong look, "is that there is some leader or ruler among the cast-out races that is binding them together for a single purpose, probably to take these lands for themselves."

Dareum's face scrunched in thought, "What's this all based on?"

Holbrin and Tyrnimar glanced at each other and spoke simultaneously.

"Assumptions," said Tyrnimar.

"Conjecture," said Holbrin.

"Conjecture…?" Dareum puzzled at the word.

"Why–" Garven blurted it out before he could stop himself. He looked at the ground sheepishly, turning red from embarrassment at barging into a conversation amongst his betters.

"It's alright, Master Garven," Dareum assured him, "it's a good question."

"The cast-out races live in very harsh areas in the hills and mountains with little in the way of hunting and farming. These lands are much easier to make a way," said Holbrin.

That's not what I mean, Garven thought uncomfortably.

Holbrin studied Garven. "You meant something else, something deeper, yes?"

"Yes, sir," said Garven tentatively. "I mean, why are they doing this *now*? Why not last summer or ten years from now? What caused them to act? The difference between the areas hasn't changed."

"Keenly put," said Holbrin who glanced at Tyrnimar, eyebrows raised in unspoken question.

"So much is uncertain," said Tyrnimar. "Let it be assumed by us that the reasons for these lands being wanted by them now are the same as they were before being cast out, then the reasons being based on their religion is what would be said by me."

"But their religion has not changed, has it?" asked Garven.

"No, by way of course, it has not," said Tyrnimar.

"Then it still leaves the 'why'," said Garven.

"Being visited by their own god could be the 'why'," said

Tyrnimar.

"Visited by their own god?" said Dareum incredulously.

"Yes," said Tyrnimar, plainly not understanding what was unclear.

"The gods visit people?" Dareum said distantly, seeming to have difficulty accepting the idea.

"Surely, just as humans were created by their gods, elves were created by their gods, so too were orcs created by their gods."

"You are saying that the orc god visited them and made them do this?" said Dareum gravely.

"More likely a demon," Holbrin broke in smoothly, "masquerading as their god."

"A demon?" Dareum repeated in disbelief.

"Is it so unbelievable next to a dragon?" asked Holbrin soberly.

"I suppose not," Dareum bleakly conceded.

Garven noticed Mkaela, who was walking near enough to hear, look away. He also noticed Tyrnimar attempting to be discrete while squinting at Mkaela.

"So, you're saying that a demon pretending to be a god visited some creature more powerful than several orc kings and is making them all do this," said Garven, with an eyebrow raised at Tyrnimar.

"Yes," said Holbrin and Tyrnimar in unison.

"How do you know it wasn't a demon pretending to be the orc god that visited the orc kings and made them cooperate, or just one orc king?" asked Garven.

Holbrin and Tyrnimar glanced at each other before Holbrin spoke. "We do not know. As my friend said, this is largely based on assumptions. If we are at least half correct, then we know enough that we can prepare," he said, looking at Dareum, "assuming that your father can successfully secure help from Prince Gerald. I truly hope that the Lady Covendran was persuasive."

"I think we can be assured," said Dareum ruefully. "She can be quite persuasive with even the most stubborn. My mother has this way about her. You end up agreeing to do things you were so set against just moments before."

"It is seen by me," muttered Tyrnimar under his breath, but only Garven seemed to hear.

"You wanted to talk about something else?" Dareum asked Holbrin.

"Ah, yes, the sentries." said Holbrin, "Your man took a bit of a risk yesterday, really. He put us all at risk."

"What risk? What do you mean?" said Dareum.

"You did not know?" Holbrin said in mild surprise.

"Know what?" Dareum said, becoming insistent.

"The sentry patrol did not spot your militia first, they attacked the sentry patrol and took a head as a trophy," said Holbrin.

"What!?" said Dareum, angrily.

His Lordship is about to be at it again, thought Garven.

"They were under the leadership of your man, Orn," said Dareum.

"Orn!?" Dareum was getting angry.

"Sir, your voice, please," cautioned Holbrin.

"Orn!" Dareum called. "*Orn!*"

Orn Blar'ail broke off from a heated discussion with Taram. Taram was speaking quietly but angrily at Orn, but Orn was laughing and waving it off while he made his way over to Dareum. "Yes, My Lord," he said. He stood in his yellow trousers, stained brown with mud and grass, his plain workman shoes with dents from dropping roof tiles on them over the years, and his brown patched tunic. He stood with his feet wide and a hand resting comfortably on the axe stuffed through his belt. There was a quiet challenge in Orn's answer to the summons.

"What are you doing seeking out those orcs for a fight? Why are you putting us all in danger? What if one of those sentries got away and brought the whole damn horde on us? Why are you giving any orders when I put Arbera in charge of you four?" Dareum accused.

"Relax, My Lord," Orn waved off with a laugh, but there

was defiance in his eye. "There were four of us, two of them, they didn't see us, we were giving 'em what they deserve. We took heads, too."

"You did *what*!?" Dareum hissed.

"Look, what's the problem, My Lord? We gave it to 'em. None would be the wiser," Orn paused searching, "if it wasn't for that pointy-eared tart!" Orn pointed. Garven followed the line of his finger to Arynn.

She must have seen and told Holbrin, Garven thought. *Can't let this get out of hand.*

Garven took two strides up to Orn before the weight of Dareum's outrage caused everyone else to take a threatening step towards Orn. Sensing the sudden change in atmosphere, Orn held up his open hands, "I'm sorry, My Lord. I made a hasty act." Mockery, insincerity, and resentment smoldered in Orn's eyes.

A moment passed in silence as Dareum's burning gaze bore into Orn. The tiler gradually broke the challenge and looked down. "See to it that you are. I will deal with you when we return," said Dareum. Turning, the young lord addressed Arynn and Garven. "Make sure to take us back to where we left the dead. We owe them a proper burial."

As the Serna Militia resumed movement, Garven and Arynn moved towards the front to take the lead again. Garven distinctly heard someone mutter 'witch-lover.'

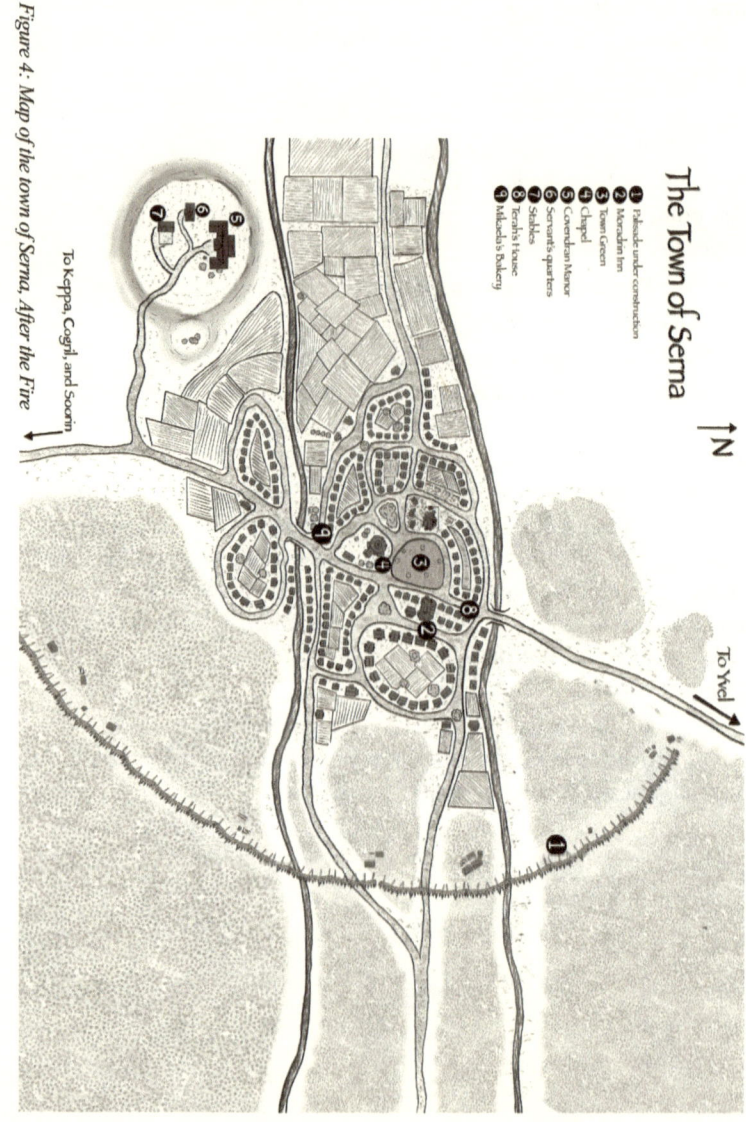

The Town of Serna

↑N

1 Palisade under construction
2 Meridian Inn
3 Town Green
4 Chapel
5 Covendian Manor
6 Servant's quarters
7 Stables
8 Terah's House
9 Mikaela's Bakery

To Yvel →

To Kappa, Cogril, and Soorm →

Figure 4: Map of the town of Serna, After the Fire

Chapter 8

Library at the Palace of Yvel, Yvel City, Yvel Principality.
By the Human Calendar, Weddingday, third week of Talinochis, 793.
Rays of sunlight peaking through the late winter clouds, same morning.

"I'm off, then, my friend."

"Do be careful," said Nicholas.

"Oh, fear not. I'll be with the *Prince*," said the Blue-Eyed Man with an eye roll.

"Be not such a brat!" Nicholas scolded indignantly. "They can see in the dark, you know."

The other man was silent. He paced and looked at the library floor while sipping his coffee. "Oh, I suppose you're right," he said abashedly. "I'm no Berin the Great, but I could be of more use to him on one of the other expeditions. The Prince is sending companies and battalions all over the border. He could send me to Borly to command the battalion there."

"He could, but Mot Gundr'ail, *his general*, is perfectly capable of handling those battalions and the sappers," said Nicholas in a conciliatory tone.

"Oh," said Nicholas, crestfallen, realizing that his friend had become, once again, distracted by sweets. He waited as the Blue-Eyed Man picked through more of the pastries.

The Blue-Eyed Man's head whipped up in surprised amusement. "What's this? Oh," he chuckled. "*Oh*, what's *this?*" He became distracted by a sweet bread topped with mashed hazelnuts mixed in thick cream.

"What do you mean 'they can see in the dark'?" the Blue-Eyed Man asked while he was chewing, changing the subject.

Nicholas sighed. "I mean I have numerous accounts, some informants further in our east, and some foreign contacts that all generally agree that orcs can see in the dark. Some say they see in the dark the same as they see in daylight. Some say that light is simply brighter to them so that what is too dark for us is not too dark for them. Some say that they can see heat," Nicholas said.

"Mmph," the Blue-Eyed Man exclaimed around a wad of chewed up pastry. "Read same thing, especially about the body heat. Several accounts, Berin the Great's campaigns and the dissolution of the old empire. Even have a long essay about how the orc eyes work by a Dwarven medicine man."

Nicholas looked at him long and hard. "Then why did you ask if you already have all of that?"

"Oh, I haven't actually read the essay from the dwarf yet. It's in Dwarven. It'll take me a bit," the Blue-Eyed Man said.

Nicholas continued his long stare. "You read Dwarven?"

"A bit. A few in the Crown Guard do. It'll take me a while." The Blue-Eyed Man smiled while finishing chewing the pastry.

"Somehow, I think you're trying to distract me from what we were speaking of and I just want you to not take this lightly and be careful," Nicholas said bitterly.

After washing down a bit with more coffee, the Blue-Eyed Man continued. "Don't mistake me, friend. I've nothing to prove, it's just going to be boring–"

"Boring. Of course," Nicholas muttered.

"–sitting there, watching the Prince actually *command* troops while doing nothing myself. I can't even fight in this little constabulary action; there will be two whole battalions there and the Crown Guard. And that's another thing! Why are there so many troops going to Serna? I mean, I was there when the Lady Covendran gave her petition… I can't describe why it's so compelling, yet if you examine the facts, their situation is really no worse than Borly, Keppa, or any of the smaller villages near the eastern woods."

"You never change," Nicholas grumbled. "I would hardly call this a little constabulary action. Have some perspective, my good man. Orcs have not come out of the hills in this number for *centuries!* Surely, it will not be over with a few skirmishes. I have reports from some Dwarven merchants that pass through. If there is one thing that orcs are undeniably better than us at doing, it would be breeding. They tell me there are whole cities of orcs."

"That doesn't sound so bad," said the Blue-Eyed Man, "except for the ugly part," he added ruefully. "Where are these dwarf merchants now?"

"My *point*, dear sir, is that even if you kill them all in a few battles, more will come. They would not send hundreds for no reason. They want something," said Nicholas.

Finishing the hazelnut sweetbread thoughtfully, the Blue-Eyed Man spoke. "I suppose you're right. There will be enough opportunity for adventure... in fact, if what you say is correct, then the Crown Army will be consumed. If more than these few hundred come, then there would need to be a new levy. The merchants' council will protest and block wherever they can... this may be more of an opportunity than I realized..."

The Blue-Eyed Man walked over to the table at which Nicholas was seated, its surface laden with books, maps, and documents. "Where is that ledger?"

"Over there with the almanac. You don't mean to–" began Nicholas.

"I do. I want you to make the necessary arrangements with the other ministry."

"But the Prince–" Nicholas protested.

"Will never know. If he does find out, it will be too late and he may well thank us for the result, if not the method," said the other man.

Nicholas was silent for a moment while he considered his friend. "I hope you know what you are doing. I am the Prince's man, first."

"That you are. And so am I, my friend, but there is only so much power in the world and we'll need all we can get in the coming days, if you're right."

***

Outside the town of Serna.
By the Human Calendar, Restday (tenth day of the week), third week of Talinochis, 793.
An overcast, late winter morning.

Almost there, Garven thought. He was exhausted. They all were. *Well, maybe not the elves. Nothing seems to worry them.*

Garven held aside a low branch from a beech tree for Dyram to pull the makeshift sled carrying Jorn Baydran's body. Garven felt that he was looking at the leaves of the beech for the

91

first time in the afternoon light of the cloudy day, noting how the shape of the leaves so closely resembled the heads of the arrows that his newfound companions carried.

"Thanks," Dyram grunted as he pulled Jorn behind him. They could hear the sounds of the town from where they were. Garven continued to hold the branch aside for the rest of the party. Turaean and Arynn were the next to pass him. Turaean looked ahead towards the town while passing him. Arynn spared him a brief smile of thanks. Garven looked after them for a moment, *I wonder what–*

"Hold it back a bit more, man." Garven started, whipping his head back to Taram pulling another sled. Taram passed, as did Baryn pulling his own wife behind him on a sled, pine boughs covering her body. Baryn would break into sobs periodically. Everyone had grown to ignore it quickly, though for many it was due to their own grief at their own friends and loved ones. Orn and his small group of newfound cronies passed him with cold glares, followed by Dareum riding Creasan. The rest of the militia and the elves followed.

Orn was the youngest man in what had been a large family. He was fully twenty-three, though he seemed older because of how soon his beard had come in. Garven remembered being jealous of Orn. He was fifteen years old when it grew in, when most other boys were sprouting whiskers at best.

Orn's brothers, sisters, and cousins had all married. That was one thing that Garven had in common with Orn. Both of their families never wasted a day in asking when they were going to get married, or suggesting one match or another. Orn was rarely fun to be around for Garven, which is why Orn worked tile-laying alone, but he imagined that those questions did not improve his moods.

Garven followed at the back of the patrol now. The woods ended thirty paces away from the town's edge. The trees had come up to the eastern edge of the town when they left almost a week ago. A wall made up of logs driven into the ground like pickets beginning on the east side of town was being extended around to the north and south. It used to smell clean here. In town, the stink of the tanneries and other industry quickly faded past the edge of the forest. A week ago, there was nothing but smoke and ash to fill his nose. Between the new edge of the tree line and the growing wooden palisade, the smell of ash lingered faintly and mingled with the scent of sap from the freshly cut stumps he passed as he followed everyone else.

The familiar smells of the small, once-prospering town emerged to greet him. The burned buildings had been torn down, and townsfolk were finishing clearing away the wreckage and debris. They looked exhausted, each and every one of them, just as exhausted as he and his fellow militiamen. Not the elves, though. Arynn and the others looked just as pristine as the day they had walked into town, even if there was a leaf clinging to her silver hair.

Garven saw Lord Koval come out to greet them. He looked exhausted. Garven could almost swear there was just the slightest touch more grey in his beard. He looked different in other ways, too, though Garven could not quite place it, as he briskly strode up to meet the column with Lord Dareum at its head.

He could not hear what they were saying, but he could guess. Korane would have told Koval about some of the people they saved and the ones that they found when Dareum sent Korane back to town with the Lin'ail sisters, Alis, and Damarus. They had set out to get back twenty-five of their people. They found four dead, saved four, and lost four from their patrol of thirty townsfolk and eight elves. Twenty-one townsfolk were still missing. All twenty-five were not coming back.

There goes trouble. Garven watched as Orn slipped off with few of his cronies, newly joined by Amryst Veradran, no doubt to get Elder Dum'ail, *come what may.* Garven walked closer as some of the townsfolk left their work to greet the returning militia patrol. He heard some cries and sobs as people learned of more friends and loved ones that would not be coming back. He could hear Dareum and Koval speaking.

"What do you mean 'powers'? You make it sound like there we have a bunch of witches," the Koval said, chuckling uneasily.

"It's just that, father." Dareum paused uneasily. "We have witches among us. They saved us."

Koval stared at Dareum for a long moment before

speaking. "You saw this? You're certain."

Dareum looked down at the ground. "Absolutely."

"Tell me what happened."

Dareum recounted the second skirmish with the orcs, nearly being overrun, being saved at the last instant by Kora's firecasting, and Mkaela saving Baryn and Dareum's horse, Creasan, from bleeding to death.

Garven glanced around and spied Baryn sitting on a log meant for the palisade, staring at the ground next to the covered litter bearing his wife. What would he do, Garven wondered, with his wife dead. Turning back to the conversation, Garven could see Koval's eyes casting about for Kora and Mkaela. Mkaela averted her gaze and Kora cringed away from it and hid in the consoling embrace of her sister Ayza. Baryn seemed not to recognize or care if anyone took notice or issue with him. Garven felt a shiver down his spine as Koval's gaze passed him to finish back at Dareum. Dareum's downcast face met his father's gaze for a moment.

Koval strode over to Kora, who shrank away from him in Ayza's arms, against the timber and clay side of a shop-turned quartermaster office. "Can you make her show me what she did and how?"

Dareum stared at his father, mouth slightly agape in surprise and trepidation. Garven noted a hint of impatience before Koval knelt before Kora. "Fear not, child. I will not hurt you. I only want to see what you can do with my own eyes."

Kora screwed her eyes shut, clutching her knees to her chest. "Father, she's been inconsolable for most of the trip or mute. Especially when we realized we couldn't get the others back," Dareum said.

"Fear, My Lord."

Garven turned with Dareum and Koval towards Mkaela.

"She was terrified when the fire flew from her hands and now, she's terrified of it. So scared that she can't even speak."

"Fine, then, show me what you can do," the Koval said.

"My Lord, have we any injured right now?" Mkaela said.

"Hm. No. Describe how you did it, then."

Mkaela seemed to hesitate and deliberate for a moment, eyes darting minutely. "It… just… feels right, My Lord. At least now, it does."

"*Now* it does? This just happened, did it not? Master Baryn and my son's horse."

Mkaela was unable to keep her gaze anywhere but the ground and seemed conflicted. "I have used it before, a week ago during the raid and the fire."

"On whom?"

Mkaela hesitated before answering, "Baswyn Gerndran… Damerwyn Perndran… Rielan Yidr'ail… and Amryst Veradran." There was a murmur through the crowd. Garven remembered Baswyn, Damerwyn and Rielan together and hysterical that they were alive the morning after the fire. "I couldn't save Danick Isrdran or… someone else." She ventured a look up at Koval before returning her gaze to the ground.

"Who was the someone else?" asked the lord.

Mkaela's face twisted for an instant in a memory of pain. "I couldn't recognize her." She hesitated. "There was too much blood on her face, My Lord."

Koval regarded her for a moment. "That's all fine, child. It felt right, you say? I–"

"Stand aside, My Lord, and we'll dispense rightly with these witches." The crowd turned. Elder Dum'ail approached at the head of another crowd, closely followed by Orn, Amryst, and some of those who had backed Orn on the patrol.

"Stand aside?" Lord Covendran replied calmly.

"From the witches!" Elder Dum'ail and his mob drew up. Koval stared at him blankly. The elder hesitated. "Surely you do not suggest harboring witches?"

Koval continued to regard him evenly. The elder hesitated and his mob began to murmur. He said in a low voice, "I am willing to overlook your son's indiscretions and–and those of the other townsfolk. They were clearly under the witches' influence and made to protect them."

Koval looked at the elder sidelong as he idly scratched his

beard. The elder bristled at the disregard. "I am looking at the safety of this town! Are you taking party with witches?"

The lord's face lit up with an animated, almost amused, light, "The safety of this town, you say?" He took a step towards the elder. "Strange, because I thought *I* am charged with the safety, well-being, and prosperity of this town. The Crown Prince grants title of Lordship over Serna to the House Covendran, not its chapel's reverend."

"I–I am still charged with the spiritual guidance of this town to ensure it does not fall to heresy and immoral practices!" the elder said through a spluttering protest.

"Yes, let us talk about the spiritual guidance that you have graced us with over the past week. Where were you when the orcs came?" The elder took a step back. "Right, you had fled into your stone chapel, one of the only stone buildings in the town, and barred the doors. How do I know this? Because we tried to find a place to put all of the wounded when we were fighting the fire." Koval took another step, backing Elder Dum'ail into the crowd, "I remember a thing of scripture, too, from Saint Kostray's essay, I believe. Did he not say to 'help others in need' and 'lend a healing hand'?"

"You're taking up with the witches," the elder said faintly as his back pressed into the crowd. The crowd was also receding from Lord Covendran's approach. From the corner of his eye, Garven saw Tyrnimar and Holbrin exchange another one of those knowing glances and then Tyrnimar whispered something to Eevarel. They, with Arynn and the other elves, stood back from the two crowds, watching the confrontation between the lord and elder.

"Surely, for you are not a warrior, you would flee from such a frightful scene, even as the town burned." A soft sob escaped Kora, punctuating Koval's words. "But even the day after, you remained in the stone safety of the chapel. You only, finally, emerged at the end of the next day and what was your quest of communal benevolence?" He let the question hang in the air for a moment. "Ah, yes, you were hungry."

"You *have* taken up with the witches!" the elder said, aghast.

"Had you studied the purpose of your position here, you

would either conduct yourself properly at the beginning of this or, in the event of doing what you did, at least stay out of the way. But you are clueless and useless. It's because you come from that useless, moneyed stock from the north. You're not even Yvelian, but your Kangadian hide pretends to have our interest at heart."

"But–" the elder spluttered.

"You say we have taken with witches? I say you have forsaken the Book! I revoke your mandate, sir."

The elder drew himself up in indignation, "Now see here–"

"You have no chapel here and no say in what happens. I cast you out!"

The elder blanched for a moment before his face twisted in rage. "We'll see about this!" He turned and forced his way through the crowd, leaving Orn and the others speechless.

Koval let what just happened sink in for a tense moment. "So, Master Orn, pick your lot. Go with that useless man or stay here where there's *real* work to be done." He took another step, this time towards Orn.

Orn, the Rollodrans, the Veradrans and his other fellows, broke the confrontation. Orn averted his gaze. "As you wish, My Lord."

"Good," replied Koval, smiling magnanimously, as if the conversation had just begun. "I'm sure that Master Beren has an endless list of tasks and not enough people to get this town armed and fortified. And while we're at it, the actual new year is upon us this time. Mayhaps we can spare a bit for a feast tonight."

***

Mkaela reached towards the shadow in her mind. *Why did you want me to hide you?*

WHAT YOUR OTHER PEOPLE CAN DO IS DIFFERENT FROM WHAT YOU CAN DO THROUGH ME, AND YET, SOON IT WILL BE THE SAME.

What does that mean?

THERE WILL BE A TIME WHERE I MUST LEAVE YOU. YOU MUST BE ABLE TO DO THE SAME ON YOUR OWN. THAT TIME SOON APPROACHES.

But how? I couldn't do any of this without you?

I HAVE ONLY AWOKEN YOUR INNER ABILITY AND HELPED IT. IT IS YOU THAT WILL CARRY ON. THERE ARE OTHERS I MUST HELP BEFORE IT IS TOO LATE.

Others? Wait, that doesn't explain why you didn't want me to tell them about you. And too late for what?

LOOK IN YOUR OWN HISTORY AND YOU WILL SEE THAT WE ARE NO STRANGERS.

When will you go…?

Mkaela's was jolted out of her reverie as Baswyn embraced her tightly and collapsed sobbing. "Thank you," she sobbed weakly, "it was you. Thank you…"

***

Eevarel watched as the crowd dispersed and the tension in the air abated. Master Beren, the merchant-turned-quartermaster, had come out and started issuing orders for work priorities. Taram and Dyram took it upon themselves to organize the townsfolk into groups for work, some stuck with Orn for their assignments. They moved off to clean the fatigue of the journey away with a meal and a rest before beginning work.

She looked at the late afternoon sky and wondered if they would get to work the same day. Eevarel looked around, noting the trails of ash where entire buildings had burned down and the townsfolk had dragged the ruin away. Fields of stumps where the pristine forest had been the town's friendly neighbor and piles of logs dotted the perimeter of the town as it grew a wooden palisade as a protective skin like a scab over a wound. The smells and noise from the smith and tanneries rang of urgency. Clearly, the townsfolk that had stayed in Serna had not had an easy time.

She turned back to Tyrnimar's and Holbrin's whispered debate in the Elven tongue, "… Comes to a point that it cannot be denied," Tyrnimar practically hissed.

"Whether they can do it and we are simply lending

assistance as a good neighbor is wholly different from using it ourselves, Tyrnimar; I will not speak on it again. Not unless we have some new mandate from the Guardian Council. Our main purpose is to observe. You have a point on the Ways and I appreciate your youthful enthusiasm for reminding an old man like me as to their purpose, but there are aspects of the Ways that warn of caution, lest we create a monster."

"But! It can be–"

"No, it cannot," Holbrin said firmly with an air of finality. "Now, if you would excuse me, I have a question to ask of our gracious host, the Lord Koval Covendran of Serna."

Eevarel noticed the human named Taram glancing in their direction every now and again. She started to turn towards him but he looked away to hustle some of the mob's stragglers off to their meal. She pursed her lips thoughtfully before turning her attention towards her real desire of the moment.

"Tyrinmar." Her words made him flinch in surprise, having been roused from his poorly masked frustration and glowering at Holbrin. "Remember the day before we got here when we stopped on the roadside for camp and you made that tea?"

"It is recalled," Tyrnimar said cautiously.

"What was in it?" she asked.

"Flowers grown by this area, white, yellow, and purple flowers or their blossoms."

"Why did you brew that tea? It took some time for you to find all of those flowers."

He eyed her askance. "The weariness of the road is washed away, the air is more cleanly breathed, and the smell was enjoyed."

"Perhaps you should make some," she said earnestly. "It would probably help."

"Helpful, it would be," he admitted.

"You should be sure to make some for yourself, too," she said.

Tyrnimar gave her an exasperated look at her over his shoulder as she flashed him a sarcastic smile.

Chapter 9

The town of Serna, Yvel Principality.
By the Elven Calendar, 90th day of Winter, 18030.
By the Human Calendar, Restday, third week of Talinochis, 793.
A late winter evening.

Elder Dum'ail left Serna that evening with two other townsfolk and two precious horses. Lord Koval let them go. 'Church property,' he had said, regarding the horses. Dareum had watched them leave before he supped with his father in their modest dining room underneath a large, shuttered window. In the summer, it would be overlooking the town, but the cold of winter lingered to the last and the window was shuttered and draped with coverings to keep the heat inside. This was their own New Year feast, though they would make the rounds with the townsfolk later on. "Are you sure it was alright to give him the heave like that, sir?"

"Aw, his mother was a Berk, I bet," said Koval.

Dareum eyed his father over the steaming bowl of turnips in creamy chicken broth and spice paste. His father had aged in the last week. He had noticeably more grey in his black hair and beard and a haggard set of bags hung under his eyes. He never seemed to take his hunting boots off, the tooling in the down-turned tops buried in caked, ashen mud. He wore his green riding breeches, but Dareum noted that he walked through the town to check work. The main item that marked him in town was his blue-grey cape with white embroidery around the hood and trim, which was draped over an unoccupied chair at the table.

The last chair was occupied by Judane. She had aged as well. Though she was not yet seventeen, she sat and ate with a solemnity about her that had not been there a week or two ago. Dareum grimaced internally at the early changes the situation was forcing on everyone. Judane used to amicably chat through meals; even when no one else wanted conversation, she would carry it. Now, though not as messily as their father, she ate with purpose. She now favored her dark neutral-toned riding dresses and skirts over the house dresses of white or yellow.

Koval tore a chicken leg apart with a fork and knife before efficiently stuffing it in his mouth. Dareum ate efficiently, too. He hadn't had a warm meal in a little over a week.

"Um, how've the fortifications been coming, sir?" Dareum asked, uneasily shifting the subject.

"It will still take another two months to finish the wooden wall around the town. I'm hopeful that your mother will return with aid from Prince Gerald. I can't imagine we're the only ones with this problem." Koval paused. "And yet, your mother always seems to get her way with people."

"So do you, sir," Dareum said.

"It's different," he said. "She's better at getting people that owe her anything to help her. I'm better at getting people that are supposed to do what I say to actually do it."

They ate in silence for a few moments. "So, Judane," Dareum started, hesitating. "What have you been up to?"

She stopped eating, but said nothing. A moment passed before Koval smiled awkwardly. "She's been riding every day and practicing the sword. Seems like she wants to be just like her brother: riding off, saving people, and fighting the baddies," he said ruefully.

"It's a good example to the people, sir. We don't have time for useless people anymore," she said tersely.

"And how does it get used?" Dareum cut in. "Are you going off fighting now? Great way to get yourself killed," he said heatedly.

"Am I not also a captain in this militia!?" she challenged.

"Darups. Judy. Calm down, both of you." Koval fixed them with his fatherly glare. "You're one to talk. Holbrin spoke very highly of your boldness and bravery, but I can see between the trees what he meant. I know how your temper is." Dareum stared at his plate in silent indignation at being chided. "But there is room and opportunity for improvement," Koval continued. "Master Holbrin has agreed to assist in training our new militia in basic weapon handling and formation fighting. He has also agreed to provide for your specialized instruction on the sword, archery, and fighting from horseback."

Dareum felt just a little more tired, but Judane perked up. It was the first time since he had returned that she seemed to feel anything resembling excitement. "Master Holbrin will teach us?"

"Not quite," said Koval. "He will provide for your training. I believe that he said, what was her name, Mistress Irduin, will instruct you on the sword and fighting from the saddle and Mistress... Eevarel the bow." He gave them both a pointed look. "You're to do as they say." Dareum felt a shiver down his spine.

"Yes, My Lord," Dareum and Judane said in unison.

They ate for a few moments before Koval broke the silence again, "Master Holbrin is going to need some people to help run the rest of the militia. Any ideas?"

"Taram, sir," said Dareum. "He can fight, though I don't know where he learned."

"No one knows, son," Koval said. "Taram's not from here. He came to town a good ten years before you were born. He always kept to himself. He wasn't unfriendly, but he wasn't too friendly, either. Always got the impression that he'd run from something. But, what can I say? He always worked hard, never got rowdy with drink."

"He never married, either, did he?" Dareum said.

"No. Never saw him take an interest in any such thing. In fact, he mostly looks the same now as he did when you were just a baby boyo. Hasn't really changed in his look for over thirty years, I'd say," said Koval, pausing in thought before bringing himself back to the moment. "Anyone else?"

Dareum thought for a moment with Judane watching him while she pushed aside the remains of her roasted pheasant and sipped her wine, "Dyram."

"Dyram Torin'ail?"

"Yes, sir." Dareum felt his stomach clench at his father's tone.

"Are you sure? He's got a speck of the trouble-maker in him. You remember the fight at the winter festival?"

Dareum looked at his plate in silence for a moment before he took a deep breath. "He stood his ground, sir." Dareum ventured a glance up from his plate at his father.

"Ah, there I go again," Koval said, "Dyram will be a tenman in the militia. Any others?" Dareum frowned in thought. Koval spoke after a moment. "What about Orn?"

"Orn!?" Dareum said in surprise before catching himself. "Uh, sir, he took unnecessary risks on patrol and he tried to kill Kora and Mkaela!"

"Mind yourself, boy," Koval said coldly.

Dareum's father seemed to have some kind of mystical power over him when he took this tone. Dareum found himself sitting in sullen silence as his father lectured them. Judane was also looking away, lips pursed in discomfort.

"You don't see this because you're young, but this is how you gain control over people, especially people like Orn. He wants power because he is weak, so you give it to him but make sure you hold the string. That way, his strength can be taken away. He can be a tenman as long as he pleases me." Koval shrugged and frowned. "The moment he steps out of line, he'll be in someone else's ten digging holes in the ground and being yelled at. He'll know that and stay in line. Orn seems like the kind of man who takes a bit too well to power, so you give him just a little," Koval said with a sense of finality.

He looked between the two of them for some kind of agreement. A moment of tense, awkward silence passed. "Why do you two always get like this when I'm trying to teach you something? Hm? It must be something about me, right?" he said, throwing up his hands in frustration and exasperation. Koval got up and left, leaving Dareum and his younger sister in silence.

They sat in silence for a few moments before Judane spoke, "He's always like this when Mother's away."

Dareum stayed silent a moment longer. "Yeah, but that's just how he is. It'll be good to have Mother back," Dareum said. "I'm worried though."

"What about?"

"When Elder Dum'ail comes back."

"You think he will?" Judane said.

Dareum nodded. "I'm afraid that he'll be back with Knights of the Church and make Father burn Kora and Mkaela as witches. And then there's the knights themselves. You know how they can be."

Judane ate another mouthful and gulped it down. "Happy New Year."

***

The town of Serna, Yvel Principality.
By the Elven Calendar, fifth day of Spring, 18030.
By the Human Calendar, Breathday (fifth day of the week), first week of Ers (first month of the year), 794.
An early spring day; sunny with a cool breeze.

Half of a week had quickly passed since the patrol had returned. Lord Covendran had mobilized the entire town. The new militia trained and drilled for most of the day when they were not fortifying the town, cooking food, carrying messages, or other related tasks. The furnaces at the smith and the tannery burned long into the evenings, and the smoke of their industry hung about the town longer each day. The construction palisade began to crawl along the perimeter of the town, but it would still take another month or two at the rate the townsfolk were building it.

The nobles of the town were not exempt from labor, either. Dareum and Judane Covendran trained sword and bow, sparred, and rode, morning until past sunset. At that particular moment, Jovaela could see Dareum Covendran face down on the ground, too tired to care about smearing mud on his face, his chest heaving, and sword just out of reach while Irduin stood over him with her snow-white skin and silver hair and her terrible unforgiving eyes of violet. Her own sword rested easily against her shoulder, held by one hand, the other brushed hair aside before resting on her hip, waiting for him with the patience of a tree to rise and resume training. Even Koval took a lesson or a sparring match when he was not supervising the fortifications, the training, managing the supplies with the quartermaster, Beren Enkr'ail, or resolving disputes between his exhausted townsfolk, cowing them into fearful silence with a few words.

That was not Jovaela's concern right now. Well, mostly not her concern. Right now, she had to find Holbrin. She searched through the town green which had been transformed into a supply yard and the workshops where craftspeople toiled to equip the militia, finally finding him in the common room of the Moradran, which Beren Enkr'ail had transformed into militia headquarters. He was in conference with Koval and his quartermaster. Seeing her, Holbrin excused himself as his company absently bid him farewell. They continued to pore over ledgers of supplies and fortification plans.

Jovaela and Holbrin quietly walked away from the inn before Holbrin spoke in Elvish. "Yes?" His voice was like stream water casually flowing by rocks as he walked with his hands clasped behind his back.

"I want to show you something Bierien told me about."

"You mean the war masks?" he said.

Jovaela hesitated. "You knew?"

"Yes, Bierien told me this morning."

"Then why did she tell me about it?" Jovaela wondered out loud.

"Probably because she quickly realized that I was not going to do anything about it."

Jovaela turned to regard Holbrin as they strode towards the workshops they were discussing. "How is it that you are not going to do anything about it?"

"It is not my place–not *our* place–to tell them what they can or cannot do. We can advise, as Bierien did when they asked how to cast a solid object in metal. How was Bierien to know that they would then take the heads and skulls of dead orcs and use them to cast the faces of helmets?" He paused thoughtfully. "Though, Bierien is quite a skilled instructor if she can teach that to a workshop full of people more accustomed to making nails, horseshoes, and barrel bands."

"Are you so certain? Why do you think the Guardian

Council sent us here? We see things clearly that they do not by virtue of our longevity. Their short lives cannot see the weight of their decisions. Do you not perceive the import of this situation?" Jovaela challenged.

"What would you have me do?" Holbrin kept his placid face forward, hands clasped behind his back, and made no outward indication that he was talking to anything besides the air in front of him, save him piercing her with a sidelong gaze. "Go in there, demand that they stop, ignore their inclination, and remove the reasons they are doing this?"

"This will not lead anywhere well for them," Jovaela retorted.

"You are correct, but that is the measure of them."

"You are letting them have magic!" she insisted.

"Only what is already theirs. I could not take it away from them if I tried and you know that. It is in their blood." Holbrin stopped and turned to face her. "What would I do? Kill the ones who have discovered their own power? We might both be dead if they did not, I would add–this is a far throw of the spear from actively coaching their blood magic, which none of us can, or teaching them book magic, which I have already dealt with against such a notion." Holbrin resumed walking at the same pace as a calm stream. "But even if I could, and were inclined to take it away, what happens at the next skirmish or raid, let alone a battle? When they are in danger of getting overrun again? They would die."

"Then we help them prepare so that it does not happen."

"We cannot prepare, even just for ourselves, for every possibility. Who are we to deprive them of the means to survive that they already possess?" Holbrin said.

Jovaela fumed. Fumed to Holbrin. Though for all of the barbs they traded, to anyone not fluent in Elven, it sounded almost melodic, with graceful sounds in phrase combinations that naturally flowed into each other. It was the body language that was more telling. Jovaela stood, feet apart, hands on her hips, the breeze fluttering her long, black hair, making it seem like thick smoke curling from smoldering embers. Holbrin had walked a few paces past where she had stopped and had turned to partially face her, hands remaining clasped behind his back. Face as placid as his hazelnut-brown hair.

Jovaela and Holbrin had not directly worked together before this journey. Holbrin knew of Jovaela in passing acquaintance, but more by reputation–particularly of her temperament. Jovaela could become quite insistent. "You know what happens if they gain greater control of it."

The sounds and smells of labor and industry clanged and reeked around them, but the street between the workshops was thankfully empty besides the noise and the smell of ash and boiling hides, and themselves. "Indeed, I do, Jovaela. I have seen it, after all. Bear in mind the differences between then and now. While this is very troubling, it is not completely unprecedented that humans– or any other type of creature–can awaken their own blood magic without a regimented ritual. Need I remind you that such rituals are forbidden among our people and unknown to others, just as book magic is a secret kept by our people. Then there are those other forms that Tyrnimar dabbles in… madman he is for it, too."

"You are avoiding my statement," Jovaela insisted vexedly.

Holbrin showed his own frustration with a quick, heavy sigh before continuing. "Indeed, I do prattle on. What is happening is within the realm of the possible without our intervention or even our knowledge. If we let it happen, it will very probably die out. Each of the blood magi here could be killed as witches by their own religion–a shame that they cannot accept such people from within themselves, but unsurprising given the bloody legacy–or, in this particular circumstance, be killed in the fighting."

Holbrin brought his hands forward from behind his back and reclasped them in front of him. "What makes this different, is that this power has awoken from within them because they have been attacked. Eight centuries ago, powers were flourishing by conflict and competition amongst themselves, where they strove, competed, and bloodied each other over petty goals. Here they struggle to survive. It is on the same basis from which their powers awoke that we help them. To survive."

Her burning, black eyes met his icy blues. "Note this, Holbrin Arozrien of the Red Order. This is a path to ruin."

He regarded her for a moment, before answering. "I note your objection, Jovaela, but I will not yield on this. I must thank the equally passionate, if somewhat more demure, Tyrnimar for reminding me of the Ways. As well as I know them, it is sometimes easy to forget their core purpose or take pieces of them in convenient context by separating them from their greater meaning. The Ways are clear, we have an obligation to help decent people," he said. "That aside, I need your help. Can I continue to count on your help?"

She glowered at him for a moment. "Yes," she said begrudgingly. "You are charged with the responsibility of the Lead Traveler."

He nodded in gratitude. "Good." He turned, continuing towards the workshop where Bierien had been coaching the smiths of Serna on their newfound crafts of smithing weapons and armor. "I am surprised that Bierien was able to instruct them on such complicated techniques without imparting other knowledge that our people retain as a secret."

Jovaela hastened to catch up with him, shooting him intermittent, irritable glances that Holbrin pretended not to notice. They entered the smithy to the smell of ash, steel, fire, smoke, and blood. A small pile of charred orc heads and skulls lay in a pile in a steel bucket, wet from their dunks in the quenching bucket. Five townsfolk labored in the smithy and a sixth lurked in the shadows. Bierien was coaching two of them through the forging of an axe blade.

Her silver hair was kept from the hazards of the workplace in braids and tied behind her. Grey eyes glowed gold in the light of the forge, but she looked tired. Next to her, and looking much older, were the men and women of the town toiling to arm it. A woman briskly ducked in to retrieve a bucket of freshly forged arrowheads and toted them off to affix them to arrow shafts and fletching.

Holbrin recognized Arbera Rollodran and Baryn Kevr'ail, both of whom had been part of Dareum's militia patrol. Baryn was polishing the face of a helmet cast in an orc's face. *I worry about what some of these people will become.* He grimaced internally before peering at Arbera Rollodran. He had seen her side with Orn and cheering him on to kill Kora Orint'ail for being a witch about ten days ago. He had not known they were smiths, but decided that it was probably a recent decision.

Holbrin then reached for the third one he recognized, lurking in the shadows. "Alright, Master Ziek, I think it is time we find a more gainful occupation for your time." Holbrin spoke in Eklendan. Ziek shrilly protested as Holbrin led him from the smithy by the ear.

"I *just* want to help. Why can't I stay in there!?" he protested.

Holbrin set him down against the stone side of the building. The smithy was one of the very few stone buildings in the town, on account of the craft inside it. "You want to help?" he interrogated.

"Yes," Ziek sulked.

Holbrin pursed his lips for a moment before switching back to Elven. "Jovaela, where are Turaean and Arynn? They have been scouting the area with those two humans, yes? What were their names?"

"Korane and Garven."

"Yes." He switched back to Eklendan. "Please take the intrepid Master Ziek and entrust them to their tutelage."

Jovaela fixed him with a stern eye before hauling him off towards the forest. Holbrin heard Ziek ask in the distance, "What's intrepid mean?"

Holbrin turned back to the smithy to see Bierien's serene face smeared with soot from her labor and instruction... though, serene was not exactly correct. Bierien was more the type to continue to look at a person until that person said what she desired.

"Hello," he said pleasantly, in Elven. She was looking down at her hands as she wiped them with a cloth and she looked up at him when he spoke. Only her eyes moved, then she looked back at her hands, finished wiping them, and stuffed the cloth into a pocket in the leather apron she wore over her red tunic and breeches. She continued to look at him, as if he was a petitioner in her domain.

Right to it, then. "You were hoping that Jovaela would

force my hand on some matter?" he began.

"Yes, that would have been nice."

Holbrin sighed internally. "I would be greatly entertained by your recommendations for how I should instruct these people to deal with the situation they are in aside from military advice."

"Well, I leave it to your wizened discretion, then," she said flatly.

"I recognize that this is a contentious combination of circumstances, and I will accept responsibility for the part of my decisions in the outcome. I believe we must help these people survive."

"Yes, I understand that Holbrin, but I do not understand allowing them to give in to hatred like this."

"This is part of all of us, even us in certain circumstances." He paused. "It saddens me that you had to see the beauty of your craft be turned into such a grotesque product."

She grimaced. "At least they took to it quickly and performed the techniques correctly."

"How does it stand?" he asked.

"Give it another two days and they will have enough mail shirts for three of their tenmen, though only four links in one. That is all that time allows. The rest will have to make do with gambesons and hard leather jerkins and skirts to go with their shields. They will have arms one way or the other, whether taken from the dead orcs, made at this forge, taken from the quartermaster's stock, hunting spears and bows, or repurposed tools: they will have arms."

"It will have to last until their Prince arrives with his army. We will need some expedients for ourselves, as well–makeshift arms and armor for the time being. Strangely, none of us anticipated fighting a pitched battle when we left," Holbrin said wryly.

"I will set some aside and see what I can do for their quality," Bierien said dispiritedly.

Chapter 10

The Stone of Rykooth, high in the shelter of the Kaskev Mountains.
By the Goblin Calendar, early in the Fourth Moon Cycle, 3114.
By the Human Calendar, Restday, first week of Ers, 794.
A windy and chilled early spring evening, under the rise of the liberating
moon.

"Great One, a party of orcs is entering the gates. They bear the shield mark of flames."

Oygariyet turned from the table of maps that he was studying with Indariyet and his First, along with ledgers written in the angular characters of Goblin. "Ah, the Borys-Karang, with a report on their reconnaissance raids, no doubt. Very well."

He pointed at his Fourth, who waited obediently on a bench by the door to the slave room and kitchens. "Go tell them to kill a fresh griffon for a feast. And fetch a keg of ridin." Oygariyet was feeling welcoming, and eagerly awaited their report. The staff ordered the house slaves about as they tidied the feasting table on the other side of the throne room.

Indariyet and her First received and lodged the Borys-Karang entourage and conducted them to the throne room just as the griffon was almost ready. Oygariyet waited atop the dais, standing in front of the throne of the Stone of Rykooth.

The throne was an old thing, made to fit the line of the previous masters of the Stone of Rykooth: wide, squat dwarves. It was wide enough to seat an orc, and made of stone with a high back to make anyone seem tall. The chairback of the throne had nine blocks carved on its edge, and its back was a relief from a larger stone piece. One of the blocks in the middle and four one each side. The block on the right corner was badly chipped.

Oygariyet remembered the fight eleven winters before when he, his previous Third, and thirty or so of his warriors broke through the doors into the throne room as the Dwarven defense collapsed. He remembered chipping that throne with his mace while

113

pursuing cowards who cared more for living than the honor of death in battle.

Oygariyet's guards held the doors open as Indariyet led in the procession, drawing his attention away from his memories. To call them a procession would make the entrance seem proper. Still, their hulking green forms lumbered in. Their king, the Borys-Karang, stood there, in a practical, unceremonious way, but Oygariyet liked that about him. There were other orc kings, the Destroyer or the Ravager, for instance, but the All-Consuming Flame was the one that could bring the others into line.

It was all work with this one. His once brown boots, now blackened with use and mud and blood, ended a few fingers below the knee. A skirt of hardened leather strips, reinforced with steel rivets, covered his legs and were surely held with a belt, but it was covered by a coat of mail. Plates and segments of more reinforced leather covered his shoulders and arms down to his wrist. Scars crisscrossed all of the skin that Oygariyet could see on the Borys-Karang's hands and face. Several scars crossed over the eye socket, particularly on the left eye, but orc eyes were set deeper than most, so they could sustain such wounds without losing the eye. Usually.

The oddest thing about him was that his lank, black hair had thinned so that he was bald on the top of his head. The vast majority of orcs never lived long enough for such a thing, and those that did rarely kept all of their limbs. This one must have been almost forty winters and had shrewd eyes. He carried a long-hafted axe resting on his shoulder. The other orcs filed in after their king, some bearing shields with brightly painted flames engulfing a figure of indeterminate race. One warrior scurried up to catch the axe as the Bory-Karang absently let it drop.

"I see the Great Oygariyet," the orc king said in his own language, a dialect of Orcish particular to the Liberator's slopes of the middle mountains.

"The mighty Borys-Karang, at last. I want you and your warriors to take this meat with us to melt the cold from your bones and hear your words," replied Oygariyet in his own accented Orcish. He had learned this dialect quickly, but it was easy enough to master as he already knew two other dialects. What he always found difficult about Orcish was not the pronunciation, accent, or words, but rather, the lack of words and ideas.

Orcs had no words for ideas that were of no use to them. There was no way to give thanks to another, because the orc people took what they wanted. There was no way to welcome a visitor because they either came when they were told to or came to take something. Several times, Oygariyet had felt at a frustrating loss of words in giving orders to his relatively new subordinates. They lacked so many customs necessary for basic cooperation, let alone showing any respect for others, that he wondered that they had not all died out killing each other.

The Borys-Karang waited, expecting something. After an awkward moment, Oygariyet formed his hand into a knife and pointed over to the feasting table. This was a guess, but it turned out to be clear enough as the Borys-Karang moved, other warriors ambling after him to take seats at the table. Oygariyet glanced meaningfully at Indariyet, and the other tribe leaders, along with their Firsts and Seconds, moved to the table and seated themselves.

House slaves moved from the wall shared with the throne and served their respective masters. Those not prosperous enough to have slaves served themselves. Indariyet's peg-legged Orcish slave shambled over and ripped pieces off of the roasted griffon and placed them with care on the copper plate before her. Three of Oygariyet's own slave women were placing food and drink before him. The salted roast griffon gave off a savory aroma that caused him to anticipate the taste.

The hair on his red-skinned beauty was growing in nicely, but it had a long way to go. The greyskin was doing fine, but there were plenty of greyskins in his own tribe. His favorite poured him copper cups of goat milk and the strong drink called ridin, made from fermented roots, and mixed with the boiled blood of the griffon for flavor. Oygariyet affectionately caressed her cheek and she looked at him as he brushed a thumb over her lip. He lingered for a moment and then shook himself from distraction when he realized that all of the others had food in their bowls. He began eating without comment, which signaled that all others could start.

They dined in silence, with no conversation or sounds save the clang of utensils on copper plates and cups being placed on the table after a drink. Oygariyet noticed that his guests seemed to greatly enjoy the food. He pitied them a moment because he knew they had no words to express the sensation. Orcs' lives were short. They either met early violent ends, or aged very quickly. The Borys-Karang was quite the oddity to live so long that he began to bald. Despite clearly enjoying the food, the Borys-Karang's hawkish eyes darted about, assessing the hobgoblins across the table from himself, his own subordinates, and even the slaves waiting with patience and discipline along the wall behind Oygariyet.

When they finished dining, the griffon carcass was picked clean. One of the Borys-Karang's minions was gnawing on some gristle and noisily sucking the salty juices and marrow from the bones. The Borys-Karang looked up at Oygariyet. There was no direct challenge. He was waiting to be bid to speak. "What did your warriors find in the human lands below?"

"Very little warriors," he replied while sipping his own cup of ridin appreciatively.

Oygariyet assumed he meant 'few.' "Any mounted warriors?"

"Only a little. Only at two places. Most run from us. Very few fight. We took many slaves."

Oygariyet frowned in puzzlement. *Where were their defenses? Surely, they will not just roll over like an eager harem and let us take their lands and their flesh…*

The Borys-Karang continued, "The Borys-Karang ordered more scouting without fighting." He made no attempt to conceal his facial expression, conveying that such a thing was a very boring prospect. "The Borys-Karang knows that they prepare an army to move in many directions. A great challenge." The Borys-Karang gestured with a backhand towards one of his entourage that had escaped notice despite being seated at the table, almost across from Indariyet.

Oygariyet looked at him for a moment before speaking. He seemed to be a peculiar orc. He was short and wore a sleeved vest of hard leather. For an orc, he was not young, and shared something similar to the Borys-Karang's shrewdness, his eyes darting about in constant assessment. He kept a bow slung on his back. Oygariyet could not see below the table, but there were none of the heavier weapons that most orcs favored, and he had a leaner musculature than his bulkier companions.

"You have something more to say for the Borys-Karang?" Oygariyet asked.

"Yes. The humans in their central place. They call it the 'Place-called-Yvel.' They will move…" the smaller orc made a face and, to Oygariyet's surprise, turned to the Borys-Karang and said, "I will use his kind of words to make this easier." The Borys-Karang lazily waved in assent while continuing to sip ridin.

The smaller orc continued in Oygariyet's own dialect of Goblin. "The humans from the Place-called-Yvel have split their army to march to the left and the right to reinforce several places. It would be easier to tell it to you if we could look at your maps, Great One."

Oygariyet, surprised by the smaller orc's linguistic versatility, hesitated for a moment before rising. He waved all of the others down, saying in Orcish, "Eat and drink more or look at other table," and in Goblin, "Take ease, but come and look if you want." Oygariyet rose with the smaller orc, Indariyet, his own First and Third, and Indariyet's First.

Reaching their maps, the smaller orc began. "I must apologize, Great One. I began my report from the middle instead of the beginning because the middle is very interesting. I wish to start again from the beginning."

"Very well," Oygariyet permitted.

Gesturing to the right side of the mountains, where winter was stronger and the mountains met the water, he pointed to the lower lands. "This large place is called 'Place-called-Markia' by the humans. The reconnaissance raids have not met any serious resistance and have raided many towns and villages. The Gezierad orcs will continue to press down the Mountains and hills into the lower human lands."

Oygariyet eyed him suspiciously. The smaller orc shifted in slight unease as he spoke. "The Gezierad sent a messenger. The Borys-Karang received the messenger on your behalf, along with several other of the orc king messengers."

Oygariyet slowly turned towards the Borys-Karang, who

was eyeing Oygariyet over his shoulder. "Great One, the Gezierad and the other orc kings view the Borys-Karang as first among them. They reported to the Borys-Karang first and view the Borys-Karang to share favor with them."

Oygariyet turned in surprise back to the smaller orc. "That is actually such a consideration?" he asked, letting a small amount of surprise into his voice. *This may be a problem later. He spreads the skin out in a way that makes it seem as though I need him to have the others...*

"It is, Great One," the smaller orc said, half turning to Oygariyet.

Oygariyet examined him for a moment. "Very well. Continue."

"Thank you, Great One." The smaller orc gestured back towards the map. "Moving to the left, the Borys-Karang's own warriors have constructed bridges over these rivers here, here, here, and here." He indicated four places on the map. Indariyet leaned with a pencil of ash to mark the map with notes. "The Borys-Karang's raids have made it within eyesight of this city," the smaller orc continued, indicating one close to the foothills, "known as the 'Place-called-Versingit' by the humans there. Looking further south, this forest can be very dense and will slow movement of large armies. The Borys-Karang's raids have not made it to the Place-called-Yvel, but have raided smaller towns and villages."

"You said this place was more interesting."

"Ah, yes, Great One," his eyes lighted with excitement, "some of the humans here have magicks."

"Magicks!?" exclaimed Oygariyet.

"Yes, Great One, but it is not very powerful. Not yet."

Oygariyet contained his consternation after his initial surprise. *This is quite a set of surprises. A well-spoken orc, a people that don't defend themselves, and magicks among mortals.* "Will it affect the future?"

"If you give them time to get strong, Great One, then they will get strong," the smaller orc stated simply.

Oygariyet considered for a moment before deciding to

offer comment on it later. "Very well. Continue."

"Further to the left here," the orc said, pointing to a city marker at the foot of the mountains and another one almost due closer, nestled in the mountains, "are the human cities 'Place-called-Soorin' and 'Place-called-Ardara.' The humans in the Place-called-Ardara have relations with the dwarves of Medria to the left. The Borys-Karang may be able to seize the Place-called-Ardara. The approaches from the Mountains make it easy for him to gather many forces close by."

"Who will he use?" Oygariyet asked.

The smaller orc hesitated, looking past Oygariyet. Oygariyet turned to see the Borys-Karang standing immediately behind him. Oygariyet was unflustered in his own domain, but he conceded to himself that he had been so immersed in the smaller orc's information that he had not noticed the Borys-Karang rise and approach. Oygariyet turned and asked him in Orcish, "Who will you use to take the Place-called-Ardara?"

"The Derz, the Tiralk, the Peradek, and the Drell."

"The Drell? That is not an orc tribe."

"The Drell are small lizard men."

"You will do this. You will also take one of my warriors with you to watch and take messages."

The Borys-Karang considered Oygariyet for a moment with a plain face, looking Oygariyet directly in the eye, holding his gaze before dropping his head in submission. "I will take your warrior," he acceded.

An orc from the table called a wordless protest, rising. He took some swaggering steps, drawing out a long, square-tipped sword. He wore no armor, save thick skins tied and loosely stitched around his waist, leaving his legs free to move and his arms and shoulders unhindered by bulk. The sword had a two-handed grip—two-handed for an orc—and he was a particularly bulky specimen.

"The great Borys-Karang does for this hobgoblin," he jeered. "So weak!" He continued approaching, around the ceremonial firepit, burning only at embers. "I am the Baki-Norn. By my breeding spheres, I am blessed by the gods and I will kill you, weak hobgoblin, and I will be the Great One, and I will send the

Borys-Karang to do this and that and I will take his slaves as mine–
not that they last with me," he guffawed.

Oygariyet was very comfortable. Even though he had not
had a fight like this since the challenge from Arkiban, he spent time
in the practice yard every day and it was an honor for his warriors
to spar with him. It was an even greater honor if they could best
him, though that was rare. But against this filth?

The Soulblade, the sword entrusted to him by Leriyet
himself, symbol of their holy mission, slid out of its scabbard in
his right hand, his left hand lifting his spiked mace from its loop
and resting the haft over his shoulder as his blade guarded him. The
Baki-Norn swaggered forward until suddenly springing into action
ten or so paces from Oygariyet with a two-handed overhand strike.
Oygariyet's smaller blade, a little more than half as tall as he was,
able to be used one or two-handed, met the Baki-Norn blade to
guide it harmlessly down to the stone floor with a loud clang and
trapping it there.

The Baki-Norn looked up in surprise to see Oygariyet's
spiked mace crash into the crown of his head with Oygariyet's own
overhand strike, knocking him to the ground, empty-handed with
blood streaming from his dented head. The orc hollered as his blade
clattered to the floor. Oygariyet noisily kicked it aside, slashing
and chopping at the Baki-Norn's legs as the orc fruitlessly tried to
scramble away, emitting panicked moans. Oygariyet crushed one of
his knees as he hollered in pain. He began to crawl on his elbows
until Oygariyet crushed his left hip. The Baki-Norn could not move
for the pain.

Oygariyet knew enough of Orcish custom to observe
what loosely held as a formality for a public challenge like this. He
shouted at the Baki-Norn, but it was for the benefit of the other orcs
in the room. "I am the taker here! Not you! You are weak and I am
strong!" Oygariyet lifted his spiked mace high and let the weight
of it pull down onto the Baki-Norn's head again and again until
the Baki-Norn's skull caved in. The sound of blood spurting and
Oygariyet's breathing were the only sounds echoing in the room.
The Baki-Norn's blood had spattered on Oygariyet's hands and
arms.

Oygariyet looked up at the Borys-Karang. *He's smiling at*

this? The Borys-Karang had a downcast face, but his eyes looked at Oygariyet levelly with a small smile on his face. A thought occurred to Oygariyet. "By Leriyet! You did that to do that," he said plainly while suppressing his frustration at the limitations of Orcish.

The Borys-Karang approached unthreateningly and in a lower voice he said in accented Goblin, "he would have challenged me, Great One, and he had other ideas than following you. I knew his pride was too much to see an orc taking orders from any but another orc."

Oygariyet schooled his anger to calm. "Do not deceive me again. Not about your own internal rivalries–I expect you to deal with that yourself–not about your knowledge of language. Nothing at all."

"As you wish, Great One."

Oygariyet paused for a moment. He brought himself back to the moment. There was fresh blood on the floor. He had to savor it. Another honorable triumph in challenge-combat. He would celebrate with the pretties tonight. Sensing his thoughts, his favorite brought him another copper cup of ridin. He handed his weapons to his now well-trained goblin slave he knew would be waiting. The goblin would take his weapons, clean them, and return them to him in but a moment.

He took the cup from his favorite, cupping her face in his other hand, smearing the Baki-Norn's blood over her mouth as she looked at him. *She's getting hungry*, he mused. Sighing contentedly, his temper subsiding, he turned to the Borys-Karang and spoke in Goblin. "What will become of the Baki-Norn?"

"They will become mine. I will choose a new Baki-Norn, but they are now mine. They will be Pev'Baki-Norn and Borys-Karang. The Baki-Norn that I choose shall be my Garad'dai Borys-Karang."

"Oh? And not mine for making that problem of yours go away?" Oygariyet said.

"The Baki-Norn are difficult to manage, Great One. Not because of their strength or anything like that, but because they are very direct. It is difficult to get them to do anything but be direct. Their reconnaissance raids have blundered the most and they have lost the most warriors. I have had to give some of my own Borys-Karang. There are also the Talz and Dren-Berz there."

"The Talz?" Oygariyet said. *The Talz are further to the right along the Mountains.*

"The other Talz, Great One, the orc tribe," the Borys-Karang said.

"Oh," said Oygariyet. "Well fine, then. Proceed with taking that Place-called-Ardara. Begin reinforcing the other forward camps to begin seizing worthy places and expand the range of the reconnaissance. Select another human place to seize after the Place-called-Ardara–but I will not easily forget this annoyance with the Baki-Norn!" Oygariyet paused, considering for a moment. "This smaller one, is he one you use in your place much?"

"No, Great One," said the Borys-Karang, "he is useful, but he is not of the Borys-Karang. He bargains and trades."

"A trader?"

"He trades tasks. Very skilled at reconnaissance," he said eyeing the smaller orc purposefully, who smirked mischievously, "and knows many dialects, as you have seen, Great One, even some of the human ones. Has been to many places. Even to the Place-called-Ikria."

"Indeed," said Oygariyet, appraising the smaller orc. "I thought it odd that you would have someone speak in your place who looked smaller and weaker than those who clearly led tribes or wanted to."

"There was a purpose to that, as well, Great One. He leads no tribe."

Of course, Oygariyet thought, *he used the smaller one to agitate what was the Baki-Norn.*

"He will be free to make another bargain very soon, Great One. Mine is done with him, now. He even has a name," the Borys-Karang said.

Oygariyet looked up, "I thought you said he led no tribe." The Borys-Karang simply nodded towards the smaller orc, now free of contract.

Oygariyet turned his head to regard the smaller orc once

more, "You have a name?"

"Grotis, Great One," replied the smaller orc.

"Alone?" asked Oygariyet.

"That is the meaning of the word in my first language, Great One," said Grotis, as they continued conversing in Goblin.

"Who gave you this name, then?" Oygariyet asked.

"I gave it to myself," said Grotis.

Oygariyet stared at Grotis for a moment. "I was going to say that would be rude and dishonorable, but I had to remember that would only be within my own people. I suppose among yours, it would simply be bold."

Grotis smirked again. "I am a tribe of one, Great One."

"By Jirmishik, I have brought you a gift from one of their raids, though, Great One," said the Borys-Karang, drawing Oygariyet's attention and reasserting himself.

"Oh?" Oygariyet said disinterestedly, still fascinated with the bold, small orc.

The Borys-Karang motioned for one of his other orcs to approach. This was clearly some hand gesture that orcs understood, but Oygariyet had only seen it a few times and did not know its meaning. The orc went back out into the hall and returned with three other orcs and two walking creatures.

These would be humans, I suppose, a man and a woman. They cowered before him in their bonds of heavy rope and tattered clothes. They looked exhausted and terrified. *What a prize! Her skin is the color of clean wool...* He reached out and grabbed her face by the jaw, smearing blood on her. She whimpered and tried to shrink away from him, but backed into one of her Orcish captors. He regained his hold on her jaw and thrust his thumb in her mouth as she continued to whimper in terror. *Completely untrained, though.* He gave his favorite a meaningful look.

Oygariyet turned his gaze back to the Borys-Karang, "I thank you for the gift, but you are trying to distract me." The Borys-Karang smirked just so slightly at being caught in the act. "You will still take my warriors with you to observe, take messages, and command in my name." Oygariyet gave a throaty sigh, gripping the jaw of the whimpering human female. "You may consume the Baki-Norn," he said distractedly.

"As you wish, Great One," the Borys-Karang said.

Oygariyet turned to his First. "You, the Second, and the Third, prepare to travel. You will be given names and sent to carry my name." Their eyes all shone with the excitement of such a blessing, just as Oygariyet lamented that he was sending them out before he was comfortable with their capabilities. They were a fine staff, had fought well and bravely, but it was a different level of experience and maturity required to be leading clans, albeit those of orcs. Still, propriety demanded that he respect their faithful service to him, their loyalty, and their seniority.

The Fourth would become his new First, and he and the First would have to pick a new Second, Third, and Fourth to serve him. "You will have capes made and gleaming helms to mark you," he said as he turned to his new First. "See that the smith properly outfits them with fine armors. Tell Indariyet to give each of them a warband of cavalry. It would be an insult to each of them and the troops they command for no one to carry their honor." Oygariyet turned, knowing that his new First would be eager to please in order to prove herself.

Back to his two new slaves. The man was mildly interesting. *Perhaps I will give him to Indariyet.* He eyed Indariyet who was clearly thinking the same thing... *in exchange for something.* But now he focused on his new female. *Four of them now, what to do? I will have to take some herbs for stamina.*

"Great One," the smaller orc said, "most humans are given names by their birthers."

"They *all* have names?" Oygariyet said skeptically.

"Yes, Great One."

"What is hers, then?"

The smaller orc approached the young human woman with her yellow, tangled hair, and her dirt-and-tear-streaked face as she shrank away from him against her implacable captors. She wore a tattered dress that swayed in the breeze as she shambled with the limp of someone who had done the majority of the walking in her whole life during the past few months. While she was by no means as short as a goblin, she seemed short for a human. Terrified brown eyes darted this way and that from under her locks of matted hair. The smaller orc spoke to her in another language that Oygariyet did not know and gently prodded her with words until she spoke once.

"What language is that?"

"The humans have many languages, Great One, on both sides of the Mountains," he explained. "This one is from one of the places near the Place-called-Yvel. They seem to speak the Markia and Eklenda dialects of human tongue there."

Oygariyet grunted in acknowledgment. "And her name?" Oygariyet said proddingly.

"Her name is Selonikah."

Chapter 11

The town of Serna, Yvel Principality.
By the Elven Calendar, thirteenth day of Spring, 18030.
By the Human Calendar, Weddingday, second week of Ers, 794.
A few clouds block the sky as twilight fades to stars on an early spring
evening.

Kora continued to sob into her Ayza's chest. Ayza, Kora's brown-haired, older sister stroked her sister's red hair, taking her forelocks and binding them in cord on either side of her face while smoothing out tangles with a brush. Tyrnimar looked on from across the green in the evening twilight.

It had been another hard day of work and preparation. The palisade continued to crawl at a snail's pace around the town. Nearly everyone trained as militia, and aside from Lord Covendran's order to do so, the townsfolk had their own reasons. Some feared a return of the orc raiders; some were determined to never be caught unawares again; some fueled by anger or revenge. Some had nothing else anymore, their families dead and livelihoods burned to the ground.

Kora and Ayza only had each other now, their parents among the casualties of the raid a month prior, their home consumed in the fire from the raid. They were not alone in these circumstances. Baryn Kev'rail's wife died fighting next to him on a militia patrol. He believed he should have died with her, except that Mkaela Ran'ail, another woman in the town, had saved him with her newfound supernatural abilities.

Tyrnimar found Mkaela's aura stranger than the other people of Serna who had unlocked the use of their own blood powers. Like most people, Kora had several auras that Tyrnimar saw as different colors swirling about her like smoke or translucent sheets of light fabric, swaying in gentle breeze with their movements and emotions. To see most auras, he had to concentrate, but some were strong enough to jump out at him. Some of the auras surrounding Mkaela were very bright and outshone the other ones around her.

Tyrnimar turned the page in his growing handbook of aura meanings that he often recorded. He had started with a bound book of blank pages and estimated that he had filled in one tenth of the book just from his time in Serna. He took a sip of his evening tea of yellow and purple flower buds before scrawling another note.

The tea. Since they returned from the scouting patrol with Dareum Covendran, Eevarel had started taking tea with him in the evenings, or, more accurately, Eevarel came to take his tea from him and he had to make more. At first, he started trying to make his tea earlier or later and drink it in secret, but his powers of stealth paled compared to hers of detection. She would find him just as he had settled somewhere he thought to be secluded, sit with him, and thank him for making tea for her and finding a relaxing place for her to enjoy it. She would smile at him in that truly infuriating way, knowing that he would allow her to partake out of an adherence to propriety and manners.

Shaking off the distraction and the impending frustration, he resumed his concentration and studied Kora. The Firecaster aura was clearer now than before the patrol, a stark difference, but even when he first saw her aura, it had not been as nascent as most other beings. An aura of sadness and determination was also there, just as it was for most of the other humans in this town.

Other auras were difficult to see, being covered up by the more powerful emotions or natures. *An example to be considered*, he thought to himself, *to be presumed would be that the aura of love that would be held between a man and a woman who had been joined by marriage for some time could be observed, yet it is not seen.* His travels in the human lands had shown him the great variation of emotions. While the colors generally conformed to the emotions, it was not a hard rule. Some emotions shared colors, and the nuance of the same emotion adjusted its shade and brightness. Generally, the stronger the emotion, the brighter the aura was, to the extent that it could mask other auras–even ones of nature. Often humans' emotional auras masked the auras of their undiscovered blood magic.

An aura competing with Kora's Firecaster aura and

the auras of sadness and determination was that of guilt. Kora had a very strong aura of guilt, stronger than most of the other townspeople. Tyrnimar leaned forward slightly as something caught his eye. He could see the aura of love between the two sisters, Kora and Ayza, but there was something about their bond–a strain upon it. He focused a little more while expanding his view to consider Ayza's auras as well.

"There you are," said that familiar voice in Elven.

Here she is, Tyrnimar dismally announced to himself. Eevarel had come upon him unawares, once again. In addition to her superior powers of detection, she also far outstripped him in powers of stealth.

"You picked an odd place today; this does not seem very relaxing," she said.

Tyrnimar looked over, noticing Taram, who was sitting on an overturned wooden crate taking his evening meal in a large tin bowl. He seemed absorbed in his own thoughts, just as Tyrnimar had been a breath beforehand. Standing in the fore, Eevarel approached in deceptively slow strides, leaning over and taking his wooden-handled, tin cup of tea.

"You drank some of mine," she accused.

Rolling his eyes, Tyrnimar produced a gourd bottle that had been lined with copper through the magically-enhanced craftsmanship of their people. This was one of the few items associated with the use of magic that Holbrin permitted him and the other travelers to bring, aside from their swords, of course. Swords, bows, arrows, and armor could be explained away through secret crafting techniques, but an inquisitive craftsperson among humans would simply ask 'how was the copper placed into the gourd without burning it completely?' Questions with which Tyrnimar preferred not to address.

Still, the copper lining was subtle enough that Holbrin had permitted it. Tyrnimar produced this bottle and another tin tea cup. This was an adjustment that he had to make. Tyrnimar puzzled for a moment. *Is this the fate to be accepted by me?* He could not hide from Eevarel pirating his tea, so he simply made enough for both of them. She smiled at him in that grating way that she did when she knew she was interrupting him from something.

"I am surprised you chose a place like this, with all of these people around."

"Please," he implored, "a moment. There is a task that must be completed by me and notes which must be recorded."

Surprisingly, she sat back with uncharacteristic patience. He looked at her for a moment and colors began to swirl around her. His eyes widened with surprise before he looked away, schooling his face to calmness, *about what or whom that is causes great curiosity. Whoever it is... their doom at her hands will be faced by them.*

Tyrnimar mentally shook off that impression and turned back to his task, focusing on Kora and Ayza. He gazed at them for a few moments, noting the colors, brightness, shades, and movement of their auras. Something caught his eye in Kora's aura. Then another something in Ayza's. It moved. It was grey and nearly completely translucent, very difficult to detect, *and yet such strength is possessed!* Tyrnimar madly scribbled notes as quickly as he could while maintaining the required integrity of his penmanship. After all, what was the use of recording knowledge if it could not be read?

"There."

"There?" Eevarel said, reminding him of her presence. The sun was significantly lower and setting now.

"Yes, the task has been completed," he said.

"Well, I am glad," she said with mild irritation. "You took a long time and your tea is cold."

"Waiting is not required for you," he said. "The tea you have could have been drunk without delaying for me."

"You are right, I did not have to delay for you. I will not always, either."

Tyrnimar looked at her for a moment. There was an edge to her that eluded him. She lost her patience at his muteness. "So what did you find?"

Speaking in Elven, he answered. "Extreme guilt is being felt by the Firecaster."

Eevarel pursed her lips thoughtfully. "I would think that

most of these people are feeling a kind of guilt that comes when they lose a loved one like this."

"No, a different quality is held here," he said. "What is meant is that kind of guilt is seen everywhere, but in the woman, Kora Orint'ail, another kind of guilt is being carried by her, and of great weight."

Eevarel furrowed her brow, but Tyrnimar continued. "Also, and something which would be wanted to be known by Holbrin, Ayza has also unlocked her own blood magic and more maturity in it has been achieved by her. Some kind of power over air is had by her. It has not been seen by me, so it is difficult for what it is to say."

Eevarel nodded. "Anything else?"

"They are only half-sisters, not full," he said. Eevarel raised her eyebrows at that one. "Well, that would be a bit of town gossip," Eevarel said, "but I do not think that is really anything that Holbrin would need to know."

"Agreement from me is had," Tyrnimar said. The two of them drank their lukewarm tea with the sunset as the townsfolk finished their work for the day and retired for their evening meal. Some still practiced with wooden weapons on the town green. Tyrnimar collected the tin cup from Eevarel with a small smile from her and placed it into his leather bag. The two rose and wandered back to the Moradran Inn where all the elves lodged.

The pair arrived to see most of their fellow travelers eating outdoors at the hastily built tables. Since the common room of the Moradran had been commandeered by Lord Covendran and the merchant-turned-quartermaster, Beren Enkr'ail, the kitchen at the Moradran served tables out front, despite the lingering chill in the air. Trinien saw their fellow travelers first and waved them over.

"Ah, good. I was wondering if you started taking up like some of the others?" he said.

"What do you mean?" Eevarel said to him.

"A few of our Travelers have started taking some of their meals with human friends and counterparts."

"Oh?" Tyrnimar said curiously.

"Arynn and Turaean are still out with those human trackers, Garven and Korane, and that human boy that Holbrin threw at them, Ziek–the one that we met on the way into town," Trinien said. *So long ago that seems*, Tyrnimar recounted. "Irduin and Eevarel take lunch with Judane and Dareum Covendran." Eevarel shrugged and smiled in answer to Tyrnimar's questioning look. "Sieraean joined them to help with the boy, Ziek."

"Convenience is made by taking lunch. Another story is told by dinner," Tyrnimar said.

"Sometimes Holbrin dines with Lord Koval," Trinien said.

"That would be, between times, expected," Tyrnimar said looking around, "but that evening meals with humans are taken by Arynn and Turaean is surprising to me."

"Would you join me or would I be an obstacle?" Trinien asked, flashing a knowing smile at Eevarel.

"You are joined. Where is Bierien?" Tyrnimar said.

"Bierien has already gone to meditate," said Trinien. The two of them sat down. Trinien had a tea cup of very black tea and a plate that had held his evening meal.

"What is held by that cup?" Tyrnimar asked.

"A human drink I tried when we were passing through Vostind called coffee," said Trinien.

Eevarel looked at him. "You like it?"

"Sometimes," said Trinien. "I have taken to trying it everywhere we find it."

"Why is that?" Eevarel asked.

"The humans in different places prepare it differently. I am thinking of preparing and publishing a study of the different methods of its preparation," said Trinien.

"An interesting thing has been said. It is made differently in what way?"

"Different places bake the seeds in different ways. The brewing is similar to tea, but the techniques are different," Trinien explained. "Sometimes humans will add herbs or spices, even other tea leaves, to the coffee while brewing, and the humans of different places all seem to have their own style. Each nearby place is similar to the last, but never exactly the same."

"So, you like it," Eevarel prodded.

"I believe I do. The style here is to brew it in sheep's milk instead of water," said Trinien.

Tyrnimar sat pensively. "It will be tried."

"I will have some brought for you," Trinien said, waving to the barkeep through the window.

The three sat for another hour. Trinien was content to enjoy another cup of coffee while Tyrnimar and Eevarel ate roasted turkey and herbed turnip soup that seemed to be a staple of this town and several other villages near Yvel that they had visited on their route. Tyrnimar tried the coffee, poured from a pot into fresh cups for them, making an indecisive face.

"Things are different here in Gersh," Trinien began.

"What do you mean?" Eevarel asked. Tyrnimar took another tentative sip of his coffee.

"This area in between. When we came through the pass in the north, we were in Markia, the land of the Marin humans. We came south. You remember when we arrived in Versinth?" Trinien asked.

"There is memory," Tyrnimar acknowledged. "What you speak of is known."

"Well, it is not known to me!" Eevarel said insistently.

"Basically," Trinien began, "on this side of the Kaskevs, the various kingdoms of humans are dominated by particular types of humans, much like it is east of the mountains."

"Right," said Eevarel.

"But in the middle of the lands here, south of Markia and Berkmar, east of Tamarkand, north of Eklenda and Daeara, is an area that is not part of any of those kingdoms." Trinien explained. "All of the different types of humans from those kingdoms are mixed up here. This town, for example, mixes the Marins from the north and the Eklendans from the south. That's why some names end in '-ail,' for Marins, and some in '-dran,' for Eklendans." Trinien paused and Tyrnimar spluttered into his coffee, choking and hacking.

"Sorrow is had by me," Tyrnimar managed after a moment while holding back another fit of coughing.

Trinien went on, unperturbed. "But the Marins here are different from the ones of Markia. The accent of their language is different, the food they prepare is similar, but in some ways is similar to the food that Eklendans prepare here. That soup, for example–Eklendans seem to have a traditional dish of steamed turnips with herbs, but the Marins frequently prepare them as a soup," Trinien continued, as Tyrnimar poured himself another cup of coffee. "The soup here is turnip soup with herbs, prepared in a kitchen owned by a married couple of an Eklendan and a Marin. That one over there," Trinien said, pointing to a long, narrow stall built off of the side of the Moradran Inn. A small cooking area was positioned against the side of the inn, with a long counter on the street side. A slanted wooden roof extended over stools at the counter, and a few townsfolk in hastily-constructed militia armor sat at the counter eating soup and drinking ale.

"How do you know that one is Eklendan and one is Marin?" Eevarel asked.

"The wife has a narrow nose and blond hair, characteristic of many Marins," Trinien said, "and the husband has a narrow jaw and black hair, characteristic of many Eklendans."

Eevarel paused thoughtfully. "But I see other people here with brown hair, or red hair, like Dareum and that young woman, Kora Orint'ail."

"The brown hair can be either one," said Trinien. "Red hair is uncommon in Eklendan lines, but it happens. It is unheard of in Marin lines." Eevarel gave Tyrnimar a meaningful look.

"Though, I am not sure how this separation began, between the human kingdoms and these in-between lands," said Trinien.

"'Broken' or 'shattered' is the meaning of 'Gersh' in Old Paetic," said Tyrnimar. "The reason the name was given–"

"My lords and lady," broke in another voice, speaking in the Marin dialect. They all turned to see Dyram Torin'ail, wearing a mail shirt hanging halfway down his thighs. The front and back parted at the hips, and wide sleeves reached most of the way to his wrists. The bulky form meant that he wore a thick gambeson underneath. He wore a surcoat over the mail, colored in quarters of blue and white to represent the House Covendran. A belt over the surcoat held his scabbard, and a conical helmet with a wide bar to protect the nose perched on his head.

Those have been quickly made, Tyrnimar remarked to himself. Dyram had been appointed a tenleader in the Serna Militia and was clearly on task for the night watch. "Your Master Holbrin wishes for your presence, as many of our own people attend the Lord Serna."

"What is the occasion?" Trinien asked in Marin.

"A thick column approaches from the north with the Prince Gerald's colors riding at the front. Their pioneers are already marking their camp."

Chapter 12

The town of Serna, Yvel Principality.
By the Elven Calendar, thirteenth day of Spring, 18030.
By the Human Calendar, Weddingday, second week of Ers, 794.
An early spring evening, mostly clear in the twilight.

The Blue-Eyed Man rode into the formerly sleepy town at the head of the column, in the shadow of his prince and the rest of the prince's entourage. He had not had a pastry in a week. He shifted in his saddle, eyeing the growing palisade creeping along the edge of the town. *That's a major investment of labor*, he observed, still skeptical about how far and deep the effects of this constabulary action would go. On the one hand, if his friend, Nicholas, was right, the palisade was not only a necessary investment, but it might be too *little* defense and too late in its construction. On the other hand, of the scale… *It could certainly make for interesting times*.

The Blue-Eyed Man caught up to Prince Gerald and nodded to him before peeling off to direct the soldiers behind him. He nodded politely to Lady Serna, Mariss Covendran, and the two townsfolk-turned-militia that had escorted her to Yvel and back. The Blue-Eyed Man could still not figure out what manner of argument she had laid out to the prince that he would send two battalions and his own person here, when he sent single battalions or less to most of the other towns and villages that asked for help.

Returning his courtesy with a small, friendly smile, he found himself being wrapped up in her spell. *How does she do that?* Shaking off his own desire to turn from his duties and ride with her to talk, he met the First Battalion leader, Lord Gunst Ver'ail, riding under a checkered banner of blue and gold. They spoke briefly before the Blue-Eyed Man pointed to the area of town marked by the pioneers for his battalion.

They rode past three companies of mostly young men, some young women, and a few older, stretching into their middle years. Those would be the harder ones that decided to make a career of it. There would be a few good ten- and fifteen-year men and women amongst those three hundred or so shieldbearers. He repeated the same exchange with Lord Dorvin Arladran, riding with his red and white striped banner, pointing out the remaining areas and watching the other battalion pass.

This one only had two companies. Both were nobles of Yvel and had petitioned the prince for the honor. There were a few other nobles in the ranks, having won a petition to be a company leader. *Still, this will be much different for them than what they're used to... bandits and border skirmishes with the other sovereigns.*

Turning his horse, he cantered back towards the prince's party, who was greeting the local lord. The man rode up about twenty paces behind the party and dismounted. Wearily, he adjusted his breastplate and removed his helmet while taking his place as part of the prince's entourage.

Prince Gerald spoke. "–Make for movement first thing in the morning. We would sup with you." He was speaking in Eklendan to another man, roughly the same age as the prince, maybe a little older. His black hair was greying on his head and especially in the beard. The beard was becoming a bit scraggly with neglect, *probably from running his town like an army for the past month*, the Blue-Eyed Man noted. There were deep lines under his eyes and down both sides of his mouth to the jaw. That would be Lord Koval Covendran, husband of Mariss.

Beside him was a tall, strapping man with red hair, a bit younger than the Blue-Eyed Man himself. The Blue-Eyed Man was in his mid-twenties; *mid-twenties without a wife!* he grumbled to himself, as he looked past the younger man to a slightly younger woman. *Those eyes!* He masked his fascination with the hard-eyed young woman with her olive skin and dark brown hair tied behind her for practicality.

Her dark brown eyes smoldered with energy. The man appraised she had been taking plenty of sword practice over the course of the past month. She wore a sturdy grey riding coat with a brown skirt hanging down under it. Black boots peeked out from under the skirt. *Bah!* he chided himself. *Father wouldn't approve of me cavorting about with a country noble and besides, what would the* Prince *think of her? Still... I wonder what she's like...*

138

The man brought himself back to the moment as Prince Gerald was about to introduce his retinue. "Here I've brought two battalions of men, each commanded by Lord Gunst and Lord Dorvin. I've formed them into a regiment commanded by two of my sons, here, the Prince-Heirs Arnold and Oswald." The Blue-Eyed Man stiffened at those names. "I've also brought my own Crown Guard, led by Sir Virek and Sir Harl. And lastly joining us is Sir Reverend Merik, of the Military Order of Saint Graffin the Defender." The man noticed some of the townsfolk shift at the mention of an Ornethian Knight. *Is something afoot?*

"Thank you, Your Grace," replied the older man, who kept giving sidelong glances to Mariss. *That must be Lord Koval Covendran. He relies on her*, the man noted, observing Mariss' warm and affectionate smile at her husband. "And thank you, sir knights and Sir Reverend. Of course, you have met my wife, Your Grace, the Lady Mariss," Koval said.

"Yes, of course," replied the prince. "She laid out a most convincing argument that Serna and its defense was of vital importance to the survival of Yvel."

"She can be most persuasive, Your Grace," continued Koval with a tired smile. "I've relied upon her moderation for a great many years. Here also is my son, Dareum, who led a reconnaissance patrol to locate the orc encampment."

"Indeed," said the prince. "Will you show us on the map later and make a full report?"

"As Your Grace wishes," said Dareum. The Blue-Eyed Man noted his bloodied knuckles and a weariness to his posture. *He's been training quite hard, I imagine. I wonder if he always had or if he's just survived so far on luck.*

The Blue-Eyed Man took the fleeting chance to report, whispering in the prince's ear. "The battalions are settling into their positions and setting sentries. They will be done within the hour, Your Grace."

"Excellent, thank you," Prince Gerald said to the Blue-Eyed Man.

"Here also is my daughter, Judane, captain of our newly formed militia," Koval continued, before moving on to other figures at whom the Blue-Eyed Man had been furtively glancing. "And here, Your Grace, are some new friends that have been an immeasurable help to us, not just in direct assistance, but in helping teach us ways of war, training our people to fight, producing arms, planning the palisade, and more." Koval stepped over to a group of elves.

At the forefront was a stately fellow with long brown hair tied in the back and eyes to match a demeanor that reminded the Blue-Eyed Man of a calm morning after a nightlong snow. He wore a brown cloak over a red tunic with silver scrollwork embroidered around the collar. The man remembered Nicholas saying something a long while ago, that elves wore certain colors while they worked to represent what they did and their accomplishments. He saw tunics of red, blue, green, and yellow.

Ah, but I could take one of them home... same problem as before, though. The Prince would never have it, grumbled the man as he gazed longingly at the pristine beauty of the Elven women. His gaze lingered on them as Koval introduced a few of them, but the Blue-Eyed Man was not paying attention and barely kept his face neutral. The lord introduced his quartermaster and his tenleaders. That brought the Blue-Eyed Man back, though he still cast a discrete eye back towards Judane and the Elven women every now and again.

Koval was saying that he had fifteen tenleaders, and fourteen of them had seen fighting with the enemy. Three of them had seen additional fighting in the recent attack. The Blue-Eyed Man noted those three that stood, two uncomfortable at the attention and one that looked further on in his years. Despite his distraction, the Blue-Eyed Man noted that the town reverend was not present. Surely, they must have one for the chapel that the man could see from where they stood.

"Excellent, Koval. We're sure to give it to those greenskins," said the prince. "Now, let's see to that sup and your maps table."

***

140

Evening passed very quickly. The people of Serna did their best to provide an ample spread for their guests, with fresh boar for the Crown's party and other game for the soldiers of the regiment, but the Blue-Eyed Man could tell that their stores were stretched by the quantity of vegetables in the stews and the reliance on the quantity of meat for the meal.

Normally, at least in regions near Yvel, sup had a great deal of bread. Some had herbs baked in, some incorporated larger portions of butter in the dough, and there were a few other variations that he would have enjoyed. There was a certain pleasant quality to the food that commoners ate that, try as he might in asking, he could never get the palace kitchens to replicate. This was a rare chance for him to sample that at which his peers, his betters, and even his lessers would sneer.

The Blue-Eyed Man ate a few items, but finished the meal somewhat unsatisfied. He sat at Koval's map table as Dareum spoke about his encounters into the woods to the east and into the beginnings of the hills of the Kaskevs. The Blue-Eyed Man asked questions about troop numbers, arms, wagons, horses, and other things he felt necessary for a commander to know prior to battle. Still, he felt his professional curiosity was still hungry.

He was glad when the manor's guest quarters were easily exhausted by the Crown party and he begged off, allowing others to take the lodgings in favor of taking a room at their remaining inn. He was leading his horse off the line when he caught a glimpse of the prince looking after him with that disapproving stare and slightly raised eyebrows that the man knew too well. *Ah*, thought the Blue-Eyed Man, *he knows me so well. He shouldn't worry. I'll behave. Please, Your Grace, grant me this quest for a pastry and the eve of our embarkation!*

The Blue-Eyed Man heard someone call out. "Oswald!" The Blue-Eyed Man ducked into the shadows, pulling his horse along. *No sense in getting wrapped up in that*. He led his horse down the hill and was making his way towards one of the few remaining three-floor buildings in town when he heard footsteps catching up to him.

"Um, please, excuse the intrusion, y–" another man began.

"Please, good master, just 'sir' will do," the Blue-Eyed

Man said. "Formalities are the death of me."

"Oh, well, that is," the other man fumbled, "uh, y–I mean, sir–"

The Blue-Eyed Man noticed the other man's Eklendan was accented with Marin, so he switched to Marin. "It's fine, man. Out with it."

The other man was surprised for an instant at the change, but seemed to welcome the change into his own, more comfortable language. "Sir, my name is Orn Blar'ail; I am one of the tenleaders here in Serna. I was on the reconnaissance patrol."

"Ah, splendid!" exclaimed the Blue-Eyed Man to Orn. "I was so hoping to speak with one of the tenleaders from the patrol."

The man hesitated. "Yes, sir, as you wish. Uh, if I may, what I *really* wanted to talk to you–"

"Yes, yes, in a moment, good master. I hear that one of the tens had a very close look at the orc camp. Got a good look at all of them, eh?"

"Right, y–I mean–sir. I tried bringing this to your b-brother and he told me to bring it to you." Orn was looking frustrated and clearly wanted to talk about something else, but the Blue-Eyed Man pressed Orn with his own questions.

"So," the Blue-Eyed Man continued against Orn's uncertain protestations. "How big are they, really? Are they really two hands taller than the tallest of us? Are they really dumb like cats and dogs?" the Blue-Eyed Man probed, then to himself, "a wonder they can even fashion clothes and sticks for weapons at that level."

"N-no, sir," answered Orn. "Well, yes, sir. They are that tall and strong to match. Very much all of them, I say. But they're not dumb, sir. They seem just as quick witted with a sword or a spear as any. Only ones that clearly outmatch them are those point-ears."

"The elves?" said the man.

"Yes, sir, those. I'll hand them that. They can fight and fight well. Every one of them," said Orn, "but, sir, what I *need* to tell you–"

"A moment, good Master Orn, I beg you," insisted the man. "Were they all just naked with spears and such?"

Orn hesitated. "No, sir. The ones that attacked us here wore animal skins for armor, but they had swords and spears of steel, and steel-tipped javelins and throwing spears. A few had two-handed clubs."

"Right," said the Blue-Eyed Man.

Orn continued. "But some of the other ones that we met later were wearing armor of boiled leather, and had small bows—like Eklendan bows." Orn paused. "We met another one who was different from all others."

The Blue-Eyed Man stopped walking and half-turned towards Orn. "In what way?"

"He spoke our language," said Orn.

"Which one?" asked the man.

"Eklendan, sir," answered Orn.

The Blue-Eyed Man looked at Orn for a long moment. "How did that come about?"

"He wanted to parlay and exchange information."

"He what!?" exclaimed the Blue-Eyed Man in outright surprise.

"Yes, sir," said Orn. "He said he did things for the orcs for pay and said he would sell us information on them. He also said that he didn't really care about them. Well—no, wait—he didn't make me think that he cared about them from the way he gave his words, sir. He traded us information about the orcs."

"What did he take in exchange?" asked the Blue-Eyed Man.

"He took a rubbing of an arrowhead from one of the point-ears," answered Orn.

Did he, now, mused the Blue-Eyed Man before answering. "Well, that doesn't make any sense."

"That's what I thought, sir," said Orn. "No sense at all."

"So, tell me more about him," said the man.

"He said his name was Grotis—" Orn began.

143

"He had a name!?" the man exclaimed again. *I've got to meet this one! Nicholas won't believe it! Nicholas said that they don't have any names.*

"Yes, sir, uh," Orn continued, "and he also wore a padded gambeson with pieces of boiled leather and steel splints. He had a horn bow and a small sword."

"Did the other orcs have any shortswords?" pressed the Blue-Eyed Man.

"No, sir, only large ones, usually two-handed. Maybe a shield here or there, but mostly large, curved swords and some with square tips. Every now and then some of them would have a knife, but they never fought with it."

"Hm," said the Blue-Eyed Man thoughtfully as he resumed walking towards the inn.

"But, really, y–I mean–sir, I need to tell you something else," Orn resumed.

"Oh, alright, man, out with it, then," the Blue-Eyed Man relented.

"There are witches here, sir."

The Blue-Eyed Man stopped walking again and turned slowly towards Orn again. "What did you say?"

"Honest, sir. Witches."

"How do you mean, good master?" asked the Blue-Eyed Man.

"There are two of them, sir. There's Kora Orint'ail," he said, pointing to a house down one of the smaller streets. "She's lost her parents, but she's a witch, that one. She shoots fire out of her hands."

No... "Go on man, there are others?"

"Yes, sir," Orn said eagerly, taking the question as encouragement. "There's that Mkaela Ran'ail. She makes deals with the Pit and gives dead people unnatural life! She lives over there." Orn pointed to another house down another quiet lane.

"What do you mean?"

"She makes deals with the Pit. She sells their souls and

the dwellers of the Pit. They bring them back to life when they should be dead. Our town elder, Elder Dum'ail, has already ridden off because Lord Dareum and Lord Koval would not listen. They've given in to her spells! They're bewitched!" Orn finished breathlessly and clearly desperate for the Blue-Eyed Man to listen and run back to the prince with this news.

It would be... The Blue-Eyed Man laughed a bit; a light, amused chuckle. "Good, sir! There's no way that such a pious town with such pious folk as you would let such monsters walk free to ruin good people. You, sir, are exhausted,"

"No, *sir–*" Orn insisted.

"No, sir, *indeed*," the Blue-Eyed Man said, chuckling a bit more. "There's no way such creatures would be allowed to live. I would have to see it for myself." A thought occurred to the Blue-Eyed Man before he continued. "And don't be stirring up trouble with the reverend knight and your stories. We march tomorrow and we need clear heads and full stomachs." The Blue-Eyed Man showed him away. "Off with you then and get some rest. You are clearly exhausted. You need a good meal, a washing, and some good sleep," the Blue-Eyed Man ordered, dismissing Orn.

Orn had an extremely sour look, poorly masked, as he paid his respects to the Blue-Eyed Man and bade him good night as tactfully as he could through his broiling frustration.

That would be too good to be true. Witches from old? Like from the Imperial Secession Wars, eight hundred years ago? I'll be on the look, but such potential! He nodded to himself. *Good to know about the elder. True or not, it would be quite a bother to have church knights poking their heads in with an inquisition. I may be able to...* The Blue-Eyed Man smirked to himself as he finished his walk down to the inn, the Moradran, as he had heard it was called. He led his horse to the stables and handed the reins to a flustered young stablehand before approaching the tables.

It struck the Blue-Eyed Man as odd that the tables for a common room would be outside of the inn, but they all looked newly built. Each table had a lantern. There were only a few glowing lanterns at the few occupied tables; all others were dark and vacant. He spotted several people from the reception at the manor and made a decision.

"May I join you?" he asked, discouraging several people from rising out of courtesy with a wave of his hand.

"Of course, y–" one of them began.

"Just 'sir,' please. I don't like to dwell on formalities, much or overly," said the Blue-Eyed Man.

They hesitated before another answered. "As you wish, sir. Of course, you may. We would be honored."

The Blue-Eyed Man had to contain his delight, sitting at a table across from three Elven women, his eyes furtively drinking gulps of them. There were a few others at the table: two other Elven men, a human woman, a human man, and a boy from Serna.

"Join me for some coffee, sir?" asked one of the Elven men.

"Yes, actually, that sounds a delight," answered the Blue-Eyed Man. "Who does me this honor?" The palace kitchen chased the fashionable styles from Eklenda, where they brewed coffee in hot water. But in smaller towns in Yvel and further north, they kept with the Marin style of brewing coffee in goat's milk. The man much preferred the rich, creamy flavor to the coffee, but try as he might, the kitchen would not abide his wishes to dispel with fashion.

The others were having ale or mead. It was difficult to see in the lantern light, but he was sure that the elf woman sitting directly across from him wore a red tunic with green embroidered scrollwork at the collar and cuffs. The other two Elven women were in red tunics with silver embroidered scrollwork under their cloaks of brown or grey. The elf offering coffee wore a golden yellow tunic with red embroidered scrollwork. The last one, looking into his cup of steaming drink, wore a blue tunic with silver scrollwork interrupted by the strap of a leather shoulder bag. The human man and woman wore green and olive tunics with hoods thrown back. Each of them had an assortment of bows, arrows, and swords of varying lengths. The boy wore a brown tunic and had his own steaming drink.

"Trinien Orsir, sir," answered the elf.

"Would you happen to have any donuts or such?" the Blue-Eyed Man asked. The others at the table shifted uncomfortably, clearly not wanting to tell the Blue-Eyed Man no, but not having another truthful answer.

"It's fine. I imagine the stocks are pretty thin and there isn't time for making things like that," said the man, slightly embarrassed at having shown his entitlement.

The Elven woman sitting further from him rose and leaned over the table with one hand, pouring a splash of hot mead from a covered clay pitcher with the other. "There, sir," she said with a friendly smile. "That should fix your sweet tooth."

"Is this what you're having?" asked the Blue-Eyed Man.

"Me? Oh, no, sir. This one makes me tea from flowers every evening," she said, indicating towards the elf staring into his own cup. The elf man seemed to try to curl into himself a bit more and make himself even smaller, covering a grimace with his shoulder.

Ah, well, not like I could've taken her anyways, thought the Blue-Eyed Man while raising the coffee. *A man can dream, though, right?* "That's about right," he said approvingly, *and it is. Could do without the bite of the mead, but the sweetness covers it.*

"What's the Prince like, sir?" asked the boy abruptly.

The human woman shushed him. "Mind yourself!" she hissed at him, "I'm sorry, sir–"

"It's alright, good lady," said the Blue-Eyed Man and then turned slightly to the boy. "And what's your name, good master?"

"Ziek, sir," answered the boy.

"Well, you're a bold one, Master Ziek," said the Blue-Eyed Man. "The Prince. Hm. Well, he's a very wise man with a good heart. Very brave, too." He shifted the subject. "Tell me, were you one of the brave souls that fought the orcs in the woods?"

"No, sir," said Ziek, disappointed at the conversation shifting away from his preferred topic. "But I was wounded in the attack! Wanna see my scar?" Ziek was starting to pull his shirt up when the human woman swatted his hands and shushed him again. She was a bit older than the man himself, maybe somewhere between thirty and forty years, with the narrow jaw, black hair, and olive skin of an Eklendan, but the boy had brown hair and their faces said that they were not related. When she looked his way, her dark eyes burned in a way that surprised him. *Hm... tasty as she seems, she doesn't seem to have any room in her head for anything but killing greenskins. Suppose most of the locals would be like that. That means Judane would also...*

"Oh, no thank you, brave Master Ziek," said the Blue-Eyed Man, "but I crave to have more knowledge from those that fought the orcs and scouted their camp. We will march tomorrow, though it'll take near a month to move this many troops through a forest without a road."

"We'll answer your questions as best we can, sir," said the other human man. He seemed quiet, but unflustered by his presence.

"Most excellent! With whom do I have the pleasure?" asked the Blue-Eyed Man.

"My name is Garven, sir. I am one of the huntsmen of this town. This is Korane, the militia scoutmaster. I am apprenticed to her." The woman who was policing Ziek nodded to the man at her introduction.

The Elven woman spoke. "My name is Eevarel, sir," she said, before motioning to the woman across from Garven followed by the one directly across from the man. "This is Arynn and Bierien," she said.

"I was not on the patrol, sir. I was here helping the townsfolk arm themselves," said Bierien.

Clapping a hand on the shoulder of the Elven man who seemed to want to be somewhere else, Garven continued. "And this one is Tyrnimar."

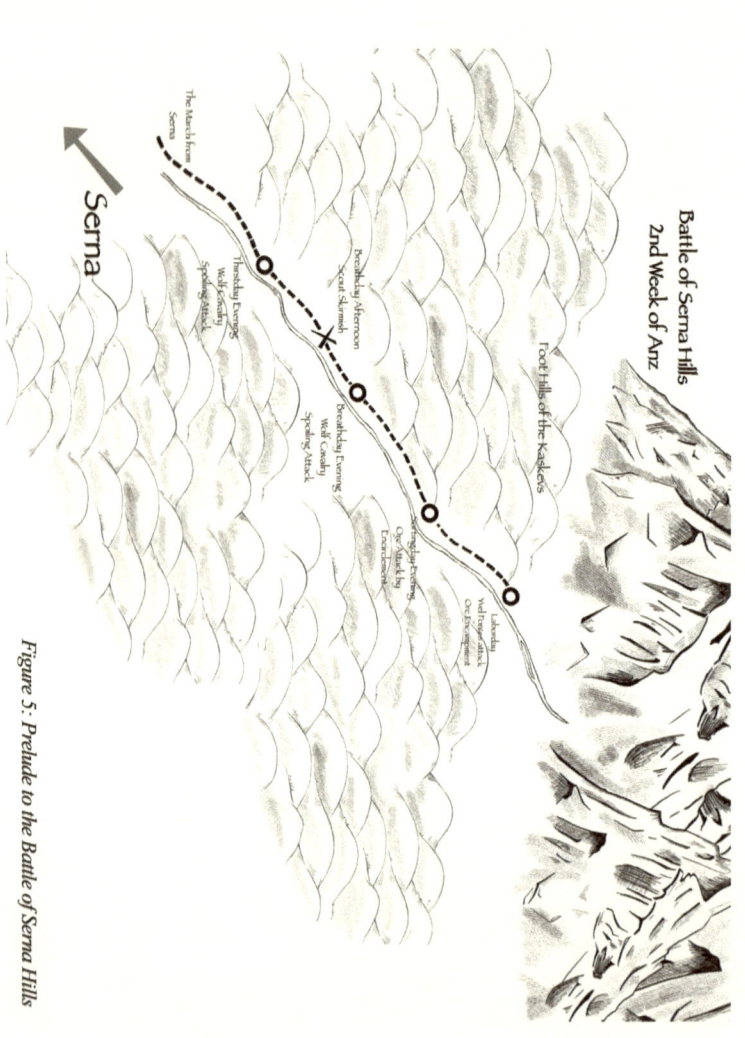

Battle of Serna Hills
2nd Week of Anz

Serna

the March from
Serna

Scout Skirmish
Breakthru/Afternoon

Breakthru/Evening
Wolf Cavalry
Spoiling Attack

Thursday Evening
Wolf Cavalry
Spoiling attack

Foot Hills of the Kaskeis

1st day Evening
Orc Attack by
Encampment

Saturday
Vwd Incursion
Orc Encampment

Figure 5: Prelude to the Battle of Serna Hills

Chapter 13

Encampment of the Pev'Baki-Norn in the foothills, middle of the Liberator
Side of the Mountains.
By the Goblin Calendar, middle of the Fifth Moon Cycle, 3114.
By the Human Calendar, Thirstday (fourth day of the week), second week
of Anz (second month of the year), 794.
A spring evening, mostly clear in the twilight.

Hearing the approach of a rider outside, Dariyet shifted in his plated mail and looked up from his map table. He had only arrived half of a moon ago with the new subleader from the Borys-Karang, known as a garad'dai, in order to consume the Baki-Norn. In that half-moon, his neatly trimmed black hair had become scraggly and unkempt. The scruff on his cheeks caught in the links of his mail hood and ripped out. *Of all the things to overlook*, he had grumbled to himself.

The subleader informed the orcs of the Baki-Norn that they were no more and that they were to be consumed by the Borys-Karang. After dealing with the challengers, the Garad'dai oversaw the remnants of the tribe in the name of the Borys-Karang in his absence. The Garad'dai Borys-Karang brought them to what passed for order among the orcs, though Dariyet had to step in and provide additional direction. Though this orc, the Garad'dai, was not from this low tribe of near-savage orcs–he was properly from the Borys-Karang–he was still an orc, and could only do so much in Dariyet's eyes.

This was not the honor that Dariyet had dreamed of, yet it would be a great insult to refuse an offer from the Great Oygariyet. He had accepted the appointment with the pride of being chosen by the great one. Besides, Dariyet knew Oygariyet to be the great one for a reason. That Oygariyet knew this was a less-honorable appointment–to lead these unsubtle, unsophisticated savages, instead of the fine hosts of his own kind–was clear by the very fine war gifts the great one had given to Dariyet and the others sent to mind this cluster of chattel, almost as an apology.

151

Still, the Garad'dai Borys-Karang was useful. Dariyet and the orc had come to an arrangement. Dariyet would set the requirements, and the Garad'dai Borys-Karang was generally reliable about accomplishing them and enforcing some measure of discipline.

Dariyet was especially thankful for having the Garad'dai to do this because, unlike his own kind, or even humble goblins, orcs traveled to war as an entire tribe–slaves, children, females with child, and all; whole households, or what goblins would consider a household. Hobgoblins, and even goblins, had the sense and decency to leave ones that had no immediate business in battle well away from it. *These orcs… not as much. Perhaps these difficulties were why Oygariyet the Great had bestowed such lavish honor gifts.*

The war gifts were quite fine. Dariyet had taken his pick of the finest plate from the smith's pile at the Stone of Rykooth. Its pauldrons were covered in leather tanned and stained dark with the blood of captives that had not been sufficient for the honor of slavery, and its sleeves were constructed of steel segments down to the wrists. Multiple layers of leather made from the skins of those captives made his armored skirt, reinforced with steel. The same material was used as the barding for his mount, a well-bred great wolf, from the great one's own houndmaster.

The last gift was the grandest, though. He felt himself flush with pride at the memory of the great one awarding it when the Oygariyet raised him from being the First to giving him his own name. It was a cape, made of the overlapping skins of five of those unsuitable captives; for if they could not serve the tribe in life, they could at least keep the rain off its leaders' backs, thus providing use to the tribe. By Leriyet, the great one was always so resourceful in his kindness, ensuring that everyone had a chance to contribute.

The skin of the faces of those captives formed the center of the surface layer on the cape, so that their faces would see to glory in the wake of the path of Dariyet. Dariyet wore it everywhere to show honor to the gift the great one had bestowed upon him, as well as the plated leather and breastplate. He could tell that some of the orcs, formerly of the Baki-Norn, perceived him as weak for hiding in a skin of steel, namely by receiving three challenges since he arrived.

While winning the challenges was easy enough, Dariyet

felt little honor in it. It was like winning an argument with a fool. Dariyet had the Garad'dai Borys-Karang put an end to the challenges. He only had so many troops, and even troops of mediocre quality should not be squandered in pointless, foregone challenges when they could at least find some sliver of honor through dying in conquest. Though, after his victories, he did enjoy that the orcs gave him a wider breadth, and he had won two orc female slaves from the third challenge. They were nice enough. Nothing he could show off with pride back at the Stone of Rykooth, at least not as his favorites, but it was a humble start for Dariyet in his own name.

Dariyet shook himself from daydreams and brought himself back to the messenger approaching his table. He had set up his orders room in the ruin of a cluster of stone houses with the trace of an old wall. Still, there was shelter from the rain, using the upper floor as a roof over the ground floor. Spread across the table were the maps of the areas they were soon to seize, in the direction of the setting sun. Some showed neighboring areas, most of which were the responsibility of the Borys-Karang. But they would not be alone; others, like himself, were sent by Oygariyet to accompany those groups of Borys-Karang orcs or others.

To the left part of the map was the Borys-Karang's attempt to strangle and seize what was known to the humans as the Place-called-Ardara. Dariyet knew of some other groups of orcs further to the left and right along the mountain spine, but he suspected there was more that he did not know about. He wondered how those other hordes of orcs traveled. The Baki-Norn had been a small, wandering tribe, so the whole tribe laid out upon the field around the ruins–warriors, females, children, their filthy possessions and all.

The cavalry leader had a quiet pride in her stature and her step, yet she approached in deference to his higher position. "A host approaches, Great One," she said, though she was not merely a messenger. She was the leader of the wolf cavalry that Oygariyet had given to Dariyet from the Wiridil tribe as his own special troops. Out of respect, she had removed her helmet to speak to Dariyet, revealing that she had colored her black hair purple with berry juice, a signal to the other warriors in her warband that she made sport in their times of rest and recreation. For her duties leading the cavalry, she kept her hair tied back from the blue skin of her hard face so that it would fit tidily into her helmet. She still wore her mail shirt and had all of her weapons and implements for fighting, riding, and scouting hanging from her or on her wolf, who was waiting lazily outside in the courtyard.

"A host? They come to us?" Dariyet asked. "*Good!* I was thinking they would be dishonorable opponents when they looked at us a moon ago without fighting. Now, how many?"

"There look to be seven to eight hundred to fight on foot, most of them well-equipped, and another fifty horse cavalry, among the humans. They also have a small number of elves with them, Great One."

"Elves?" repeated Dariyet, intrigued. "This will be *very* interesting. How soon will they be here?"

"Three days, Great One, at their rate," she said. "Supply carts drawn with other animals follow them."

Dariyet pondered for a moment, scratching a bug bite on his neck. He looked at the segment of the map between his camp with these Borys-Karang and the Place-called-Serna, which he was to seize. Normally, he would be all too happy to meet the host head-on in an *ultimate* contest of wills between warriors, proving to himself again what had been proven many times before.

"What are your orders, Great One?"

Dariyet pondered more, though. The cavalry leader stirred, but he held up his hand for her patience, which was his due. These Borys-Karang that he had, while they were greater in number than the human host approaching and greater in size and strength, he had been told, but... still. The humans' numbers were not without end, and he knew he would lose a significant number, especially if their horse cavalry had their way. Dariyet also knew that it would be far from over after seizing the Place-called-Serna. Seizing the town was more like moving the camp forward than reaching victory. It would be a small victory, but certainly not the final one... and perhaps as significant as stepping on the crushed head of an enemy warrior on the way to killing them all to the last one. "How are their scouts?" he asked.

"Their scouts have talent, but they are on foot, Great One," she answered. "They saw us, but we were too fast for any of their horses to catch us."

"Tell me about their horses," he said. "Are they light or heavy?"

"They have some of both, Great One, mostly heavy. The ones that are well-equipped wear coats of colors and designs like most of the warriors on foot. The ones that do not wear those coats are mostly light or medium horses. Those riders have mail, leather, or padded coats and the horses usually have no armor. The horses seem like they would be strongest in the open, like in a field. They have strong legs and bodies, but they are clumsy in the woods."

Dariyet had decided. "We shall use our strength to benefit our pet savages and use their strength for our purpose. Pull the other scouts in to assemble our cavalry, and send the Garad'dai Borys-Karang to me."

***

Dusk

Julian Panr'ail was rubbing down Pine, his roan mare, at the end of another day on the march with the Prince's Army and the newly formed Serna Company. He had escorted Lady Mariss Covendran to Yvel to ask the prince for help and returned with Mariss and the prince's contingent to find his town being turned into a fortress, though there had been a long way to go towards completing the wooden palisade when they were departing for the march. He missed the quiet life raising cattle, sheep, and horses on his family farm, west of Serna, but there was no going back to that now. At least, not for a few years.

Julian had no illusions about this being over quickly. Aside from the rage and boiling anger from the raid–almost two months ago–Julian nursed an unspoken resentment that, even if he lived through this, the orcs had stolen years from his life that he would have to watch with fewer and fewer of his friends and family.

A few paces off, his cousin Ervan was rubbing down his own horse and boasting to Liri Venodran about how he should have brought more javelins for all of the orcs he was going to kill. Julian shook his head and smiled grimly. It was not simply that Julian was taller than Ervan–Julian was taller than most Sernans–but Ervan had always been the child between them, despite being the same age. Ervan had the same brown hair as Julian and so, years ago, they were sometimes mistaken for each other when spotted from afar.

Julian and Ervan made up a large part of the small light horse detachment of the Serna Militia Company. Liri, who had also attended as an escort for Mariss, rode with them as well. Lastly were the younger and elder Lords Covendran, when they chose to travel and fight with the horse detachment rather than joining most of the company on foot.

Lord Koval had been given the honor of riding as part of the Prince's Crown Guard, comprised of medium and heavy horses, and Dareum was busy commanding the whole Serna Militia, including the light horse, with the younger Lady Judane assisting. Holbrin's elves formed a separate contingent, which seemed to loosely answer to the prince, the lord of Serna, and itself. Julian was confused by that arrangement, but it seemed that the elves were agreeing to requests rather than taking orders. Most of the elves had arrived with horses, but Holbrin suggested that they were more valuable to the army as archers. The Sernan Militia Company had been temporarily given to Arladran's Battalion as reinforcement, to make two battalions of three companies each.

Julian and Liri had been on the road almost two months, since the day after the orcs raided their town, but Ervan was not yet used to traveling this much. He had been on the march with the rest of the company and the Prince's Army for almost four weeks. They were following the trail that Dareum's patrol had taken when pursuing the raiding orcs back to their camp, though to call it a trail was not altogether accurate. This was a wide draw–a low ground gap in the hills, sloping downward–that eventually led to the foot of the Kaskev Mountains.

The draw was lightly forested with various bare broadleaf trees and bushes that were just now budding, a few pine trees, and patches of ground vines. A stream lazily wound its way through it. Ervan had embarked upon the march with his own stream of bluster about how he was going to give the orcs some of their own bread. He made sure to ride closest with Julian and keep Julian on the flank so that he would take the brunt of the incessant boasting. After the second day on the march, it mysteriously transformed into hourly boasting.

Julian shook his head with a small, internal chuckle. The rain two days ago brought Ervan to a slightly higher sense of misery and Julian was relieved that his boasting came up only when he thought back to the raid and got angry.

The sun was already behind the mountains by the time the Prince's Army moved into the place marked by their pioneers, and the day was done. Julian had never considered how difficult and slow it was to move this many people through the wilderness with trees and streams breaking up the column and no room for the horses to fight, really–especially the heavier horses that the prince had brought, along with their with barding and knights and men-at-arms with plate.

Julian was leading Pine to a patch of grass for her to eat. He could really go for some of his aunt's plum pie right now, but that would be for later, he told himself. If he lived through this, there would be a little bit of time for pie before the next big fight. If he died, he would not need the pie anymore and would not be able to complain about it, either. He heard commotion and shouting further down the line, towards the front, and he turned in its direction to see. The torches that lit the perimeter of the large camp flickered as large figures flitted past and Julian began to hear the clang of steel.

"COME AND GET IT!" shouted Ervan, as he speedily climbed into his saddle and spurred towards the noise. Following, Julian vaulted into Pine's saddle, feeling exhilaration for the first time in two months. He snatched a spear, an orc spear he had taken up after the raid, trailing Ervan. Liri followed him on her own horse.

As they drew nearer the commotion, the camp was in turmoil. Armored figures with helmets covering their faces–must be orcs–rode giant wolves tearing through the camp. The wolves loped gracefully as their riders slashed, hacked, and crushed anyone they could reach, stopping every now and again to throw a short javelin.

The three human riders spurred their horses ahead, but

trees, roots, and rocks seemed to mock them as they struggled to reach the fray. The wolf-mounted orcs dealt a few more wounds and turned, bounding back through the camp from the way they had come. Julian gritted his teeth. *Stay and fight!* A scream from behind brought his head around. Liri was falling from the saddle, spurting blood while one of the riders dashed behind her brandishing a shortspear.

"Stay and fight!" he called after it, wheeling Pine around.

"HERE IT IS!" shouted Ervan as he hurled his spear after it. The spear sunk into the ground and Ervan howled in rage, speeding after the rider while drawing an axe.

"No, wait!" called Julian. But it was too late. Ervan was building momentum after the riders, passing the light from the torches, and speeding into the darkness. He was there for an instant and suddenly disappeared from view, leaving only the sound of a screaming horse. *Damn it! The fool!*

The wolf riders were gone as quickly as they came. Julian dismounted and ran in the direction Ervan had rode, and found exactly what he dreaded, about twenty paces past the torchlight. Ervan's horse had tripped on the dark and uneven forest floor, strewn with rocks and gnarled tree roots. It twisted and screamed on the ground with a broken leg. A few paces ahead, Ervan laid silently with his head twisted at an unnatural angle.

***

The glow faded and Mkaela withdrew her hand as the soldier began breathing normally, concealing her talent under her cloak. She rose, pulling the cloak up and briskly walked away, both searching for other wounded to assist and removing herself from the view of the soldier before he woke up. Mkaela was not eager for the questions and the witch-calling. She was lost in thought when she bumped into someone who turned.

"Orn!" she said. Orn looked at her disdainfully. "I…" she hesitated.

Something seemed to occur to him and he broke a very small smile. "Come quickly. Someone's hurt. You can help them."

"Alright," she said skeptically. "Show me." She was nervous about his intentions, but she nonetheless followed for about fifty steps through the camp, winding around trees, collapsed tents, and overturned cookpots and supplies. He led her to a crowd of people forming a ring. Mkaela stopped. She was afraid. There were a lot of people and there was no way she could hide what she was doing.

Orn looked at her over his shoulder from the edge of the crowd. "What's the matter?" He half turned towards her. "You help people, right?" He smiled in mock encouragement.

Someone in the crowd turned to see what the noise was behind them. "There you are! Did you get the Prince's Surgeon?"

"Even better," said Orn with bluster, indicating towards Mkaela. She drew back further, eyes wide with surprise and fear.

Kostray, help me! He's trying to get me killed! Mkaela fretted.

SOMEONE NEEDS HELP, the presence in her head commented. WILL YOU NOT HELP THAT PERSON?

If they see me do it, they'll kill me as a witch!

WILL YOU ONLY HELP OTHERS WHEN IT IS SAFE? HAVE WE NOT DECIDED THIS BEFORE?

The man in the crowd that had spoken to Orn gave a vexed sigh. "Look, I don't care how good your village medicine woman is or if you want to take her to bed," he said sharply. Orn was taken aback by the scolding, but it continued. "We need the surgeon now, or Sir Merik will die!"

"Here, now," Orn began to protest, "I don't want–"

"Never-*mind*!" he hissed. He motioned at Mkaela. "Here. You're better than nothing. Do what you can for the reverend knight while *I*–" he glared at Orn with coldly burning blue eyes, "–go find the surgeon."

The man stormed off unquietly muttering curses, looking this way and that, no doubt in quest for the prince's surgeon. Orn and Mkaela watched his departure for a few breaths, when someone else from the crowd called to ask if the medicine woman was going to help or not. Orn gave her a baleful, burning stare before it twisted into that same small, cruel smile. "Go on then, *medicine woman*, you'll help the reverend knight, won't you?"

Mkaela swallowed and passed into the crowd. Soldiers and the reverend knight's squires parted way before Mkaela. Sir Merik sat, leaning against a tree trunk, wearing an undyed, grey gambeson over dark colored breeches and leather boots. He looked to be on the edge of thirty years old, with short-cut blond hair and warm-toned skin with freckles that was paled from his wound. His face was contorted and his eyes squeezed shut in pain for the short spear stuck in the side of his stomach, the back of the head just peeking out of the padding of the gambeson. Dark red was blossoming from the spearhead and he breathed hoarsely with pain.

The shaft was shorter than most fighting spears and seemed meant to be thrown by a rider. Mkaela had seen a few of these spears throughout the camp. She knelt next to him, hesitating with everyone in the crowd looking on with nervous, dreadful expectation. She silenced the crowd with a deep sigh, placing one hand around the spearhead, the other grasping the shaft, and concentrated. Nothing happened for a moment and the crowd began to murmur nervously again.

The glow of light began faintly. As its brightness grew, the crowd silenced again. The glow encompassed a hand's breadth around the spearhead and she began drawing the spear out from the blood blossom on his gambeson as she stopped the bleeding, knitting the flesh inside before closing the wound. It was over in a moment that stretched for days. She cast the spear aside and withdrew her hand slowly, wishing that no one could see her now, wishing that she could be any place besides right there, even as her eyes met with the shocked and stunned expression of Sir Merik. She could see Orn sneering with triumph from behind the edge of the crowd.

"She's a witch!" cried a man. Orn's sneer blossomed into a smirk.

"A witch!" echoed another.

"NO! This is a blessing! Can't you see? Sent by Orneth!" said a third. All eyes locked on a brown-haired young man, a spearbearer in the prince's livery.

"He's a witch-lover," called someone else in the crowd.

"No, it *is* a blessing," cried yet another. The voices grew louder, tumbling over each other and rising. Mkaela shrank against the ground, breath short with fear. Sir Merik slowly rose to his feet, back still against the tree, his gaze fixed on Mkaela with a mix of shock, horror, and awe.

Amid the shouting, one voice rose abruptly. At first, it was difficult for Mkaela to pick out, but the other voices gave way to its authority. "Silence!" called the voice, firm and clear. Mkaela looked up as the shouting subsided. She recognized the caller; heir to the Crown, Prince-Heir Arnold of Torg'ail, closely trailed by his brother Oswald of Torg'ail.

Arnold wore a red cape with a grey chevron across the back, which swirled about him as he stalked towards the crowd in his coat of mail and a belted sword. His air permeated anger as his icy eyes froze any protests before they were given voice. Brown locks swept back to reveal the long, narrow nose so characteristic of Marin heritage, though he was a bit taller than most Marins, or even Eklendans. The prince-heir took in the situation as all eyes fell upon him and the crowd yielded control of the situation. "Now, what's this about?" he asked, in a manner more even than his previous tone.

"That one's a witch!" called a man. "She used her witch charms and hexes on Sir Merik and turned him to Pit meat!"

"I am no Pit meat!" retorted Sir Merik, abruptly pulled away from his fascination with Mkaela.

"Here now, Sir Merik!" said the prince-heir, cautioning. "And you, mind yourself," he warned the other man. "Now, what actually happened?" He scanned the crowd and pointed to someone else. "You! What happened here?"

"Uh," stammered the man that the prince-heir had pointed out. "Well, Your Grace, Sir Merik was wounded by one of the wolf riders–by a javelin–and, um, in the gut, that is, sir–I mean–Your Grace, and, um, this woman came about and laid her hands upon Sir Merik where he had the slash–the one in his gut that is–and, um, then it glowed up and Sir Merik looked like he wasn't wounded anymore." He hesitated. "Your Grace."

The prince-heir listened intently, showing no reaction, thinking for a moment. Then he looked down at Mkaela. "And how did you come upon this? Just happened to be walking by, looking for men to bewitch?" he asked quietly, yet everyone heard the words in the tense silence.

Mkaela hesitated, but someone else called out.

"He brought her here, Your Grace," said the first man, pointing to Orn, who was trying to hide in the crowd. "This witch-lover." Orn's triumphant smirk abruptly melted as the crowd parted to display him to the prince-heir. "We sent him to find the Prince's Surgeon for Sir Merik and instead he brought this harlot," the man finished.

"Your peace, man!" Prince-Heir Oswald scolded the man as Prince-Heir Arnold turned towards Orn.

"Is this true?" Prince-Heir Arnold asked calmly.

"Yes, Your Grace," Orn answered.

"And why did you get this woman instead of the surgeon?"

"Well," Orn was clearly flustered, "because, y–Your Grace, I knew she could help Sir Merik."

"… Indeed," said Prince-Heir Arnold. He folded one arm across his chest and held the fist of his other hand to his chin in thought, thumb under his jaw. He paced for a moment before speaking again. "Sir Reverend?"

"Yes, Your Grace," Sir Merik said calmly, but uncertainly.

"Isn't there a passage, a verse, in the Book of Graffin? How did it go? 'When people remember the forgotten ways, turn near death to life, defeat to victory, there shall be the sign that, born of jealousy, will come an echo of the denizens of the Pit into the lives of all people, but those who remember will be the best and the worst. Peoples' salvation and damnation.'

Sir Merik glanced aside recalling his memories. "Yes, Your Grace, there is such a passage. Though, it reads 'rememberers' instead of 'those who remember'."

"Is it not storied in a variety of holy texts of people being able to use magic–including the power to heal grievous wounds?" asked the prince-heir.

Sir Merik hesitated. "It is so written, Your Grace." Sir Merik looked down, seeming to struggle with himself. "So you say, Your Grace, this is a sign?"

"I say it could be," said Prince-Heir Arnold.

"How can it be?" asked Sir Merik.

"Sir Merik, you are sworn to one of the orders that fight for the Ornethian cause, correct?"

"Yes, Your Grace," Sir Merik said stalwartly, as if the prince-heir was questioning his faith.

"If this is not a sign, then what would a sign look like?" the prince-heir asked quietly. "Do you not really believe what is written?"

"I do, Your Grace, but…" Sir Merik struggled and the crowd watched, captivated. "There have been many witch burnings over the centuries. They were not signs."

"Indeed, Sir Merik, there have been, but how many of those witch burnings have been about 'witches' healing people from near death?" the prince-heir said. "Come now, look into all of those cases and you will find that the lot of them are about cheating wives, husbands, adulterers, and temptresses, charlatan doctors selling no-good cure-alls, farmers that do too well better on their harvests than their jealous neighbors, and all that like. None of those were really actual witchcraft–and if they were–none so clear a use of magic as this."

Sir Merik struggled at the prince-heir's words for a moment, but the prince-heir finished the discussion. "I ask you again, Sir Reverend, if this is not a sign, then what would a sign be, if not real magic–magic that saved *your life*, no doubt!"

Sir Merik relented. "You have it, Your Grace, this is a sign. It must be." The crowd gasped at his concession: some with relief, some with horror. Mkaela felt as though she were listening to a conversation about someone else, about people she did not know. Numb from the tension of the crowd crushing her, and disconnected from herself. The crowd began to murmur.

"So be it, then," announced the prince-heir. "You agree, Sir Reverend? This is a sign."

"A sign it is," Sir Merik further relented. The crowd murmured further.

"Disperse!" called the prince-heir to the gathering. "You must have duties about beyond milling about here, no?"

"But what about the other witches?" asked the first man.

"What other witches?" asked the prince-heir in reply. The dispersing crowd turned to hear this.

"There is another witch that can call the fire of the Pit–and there's sure to be more, Your Grace."

"Your Prince and the Prince-Heir will believe it when they see it, good man. For the time, we will count this as a blessing on our side–as I'm sure *you* would if *your* own gut had been sliced open." The other man sullenly bowed his head and took leave.

The prince-heir looked down at Mkaela. "The Prince would do well to hear about your powers, young lady, and the Prince-Heir would be honored to escort you. You," he said, pointing at Orn, "fetch the Lord Serna and the Lord Covendran, and present them to the Prince to explain this.

"Mkaela!" A man, Julian Panr'ail, stumbled through the crowd. "Mkaela! Help! Come quick, it's Liri and Ervan," Julian said breathlessly, shoulders heaving from exertion.

Prince-Heir Arnold pondered for an instant. "Explanations can come later; you have a calling, young lady." No one caught the wink exchanged between the brothers that were heirs to the prince.

***

The Blue-Eyed Man separated himself from the crowd and approached Mkaela, reached out for her hand, and helped her up. "The Prince-Heir tries to be reasonable. The Lords Covendran can explain the situation to the Prince. Off with you, then, and for good cause."

Mkaela took the Blue-Eyed Man's hand to help her unsteadily to her feet. "Thank you, y–"

"Please, just sir. Formality. Despise it," said the Blue-Eyed Man. She smiled and curtsied before rushing off with the other man from her town. The Blue-Eyed Man recognized him; Master Panr'ail, he thought, one of Serna's militia that had escorted Mariss to Yvel to plead their needs.

The Blue-Eyed Man struggled to contain his glee, presenting an outwardly calm and disciplined demeanor, while internally he rejoiced. *A true Healer. I wouldn't have believed it if I hadn't seen it. So, it's actually true. They've a Firecaster, too? Oh, this really is too good to be true. Oh, thank the Prince-Heir for paying attention to his scriptures, and thank the poor Sir Merik for being too dazed to think.* He rolled his eyes and shook his head with a smile. *A sign, indeed! Pf! Still, looks like I'll have to worry about that Church inquisition after all. Hm. I wonder if I can...*

"You there!" said the prince-heir, pointing at someone leaving the tense scene. "Fetch me Lord Arladran and Lord Ver'ail. They're sure to try another raid every night. Hop to it!"

The Blue-Eyed Man had watched the whole scene from the shadows until entering the crowd towards the end. *And then, there's the troublemaker.* As the crowd continued to melt back into the camp, the Blue-Eyed Man discretely picked up one of the short throwing spears from the wolf riders and tucked it away before sinking back into the shadows from whence he came.

Chapter 14

Higher foothills, middle of the Liberator Side of the Mountains.
By the Goblin Calendar, middle of the Fifth Moon Cycle, 3114.
By the Human Calendar, Breathday, second week of Anz, 794.
A windy afternoon, the next day.

The wolf cavalry leader spied the human army ambling through the trees from the crest of a hill, where she laid upon her belly to avoid being seen. Her wolf chewed on a rabbit she had shot with her bow earlier, before the invader in the sky's peak. She watched the humans mill by like ants, generally following the stream up the draw.

They had become much more careful after last night. No doubt they would have sentries tonight. Their ranks were only slightly thinned, though she was sure the raiders had given more wounds on the humans than their losses reflected. Still, they had inflicted a few casualties on the humans... better than nothing.

She absently reached over and plucked a bundle of dark blue berries from a small bush. They hung in bunches of two or three berries on bushes of knee height. She was not familiar with these plants. They did not grow higher in the Mountains, but she was thankful they were here now, so early before the warm months. The skin of the berries was a dark blue, but the insides were purple, and purple coloring is what she sought. They made such an erotic color for her hair. She was sure to use them tonight.

She carefully packed them away and looked again. She had seen their far scouts pass by a while ago and she spied a few of their close scouts ahead. Three in the front. One, no, two on the far slope of the hill on the opposite side of the draw along which their army plodded. That meant there would be one, two, or three scouts on this hill. Where were they... *there*. She spotted two together. An elf and a human–a female and a male. *They are too close together to guard the flank. There must be another...*

And then she saw the other scout–a human female with

the hair of a raven and eyes that blazed cold hate at her, her bow already drawn. They stared at one another for an instant. The arrow loosed, screaming towards her, and lodged neatly through the muscle under her knee.

The cavalry leader yelped in surprise and rolled behind the trunk of a small needle tree, hastily fitted an arrow to her own bowstring. This could be an honorable death, but she preferred to use the berries tonight and have many other nights like it. She lunged from cover, loosing the arrow in the general direction of the enemy scout, and staggered towards her wolf, who was alert and low on its paws, uncertain of the direction of danger. She stumbled, the arrow shaft catching on the small branches of other berry bushes.

She winced as she kept low to the ground again. The wolf barked and snarled off to the side. She was close to escape. She bent herself in half to untangle the arrow shaft from the bush, then broke most of the arrow off on either side, both entry and exit, so that it would not catch on anything else. She would have to pull the rest of the shaft out when she had time and bind it with a compress. Hearing the scream of another arrow, she rolled again, this time behind a rock.

She hauled herself up and lunged toward the wolf just to see it scrambling on the ground, frantically pawing at an arrow sticking out of its neck, spurting blood on the dry ground. She looked up in time to see the woman with hate in her eyes lunging through the air at her with a skinning knife, leading for her face. The cavalry leader almost dodged, but was hobbled by the arrow shaft in her leg. The knife slashed across the side of her jaw but bounced off of the taut sinews in her neck. She twisted her head aside while smashing the heel of her palm into the side of the human woman's head as she continued her descent onto the cavalry leader.

Moving quickly, the cavalry leader wrested the knife away from her attacker and slashed the woman deeply across the outside of her leg. The human woman tumbled to the ground, gripping her leg in pain and trying to hold the blood in. The wolf weakly pawed at the arrow, no longer having the strength to stand as it neared its death. *This will be a very long walk.*

The cavalry leader hobbled over to the human woman who glared at her with contempt, daring her to finish the job. She would not be able to stand with a cut that deep, let alone defend herself. She held the blade close to the human, but the woman did not flinch. The cavalry leader gave her a sardonic smile and flicked the tip of the knife across her cheek. She did flinch at that.

"There," she said. "We match now." The cavalry leader knew the human female did not understand her. "But we both get more nights with men and women or whoever we want to love today." On a whim, she grabbed the human female's raven-black hair and smashed her own face into the human's, roughly kissing her before shoving her back to the ground. "Maybe you can come play sometime when this is done and take each other for a night's sport."

The human woman spat at her and shouted harshly, probably cursing her. She flung the knife to stick in the ground paces away and, with a chuckle, began the long limping walk back towards the camp.

***

Encampment of the Yvel Regiment in the higher foothills of the Kaskev Mountains, east of the town of Serna, Yvel Principality.
That evening, in fading twilight.

"I don't *know* why the torches have to be this far out, Orn," said Dyram irritably, "but those are the orders from Lord Arladran! You heard them the same as I did *and* you heard Lord Dareum tell us to do it, too. And mind the rest of the implements!"

"Witch-lover," Orn muttered under his breath.

"You have something to say, Orn?" Dyram's voice matched his resting sour-faced expression.

"Oh, no," Orn said sarcastically, adjusting the helm hanging at his belt. It was one of the pieces with the face cast in a slain orc's face. Fully a half of the militia's helmets were cast in orc faces for steel helms, or leather stretched about their faces or skulls on leather masks or leather shield coverings. Dyram was fairly sure that the elves were not pleased at some of the smiths' use of their newly learned skills. "I wouldn't dare question any of my betters, Dyram, and I certainly know you wouldn't, no matter what they say."

Dyram glared at Orn with his ice-blue eyes. "Fine, Dyram," Orn relented, rolling his eyes, "the torch stakes go on both sides of the stream. I got it." Orn turned to gather up his squad to install more torches along both banks of the stream.

The stream that wound its way up the draw they had been following abruptly curved across their path. It was no major obstacle for the army to cross, though the cavalry would have to walk their horses across. One of the prince's sons, Arnold, had insisted on stopping there. Or had it been Oswald? There had been shouting amongst him, the battalion leaders, and a few others. Prince Gerald had put a stop to it, scolding them that their soldiers should not see their leaders arguing, but everyone saw it and saw the prince shaking his finger at them like boys who broke their mother's dish.

Whatever got said in quiet after that was a mystery, but the army still stopped for the day and made preparations for the night. With this extra row of torches on both sides of the stream, the sentries would have further visibility to see the wolf riders, and archers and crossbows would be at the ready all night. Dyram was skeptical about it, figuring that the wolf riders would see the preparations and just go around, but Taram had said the prince's son had a good idea and left it at that.

The torches curved all the way around the camp, in case the wolf riders attacked from another direction. But for some reason, the prince's son really thought the wolf riders would–and really wanted them to–attack from the east, uphill, the direction the army was marching towards. Dyram was not sure.

Until the past month, he had only known the nobles in Serna, the Covendrans. It did not take long for Dyram, for anybody, to see that each noble thought that their own idea was the best and made sure to let you know it. Dareum and Judane seemed different, but they were the same age as Dyram was himself. Dyram did not see why that made a difference, but Taram told him that they were at an age, all in their late tens or early twenties, that more easily accepted change without understanding it, whatever that meant.

"Let's go, you two." Dyram called to two militia from his squad; Baryn Kevr'ail, who had lost his wife on Dareum's patrol, and Amryst Veradran. Dyram was nervous about Amryst because she clearly preferred Orn. Orn's ideas, Orn's words, Orn's company. She had sided with Orn on Dareum's patrol and wanted to kill Kora and Mkaela. Dyram was nervous that he might find Amryst's knife in his back if he had to confront Orn again, but Lord Covendran had made it clear who was assigned to which squad and made those eyes at even the whisper of a question on it. Dyram shook himself. Something about Koval's eyes always gave him the shivers.

"Make busy in the streambed." The two of them put in their last torch post, lit the oiled wick, and got into the streambed for the rest of the work. *At least Mkaela saved Liri.*

***

Later, after darkness falls.

The wolf cavalry subleader grinned. This was his chance to prove himself to Dariyet to be the cavalry leader. The wolf cavalry leader had not returned from her scouting mission today and it was widely believed that she had met an honorable death. Still, while the cavalry subleader was pleased at the leader's honor, she had quite an appetite for sport, and their fist of one hundred and twenty wolf riders would not quite be the same. There would still be sport, but it was different when the cavalry leader led and participated.

He brought himself back to the moment. One did not become cavalry leader, chosen as first, or earn a name by feeling sorrow for the fallen or envying their glory. The sun had retreated from the night some time ago. He could hear the human army a few hundred paces away, attempting to be cautious. They placed their torches further out, and more of them, but it made no difference. The strength of the wolves would carry them the added distance in a breath.

The wolf cavalry subleader shifted under his vest of overlapping steel plates and pulled at the collar of his mail shirt to adjust where the mail sleeves fell before looking up. Before him, aside from his own wolf–a majestic creature built of power and discipline encased in plates of hardened leather–was the rest of the wolf cavalry: one hundred and eighteen armored hobgoblins, astride these great beasts. With a thrill, he walked to his mount, placed his left foot in one stirrup and hauled himself atop.

The subleader let out a sharp whistle, a common sound to some of the night birds, bringing all attention to him. He picked up his helmet from the saddle pommel and raised it high. Silently and wordlessly, the other wolf riders mounted their steeds and donned their helmets. The subleader slowly laid his helmet to rest on his head and nudged his wolf forward with his knees. He heard the soft patter of one hundred and eighteen wolves behind him quickly gain speed as his own wolf broke into a sprint.

He entered the outer layer of torchlight and was almost past the ring of torch posts before the first calls of alarm from the surprised sentries sounded. Arrows had not even flown as he was leaving the outer layer of torch light, bounding down into a streambed. He let out a yip of laughter from the exhilaration, turning to a yelp of surprise as his wolf yelped and stumbled, making wet sounds in the streambed and pitching him forward.

The subleader landed on his back, the plates of his vest clanging. Other wolves and riders began to pile up on either side of him, screaming and groaning. On his back, sprawled on the bank of the streambed, he lay lamenting. He feebly reached with both hands to feel about the sharpened wooden stakes that he had landed on, piercing his chest and right leg. *Shame*, he thought sorrowfully. *Shame to die on the first attack I led before killing a single enemy soldier, to die first, to die on a fortification instead of by the hands of a skilled enemy fighter*.

The stream only trickled this time of year, before the rains closer to the winter began, but the stream would swell with all of their spilled blood. The wolf cavalry subleader closed his eyes for the last time and a single, indistinguishable tear of shame trailed downward over his forehead. The sounds became dimmer and distant. He was unaware of the other wolves that had piled up on top of him until some were finally able to cross the river of stakes.

***

Sounds of alarm filtered through the camp, but despite their warning, the Blue-Eyed Man smiled to himself. Smiled at being right, and smiled at the opportunity to butcher two pigs with one knife. Some of the wolves had broken into the camp, but quite a few had impaled themselves and their riders on the stakes that had been placed in the streambed.

Nicholas was right. The enemy could see very well at night; far better than any of the humans. But just as any human struggled to look at the sun, these creatures–orcs, he supposed–had trouble seeing dark areas in the shadows of the brighter torchlight. The wolves had been moving too quickly for any of them to stop. It seemed that a few who were committed to the attack broke through, running over the bodies of their dead and dying comrades. Others changed direction at the last instant and were probing the perimeter for an opening, but the alerted sentries, which had been wisely bolstered with those elves from Holbrin's band, were harassing them with arrows, crossbows, and throwing spears.

The Blue-Eyed Man moved through the shadows of the trees and the camp tents, staying close to the sounds of fighting. He knew a certain ten of the Serna Militia was posted on this side of the camp–he had personally ensured that it was posted here. *There*. He recognized some of the squad members with whom he had spoken with in Serna, and recognized one of them from the crowd when that girl healed Sir Merik. He hefted a throwing spear he had taken, that one of the wolf riders had thrown yesterday, and made sure of his target as the wolves raced around in a frenzy.

He threw the spear and watched it arc gracefully through the air, glad of all of his time in the practice yard, and found its target. The spear sunk into Orn Blar'ail's chest, piercing the large piece of hardened leather meant to protect his chest, sinking in with enough force to emerge on the far side of his body. Master Orn's face registered surprise as his eyes glazed over, dying before he was fully on the ground. The Blue-Eyed Man quickly and silently glided away, satisfied at having eliminated a threat to his new pet witches.

***

The wolf and its rider frantically thrashed about the camp, trying to find a way out. Everywhere it turned it was stopped by spears, swords, and angry shouts. Tyrnimar gripped his sword, forged in the furnaces of his homeland. He barred its path, lamenting yet again time that he could not use magic. *So much easier would be this, if magic could be used!* The rider, garbed in mail, regarded Tyrnimar and hastily urged its mount on, raising its axe.

Tyrnimar advanced, the blade dipped low to his right side and behind him. His hands moved about each other, rotating the blade about his body, meeting the axe haft and batting it aside. The blade hung high, arcing over Tyrnimar's view of the rider. The hands rotated again, flicking the blade, and rapping the rider on the helmet with a loud clang. The rider carried the momentum of his axe strike around, unfazed by Tyrnimar's jarring hit, and the axe sailed again downwards towards Tyrnimar.

Tyrnimar dodged, narrowly avoiding the axe and feeling the wind from its arc. The wolf, head and snout covered in plates of steel with a goring spike in its forehead, growled and nipped at the elf as he pivoted around and the wolf circled him. Reading the color of controlled fear radiating from both rider and wolf, he rushed forward, pressing the attack on the rider. He sought an opening as the rider flailed its axe and mailed hands to fend off Tyrnimar's blade. *There!*

The opening presented itself, the hands moved, connecting the blade with the wolf's right foreleg and dragging it across bone, opening skin and sinews. The wolf yelped, tumbling onto its side, taking its rider with it. Tyrnimar leapt over the squirming wolf and stepped on the scrambling rider's helmet, forcing the head back. He plunged his blade downward using both hands, breaking mail links protecting the neck to pierce the rider's throat.

The wolf scrambled, knocking Tyrnimar over, and his sword clattered to the ground out of reach. Another wolf and rider rushed by, similarly seeking an exit. The wolf rolled its massive form over Tyrnimar, pressing the breath out of him. Its anger at Tyrnimar for slashing its paw seemed to be overpowering the pain it felt as it glared at him and snorted. Thinking as quickly as he could,

Tyrnimar grabbed the goring spike, jerked the plates aside and punched the wolf in the eye. The wolf jerked the other way in pain and scratched at its face far enough for Tyrnimar to snatch a dagger from his belt and plunge it into the wolf's same eye. It shuddered and lay still.

Tyrnimar could still hear fighting nearby, but was once again exceedingly grateful to Eevarel for forcing him into all of those painful hours of sword practice. The dead wolf was still pinning Tyrnimar to the ground by his legs, but he was out of immediate danger. He noticed that allied soldiers had formed a ring around his apparent duel with the wolf and its rider, and were now cheering at something. Five of them quickly approached to help him push the wolf off, while the others ran towards the other fight a mere twenty paces away. The soldiers were forming another ring around two combatants. Tyrnimar craned his head around to watch as he was freed from the wolf's weight and helped to his feet.

The two combatants were the other wolf rider and a tall human soldier. *No!–not a soldier, one of the Princes-Heir! Arnold!* Tyrnimar recognized the human. *Those colors have what meaning?* he puzzled. The prince-heir wore a mail shirt and sleeves with steel plates around his neck and over his shoulders. Steel gauntlets and greaves were hastily donned over a white undershirt and blue riding breeches, which could be seen hanging under the mail shirt and behind the greaves. His head was bare as he waved off the other soldiers.

For himself, this is wanted by him? This could be ended by the other soldiers in a breath! A longsword gripped by his right hand, resting over his shoulder, blade straight and tall. His left hand rested easily on his hip. The prince-heir's back was to Tyrnimar, but slightly turned. Tyrnimar could make out the corner of a bemused, even unconcerned smile, as if he was looking at an afternoon snack he was about to enjoy.

Behind the wolf and rider were three human soldiers behind it and two others crawling to the edge of the crowd, being helped by their comrades. The wolf's head was protected by steel plates similar to the one which Tyrnimar had finished off, but with no goring spike. Instead, the wolf wore more barding, but of hardened leather. It snarled at the soldiers around it as the rider controlled it. This one wore an angled breast plate and helmet with mail over its arms and legs, with leather gloves. It sported a round shield and a curved, one-handed cavalry sword.

The prince-heir hefted his sword in both hands and raised it in salute. The rider clapped his sword against his shield and pointed at its opponent. The prince-heir advanced, holding his hands high. He let the tip of the sword dip low across his body while pointing forward in the high guard as he advanced and circled toward the rider's shield side. Then, he circled tightly and moved further in.

The rider urged the wolf to circle faster, but the prince-heir abruptly brought the blade high and crashed it onto the rider's shield, knocking him from the saddle. Bringing the blade around again, it sliced into the wolf's neck, behind the steel plates, parting the hardened leather and severing his head most of the way through the neck.

The prince-heir casually placed a foot on the collapsed wolf's head to wrench his blade free while the rider tumbled and scrambled to its feet. The prince-heir shouted at the other soldiers to stay back. Finishing freeing his blade, he waited for his opponent to regain his footing and saluted him again. The rider was as tall as the prince-heir, who towered over most other humans, and elves too, for that matter. The rider hesitated, then clapped its shield again with its blade, pointing at the prince-heir.

The prince-heir held his sword with one hand on the hilt and one gauntleted hand halfway up the blade. The rider presented its shield first, blade held low under the shield as they moved towards each other. The prince-heir reached with the blade tip to catch the top of the rider's shield, circled to the shield side, and moved the hilt of the blade upwards. He deftly used the blade to block the rider's strike, then struck the rider in the helmet with the crossguard of the sword. The rider struggled and the two grappled, unable to gain enough space to make a clear strike at each other. They stood for a moment, each trying to force the other down. The prince-heir was grappling his opponent with his sword held across his opponent's back, the metal of their armor grating together noisily in stalemate. Suddenly, the prince-heir released the hilt of his sword and reached his opponent, drawing his opponent's own dagger, stabbing him in the armpit and then the neck.

As red blood poured down the rider's left side, it loosened its grip on its sword, dropping it, and sagged against the prince-heir. He let his opponent collapse onto the ground and rolled it onto its back.

"Let's see what these orcs look like, then!" called the prince-heir. Placing his own sword on the ground next to his now harmless opponent, he reached down and removed the helmet amid the sounds of labored, wet-sounding breathing. Gasps in the crowd emitted as the torchlight revealed blue skin.

Tyrnimar recognized a face like this. Blue skin, smooth with youth, despite the grey hair. Not at all the face of an orc, but that of a hobgoblin from the western slopes of the Kaskevs. Tyrnimar, propelled by curiosity, moved closer. He could see the rider looking at the prince-heir as the prince-heir gazed back. *That face is there again! As if an unexpected afternoon meal has been enjoyed by him.*

Tyrnimar looked at the dying rider. *A woman!* She glanced at Tyrnimar, but then smiled at the prince-heir. She tried to say something. A few weak attempts at forming words came out of her mouth before blood bubbled out and her eyes glazed over.

Chapter 15

Encampment of the Pev'Baki-Norn in the foothills, middle of the Liberator
Side of the Mountains.
By the Goblin Calendar, middle of the Fifth Moon Cycle, 3114.
By the Human Calendar, Breathday, second week of Anz, 794.
A cool and clear spring night, the moon high in the sky.

Another unfamiliar wolf rider approached Dariyet's
headquarters, who was waiting for this report. He put down the
rodent stew. The rider dismounted outside of the ruined stone
building and removed his helmet before approaching. He stood at
Dariyet's desk for a moment, clearly nervous.

"Out with it, rider. How was the raid?"

"It was not effective, Great One," he said, stiffening in
anticipation of rebuke.

"Oh?"

"We have lost most of the cavalry. Only twenty-nine riders
remain, with eleven of them wounded."

Remain calm. "Twenty-nine?" he said evenly. *Losing
ninety-one in a raid*, Dariyet silently lamented.

"Y-yes, Great One."

Dariyet thought for a moment before answering. "Did they
die well?"

The rider shifted uneasily, but kept his disciplined bearing,
and looked directly at Dariyet. "Many did not, Great One. They fell
prey to a trap of fortifications and sharpened sticks."

They did not even die fighting*!?* Dariyet could barely
contain his anger, but pushed it down. "Where is the human army
now?" Dariyet asked evenly, indicating towards the rider to show
him on the map.

The rider leaned over the map and studied the terrain.
Dariyet could see his eyes tracing the flow of water down the
mountains, selecting the correct stream and finding the hills. Dariyet

179

wondered how human maps would look. A good map like this would take a mapmaker a good full moon to draw, standing on the tops of mountains and hills to draw different portions of the map to a scale. Humans had no mountains to stand on and see the ground below them.

"Here, Great One." The rider's response pulled Dariyet back to the moment.

Dariyet looked at the area indicated. *About a night and a half march between them and us. What would the Great Oygariyet do?* he mused. "No matter, then. The raids achieved their purpose. They died with honor, tricks or not."

The rider stiffened, moisture collected in his eyes, "Th–"

Dariyet held up his hand. "There is much to be done. Rest the cavalry for the night. I want scouts tracking their position before the invading sun peeks over the Mountains, but no engagement. We will proceed with the next action." Dariyet turned and leaned on his map table, noting the markers on his map showing the progress of the host of approaching humans. "Bring me the Garad'dai Borys-Karang. Let the Pev'Baki-Norn do the one thing they can!"

***

Encampment of the Yvel Regiment in the higher foothills of the Kaskev Mountains, east of the town of Serna, Yvel Principality.
By the Elven Calendar, forty-sixth day of Spring, 18030.
By the Human Calendar, Sortingday, second week of Anz, 794.
The next morning.

"You were supposed to save him!" screamed the woman, flailing fists at Mkaela and spitting at her.

Mkaela, trying to fend her off, was stumbling away trying to keep the other woman from grabbing her hair. "I already told you he was already dead! There was nothing I could do!" she cried back.

"LIAR!" screamed the other woman and struck her. "PIT FILTH! WITCH! He wouldn't take your pit deals and that's why you let him die!"

"Stop!" Sir Merik called as his blocky frame rushed over,

hindered by the armor plates covering his legs and abdomen. He was only wearing his undercoats of padding and mail, and did not wear the breastplate, pauldrons, plated sleeves, the gorget, and certainly not the helmet–or anything else that would bake him in the heat of his own exertion.

The woman reached for something at her belt. "Amryst!" cried Mkaela.

Sir Merik reached them and seized the other woman's wrist and pulled it away with his thick arm, showing a belt knife that she had been drawing. Sir Merik tightened his iron grip, forcing the knife to drop from the woman's hand. His hazel eyes flashed menacingly at her before shoving her stumbling a few paces. "You had best be on your way," Sir Merik said to her. She tarried a moment before storming off, casting scathing looks over her shoulder.

Mkaela, a bit shaken, turned toward Sir Merik and squinted in the morning sunlight. "Uh, thanks–I mean–thank you, Sir Reverend."

"Think nothing of it, My Lady," said Sir Merik. Sir Merik suddenly felt at a complete loss for what to say or do. They both looked away. Sir Merik, a man of thirty-two years, had devoted most of his adult life to the Order of the Defending Saint, never thinking that in his time he would encounter someone... *someone chosen by Orneth or Graffin or Kostray*, he worried. *A sign of great peril and strife, yet also a sign of hope...*

"Uh, so, thank you, Sir Reverend. I have duties to attend."

"What? Uh–My Lady, what duties? You are a savior, you cannot be going about digging trenches," said Sir Merik.

Mkaela looked at him in apparent alarm. "Uh, Sir Reverend, really, I have militia duties."

"Nonsense. Who said?"

"It's fine, Mkaela," called a man who had just arrived, apparently looking for her. The man appeared middle-aged, over forty or fifty years. He was garbed as his fellow militia were, with piecemeal armor made up of hardened leather segments reinforced with steel plates in some places. He had scraggly black hair, coarsely swept straight back and roughly hanging to his shoulders.

His face was etched with many seasons in harsh elements. "Really. It's fine. Off be with you with the reverend knight."

Mkaela looked after the older man, but Sir Merik could not see her face. "My Lady, clearly it is dangerous for you as there are some who do not believe–" He hesitated. "Believe that you have been Chosen." He looked at her, a young girl of perhaps twenty years with, he guessed, Marin blood. Sir Merik was not sure about the characteristic looks of Marins versus Eklendans. He hailed from near Clovis, near the land of the Berks and the Tamarks and, like most of the clergy, had Berk blood in his own veins.

Mkaela seemed worried about something. "I'm sorry, My Lady, I've–uh–I've never been around someone that, uh…" Sir Merik trailed off, unsure of whether he did not know the words or it was that he could not bring himself to say the words that he knew. "I never dreamed that I would be in the presence of a Chosen."

"Chosen?"

"Yes, uh, Your Grace, I should say," said Sir Merik.

"Your Grace!?" exclaimed Mkaela.

"I can think of no better way of addressing you, Your Grace," said Sir Merik plaintively.

"What in the Pit is this!?" said Mkaela, taken aback. "I'm a baker apprenticing with the herbalist! Your Grace, I bet! Pff!' She started to walk off, changing her mind on which of several directions to go.

"Your Grace, language! And it is clearly not safe for you with that woman nearby. I should stay by your side." Mkaela looked up at the sky with tightly closed eyes. *Is she communing with Orneth?* wondered Sir Merik.

"I can get by fine, Sir Reverend," said Mkaela.

"Your Grace, that woman attacked you, and I would be remiss in allowing your holy person to be endangered."

"My holy person!? Are you *serious*?" she intoned in exasperation.

"He may have a point, you know," said another voice. They both turned to see the Prince-Heir Arnold approaching them. He was flanked by his brother, Prince-Heir Oswald on one side, and two of his squires on the other. Similar to Sir Merik, he wore plates and mail over his legs with a mail shirt and padded liner. The ties at the top of the padded liner were undone to let air into the shirt in the heat of the day. He was tall, with strength in his shoulders from countless hours at the practice yard. He normally kept his brown hair cut short, but it had grown longer and was unkempt from being on the march for over a month now. Eyes of ice regarded them.

"Your Grace," said Sir Merik respectfully.

"Your Grace," repeated Mkaela. She sounded a bit out of breath suddenly.

The prince-heir held up a hand. ""Please." He spoke to Mkaela. "Sir Merik may have a point, My Lady."

Mkaela did not say anything for a breath. "But, Your Grace, I have militia duties."

"Not anymore," he said. "I've taken the liberty of speaking with your Lord Serna and Lord Dareum. We have been given a sign, haven't we, Sir Reverend?" He glanced at Sir Merik. "We cannot risk the gifts of one of the Chosen fighting directly on the front. You will be behind the fighting with the Prince's Surgeon, using your gift."

"But–" she began to protest.

"No, nothing on it. Please stay with Sir Merik for your safety," he answered, turning to Sir Merik. "I'm sorry, Sir Reverend, but I have to ask you to stay out of the main fighting and ensure the safety of the Lady Mkaela here."

Sir Merik was speechless for an instant before he spoke. "But, Your Grace–"

"Sir Reverend, please. I think we agree on this. I know you want to fight to protect the people, but this is the best use of your skills: ensuring that the Lady Mkaela survives and is able to use her gift. You will contribute to saving more people this way, albeit not as directly as you would like."

Sir Merik's posture slumped a bit. "As you wish, Your Grace," he said sullenly.

"Thank you. Now, I must attend a planning meeting in the command tent with the Prince and the Prince-Heir. You are welcome to attend, Sir Reverend." Prince-Heir Arnold paused, glancing at Mkaela. "I suppose you both could attend or wait for further instructions from the Prince's Surgeon."

"I–" Sir Merik corrected himself. "We will be there, Your Grace."

The prince-heir strolled on, starting to hum to himself as he walked off towards the command tent. They waited awkwardly as he left before they spoke.

"Does he always talk about himself like he's not here?" asked Mkaela.

"I do not rightly know, My Lady. I only recently met him," said Sir Merik, puzzling after the prince-heir.

***

The command tent, encampment of the Yvel Regiment.

The Blue-Eyed Man entered the command tent with a few of the prince's staff and some Crown guardsmen. "Ah," declared Lord Gunst, "we are all gathered, then. We've still a day's march to do here."

"Sorry," said the Blue-Eyed Man, smiling. "Let's be on with it."

The collection of people crowded around the prince's planning table. With the prince were the prince-heir; Lords Gunst and Dorvin, the two battalion leaders, and their lieutenants as company leaders, among them Dareum and Judane of the Serna Militia. Also present were Sir Virek and Sir Harl of the Crown Guard; Lord Koval of Serna; Holbrin with several compatriots, and two scouts from the Serna Militia (the man remembered dining with one of them but the name escaped him at the moment). Sir Merik of the Militant Order of Saint Graffin stood by the entrance, and the healer witch from Serna tried to vanish into the tent wall, clearly resenting every minute of being in this tent instead of doing some lowly task.

Have to thank the Prince-Heir, that dashing fellow, the

Blue-Eyed Man congratulated internally, *for finding a competent and committed bodyguard for my investment. Sir Harl is a good find, too*. One of Sir Harl's siblings had married into a Daearan house and he had been able to acquire some of that Daearan heavy plate for himself, as well as some barding for his horse. He was the heaviest cavalryman of all the prince's appointed knights, even if he hated being a cavalryman at all. He was also the slowest. The Blue-Eyed Man did not have the best eye for horseflesh, but he could gauge well enough. Sir Harl's horse was not Daearan, and was neither bred nor trained from a young age to carry all that weight. The Blue-Eyed Man had seen Sir Harl in the practice yard, and even sparred him from horse and on foot a few times. The horse had gotten used to the weight, but it was slow. The Blue-Eyed Man brought himself back to the moment.

"Still, it is concerning, Your Grace," Holbrin said to the prince. "The presence of hobgoblins here. There may be something larger afoot."

"Share your thoughts, Master Holbrin," said the prince. "I welcome your words."

"There is normally fierce competition between orcs and hobgoblins. That there are so many orcs of different tribes working together at all is already troubling enough, but the presence of hobgoblins is altogether different."

"How so?" asked the prince.

"Your Grace, just look at their equipment alone. Not just skins and hardened leather, but mail, plates, full helms, a variety of weaponry, even barding for their mounts," said Holbrin. "Their mounts, alone! You and I have seen the same specimens, bred and trained for riding in combat. That alone takes years of dedicated effort. This is a whole different enemy than the ones that we have fought."

"True," interjected the Blue-Eyed Man, "but there are so few of the wolf riders, maybe a hundred at the most. Compared to the number of orcs, are they necessarily allies, or is there a possibility of some other explanation?"

The prince turned to the Blue-Eyed Man. "Finish the thought, then."

"Well, they could be mercenaries hired by the orcs, or we could be passing through the hobgoblin territory on the way to fight the orcs. Or even that the hobgoblins and orcs are fighting each other and view us as another contender."

"I am most inclined to agree with your idea of mercenaries, sir," said Holbrin. The elf next to Holbrin stirred, the reclusive one with the blue tunic and leather shoulder bag. The Blue-Eyed Man had eaten with him before. *What was his name again? Turnover?* He suppressed both a smirk and a craving for plum-filled pastries. "My companion has another opinion, which he is nearly bursting to share," said Holbrin flatly.

Attention in the tent shifted to the elf next to Holbrin. "Thanks is given," he began. "With the amount of cooperation over such a wide area of different tribes of orcs, which has not been seen before, consideration must be given that the reason for this cooperation may be indicated by the presence of the hobgoblins."

"Your name, sir?" asked the prince.

"What?" the elf said, startled by the question. "Oh, Tyrnimar. Tyrnimar Iquarren, Your Grace."

"Thank you, Master Tyrnimar," said the prince. "Could you say that again?"

"I am sorry, Your Grace," Holbrin broke in, "this is just the manner in which he speaks. A pattern of his dialect of Elvish."

"I see," said the prince, "Well, could you reword that?"

Tyrnimar did not suppress his glower as Holbrin spoke plain-faced, as if Tyrnimar were sipping tea next to him. "What he meant, Your Grace, is that we have not seen orcs cooperating on this scale ever before. Master Tyrnimar believes that the hobgoblins are not an accessory, but rather that they may be part of the cause."

The prince considered this for a moment. "Alright, why do the orcs not cooperate?"

Holbrin glanced at Tyrnimar, cuing him to proceed. The Blue-Eyed Man noticed a female elf against the tent wall quietly chuckling at Tyrnimar. "Cooperation could be had by them at any time, Your Grace, except that more contentment is had by them in competition with each other," he began.

"He meant that they could cooperate but normally are content and more inclined to contend with one another, Your Grace," said Holbrin.

"Yes, I see," said the prince. "Then what is the purpose of these hobgoblins that we just fought?"

"Reinforcement, Your Grace," they both said.

"Oh? You agree, Master Holbrin," said the Blue-Eyed Man.

"We cannot ignore the possibility just pointed out, Your Grace," said Holbrin. "If the hobgoblins are here to reinforce these orcs, they would be sent by other hobgoblins. This would explain why so many orcs are cooperating, because it is being orchestrated by a more organized entity." Holbrin began to pace about as he spoke, clasping his hands behind his back and looking up at the tent ceiling. "Hobgoblins also are quite competitive with one another, as well as with their neighboring races of orcs, goblin-pure tribes, lizard people of various types, even Dwarven settlements, and the like." He stopped at the end of the table with maps sprawled out for later use. "However, they have the best ability for organization in their culture and would be able to mobilize and coordinate on a much broader scale. We cannot ignore the possibility."

"That would mean this is really the opening battle in a war," said the Blue-Eyed Man.

The two elves looked at each other. "It would, Your Grace," said Tyrnimar.

"The battle for Serna?" asked Dareum.

"The battle for Yvel," said the prince grimly.

***

That evening.

As soon as the second company of Dorvin's battalion arrived at the area of the camp designated by the army's pioneers, Tyrnimar tethered his horse to a tree. He had been leading the horse all day to be at the same pace as the infantry company that Holbrin had told him to support, and left all of his traveling gear with it. Rifling quickly through the various bags and compartments, until he pulled out his small stone bowl and stone grinder, copper lined gourds, iron kettle, a small steel hook, and two tin cups. Clanking about, he scoured the rest of the camp site as the rest of the army was settling in for the evening.

He searched frantically until he found what he was looking for–flowers of white, yellow, and purple, and gathered each of them with care. He then filled the kettle at a stream after filtering the water through cloth, and made for the nearest fire. Cookfires sprouted all over the camp and it was an easy task for him to find one with space for a kettle of water.

He meticulously ground the flower petals in his stone bowl while the water heated. By the time the kettle came to a boil, the flower petals were ground to a coarse paste. He dumped them into the gourd bottle, pouring the hot water in after and corking it. Gingerly handling the iron kettle with the steel hook, he went searching throughout the camp. The sun was setting before he found who he was looking for.

"Eevarel," he said.

Eevarel turned from advising a pair of soldiers from one of Gunst's companies on their sword stances.

"It's alright, My Lady. I think that's about all we can take at a time."

"Keep practicing," she told them sternly. Tyrnimar felt a sharp pang of an emotion he was not familiar with. "Yes, Tyrnimar of the Blue," she said, approaching him.

"Your tea was not drank yesterday," he said.

Eevarel looked at him without expression for a few breaths. Confusing colors cascaded over each other in her aura.

"That is to say, your tea was made and it was not drank by you," he continued after a moment.

"Well, surely, I had duties here to this company, just as you had yours, Tyrnimar," she said.

"Yes, but," he hesitated, "my teacraft and location is always sought by you."

"Your teacraft?" she asked.

"Yes, you came so much for the tea, more had to be made. Enough tea for two people," he said.

"Yes, you provided enough tea for both of us while I sat with you," she said.

What is that color? Tyrnimar was puzzled and frustrated. "No, it is meant," he searched for the words, slightly flustered, "the tea was made for you."

"Oh, how nice of you," she said sweetly.

"No! What is meant is…" He was getting more flustered before he relented and heaved a great sigh. "Your company is sought and there is a provision of tea, newly made."

"Ah, so you come to me with tea," she said bemusedly. "You should continue this. For the time, I support the first company in Lord Gunst's battalion. You will be here tomorrow with my tea."

An outwitting. Again and again, Tyrnimar thought gloomily. *The fate must be this, lest if awaits something worse, loathe I am for it. Fate is not supposed to exist. Though, not that the fate in and of itself is minded, but rather that such pleasure at a slow feast is like what it feels.* "There was a wish to thank you after yesterday."

"Yesterday? What happened?" she asked.

"The raid. The camp was entered by some of the riders of the enemy. One was fought by me," he said. *If be this the fate for me, how will circumstances be reconciled? Different lives are lived by she and I with many obstacles.*

"Ah, yes, I heard about that. Quite the show, I heard, facing down a mounted rider all by yourself," she said gently.

Tyrnimar felt very warm. A tingling feeling began on his scalp and spread down his neck, arms, and back. He fidgeted. "Uh, yes, indeed," he said, back to being flustered.

"You should have been wearing your leathers and mail, though. It would be a shame for you to get eviscerated," she said.

"Indeed. A shame," Tyrnimar nodded. "Wait. How is it known by you my leathers and mail were not worn?"

"Did you really come just to bring me my evening tea after

I missed it yesterday?" she dodged.

That color. Tyrnimar grumbled in frustration. "The giving of thanks to you is the reason."

"Thanks? For what?" she said lightly.

Tyrnimar hesitated. "For all those hours at practice with the blade and the bow."

"What about them?" she asked.

"If not for all of those hours under your tutelage, death would have been met yesterday. The next life would be journeyed by me," he said.

"So, you are thanking me for your life?" she asked with the same light tone.

"Uh, yes?" he said uncertainly.

"Good. You are welcome."

And another.

Chapter 16

Encampment of the Yvel Regiment in the higher foothills of the Kaskev
Mountains, east of the town of Serna, Yvel Principality.
By the Elven Calendar, forty-sixth day of Spring, 18030.
By the Goblin Calendar, middle of the Fifth Moon Cycle, 3114.
By the Human Calendar, Sortingday, second week of Anz, 794.
A cool and clear spring evening, dusk.

Eevarel threw the tin cup at Tyrnimar while he scrambled to
stuff the gourd bottle and the other cup in his bag with one hand
while messily dumping out the kettle, stone bowl and grinder. They
parted in a rush, without words. Eevarel quickly made her way to
the company in which Holbrin had placed her. They were hastily
forming up as tenleaders called soldiers to their arms. Tyrnimar
stumbled and staggered before regaining his footing, still jamming
the traveling tea set into his pack and cinching the strap. His
sword-in-scabbard jangled at his belt while he ran back to the
company with which he was partnered. The howls of orcs echoed in
the woods and darkness.

Tyrnimar was once again grateful to Eevarel for helping
him harness his newfound agility, gained through daily sword
practice, as his feet carried him quickly around tree roots, soldiers'
bedrolls, cook pots, horses, weapon piles, and soldiers scurrying
about for their weapons. His tea set clanged in his bag and knocked
against his hip every other stride, but he paid it no mind. He could
see the orcs on the other side of the lines of ranks being formed by
the soldiers, but he knew the human soldiers could not see them yet,
their eyes not being nearly as keen in the dark as Elven ones.

Finding the company Holbrin had told him to help, he
darted over to his horse and equipment. He dumped his bag and
snatched his bow and quiver before the bag hit the ground, not
stopping for a pause, slinging his quiver and finishing his sprint
with a leap onto a fallen tree trunk. His breath wheezed in his throat
and he could not form words while he snatched an arrow from his
quiver, and nocked and loosed it. The orcs were howling and jeering

in their language. He could see them beyond the torchlight. The arrow flew true and pierced the skins wrapped around the waist of one of the orcs as they bounded forward towards the humans. *There must be hundreds!*

Cries and startled gasps escaped some of the human soldiers. These orcs seemed to be from the same tribe that Dareum's patrol had fought, presumably the same group that had attacked Serna nearly two months ago. Tyrnimar knew they had never seen orcs before. The hobgoblins were easier to deal with because they were all fully clad–humans did not see their blue skin until *after* the fighting.

The ring of steel and shout of voices grew louder and louder as the orcs crashed into the formed ranks of Dorvin's battalion of spearbearers. The orcs' axes and swords hacked and ground on the humans shields. Some squeezed or forced their bodies between the Yvelian spears and crashed into their shields with the last of their momentum, knocking the Yvelians to the ground. The spearbearers, relying on long days in the practice yard at muster, drove their heels into the ground, thrusting their short spears into the orcs. Some of the orcs trying to smash through the line found themselves pierced with bright speartips through the neck, stomach, arm, or ribs. Others knocked the spears aside or glided between them, bringing themselves and their opponents to the ground, punching, elbowing, and biting the shouting and screaming human defenders.

The air smelled of panic. The orc attackers and human defenders became further entangled, stabbing, slashing, punching, and crushing one another. Tyrnimar loosed arrow after arrow at the orcs behind the lead rank. The orcs did not advance in ranks–more like rushing green water–but once the orcs in front crashed against the lead rank of spearbearers, they effectively became the lead rank, leaving all of the orcs behind them to jostle and jump in efforts to meet an opponent.

The humans knocked to the ground struggled in grapple with their opponents. The orcs, who were generally taller, heavier and stronger than the humans, frequently gained the upper hand, gouging out eyes, biting throats, smashing with fists and elbows, and twisting necks and laughing at a gratifying popping sound. The grounded spearbearers struggled, some escaping and regaining their footing or drawing dirks, some scoring enough cuts and stabs in their opponents' torsos and faces to gain freedom. Others simply broke. On the ground, some screamed in fear while others scurried away in frantic search of safety, stripping off their armor, dropping spears and shields to run faster. Those spearbearers still on their feet fought desperately, barely keeping the orcs off of them, taking one or two down with strong spear thrusts.

Tyrnimar loosed another arrow. Only seven left. Another. Another. This was starting to become alarming to him. Another arrow. Each finding a target; one less orc to break through. One less drop of water in the sea. Another arrow. He hoped that Eevarel was faring better. Another arrow. Three left. He hoped Turaean and Holbrin were doing better. Another. Truly, he hoped everyone was faring better.

A great shout brought his attention from the orcs in the back to the front. A cluster of shouts. Shouts of glee and elation emerged from the orcs as they were breaking through the company's lines. The orcs broke through all five ranks towards the left flank while crushing men under their feet. The men's shouts and screams of despair rose to pair with the sound of glee from the orcs. Tyrnimar let the arrow loose into one of the forward orcs before dropping his bow. Running towards the breach, he drew his sword. *I will be had again for not wearing my leathers and mail by Eevarel,* he grumbled to himself, *if alive I still am.*

From the right, he saw Dorvin rushing up, helmeted and in plate and mail, hand axe and shield in hand. He was accompanied by two of his mail-clad men-at-arms. They dove into the fray at another penetration, closer to the center of the company. Tyrnimar approached the breach on the left flank as an orc rose from pummeling a spearbearer to death. Knocking its spear aside as it lumbered to a run, Tyrnimar eviscerated it as he passed, its intestines spilling out behind him.

Grateful again to Eevarel for countless hours of drill, he glided between two other orcs, slashing one in the leg. It fell, to be stabbed by a thrust from a spearbearer out of view. He helped another spearbearer rise. Tyrnimar raised his blade barely in time to block an axe strike that crushed him to the ground. He was kicked stoutly in the ribs by an orc he did not see, sending him rolling back a few paces and knocking the breath from him. He had no idea where his sword was, but was more concerned with staying conscious and finding breath as he strained to open his lungs.

The booted feet of the Yvelian spearbearers of Dorvin's battalion and the bare green feet of orcs shuffled and pounded the ground all around him, the dust held to the ground by the moisture of blood. Tyrnimar turned and looked around, finally drawing breath to see Dorvin in the clutches of a larger orc. One of his men-at-arms lay on the ground motionless, the other struggling and twisting under a barrage of axe strikes. Tyrnimar squirmed to his feet, finding a spear, which he gripped with both hands.

The orc had stripped off Dorvin's helmet. He struggled with both gauntleted hands to hold back the orc's grinning face. Tyrnimar made a timely thrust at an orc immediately in front of him, saving a spearbearer from being split by its axe. Tyrnimar dodged through the melee, taking a few orcs in the back or leg with his borrowed spear. He knew not to engage an orc directly with the spear–he was improvising, based on his sword drilling with Eevarel, knowing that he would lose a direct contest. He struggled towards the edge of the melee as the flank continued to collapse.

Dorvin's blood-curdling scream rang out as the orc grappling him fitted his huge hand inside Dorvin's mouth and began to rip his jaw away, spraying blood. Tyrnimar struggled on, fighting desperately. He could hear Dorvin's scream cut off as his wind-pipe tore open.

Survival took priority over escape, but that too ceased to matter, as Tyrnimar was knocked to the ground, losing his consciousness along the way.

***

Dariyet could hear the call from some of the leaders inside the camp. He waited with his remaining twenty-nine wolf cavalry outside the ring of torchlight while watching the human army react to the Borys-Karang attack on the far side of the camp. The Pev'Baki-Norn were not subtle, but he could be. The Pev'Baki-

Norn were not patient, but he was. But that was why he was here. The Garad'dai Borys-Karang was doing his part, which would soon bear mushrooms for Dariyet's patience. Dariyet did not know what the humans were saying, but he could recognize the tone. A tone of alarm; even desperation, at times.

There it is! He watched with anticipation as the humans on this side of the perimeter began thinning ranks to reinforce the mountainside of the perimeter. He waited aching moments, one grinding on after the other, as the ranks thinned enough to be vulnerable and the soldiers moving off were too far away to return in significant numbers. He raised his hand silently, feeling the stiffening of the twenty-nine riders behind him. A tense moment passed as he savored the moment–the instant–before the charge *when greatness is born!*–before dropping his hand and kicking his wolf into a run, then a sprint, his leather cape of faces flapping behind him.

The quiet rustling lope of the wolves behind him soon followed. They were barely into the torchlight before the humans with spears reacted with shouts of alarm and dismay. Forming a great spear of wolves and riders, they pierced the remaining ranks in one place, just enough for two wolves abreast, slashing and trampling the defenders. They lost two riders breaching the line, one run through, wolf and rider, with at least three spears each, the other skirmishing behind the line to tie the defenders down. The rest wreaked havoc amid the interior of the camp.

Dariyet's blood was up and he laughed in elation as he pounded through the human camp with his riders. Slashing bewildered defenders, camp lines, and flanks of tethered horses, they tore through the interior. Dariyet hurled a throwing spear into a brown-haired defender with pointed ears. *An elf!* He laughed as he recognized the pointed ears of unhealthy color. Still giddy with delight, he spotted a much larger tent. He recognized this to be a command tent, much like his own improvised command area. Shelter and space. Space to think, space to plan, space to receive multiple subordinates and issue detailed orders. With a thrill, he kicked on his wolfish mount.

Bounding forward, he cut the lines of the tent, dropping the canopy onto confused, flailing inhabitants. He trotted his wolf over and amusedly plunged his blade into each of them. One, two, three. He was starting to feel a little guilty for claiming a great victory if his opponents were going to make it easy. *Perhaps it is simply my own cunning and greatness that makes theirs seem so small?* he puzzled, as he was pulling his blade from the third inhabitant.

That rang hollow to him. He felt he was missing something. His attention was pulled around by a shout. He recognized the tone. Outrage. Indignation. A group of armored men. Mostly armored. The majority of them were missing a helmet or gauntlets or some piece of their armor, and a few were only wearing mail. The one at the center was the one shouting and pointing at him with his sword. Dariyet's mount leaped forward to the cluster of steel and humans, and he slashed at them from his mount. The wolf slammed into two of the men, putting them on the ground. Dariyet leaned over and inserted his blade into the back of one's head before it could roll over while his wolf gnawed on the other one's hand as it had reached for its axe.

There was that shout again. Dariyet turned in annoyance. It was an older human in mail and no helmet. *If you are worthy, then offer combat instead of bleat about!* Kicking his mount up to bound upon him, Dariyet dodged around a tall, strong-looking human, nearly taking a powerful sword blow from him, and approached the older human in two great strides from the wolf. Dariyet reached out with his long, curve-bladed sword and glided it between the head and shoulders of the human. The other men wailed at the death of the older human. Dariyet drove his mount away to gather his riders and wreak havoc elsewhere in the camp before exiting. He estimated he had just dealt a serious blow to the human army. *Perhaps even crippled their will to fight*, he thought in disgust. *These weaklings cannot bring me glory.*

***

Prince Gerald's head spun away from his body as the rest of him dropped to his knees and fell over.

"*NO! YOUR GRACE!*" cried the Prince-Heir Arnold.

Harl Oleandran was dumbstruck. Numbly, he regarded

his friend, Sir Virek, lying motionlessly, slowly oozing blood and grey material out of the hole in the back of his head. He watched Arnold tremble as he crawled to his father's body and clutched the body and head closely, as his shoulders shook. He was dimly aware of a sudden bright light on the east end of the camp where the companies were collapsing into rout in the face of hundreds of orcs.

"Oh, Your Grace. Why didn't you–" Arnold sobbed, "why didn't you keep your guard up…"

Harl looked on as Arnold wept. *The Prince is dead.*

"No–why didn't you. I didn't want you to go."

Long live the Prince.

Figure 6: The Witches of Serna

Chapter 17

Encampment of the Yvel Regiment in the higher foothills of the Kaskev
Mountains, east of the town of Serna, Yvel Principality.
By the Elven Calendar, forty-sixth day of Spring, 18030.
By the Goblin Calendar, middle of the Fifth Moon Cycle, 3114.
By the Human Calendar, Sortingday, second week of Anz, 794.
At the same time, on the east end of the camp.

Chaos swirled around Ayza. The orcs had come down from the higher ground in the hills and attacked in greater numbers than they ever had. The Prince's Army was folding. The militia company was folding. Soldiers and militia lay about, dead and dying, as the orcs were breaking through the lines into the camp interior.

That was when Kora lost control, three tens of soldiers to her right. Like the other times, screaming in hysterical fear, fire leapt from her hands, burning everything as she flailed her arms hysterically. Orc, soldier, militiaman, horse, tree, tent–everything within ten paces caught fire if she pointed her hands at it. She incinerated the orcs in front of her, but also the militia in her ten to her left and right. As they caught fire, she screamed in terror.

Now or never… no point in hiding this if I die anyways, thought Ayza, as she threw down her spear and raised her hands high over her head, palms forward. She could feel their air better this way, and the better she could feel the air, the better she could control it. She seized the air with her will, enough that she could talk to it. She whispered to the air and the air echoed her words back. The wind blew, then gusted, and blew. It gusted again. Each time that it gusted, the steady wind was stronger. Stronger and stronger, coming up from the low lands and blowing into the attackers' faces. Stronger and stronger until the roar of the wind was deafening, blowing dirt and dust around her.

It felt good. She had never stretched this much. She suddenly felt ashamed for thinking about feeling good amid the carnage where her friends and relatives were suffering and hundreds of others that had come to offer aid were dying. Dying why? *Because of THEM!* She seized an eddy of wind, whirling in the wake of a large stone, and grabbed an orc with it. She lifted the filthy thing high and threw it down into the sea of green in the night, sending half a dozen bodies flying.

"Because of YOU!" she screamed as she picked up another and hurled it at the ground, crushing its bones. It was her own voice screaming with her sister's now. Her wind took the flames of her sister and carried them, spreading them further out. The attack had ceased for the wind, and the orcs to their front and human defenders alike were helpless but to not be blown away. "BECAUSE OF *YOU!*" She picked up another one and wrapped its limbs with different eddies, gripping them, pulling them. The orc shrieked in terror at first, its screams giving way to pain as the limbs separated from the body. Tearing the first arm, then one of its legs, then the other, the screaming stopped with the head, then the last arm. Finally, she hurled the torso into the crowd of attackers.

***

Taram guided the orc's speartip, trapped between the bottom of his blade and the small crossguard into a tree trunk, before piercing the orc's shoulder with the end of his curved Orcish blade. While the orc was frantically pawing at the blade in vain, Taram brought down his knotted club on the orc's head and shoulders. The orc howled and whimpered as it sank lower and lower with each stroke from Taram's club. He pulled his blade free and gave it one last blow to hear the anticipated crack of bone in the orc's head.

Looking around, Taram saw that he was more fortunate than most of the defenders, embroiled in a frantic melee, outnumbered, wrestled to the ground, or bleeding to death. *Not looking good at all. Really didn't want it to end like this*, he thought soberly. Locking blades with another combatant, he traded two blows, thankful for the thickness of the club that it could deflect an axe strike at an angle. He and the other orc separated. Taram was able to look at it clearly. It was a young orc with only one iron earring.

Barely an adult. How many times over have I lived its whole life? Taram thought as they circled each other. But then the orc paused. Taram thought it was a sudden change of direction, but the orc did not move. He realized that it was not even looking at him, but past him. Maybe Taram was about to be killed from behind as he felt a chill on his back, but he seized the opportunity and lunged forward, ramming his blade through into its chest as a bright light suddenly blazed far off to his right.

Wrenching his blade free with a wet snap, he still felt that cold on his back as he looked around. The fighting had stopped. Human and orc alike were frozen, looking behind Taram in the same direction. The paralyzing chill overtook him as he was frozen by the appearance of Lord Koval standing perfectly still. His helmetless head was framed by the steel plates over his shoulders and arms over the coat of mail, the light casting severe shadows over the contour of his face. He held his sword in one hand, hanging easily at his side, the blade crossing in front of him with the point dipping low. And he was covered in blood. Spattered over his face, slowly dripping off of his blade, and caked at the crossguard. Blood was splashed across his mail and plates. He stood there transfixing everything for a moment that stretched for days.

Taram was vaguely aware of the sound of rushing winds and saw trees and branches sway in other parts of the camp but numbly noted that there was no wind in this part of the camp. The light of flames burned brighter, but Taram could not tear his gaze from Koval as the cold of winter gripped his insides.

Koval took a step forward. It was such a small, slow movement, yet it seemed so abrupt. The step lasted for ages, yet before Taram realized it, Koval had crossed a distance of thirty paces and carefully inserted his blade into the eye socket of the first orc he reached as it watched in paralyzed horror.

Something shifted in Koval. Something about him. He did not move, but Taram felt that he was able to move again. And breath. He gasped as he took air again. He had not realized that he was holding his breath. Barely able to look around, he noticed that the other defenders were also able to move again, for the most part, but the orcs were able to move again, as well. The orcs began to run, cascading from far to near. The humans were able to strike a few down, but for the most part, the orcs fled howling into the night from whence they came.

***

Judane felt her skin tingling as she desperately fought. Over the past two months of hard training and riding, she had gotten much stronger, but it was still a long way to go to match the strength of most any orc. She swung and dodged and swung again, meeting her foe, an orc a full three heads taller than her, briefly with locked blades. She tried to shift her weight to slip to its side, but it pushed her back and swung hard with his own sword, striking her across the stomach and knocking her to the ground.

The orc's sword must have twisted and hit her with the flat because she was able to get back up without even losing her breath. The orc looked surprised as she slashed it across its abdomen. It fell to its knees, trying to hold in its entrails, as she cleaved its head in two. Her skin was still tingling, but she was knocked to the ground again from behind, losing her sword stuck in the first orc's head. She rolled over and squirmed aside just as an axe crashed into the ground where she had been.

Curling her feet in, she launched herself along the ground, out of its reach. She clamored and skidded, casting about with her hands until she claimed a weapon from a fallen knight of the Crown Guard. The weapon was a long-hafted axe with a spike at the end and a hammerhead reverse from the axe. The butt of the shaft ended in another spike. She rolled to her feet into a guard position. She had neither trained with the spear nor this weapon, but improvised a stance and attack from her sword training.

The orc rushed towards her and circled around to her left. One of his allies, also armed with a forward-curving sword, joined him and circled to her right. Judane planted her stance so that neither her back nor her front faced either of them. She could not prevent them from flanking her, but she could keep them from getting behind her by pivoting with their circling.

They both attacked at once. Judane leapt towards the one on her left, jamming the butt point into its abdomen, planting her left foot on it, and ripping the point back out. The other orc reached her with its blade and her skin tingled under her leather, mail, and gambeson.

There was that surprised look again as she whirled the weapon around and struck its forehead with the hammer end, cracking its skull open. Dark, wet chunks squirted out of the orc's head as it fell. She must really thank Bierien for her help with the newly appointed armorers. Looking around at the chaos that still swirled around her, much of the militia was fleeing, dying, or dead, with meager remains struggling on.

"LET'S GO, SERNANS! FIGHT!" her brother shouted. She felt a sudden blood rush through her whole body. Not like the life-or-death surge of pumping blood, but the rush of new and sudden rage. "LET'S GO, YVEL! KILL THEM ALL!" Dareum continued, crashing into the melee. He gripped his longsword in both hands, laying foes low with broad swings that severed hands, arms, and heads.

If Judane had been able to control her sudden anger, she would have seen the fleeing militia and soldiers return and fight. She would have seen some of the wounded stand, snarling and gripping weapons, dealing blows to their enemy until they bled dry. All Judane could focus on was moving her weapon and the ringing in her skin. She barely noticed the Prince-Heirs Arnold and Oswald join the fray in their mail and plate, Arnold with his sword and Oswald with a battle axe and a blue-painted helmet, as she was more occupied hacking and beating the life out of two orcs that were now on the ground, whimpering and howling.

***

Tyrnimar's eyes fluttered open. Something was catching on his hair repeatedly. His eyes focused in the darkness and he saw Eevarel. She was reaching into his hair. She must have been stroking it. She saw he was awake, but she continued. He was glad to see her. He was glad to see anything, really. She had spatters of blood streaking her face and the boiled leather plates and straps that were the outer layer of her armor. They stayed that way, him lying on the ground with her crouched over him. He gradually became aware of the sounds around him. They were not in an Orcish camp about to be eaten. *Good. Unpleasantness would be abound if that. This… this is passable.*

"What is being done by you?" he asked.

"Nothing you have to worry about," she replied.

"Is there anger at me in you?"

"For what?"

"My mail and leathers not being worn by myself."

"A small amount," she said. "I have a new requirement, though."

"That is?"

"A helmet."

"Oh," he said. They stayed that way for a while longer before he spoke again. "Sorrow is had by me."

"For what?" She asked.

"No more tea is had by me," he said.

She smiled. "We just had some."

"Oh, right."

***

"There you are," said Holbrin irritably. It was rare for Holbrin to let his irritation show openly, but then, being half-way to summer's journey away from the homeland helping humans fight orcs allied with hobgoblins was a rare circumstance. He briskly walked towards Eevarel and Tyrnimar.

"I am glad that the two of you are alive, but there are slightly pressing matters to attend to if you do not mind." The two of them scurried to their feet sheepishly. Had Holbrin not been so pressed by the circumstance, he would have chuckled at the two of them being so flagrantly caught and red-faced about it. "Tyrnimar, go to the west flank. Trinien, Sieraean, and Parendien are badly wounded. I authorize you to use whatever means you have–but be discreet! No observers."

"Cannot they be tended by the human healer? Mkaela? The only healing means had by me require a pact with a dryad to be made," Tyrnimar asked.

"She is literally wading in wounded and it would be hours before she could make it to them–hours that they do not have… let me know what you tell the dryad."

"Yes, Holbrin." Tyrnimar started to move off, then stopped and moved in a different direction towards the unit he had been supporting, where his tools and books would be. Eevarel began to move after him but Holbrin stopped her. *Young fool that he is. Why does she toy with him so? She knows this will not endure. Pah, what a fool am I, giving him such direction!*

"Is anyone else hurt?" Eevarel said suddenly.

Holbrin fixed her with a somber look before speaking. "Turaean is in the next eternity." Eevarel's lips parted in surprise, but she said nothing. "Please go find Jovaela for me."

Eevarel left and returned a time later with Jovaela. "Thank you. Please go help Tyrnimar now." Holbrin had moved on to check on Irduin, Arynn–accompanied by her ever-present human friend, whose name escaped Holbrin at the moment–and his younger elves, Lierialuth, Lazura, and Erensed, whom he kept together, and finally Turaean's remains.

"You sent for me?"

"I did." They stood looking at Turaean's empty vessel. "I want you to prepare to return."

"For what purpose?"

"To return Turaean's vessel to his family for rites and to make an interim report to the Guardian Council."

"Are you certain you want me making that report?" Jovaela asked.

"I am," he said. "The council purposefully placed us together because of our past disagreements in hopes that we would temper each other."

"I know," she said.

"For that reason, they know that you will not be embellishing for my betterment."

"I see," she said.

"If they allow you to return to us, I would like that," Holbrin said. "We are going to need as much help as we can get. *I* am going to need as much help as I can get. Especially yours."

"Indeed," she said ruefully.

"If they allow you to return, would you be so kind as to return with proper armor and some replacement weapons?"

"I will see what I can do."

"Please do and depart as quickly as you can," Holbrin said.

"Even now?" she said in mild surprise, "in the midst of all this?"

"Yes, even now. We cannot be certain that we will survive the next engagement and the Council must be apprised."

***

"Hurry up and put her over there!" Mkaela cajoled Merik. "Didn't you have to study a long time and do chores at some temple or something?"

The wind whispered through the trees, rustling the leaves. The sound was strangely calm compared to what had ended just moments ago. Merik strained to pull another bleeding soldier along. The soldier was bleeding from her left leg, which ended in a stump above the knee. Her leg had rope tightly coiled around her thigh to stop the bleeding. "Yes, Your Grace," Merik said over the sobs of the soldier crying out in pain.

"And cut it with that! For the fifth time. I was tired of it the first time you said it," she barked at him.

"Uh," Merik put the soldier down, "I only wish to show the proper respect–"

"Well, shut it," she barked grumpily. "Do you have the rest of the leg?"

"What!?" Merik asked in shock.

"The leg! You ever seen a girl's leg?" Mkaela snapped at him.

"Uh," he hesitated.

"Go find it," she said impatiently. Taking an internal breath, she placed her hand on the leg above the stump as the soldier winced and quivered in pain. *Can I attach it if Merik brings*

207

it back? She asked the shadowy presence within her.

YES, it answered, WHEN HE RETURNS WITH THE OTHER PIECE, I SHALL GUIDE YOU IN SEEING THE WOUND.

Thank you.

YOU SHOULD CONSIDER EXTENDING THE SAME COURTESY TO THE ONE CALLED MERIK.

Mkaela hesitated. *Why?*

WHY SHOULD YOU NOT? AT THIS POINT, YOU ARE SPENDING MORE TIME AND EFFORT TO BE CRUEL TO HIM.

Well, I'm tired.

IS HE NOT?

He's not doing all of this.

NEITHER ARE YOU.

What do you mean?

YOU HAVE THE ABILITY TO HEAL THESE WOUNDS, BUT YOU ARE USING MY EFFORT.

Mkaela hesitated again. *So I can't do this without you?*

YOU CAN, BUT NOT NEARLY AS STRONGLY UNTIL YOU HAVE MORE PRACTICE TO GROW STRONGER AND MORE SKILLED.

So why are you helping? Why did you even talk to me in the first place!? She was becoming irritated.

MIND YOURSELF, it chided sternly. I HAVE ALREADY SPOKEN OF THIS TO YOU. THERE ARE WAYS THAT YOU CAN HELP. I HAVE OPENED YOUR ABILITY WITHOUT DANGER TO YOU AND AM GIVING YOU STRENGTH. SOON, I MUST DEPART AND HELP OTHERS.

So, what, you just go around giving other people your strength?

WHEN THERE IS NEED.

Oh, please, you make yourself out like Saint Kostray.

THAT IS HOW I AM KNOWN.

Mkaela hesitated for a third time. *You are Saint Kostray?*

I AM.

Oh, come on. You expect me to believe–

I DO, it interrupted. YOU HAVE PUT ASIDE YOUR DISBELIEF TO ACCEPT THAT A CREATURE OF SMOKE AND SHADOW WHICH SPEAKS TO YOU IN YOUR MIND AND DRAWS YOU INTO WAKING DREAMS GIVES YOU POWERS THAT YOU ONLY READ ABOUT STORYBOOKS–IF YOU HAD BOTHERED TO LEARN TO READ. It seemed irritated as it went on in its strangely monotonous but booming presence inside Mkaela's head. THE PROBLEM WITH PEOPLE–HUMANS, THAT IS–OF THE PAST FEW CENTURIES IS THAT YOU DO NOT ACCEPT THE PEOPLE, ARTIFACTS, AND EVENTS OF YOUR RELIGION WHEN THEY OCCUR IN FRONT OF YOU. AND YOU WONDER WHY MAGIC IS ONLY IN CHILDREN'S STORIES. I TELL YOU TRULY, THE OTHER PEOPLES KEPT THEIR RELIGION AND SCIENCES FIRMLY AND LOOK AT THEM NOW.

Mkaela was taken aback at the sudden rant and mentally blurted out. *So the other races have magic?*

SOME.

Wait. Some races have magic or the other races have some magic?

"Your Grace, I've found it," Merik returned. Mkaela actually looked at him for the first time in hours. He was caked in mud and blood from hauling the wounded and sorting through the dead. She also noticed a gash across his left hand that he had wrapped in torn cloth. He carried the severed leg, still shod in a bloody boot, the bone visible in the leg as Merik turned it.

"Bring it here," she said.

GOOD, began the shadow. NOW OPEN YOUR SENSES TO THE LINK BETWEEN THE LEG AND THE STUMP.

How?

AS YOU DID THE OTHER TIMES, SENSING THE LINK BETWEEN THE BODY AND THE BLOOD.

Mkaela concentrated for a moment. *Are you sure? I don't*

see anything.

PATIENCE. CONCENTRATE ON THE LIVING ENERGIES THAT HAVE NOT LEFT THE LEG AND THE MATCHES IN THE STUMP.

Mkaela looked again, hard, and began to see the energies calling to each other, wishing to be reunited. She drew upon the shadow's–Saint Kostray's–*that will take some getting used to*–power and connected the energies again.

GOOD. SHE WILL NEED REST.

So, how will this be different when you leave?

SOME TECHNIQUES WILL BE IMPOSSIBLE UNTIL YOU GAIN GREATER STRENGTH. YOU WILL HAVE TO LEARN HOW TO DO THINGS YOURSELF WITH YOUR OWN ENERGIES.

Like what techniques?

THE BLOOD BINDING TECHNIQUE THAT YOU BEGAN WITH IS A VERY POWERFUL, BUT TAXING TECHNIQUE. YOU WILL HAVE TO FIND OTHER WAYS OF DOING IT AND THOSE HEALED WILL NOT BE BETTER AS QUICKLY.

Mkaela hesitated. *I understand.*

The soldier's sobs subsided into relieved breathing. She briefly looked Mkaela in surprise as she came to her senses before exhaustion stole consciousness from her.

So, why me? Is this some kind of fate thing?

FATE?

... yes, fate. Is this all fated?

TRULY, DO YOU THINK THAT THE FUTURE IS ALREADY WRITTEN? WHAT WOULD BE THE POINT OF THE TIME RIGHT NOW IF THE FUTURE IS ALREADY WRITTEN? IT MAY AS WELL HAVE ALREADY HAPPENED, IN WHICH CASE, THAT WOULD MAKE IT ALL THE PAST.

Uh...

NEVERMIND.

Mkaela sighed and looked up at the soldier at Merik. He

waited patiently for instructions. She supposed it would not hurt to be nicer to him. *He's only doing what he knows to be right.* "Merik, could you please help me look for more casualties?"

"Certainly, Your Gr–" he broke off seeing Mkaela's look and corrected himself. "Uh, My Lady."

Mkaela supposed that she could live with 'my lady' for the time being. It was definitely better than 'your grace.'

"The fighting spread outside of the perimeter in some places. We should look there," she said.

"As you wish, My Lady," said Merik.

"Thank you." Mkaela felt a bit sheepish with the change, but agreed with her guest—Kostray himself, apparently—that it was a poor thing to take a bad day out on someone who would not fight back. Merik glanced at her in mild surprise but said nothing as he fell in beside her and walked towards the eastern perimeter. The smell of blood, sweat, ash, and upturned dirt was pervasive; the scents mingled with one another, blurring the boundaries between them. She heard the heaving and grunting of the soldiers, and saw the militia gathering and mending equipment, praying to the ground, thanking Orneth for continued life, or mourning the dead. There were still plenty of wounded, but mostly those that did not need serious help.

Mkaela and Merik passed through the perimeter, which was guarded by a fraction of the number it was before. Beyond the border, it was difficult to see in the torchlight, fading behind them even twenty or thirty paces away. "Let's spread out a bit, so we can search a bigger area," Mkaela said to Merik.

"My Lady…" he began, but saw her face. "Very well, but I will be nearby." He paused. "Please at least make sure that we can see each other."

"That'll be fine, Merik." Merik paced off and started searching the bodies on the ground in the dark. Mkaela meandered about the field, unaware that she was some fifty paces or so away from Sir Merik.

So, what about what the Prince-Heir said?

HE IS THE PRINCE NOW.

What!?

PRINCE GERALD HAS DIED. ARNOLD IS NOW THE PRINCE. HIS BROTHER OSWALD AND SISTER VELTHURIA ARE THE NEXT HEIRS.

Mkaela was stunned for a moment before gathering herself. *Well, what about what he said? About the signs and the best and the worst, salvation, damnation, all that?*

WHAT OF IT?

Is it true?

THE MEANING IS TRUE.

What do you mean? It's a sign. It tells the future of what is to come, right?

I TOLD YOU ALREADY. THERE IS NO WAY TO TELL THE FUTURE. IT IS NOT A PROPHECY, IF THAT IS WHAT YOU MEAN. THERE IS NO SUCH TRUE THING. REMEMBER? IT IS MERELY A WARNING. FOR THOSE WHO REMEMBER THEIR POWER. POWER THEY ALWAYS HAD, OR POWER THAT THEY CAN LEARN: EITHER WAY, THOSE WHO REMEMBER IT CAN BE THE BEST AND WORST. YOU REMEMBERED, THOUGH YOU HAD HELP.

What power can be learned? You said before that the other races never forgot…

Kostray, or Kostray's ghost, whatever it was, seemed to ignore Mkaela's question and remained silent for a few moments. Mkaela continued to search for wounded among the dead in the darkness. AN IMPORTANT DECISION IS AT HAND FOR YOU, it said abruptly.

What do you mean? Mkaela silently asked, but then her attention was drawn to a shifting form at her feet. The darkness made it difficult to see any color at all, its face wreathed in shadow and its breathing labored. Its legs were burnt away to the knee and it had a deep gash starting from the left side of its chest spanning to its right shoulder. It was an orc, by the skins draped about it and its massive form. The creature looked weakly at Mkaela.

It suddenly registered her form and made a faint squeal of terror and feebly tried to crawl away. Mkaela stood there in the darkness watching the orc struggle in vain. This creature represented the kind that had killed so many that she knew and had brought such misery, nearly burning down her town. She considered how she could walk over and end it much like a bug or some other vermin. And yet, seeing it struggle so weakly with its legs burnt away, she could not help but feel pity for it as it glanced at her over its shoulder in terror.

Should I kill it?

THAT IS FOR YOU TO DECIDE.

But it can't do anything to me. The ghost was silent. *Should I leave it?*

THAT IS FOR YOU TO DECIDE.

It'll die if I just leave it. The ghost was silent again. *What in the Pit?* She approached it. The orc turned over on its back, holding up its hands to shield itself, wheezing in terror. The noise would not have been detectable more than a few paces away with the night wind rustling through the leaves. She bent down brushing aside its weak defense. It struggled, feebly flailing, weak from the loss of blood. Losing patience for a moment, she knocked the hands aside and slapped it across the face.

"Shut up, you!" she hissed. "Let me help you before I change my mind." The orc stared at her, wide-eyed in fear as she laid her hand over the gash in its chest and closed it, covering the glow with her cloak. She repeated the process for the stumps, feeling the ghost of Kostray's power flow through her and seeing the flesh weave anew from the ash. It was not the same as before–even in the dark, she could tell its legs were still the color of ash. It gaped at her in shock.

"Now go!" she hissed again. "Get! Before I change my mind!" It gawked at her for another endless moment. She gestured with her hand in a shooing motion. Another moment went by before it started to move. It moved away, crawling at first to a tree trunk. Hobbling to its feet, its eyes never leaving Mkaela, it took an uncertain step away from her. She did nothing. Said nothing. It took another step, and another, before it started to run. Losing some of its clumsiness, it ran silently into the night, away from the camp, glancing over its shoulder fearfully.

And there. I just helped the enemy.

MAYBE SO, BUT DO YOU KNOW IF YOU WILL ALWAYS BE ENEMIES?

Could it be any other way?

PERHAPS, PERHAPS NOT. THE IMPORTANT DECISION HAS PASSED.

It did? To help it?

NOT DIRECTLY.

Then what?

YOUR ROLES WERE REVERSED, THE POWERFUL AND THE WEAK. YOU CHOSE NOT TO DO WHAT HAS BEEN DONE TO YOU. YOU CHOSE TO BE DIFFERENT THAN THOSE WHO WRONGED YOU.

So, we're not supposed to kill them after all that!?

I NEVER SAID THAT YOU SHOULD NOT FIGHT. ORNETH KNOWS HOW MUCH I FOUGHT. THE IMPORTANT THING IS THAT YOU ARE NOT A BUTCHER. A MURDERER.

Oh. Mkaela paused awkwardly. *So, now what?*

WHAT NOW? NOW I DEPART.

What!?

I TOLD YOU, ALREADY. WHY DO YOU NEED SO MUCH REPEATING? THERE ARE OTHERS THAT I MUST HELP AWAKEN. HELP TO REMEMBER. YOU HAVE SHOWN ME THAT YOU WILL PROBABLY NOT BE THE WORST.

Probably?

THERE IS NOTHING CERTAIN. THE TEMPTATION TO DO A WRONG IS AN UNDYING THING, ONE WHICH HAUNTS US ALL. IT MUST BE CAREFULLY GUARDED AGAINST. SOMETIMES WRONG THINGS ARE DONE UNDER THE BEST INTENTIONS, BUT IT DOES NOT CHANGE THAT IT IS A WRONG, THAT IT HAS WRONGED OTHERS.

When will you leave? Mkaela suddenly and strangely felt alone in a way that she felt for the first time, yet seemed familiar. She looked at the last place she had seen the black-legged orc

214

before Merik called to break her brooding.

"My Lady! I found one. Come quickly, please!"

Mkaela hustled off towards Merik.

***

Ayza came to and sat up, heaving a deep breath of relief. The bodies surrounding her registered immediately. Charred bodies all around–mostly orcs, but some humans–largely towards the front of the perimeter. She overheard Kora sobbing uncontrollably. Some thirty paces off, a group of soldiers looked on with a mixture of fear, guard, and suspicion towards Kora. Her sister was alone, curled in a ball, surrounded by ash and charred flesh, some of her own clothes burned. Ayza crawled over to her.

When Kora saw Ayza, she needily welcomed Ayza's embrace and continued to cry. "It's all my fault," she sobbed.

"Shh," comforted Ayza. "No one ever has to know."

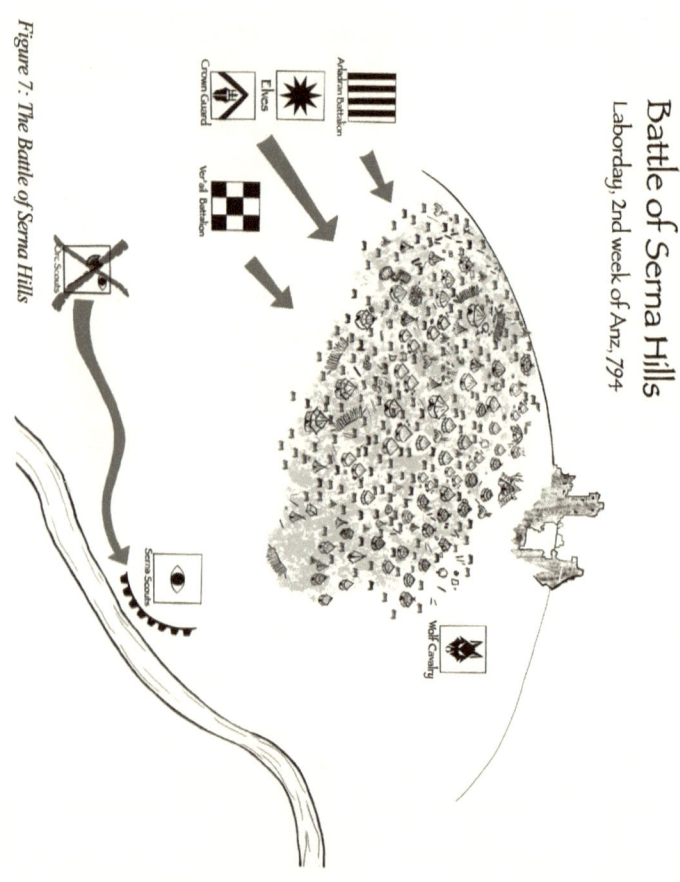

Battle of Serna Hills
Laborday, 2nd week of Anz, 794

Arbalean Battalion

Elkes

Crown Guard

Verd Battalion

Orc Scouts

Serna Scouts

Wolf Cavalry

Figure 7: The Battle of Serna Hills

Chapter 18

Encampment of the Yvel Regiment in the higher foothills of the Kaskev
Mountains, east of the town of Serna, Yvel Principality.
By the Elven Calendar, forty-seventh day of Spring, 18030.
By the Goblin Calendar, middle of the Fifth Moon Cycle, 3114.
By the Human Calendar, Laborday (seventh day of the week), second week
of Anz, 794.
The next morning; sunlight beaming through the misty mid-spring haze.

Soldiers moved about stowing pots, cinching saddle bags,
bundling tents, and breaking down the remains of their camp. The
air smelled of a mixture of blood, ash, dust, and overturned mud.
Arynn watched, having packed all of her items. Holbrin had told her
to stay with the company of humans she had assisted. She watched
as Gunst Ver'ail, a lord of theirs and their battalion leader, moved
about and inspected progress. Gunst walked with a measured step
that matched the careworn face and receding hair of a man in his
forties who was used to worrying about crop yields, coffer balances,
and a whole different brand of conflict, one far from the battles of
life and death. Their new prince, Prince Arnold, approached. His
brother, Prince-Heir Oswald trailed behind. They were having a
whispered conversation which they cut short as they drew up to
Gunst.

"We are almost ready to move, Your Grace," said Gunst
morosely, offering no greeting.

"Good," the prince said hollowly. He stood in his plating
about his legs, arms, and chest. One of his squires carried his
helmet. Arynn noted that in previous days, be it the humidity of the
morning or the heat of the exertion of wearing it all, the young heir
to the Crown would walk about camp with his leg plating, but none
on his upper body. Just his arming jacket, had there been a need to
don the rest.

"I estimate it should take us six weeks to return to
Serna, moving through this terrain and carrying wounded and this
equipment with less soldiers, and another two weeks to return to

Yvel."

"What?" the prince asked, seeming to wake up suddenly.

"Your Grace, I was saying to you that it would be five weeks–" Gunst Ver'ail began.

"You go in the wrong direction, sir," the prince stated flatly.

Gunst hesitated a moment, "Your Grace, you can't mean–"

"But I do." The prince's armored figure towered over Gunst.

"Your Grace! We can't possibly attack after such a defeat!"

"Gunst." The prince stepped closer and lowered his voice, but Arynn's keen ears could still clearly mark the conversation. "They have killed our Prince. Your Prince demands redress."

"Your Grace, with all of the casualties, we can't–"

"Your casualties are rather low," broke in Holbrin's voice as he approached from the side with Irduin.

"I beg your pardon, master elf," Gunst Ver'ail addressed Holbrin offhandedly, "but I am in consult with my liege."

"Yes, and I must intrude," Holbrin said plainly, as if confirming the color of grass. "Your Grace," Holbrin addressed Prince Arnold. The prince looked at Holbrin impassively. "I would like to extend the renewed offer of assistance from my contingent and myself in this time–"

"Accepted," the prince said bluntly but quietly.

"Ahm, yes, I would like to offer some advice from my compatriot." Holbrin made a deferential motion to Irduin.

"And you are?" the prince broke in.

"Irduin Ursani, Your Grace," she answered, "You have–"

"Your qualifications," the prince stated. It was less a question and more of a demand for continued conversation.

"Your Grace, I have studied martial arts, tactics, battles, campaigns, and wars for the past four centuries," Irduin said, unflustered.

"So, you read some books," Gunst Ver'ail broke in, "but some of us actually do this and need decisions now, not prattling

218

from well-read girls."

Irduin wore a small, polite smile, matching Holbrin's. "Begging your pardon, Lord Gunst, I do mean that over the course of my study, both practical and academic, my career spans this past four hundred years. I have written twenty-seven books on the topics, of which twenty-three are from personal experience on campaigns or study of practice."

"Irduin fought in the First and Third Beres Wars, opposed Berin the Great's campaigns, against the Vostindin in various border incursions through the centuries, and a few others," Holbrin provided.

Gunst hesitated and the prince turned slowly to him. "Your Prince holds these qualifications in good standing," he said, slowly turning back to Irduin and Holbrin. "Continue."

"Your greatest opportunity for a decisive victory over this group of orcs is now," Irduin stated. Gunst began to splutter, but Irduin continued over him as if he were a splash in the water. "To retreat now would allow them time to regroup, pursue, and harass us all of the way back to Serna." Breath left Gunst as her words sank in. "I have checked your casualties. There are some two hundred and eighty-three dead or unable to fight."

"See?" exclaimed Gunst Ver'ail. Arynn noted that he was beginning to seem desperate.

"That leaves you with just under four hundred ready to fight between shieldbearers, Serna Militia, and your Crown Guard. Over four hundred, if you include our contingent."

"Yes! Against nine hundred orcs!" pleaded Gunst Ver'ail.

"Against four hundred orcs." Irduin flatly regarded him, "The fighting over the night was indeed ferocious, Gunst Ver'ail, for them and for us. Where they had surprise and numerical superiority, we had superior armor, and more decisively, your magics to control fire and wind." Irduin paused for a breath, steepled her fingers, and continued. "In addition, Lady Judane held the line where it would have broken, Lords Koval and Dareum Covendran retook the initiative, and a healer treated your wounded and returned them to fighting ability. Without the healer, this situation would have been untenable and your casualties too great to retreat without leaving them."

The prince turned to a passing soldier. "You there, good sir." The soldier was startled at being addressed by the prince. "Get me both Lords and Lady Covendran and the company leaders from the Arladran Battalion." The soldier scurried off and returned a moment later with the other attendees. Garven arrived and leaned on the tree by Arynn, watching the exchange from the side. The two shared a quiet friendship that did not need many words.

"Glad to see you this morning," the prince spoke to the new arrivals, his tone hollow again. "What say you of our situation?"

The two looked at each other and Koval spoke. "We will do whatever must be done, Your Grace. We urge dealing with the enemy now, if we can. They did come down from the mountains in the first place. No reason why they wouldn't again."

"Prepare to attack, Gunst," the prince said quietly.

"As you wish, Your Grace," Gunst said helplessly.

"One more thing you should be aware of, Your Grace?" Holbrin said. The prince turned back to him with an impassive gaze. Holbrin continued, seeing the prince was waiting for him to speak. "I have sent one of my own back to report to our government," Holbrin said. The prince continued his wordless gaze. "So that my people may prepare in the event that this is larger than a few village raids," Holbrin finished.

The prince looked at Holbrin a moment longer. "Very well," he said, then turned. "Lord Koval."

"Yes, Your Grace?" Koval Covendran answered.

"I am giving you command of Dorvin Arladran's battalion for this battle. You will command it as your own and prepare to attack."

"As you wish, Your Grace," Koval and the company leaders eyed each other grimly.

"Lord Dareum."

"Your Grace," answered Dareum Covendran.

"You will take your father's place in Crown Guard."

"Yes, Your Grace."

"Lady Judane."

"Your Grace."

"You will take sole command of the Serna Militia company under the Arladran Battalion."

"Yes, Your Grace."

"Also, Lady Judane," continued Prince Arnold.

"Yes, Your Grace?" she answered.

"Separate out the witches and keep them back from the fighting."

"For what purpose, Your Grace?" Holbrin asked.

"I want to be able to use them separately," said the prince.

Holbrin and Irduin exchanged glances. "Respectfully, Your Grace, they do not seem to be able to control their powers very well and may not be reliable for any use."

The prince turned to Holbrin slowly. "So, what do you recommend? Put them back in the fighting ranks? You just stated that they were unreliable. Mind you that some of our dead were burnt by their witchfire. So, either I hold them out to use them, I hold them out to keep the ranks safe from witchcraft, or I put them in the fighting because we cannot spare a single spear from the fight."

"Your Grace," began Judane, "I plead you, let me keep them in the ranks. We all came to this fight for a reason."

The prince regarded Judane for an instant. "Very well."

***

Near the orc encampment, late afternoon.

"They're just up ahead, Your Grace," said Korane.

"Good, scoutmaster," said the prince. "What is their disposition?"

"Uh, disposition, Your Grace?" said Korane. "I beg your patience. I am not lettered, Your Grace."

"What are they doing?"

"They're all clustered together, licking their wounds. A few sentries in boiled leather armor with bows. Only a handful of wolves. I guess that they have riders for the wolves. There is a whole mess of them. Warriors, but also children. Lots of them. Also, Your Grace, there is easy ground to their south, leading down another stream."

"Very good, scoutmaster," said the prince. Korane was flanked by Arynn and Garven on one side and Sieraean and Eevarel on the other. Sieraean and Eevarel were filling the void left by Turaean's passing and the greater need for scouting the enemy. The stitches on Korane's leg continued to itch and the slashing ached as she reported to the new prince, a much younger man, some ten or fifteen years younger than she was.

Korane had refused Mkaela's offer to heal the slash, however she did that. Korane knew that Mkaela was a nice girl, but did not trust this newfound... whatever it was, that Mkaela was sprinkling on anyone with so much as a splinter. She did take the surgeon's cleaning and stitches, though, and limped about for the first few days, bearing the pain throughout.

"Form skirmishers. Eliminate those sentries and then move to the south and block their withdrawal on easier ground."

"Yes, Your Grace," said Korane and quickly moved out with the other scouts. She secured permission from Holbrin and Judane to use a few others for skirmishers, obtaining Lierialuth, Lazura, and Erensed from the elves and Alain Tun'ail, Marsen Fris'ail, and Lena Pardran from the militia, as well as a shieldbearer named Conwyn Extardran, who was the only surviving member of his ten. The three militia had all worked in a tailor shop owned by Marsen's family. They had lost the shop, their homes, and their families in the first raid and they all wore hard leather masks, boiled and molded over an orc's skull.

Korane's small band of skirmishers moved a few hundred paces ahead of the army. They came upon the sentries quickly–only four of them–and were able to eliminate them efficiently before they had a chance to raise any alarm. Korane noted that these orcs wore armor of boiled, hard leather, and carried small bows that seemed to curve back away from the archer. Their quivers were bristling with arrows, and they all had small hand weapons like a small sword or hand axe, along with skinning knives. She noticed Arynn and Sieraean pocket some of the Orcish arrows.

The group moved south, around the edge of the large field where the orcs lounged and moaned. The sloping field would have been sight with bursts of yellow and white wild flowers amidst foxtail grass, wild wheat, and clover, except for the mass of stinking bloody, whining orcs littering the field in small clumps. At the high end of the hilly meadow were a few stone buildings and a small ruin of what seemed to be a toppled tower. One building was still somewhat intact, with a second floor.

Korane could see that there were a number of female orcs in the camp. Lots. More than there were men. Maybe twice as many as the men or more. Some were wounded, some showed burn marks, some seemed fine. *This'll be really bad if they fight, too,* Korane fretted.

At the first sign of the Prince's Army and the militia appearing, the disorganized camp of orcs was roused. A handful–the wounded orcs–attempted to run, though it more resembled hobbling, to the south, where the terrain was easier. Korane's skirmishers were able to stop them with bow shots and a few spear thrusts close to the edge of the meadow without attracting any attention, picking off the trailing orcs first, eliminating each of them, until killing the first one. The rest of the orcs were too busy watching the Prince's Army unfold from the trees and bushes. Companies formed and closed their ranks. Some orcs mounted an assault, rushing the ranks of humans, while others stood back, seemingly unsure of what to do.

Korane spotted one of the few wolf riders a hundred paces off, wearing a strange-colored cape. It was too light to be from the hides of cows, pigs, sheep, or any other kind of animal she had seen made into leather. She could not hear over the din of clashing arms, but the rider was clearly arguing with another orc. Both were pointing at each other and the fight spewing forth from the trees. Korane's eyes were drawn back to the grinding of metal on bodies, seeing the orc assault on the far battalion break. She thought that was the one that Koval was leading. The orcs broke in their assault and fled from the ranks of humans under a hail of thrown spears and stones. The soldiers advanced ahead of the other battalion, exposing a gap between the two.

The caped rider turned, stabbing his finger in the direction of three other wolf riders and then at the gap between the two halves of the human army, shouting something at them before returning to his argument. The three wolf riders resolutely clapped their shields with their assorted swords and axes before kicking their wolves to a run at the gap, only to be met with a sheet of arrows, Korane thought from Holbrin's elves. They fell in the field with their wolves and lay motionless.

Orcs attacking the other battalion threw spears from their rear ranks, which impacted on some invisible wall in the air. *Those witches*. Korane shook herself. She paused to bring down three more orcs fleeing to the south with her arrows. The caped rider seemed to have finished its argument with the orc and they both rode off toward different parts of the fight. His cape flourished and Korane clearly saw the skin of five faces–people's faces–stretched over the center of the back, their mouths stretched agape. Anger boiled within her, but Korane knew that she had a part to do right there on the southern edge of the field.

The wind in the field in front of the trailing battalion, the one with the militia, picked up into a sideways spiral. It blew strongly towards the orcs, forcing them to step back and shield their faces. Flame began to gout along the spiral of wind, searing the orcs in the front as the wind spiral arced to its left and right, spraying flaming air over all in its path. The arguing orc was knocked to the ground by the stampede of broken orcs fleeing, some in flames, from the advancing ranks of humans. It regained its footing only to be immersed in a gout of fire. It stumbled some paces, scraping and tearing at the skin on its face before collapsing.

Korane caught sight of the prince and his Crown Guard riding out between the gap. He directed the guard to pursue the fleeing orcs with a wave, and pointed at the lone remaining wolf rider with the tip of his sword. Korane downed another fleeing orc and saw the wolf rider clap its shield with its blade and point back to the prince. They spurred their mounts towards each other, but Korane had to stop watching. The Crown Guard charged uphill to the north and east after the fleeing orcs. She could see a blue helmet among them marking Prince-Heir Oswald. A significant number of orcs were fleeing toward Korane's skirmish line to the south, as well.

Korane and the skirmishers spent several minutes loosing arrow after arrow, this time eliminating the front orcs so as to give them the most pause and force them back towards more difficult ground. It mostly worked. A good number took a few arrows and expired. Some broke through, but were speared and hacked by Conwyn, Alain, Marsen, and Lena. The rest took the message and fled further to the north under a light rain of arrows, once Korane could spare the attention.

Korane looked back, questing for the prince and the wolf rider. She saw the prince's horse with no rider. *Where is he? Don't tell me we lost another one.* Then she saw him.

***

Judane rode up from the militia ranks to the prince as he bent over his fallen opponent. The orcs were fleeing. Some paused at the east end of the meadow on higher ground to look back at the carnage of broken green bodies littering the field. Judane guided her mount to see the prince's armored opponent lying on the ground. The rider had a full helm around its head with a long horizontal slit for sight and numerous holes over the mouth area for breathing and a collar of mail draping underneath it.

The prince pulled the helmet off to reveal the blue skin and sweaty mass of coarse black hair of a hobgoblin. Crimson blood streaked from its mouth down its chin and neck and over its cheeks. It looked at the prince, and said something weakly. It sounded almost like it was asking for something. The prince grimaced in disdain as he gripped the hobgoblin by the hair and kicked him over. Holding his foe down with an armored boot in its right shoulder, the prince pulled its head up by the hair and raised a hand axe high. Judane again thought she heard the hobgoblin faintly say something.

The prince began to chop and hack, cutting through the neck from the front, splattering blood on his hands and the ground.

"Your Grace?" Judane asked tentatively. He paused for the briefest instance, glancing back at her with a face of stone before returning to his task. After a few more hacks, the head pulled free of the neck and the prince raised the head to the soldiers and militia of the regiment.

"WE HAVE WON!" he shouted at them, his cry returned with a thunderous cheer. Judane saw the face of the hobgoblin. It was smiling, or it was when it died. The smile was fading as the muscles loosened in death.

**

The cavalry leader looked on in dismay from the nightside of the meadow, further up the meadow. *Not much of a cavalry leader anymore. No wolf to ride, no brothers and sisters to lead, no great one to serve. I cannot go back to Muydiyet with such complete dishonor… rather, I do not exist to them anymore*, she thought bleakly.

"Come now," said the orc she met earlier that day. "You could be down in that."

"At least I would have honor, then," she said morosely.

"Oh, pah, what's the honor good for? You'd be dead. If you want it so badly, then just go down there and get yourself killed. Better yet, save yourself the trouble and cut yourself right here! Why did I waste my time with you anyways then?" he said in annoyance.

They watched on as the warband of orcs disintegrated. Some ran for their slave women and children; others bolted. The encampment that had been the resting place of the orc tribe wandering home drained as terrified slaves and children bolted into the wilderness, trampled or killed by other orcs, or were ridden down by the human horse cavalry.

"There's no honor in a pointless death. There is honor in reaching a goal, whether one lives or dies. Going down there now meets no goal." She sat on the ground and looked dejectedly at the dirt.

"Well, good and fine then, but what will you do now?" he asked.

She stared at the dirt for a long time before looking up at him. "I do not know. Everything that I had is dead."

"Well fine, then," he said shortly.

She sighed. "Yes, fine. Really, thank you for finding me, helping me with the arrow shaft, and making the poultice for me. The wound was starting to itch in a bad way."

"It is fine," he said irritably.

They both looked out over the battlefield from concealment. She looked towards where Dariyet's body was, his wolf nearby speared through the neck by that ruthless armored man of theirs. *At least he was kind to Dariyet*, she thought. She was surprised that he knew their customs of an honorable death of a defeated foe. She had seen the Great Oygariyet grant such a death to Arkiban the past winter.

"I know a place for people like you, people with no place to go," he offered.

After a moment of consideration. "Seems like as good of a place as any," she said.

"It is three days' walk from here," he said. "Maybe five with your injury."

"Yes, take me there," she said distractedly.

"You will need to be warm at night, too, so you do not take sick. The winds are strong here," he said.

"Not as strong as where my tribe is from." She looked over at him and shrugged. "But I will need to be warm tonight."

***

"Yes, I *do* want to look in here myself," insisted the prince.

"As you wish, Your Grace," said Sir Harl.

The prince picked his steps into the ruined compound and found his way into the enclosure, the only part of the ruin that offered shelter from the elements.

"There we are," said the prince, as some of his Crown Guard, Koval and Judane, some of the elves, and Mkaela and Merik filed in behind him. Dareum was out with the rest of the Crown Guard to mop up the remaining orcs. The prince and the others approached what they would consider a command table with an annotated map spread out on it. "Can anyone read this?"

Holbrin allowed Tyrnimar to push past. "It can be read, uh, Your Grace."

The two of them looked at each other for a long moment. "So could you please read it and tell me what it says?"

"Oh, yes, by its way, Your Grace." Tyrnimar scurried over and began poring over the map. The prince looked on, as did Holbrin and many of the others. Most were surprised at the complexity. Holbrin was only guessing, but it seemed to have notes for supply lines, boundaries of responsibility with other bands of orcs or whatever creatures in other tribes, and goals for seizure and occupation. It also seemed to note several mustering areas or major supply points in the mountains.

"The time between when this map was last noted and now is not known by me, but Ardara will soon be seized by other tribes of orcs, to me it seems."

"Indeed," said the prince. "Please take the map for further study and write me a full report. Have it ready within the week."

"Y-yes, Your Grace," said Tyrnimar, already becoming distracted in study.

The prince leaned towards Holbrin. "Make sure it's clearly worded."

"Yes, Your Grace," said Holbrin.

The prince strolled around the makeshift office, something catching his eye as Tyrnimar pored over the map and others watched. "What's this?" the prince asked. All turned to see him studying a worn carving in the stone of an archway. The archway seemed to mark a hall that would have led into the side of the hill but for being caved in. It was covered in dirt and grown over with grass, clover, and flowers. "It's old. I think it's written in Old Paetic." He turned. "Can anyone read this?"

No one answered. "Not even you, master elf?" he asked

Tyrnimar.

"Ah, no, Your Grace, it cannot be read by me," Tyrnimar answered.

"Hm." The prince seemed disappointed. "Very well."

A stir from an adjacent room drew everyone's attention. Sir Harl moved in, blade drawn and hauled out two orcs by their long, green hair. They were orc women.

"His concubines, Your Grace," Sir Harl announced.

"Ah, kill them," the prince said offhandedly.

"Yes, Your Grace," he answered.

"Wait." All heads turned to Mkaela and Sir Merik. Sir Merik's eyes were large with surprise and fixed sideways at Mkaela.

The prince turned towards her slowly. "I appreciate your boldness, Lady Mkaela, but I am not in the humor to be merciful, nor am I in the humor to be questioned at this time," he said coldly.

"But Your Grace, can we not put them in with the rest of the prisoners? They're harmless," she pleaded.

"You know this for a fact? And even if so, what of all the people–your own townsfolks, harmless folk–that their masters slaughtered? What of them? Why should there be any quarter?" Something seemed to occur to the prince. "Where *will* the other prisoners quarter?"

"Perhaps they can be questioned to provide some information, Your Grace? They were concubines to their leader," Holbrin said. "The orcs seem to be less resolute than the hobgoblins and may be more willing to cooperate."

"And then when the questioning is through? Then what? That usefulness expires," the prince pressed. "In fact, we only need one of them to answer questions." He drew his blade.

"This is not Orneth's way!" Mkaela pleaded. "We can put them to work, Your Grace. They can continue to be useful," she said, "and two can lift more than one."

The prince regarded her for a long, tense moment. "Very well, Lady Mkaela. You make a compelling argument. These two will both be in your particular care once we return to Serna. In the meantime, they will be in my custody for questioning." He turned slightly to address Holbrin. "Do you have anyone that can speak Orcish?"

"Yes, Your Grace." Holbrin sharply held a hand to Tyrnimar who was excitedly rising. "You are the only one who can read Goblin," he told Tyrnimar, before looking back to the prince. "Yes, Your Grace. Irduin, Trinien, and Parendien are all passable speakers in several dialects of Orcish. I will send them by this evening."

"*Several* dialects? Ah, no matter. Thank you, Master Holbrin," said the prince.

Tyrnimar packed up the map as Holbrin hustled him along. The two walked away from the ruin speaking in Elvish.

"What is your read on the map?"

"Good to find. Supply routes, near plans, several strongholds, one called the Stone of Rykooth, one called Kogylar. Closer to here is Kogylar. Many different clans and tribes. Orcs, kobolds, goblins, a few others. Cities, too."

"It says all that?" asked Holbrin.

"Not with exactness. The symbols and characters are recognized by me for that meaning," Tyrnimar said.

"Indeed." The two walked along for a few more paces. "What did that carving say?"

"Oh, that? It said 'strength from knowledge, freedom from strength,'" said Tyrnimar. "Is the falseness of my words known to the Prince?"

"I do not know," Holbrin replied, glancing at Tyrnimar. "You are not a very good liar, my young friend."

They walked on for a few more paces before Tyrnimar spoke again. "Interesting properties are had by the sixth sorcerer."

Holbrin walked in silence with a small bemused smile, piercing Tyrnimar with a sidelong glare. Silence, then a gentle, "what?"

"The sixth sorc…" Tyrnimar began. "Oh. You were not told by me."

"No," Holbrin said quietly, "but I would very much like to know, when you get around to it."

"Oh, yes, um," Tyrnimar fumbled, then described seeing the echo of another aura awakening.

***

The sun had set and the Blue-Eyed Man ambled forth from the encampment at the meadow. The battle had been brief, but the soldiers were exhausted and deserved a rest. Garbed in his night cape, he walked by the moonlight, pulling the hood close against the wind in the hills, and glided noiselessly through the whistling grasses into the ruin. Producing paper and charcoal, he laid the paper over the letters carved in stone and rubbed the charcoal over them to take an impression. He blew the extra flecks of charcoal off of the paper before rolling it up and fitting it into a tube, which he tucked into the folds of his cape and quietly slipped back into camp before being missed by anyone.

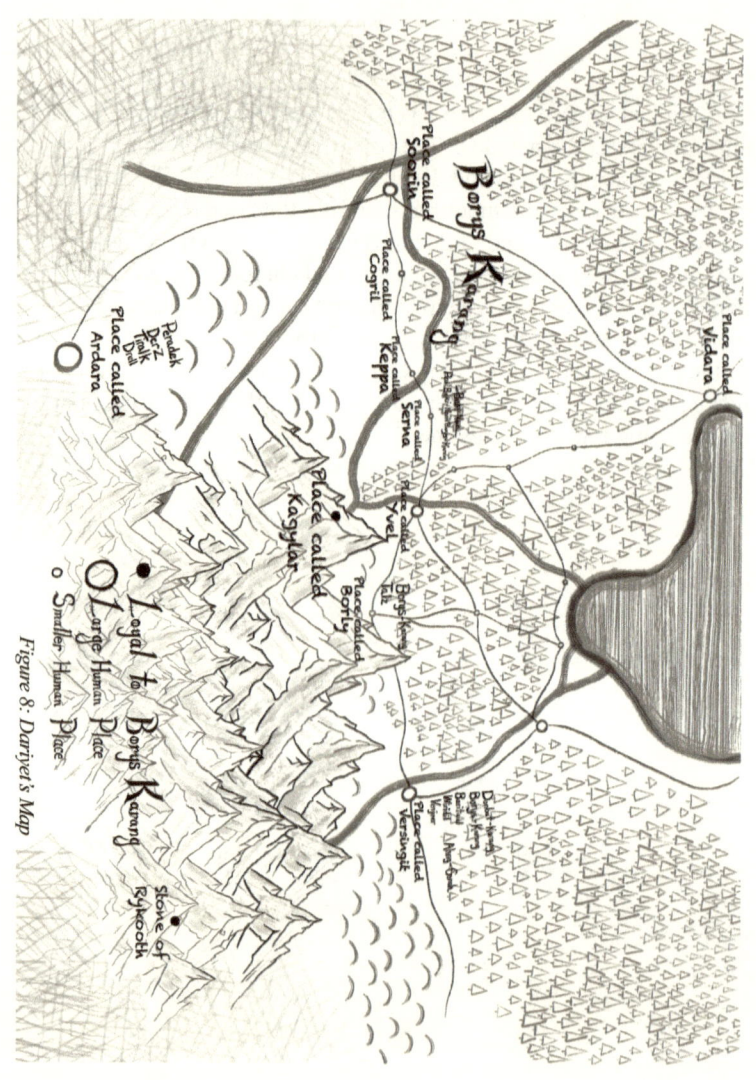

Figure 8: Dariye's Map

Borys Karyng

Place called Solorin

Place called Vidara

Place called Cogrili

Place called Keppa

Place called Serna

Pendak
Dar-Z
Teuk
Deul

Place called Ardara

Place called Kagylar

Place called Yvel

Borys Karyng

Place called Borly

Place called Versliegik

Dark worlds
Borys-Karyng
Borys-Karyng
Borys-Karyng
Naryn
Vurg
All-my-kinds

Stone of Rykootk

● Loyal to Borys Karyng
○ Large Human Place
○ Smaller Human Place

232

Chapter 19

Encampment of the Yvel Regiment in the higher foothills of the Kaskev
Mountains, east of the town of Serna, Yvel Principality.
By the Elven Calendar, sixty-eighth day of Spring, 18030.
By the Goblin Calendar, early in the Sixth Moon Cycle, 3114.
By the Human Calendar, Fryday, first week of Aiz, 794.
Two weeks later, a late spring morning with misty sunlight beaming
through the haze.

Prince Arnold tore aside the flap as he strode into the command
tent. "We've been on the march for nearly two weeks. Is that map
report ready, Holbrin?" Prince-Heir Oswald trailed his brother and
peeled off to the edge of the tent.

Irduin watched Holbrin produce the report written on
hastily bound papers. "Here, Your Grace." She readily recognized
Tyrnimar's hand. He could not stand even a few papers to
escape binding–the seven pages were pressed between a pair of
straightened sticks and bound through with string to form a book
spine of sorts. Her eyes could make out the arcs of Holbrin's
flowing script and knew that the first two or three pages would be
Holbrin's reworded version of Tyrnimar's report, the rest being
Tyrnimar's original version. She watched the prince's eyes rake it
hungrily.

He was a quick one. It was easy to assume he was all brute
and direct, but there was something else about him. Some kind
of edge. Irduin had noticed a few of the young prince's entourage
who were with him nearly all of the time: one of his clerks, Stanis
Tw'ail, who had a sharp eye for details, Aleksan Odr'ail, a knight in
the Prince's Crown Guard, and Erion Feradran, one of his squires.
Sir Garn Dandran of the Crown Guard was also commonly nearby,
as were Dame Sora Avr'ail and her husband, Sir Jaro Arvr'ail,
also of the Crown Guard. There was also a new hanger-on, Jof
Toliodran, a minor noble from Keppa who would have been tall,
slender, blond, and dashing, but for the situation. During the march,
he rode, walked, and stood with the hunched shoulders of shame.

He had been one of the company leaders in the Arladran Battalion, but his company had taken bad deaths during the recent combats, and was folded into another company. The prince had taken him into the Crown Guard to provide him new purpose.

"What's this confusion about this all-consuming flame and thrilling blood?" the prince asked.

"Those are the names of the orc tribes, Your Grace," Holbrin said.

"How many do you think there are?" the prince asked.

"How many tribes?" Holbrin said.

"Well–" Irduin began.

"No, sorry, nevermind. Foolish question," said the prince. "That's the same as asking how many villages of humans there are." He continued scanning the report. "So, this matches up with some of what the prisoners said. Dariyet was sent here to supervise the Baki-Norn, after the leader of the Baki-Norn was removed."

"Your Grace, that is not said by the report," Tyrnimar piped from the other end of the tent.

"Nor did the prisoners say that, Your Grace," said Holbrin.

"Right, but why else would the name of a unit be changed and new leadership installed. What did you say that word was? 'Garad'dai?'" said the prince.

"It's an Orcish word, Your Grace," Irduin said, "it means 'leads in the name of.'"

"Right, why would this all-consuming flame change the name of another tribe and send one of their 'Garad'dai' *and* a hobgoblin to run it?" the prince reasoned. "It seems very much like a struggle for power to me, one that these blood-happy types lost. How did you say those names again, Lady, uh, Irduin?"

"The 'thrill of blood' is 'Baki-Norn' and the 'all-consuming flame' is Borys-Karang," said Irduin.

Irduin noted Korane whispering something to Dareum before he spoke. "Your Grace? The scoutmaster here was telling me that the sentries that she eliminated were the only ones that she saw carrying shields, and they all had a burning person painted on them."

"The all-consuming flame, eh?" the prince said. "So." He paused pensively. "Tell me why the different tribes are equipped."

Tyrnimar began to speak. "Wait," the prince interrupted, holding up his hand. "This will be a long discussion, I imagine. First thing first." He motioned to a guard. "Please have the kitchen send in enough coffee for everyone. Do we have any hard bread left?"

"Right to it, Your Grace!" answered the guard who hopped off to answer the request. The prince studied the map with the report in the moments before the guard returned with coffee and those abominable biscuits of wheat and water cooked over a fire months ago. Irduin tolerated the biscuits graciously and knew that many of the soldiers lived on them, but also knew that every soldier ate them only out of necessity. There was no time for hunting for an army on the move. They were the only ration that would not spoil or mold quickly but she knew that, like herself, the soldiers thoroughly detested them with each and every bite.

"Ah, now, a secret, my friends." The prince walked to a small chest in the corner of the tent and returned with a brown clay jar wrapped in cord to keep it from breaking during the bumps of travel. "To make the hard bread more bearable." He poured a trickle of thick, deep gold fluid onto the biscuit. "There, best I can do." *Honey!* Irduin's calm demeanor neatly concealed the sudden yearning for sweetness. They all had been subsisting on the unleavened trail bread and small portions of meat hastily roasted or boiled. The sight of honey seemed like a glimpse into another world awaiting.

As the coffee and hard biscuits were passed around, the prince resumed, while the others quietly savored the unexpected sweetness. "So, I began at the wrong end; I tend to go into details, but it's the wrong way this time." He beckoned Harl, the remaining original battalion leader, Gunst, Lord Koval, and Holbrin to the map that Stanis and Erion had spread out over the prince's table. Irduin noted the others assembled were Dareum, Judane, and most of the elves, except for Lierialuth, Lazura, and Erensed. Merik and Mkaela also attended. *Lady Mkaela now, apparently*.

Irduin was uncomfortable with the readiness with which the prince had accepted this new magic, but could see that from the prince's perspective, it was useful and necessary. *We certainly may all be dead if not for the five sorcerers Serna fielded.* "So, from a broader look, we think that the orcs are being commanded by hobgoblins, right?" the prince posited. Holbrin nodded with Tyrnimar mirroring him in the background. "And the hobgoblins are not only able to command many different bands of orcs, but to form units of their own kind, and probably other similar cast-out races, right?"

"Form other units, yes, we have seen that, Your Grace, with the wolf riders, but we have not seen anything about other races," said Holbrin.

"Is it not implied?" asked the prince.

Irduin recognized Holbrin's placid smile concealing aching curiosity. "How do you mean, Your Grace?"

"This word here by Ardara," the prince replied, pointing towards the marker on the map. "There are four groups you note here: 'the fist made of very hard stone,' 'the smell of foot treads in the night,' 'the stone breakers,' and the 'Drell.'" The prince cross-referenced the names with the report. But the symbols here on the map do not match between 'first of very hard stone' and 'stone breakers.'"

Holbrin glanced at the map, turned back to look at Tyrnimar before speaking to the prince. "It could be a different word, like the difference between 'stone' and 'rock.'"

"Is it?" asked the prince.

Holbrin beckoned to Tyrnimar with deferential hand. Tyrnimar spoke. "From different languages, Your Grace. From Goblin, 'stone breakers' is translated. From Orcish, 'fist of very hard stone' is translated."

"Do we believe these to be hobgoblins or goblins?" asked the prince.

"They could be either, Your Grace," said Holbrin, "but it seems that the hobgoblins are very sparing in where they commit their own soldiers, so it very well may be that the stone breakers, 'Peradek' in their own saying, are goblins."

"My thoughts exactly, but that still leaves the 'Drell.' Why is that one not translated?"

"Your Grace has a good eye," said Holbrin. "Master Tyrnimar tells me that it is not a Goblin word. Probably a Goblin approximation of another word. The person making notes on the map clearly knew Orcish and Goblin, but did not know this other language for the 'Drell.'

"Or no written form is had by the Drell language," piped in Tyrnimar.

"Very good," said the prince. "So with all of this, the map notes the goals that the all-consuming flame was meant to–can we just call it 'the flame?'–had: Serna, of course, and Borly, Yvel, Keppa and the quarries, the Ardara mines, Ardara itself, the list goes on." The prince looked up. "That's just for the flame and the tribes that they're running. What about the other orcs? What about the hobgoblins themselves? Are they holding themselves back in case the orcs fail or do they reach beyond the orcs for even more territory?"

"This is not clear, Your Grace, but you do have a very good eye. Have you been to the university in Clovis?"

"What? No. I'm no university boy. They're much too proper," the prince dismissed. "I've always had a fascination with the greats of old and read many of the accounts. In fact, the Prince could spend hours listening to the Lady Irduin's memories of fighting Berin the Great."

"Indeed," said Holbrin. "Your Grace," he added.

"Right, so this affects not only Yvel and Ardara," the prince continued, "but probably the other cities, princes, and princesses of Gersh–maybe even beyond that."

"Quite possibly," Holbrin said.

"Before we get into the explanation from Master Tyrnimar about equipment, several matters of logistics and administration come to mind. For one, just to defend Yvel, it would require an enormous levy–one that I am skeptical our industry, trade, and treasury could support for enough time to survive this war and win." The prince began to pace, scheming eyes darting this way and that. "We will have to request aid from our neighbors, which goes without saying they are loath to lend, and some of whom will be having their own problems and won't be able to spare any." He scowled.

"Even if the levy can be met, this is going to require a spread of leadership that is beyond the capacity of myself and General Gundr'ail, especially with my father gone." He paused for the briefest instant at that. Irduin silently applauded the prince for quietly mourning while being everything that his soldiers needed him to be. "What I am speaking of is an expansion of the army, which admittedly is more of a peacetime garrison for city and road security, a few parades, and other errands. I'll need to go beyond a contingent primarily of spearbearers, but one that includes archers, cavalry, other forms of infantry–light, medium, and heavy–my own scouts instead of borrowing them here and there, leaders to manage it, and staff to administer it. Just in this endeavor, I am sorely missing an adjutant."

"Your Grace, this is a page from–" began Gunst.

"From Berin the Great, yes. That was his strength: administering his army and organizing a staff to do so," finished the prince.

"Moreover," he said, turning to Holbrin, "I don't at all mean to be ungrateful, Master Holbrin, but I find that I am overly dependent on your aid. I will need my own ability to speak and translate Orcish, and Goblin, and any of those other vile noises. Can you supply a bit more in the form of training some of my own in these matters?"

Holbrin's mouth formed into a placid smile of endurance. "Of course, Your Grace. We gladly continue to extend our hand in friendship."

"Most excellent." The prince smiled, clasping hands with Holbrin before turning to Koval. "Lord Koval."

"Yes, Your Grace?" he answered.

"I would like you to continue commanding that battalion. I may form it into a regiment with you at its van."

"Your Grace?" Koval stammered.

"The van! You know, the vanguard, the lead," the prince hissed in irritation. "As I was saying–more leaders, bigger army, all that. But I would like you to separate out your witches and have them trained separately," the prince said.

"I understood, Your Grace. I... As you wish, Your Grace," Koval said.

"Are you certain that is wise, Your Grace?" Holbrin said.

Prince Arnold turned slowly back towards Holbrin. "I believe it is necessary."

"Yes, I can see why you would see it that way, Your Grace, but these powers are very unpredictable. Very little is known about how well they can control their powers and use them safely," Holbrin said.

"That may be, but I cannot afford to not take this chance," the prince answered firmly. "We both know that we would likely all be dead if not for the witches of Serna. We also know that I am going to have a very hard time meeting a levy that will barely avoid defeat and that quite a number of soldiers would not have lived or been able to fight the next day if not for the ministrations of Lady Mkaela."

"I understand, Your Grace, but I urge caution," Holbrin said.

"I note your concern, Master Holbrin, but I truly cannot afford to not do this."

"Lord Koval, since your fine town has produced three witches that have saved us thus far–"

Six. They have not identified the Fearmonger, the Warmonger, or the Unbreakable as sorcerers, yet. And yet, surely two were just as important in saving them, Irduin observed.

"If you could look around your village for anyone else with unusual abilities, that would be incredibly helpful."

"Well, Your Grace," said Koval, "I don't know how much this is noteworthy, but we do have someone that never seems to get old."

Oh? Thought Irduin as most of the other elves discretely paid more attention. Irduin suddenly noticed Prince-Heir Oswald eyeing her. She realized that he had been watching the elves this whole time, gauging their reactions.

"Never gets old?" the prince asked.

"Yes, Your Grace, he's one of our tenmen here with us.

I've known him for more than twenty years and he looks the same," said Koval, "though he isn't from Serna. He came to town some twenty or twenty-five years prior."

"However it is, pull him aside and figure out what his situation is. If he's a power that can be used, then put him with the other witches." He paused for a moment, remembering. "Lord Koval and some others have told me of your Elder Dum'ail who took issue with the use of these powers and bandied about 'heresy.' The sort to scare you into throwing away an important tool of survival," he said, turning to the rest of the attendees. "This is a problem that we will have to deal with eventually, but I will need all of your help in doing so." He eyed Merik, who shifted uncomfortably. Sir Merik, Irduin knew, would be put into the position of choosing between what he and his organization claimed they believed in, and his actual organization, the Holy Order of Kostray of the Ornethian Knights–let alone any livelihood tied to his order and status. An unenviable position.

The prince continued. "Now, let's all enjoy Master Tyrnimar's explanation of differences in Orcish equipment."

***

The impromptu war council adjourned from the command tent. As the attendants wearily trudged out, the Blue-Eyed Man spied an opportunity. "A moment, Lord Gunst. May I detain you?"

"Of course, y–" began Gunst, his eyebrows rising to accentuate his wrinkles up his forehead and onto his scalp.

"No, none of that title stuff. Just 'sir' will do when it's just you and me," said the Blue-Eyed Man.

"Uh, yes, uh, sir," Gunst said uneasily.

"The Prince would like you to become his chief adjutant." The Blue-Eyed Man moved right to the point as he sat down and tried to casually gnaw on the hard trail bread. *By Andren, I could use a donut and some real coffee! I'll have to have some of that good stuff at Serna on the way through.*

Gunst was a bit stunned. "But, y–, I mean, what about the

battalion?"

The Blue-Eyed Man waved his hand, trying to calm down the nervous man. "The Prince understands, Gunst, please. He tries to be a sensible man and sees that you are a man with a head for numbers, figures, and administration. The Prince needs someone to help manage all of that. After all, did we not just discuss the enormity of the problem posed just by the levy?"

"We did, uh, sir," said Gunst, "but what about the battalion? What about the obligations of House Ver'ail? I would be seen as shirking duty as head of the House."

"Not at all," the Blue-Eyed Man dismissed as he sipped the muddy mixture that was provided as his requested coffee. "Not if the appointment comes from the Prince, and cites your unique talents and assets."

"Assets, y–I mean, sir?" Gunst said, "and what about the battalion?"

"That being the third time you have asked. So, fine, what *about* the battalion," the Blue-Eyed Man emphasized.

"If I ride not at its head, what will become of it? Surely it will not be disbanded in this time of need."

"Oh come, now, Gunst," the Blue-Eyed Man said, "of course not." *I have to be careful here, balance between being open to build trust, but provide enough bait that he chooses what I require.* "The Ver'ail Battalion and the Arladran Battalion will be recommissioned as the new regiment the Prince mentioned and the Covendrans lead that regiment."

"The Covendrans!?" Gunst began, indignant. "Those country...! If not for their blunders, we wouldn't–"

"Please, Gunst, please, no matter what any of us think of them, none of us could have foreseen any of this. Truly." Gunst shrugged reluctantly. "The Prince will ensure that both House Ver'ail and House Arladran are compensated for the cost of raising the battalions and that it is counted towards any levy requirements."

The Blue-Eyed Man's offer seemed to ease some of Gunst's concerns. "I can imagine those requirements will be quite high."

"Yes, indeed they will. And oh, by the course of things, you'll be the one managing those requirements. Not only in men and women as soldiers and the various crafters necessary for the running of an army, but horses, wagons..."

"Clothing," said Gunst. *Ah, there's that head for administration.*

"Ah, yes, House Ver'ail's sprawling flax plantations and sheep herds would be put to quite the test of output. Can you not see the benefits and certain... opportunities... to being on the Prince's personal staff?" The Blue-Eyed Man rose and clapped Gunst on the shoulder in friendship. "There are reasons that you are being asked. Talents and assets. The Prince needs someone that can see the larger field of battle, and there are gains to seeing the larger field."

"I think we can come to an agreement, then, sir," said Gunst with an uneasy smile.

"Good!" said the Blue-Eyed Man. "The Prince will look forward to your accomplishments." *We'll see how he does with these. I may be able to trust him with parts of the plan, but his head for numbers is still reliable, even if he plays a minor part.* "As we said, the levy is a huge task and we must ask our neighbors for help."

"The other princes and princesses? But, sir! They would never–" Gunst began.

"Of course, they won't. We all know this." The Blue-Eyed Man dismissively waved his hand to calm Gunst. "But we must at least go through with the formality of asking. Please begin by drafting four letters that will bear the Prince's seal. We'll send them off from Serna."

"As you wish, sir," Gunst said, fidgeting anxiously. "So, what about the battalion *right now*?"

And attention to detail, what more could Berin the Great have wanted? "Good man, lead the battalion back to Yvel. They value you at their head and you have earned your place in the returning parade, for sure. Once we return to Yvel, the Prince will appoint them barracks space, and change the commission of the battalion. They will all get renewed contracts, which, by the course of things, will be one of your tasks to manage–bear in mind that you will have an expansive administrative staff of your own." The Blue-Eyed Man watched as Gunst's brow furrowed in thought as the weight of future responsibilities settled on his shoulders.

"Yes, sir," said Gunst.

***

Elsewhere on the Liberator Side of the Mountains.

"Stay here!?" the former cavalry leader demanded. "I would have a better chance at… at *anything*, staying in the wilderness or even going to Kogylar."

The orc turned slowly to face her. "Why not? Leave. Go to Kogylar, if you wish. No choice on this kills me."

"Kills you?" she said, confused.

"No, I mean," he sighed, frustrated, "it is a saying in my first language." They were speaking in Goblin, but he meant in Orcish. "It rhymes in my language, too."

"I do not care! I am not staying here," she said angrily. *Not in this disgraceful place with no honor!*

"Fine." He gestured to their surroundings. They stood at the mouth of a cave on the side of a mountain with narrow paths giving access, within which dwelled a few dozen of the cast-out races. Some transient, just coming from battle, some not. The former cavalry leader—*I do not even know what to call myself anymore*—loathed this place.

She had heard of places like this. Places where cowards, outcasts, and scavengers go. The place reeked of urine and rotten meat. The one hobgoblin there had no legs and would not speak to her. He fletched arrows for the goblins and cooked some meat or forage that they would bring to him. There was one orc that seemed to think he ran the place. He walked around with his chest pushed out, smiling, kicking goblins and pushing the other orcs, many of whom were still wounded. He took what he wanted.

"If this is not to your liking, Great One, then do not stay." Then he took a step towards her, showing a bit of anger. "Oh, wait, that is true that you are not a great one and you missed a battle that your side lost! I do not care. I found you, you had a need, we made a bargain. That is all. Your leg is mostly better. I am not here to... to," he struggled to find a word, "to *fix* obstacles that you have."

"I am not saying that you are, but *this*!?" she said.

"Yes, good, then leave it. It does not kill me," he said. She glowered at him. "You are not coming with me," he said flatly.

New outrage blossomed on her face. "Of course not! *With you*," she said exasperated, before flippantly dismissing the statement. She knew that she was frustrated at feeling powerless. She did not want anyone to change things for her; she would owe a debt–and she *hated* owing debts. She stared off into the late sunlight. Soon it would be a new day with the sun retreating. She mulled her options. *I could...*

"You could start your own clan," he said abruptly.

"What!?" she said incredulously. "Start my own... I cannot–"

"Why not?" he said, suddenly curious.

"What are you making that face for? Because I cannot," she said.

"But why?" he asked persistently.

"Well," she sighed and began with concerted patience, "at the beginning, I have lost all of my wolf riders in a battle that I completely missed."

"So?" he asked.

"*So*," she emphasized, "I was in the wrong place at the wrong time!"

"So what? You missed the battle and everyone else is dead. Your whole clan, right?"

"Right," she said.

"Then how does anyone know that you were in the wrong place at the wrong time?"

"Well..." she began, "some orcs got away."

"Right, but you wore your helmet most of the time and most of you look all the same to us," he said.

"We what?" she said, bewildered.

"Ah," he fumbled. "That kills me a small amount. I want to not say that before."

She looked at him askance. "You mean, you wish you did not say that?"

"*That* is how it goes, yes, I wish I did not say that," he agreed, but seemed sheepish. "I mean, I can tell which are women and which are men."

"I gathered," she said wryly. "So where did you come up with this idea?"

"It is what I have done," he said.

"What do you mean?" she asked.

"I started my own tribe," he said.

"So, you are named?" she asked.

"I am," he said.

She hesitated a moment. "Who named you?"

"Myself," he said matter of factly.

"You cannot do that," she dismissed in irritation.

"Why can I not? I have done it," he said. He seemed proud.

"But. In your people, do you not have to kill the last owner of the name to take it. It is the name of the whole tribe and everyone is in the tribe, but there is only one that owns the name."

"Yes, but I made a new one, so there was no one to kill," he said.

"But, among your people–"

"My *people*. Heh," he chuckled scornfully, "you speak as if there is one people. You hobgoblins are proud of your blue skin, except when it is purple or red or grey; then you are proud of being purple or red or grey. Orcs do not care about being orcs. They just be and do like orcs, they do not think about it." He threw up his hands derisively, as if to push away the notions of both his and her kind. "But anyways, yes, I made a tribe and no one made me stop and if there is one thing about being an orc that is true, you can do anything that no one else stops you from doing."

She considered his words. "So make a tribe."

"Why not? There are tons of orcs around," he suggested.

"I will not make a clan of *slaves* and *cowards*!" she spat.

"Ooh, that kills me a bit more," he said.

"So how many are in your tribe?" she asked.

"Myself," he said readily, almost with a smile.

"That is all?" she asked.

"That is all," he answered, more surely with a smile.

"I cannot begin to do such a thing! I would be laughed at and scorned," she said.

"Well, that will happen if you go back as the only survivor, right?"

"It will," she mulled. "What is the name of you and your tribe?"

"Grotis," he said. "It is the Orcish word for 'alone.'"

Chapter 20

Eastern edge of the town of Serna, Yvel Principality.
By the Human Calendar, Twosday (second day of the week), second week
of Aiz, 794.
A cool and windy late spring afternoon, one week later.

More than two months after its departure, the weary column of
the regiment emerged from the tree line to return to Serna. The trees
were even further cut back giving a longer expanse for any would-
be intruders to wither under arrows fired from the palisade. The wall
itself was nearly complete, a sign of the industry of the townsfolk
and the leadership of Lady Mariss. With the passing of time, the
first gusts of cold wind blew down from the mountains,
occasionally bringing a shiver.

The sounds of music drifted from the walls as people
found their fiddles and flutes to greet the returning soldiers. As
the column unwound itself from the encasing forest, cheers could
be heard from the town. Answering cheers from the column were
stifled by tenleaders and company leaders barking for discipline.
Each soldier was glad to at last be free of the enshrouding canopy of
the forest, and welcomed the prospect of fresh supplies: beer, wine,
brandy, mead, and any other such mild to strong drink they could
have.

Julian kept his head down. Coming home was bittersweet.
His attention was drawn for a moment of fuss. The prince was
riding around the column. "Be still and ready, you stalwarts! You
will get time to enjoy life's goodness with a bit more patience.
Make a good orderly show for them, now." He rode on repeating
similar things. Julian did not catch all of it, but from what he could,
it was mostly the same.

The next two hours were somewhat of a blur. The regiment
marched to the south road and then turned north to enter Serna
through the gate. Now there was a gate. Another sign of life here
being forever changed. *We never needed a gate before*, he thought

bitterly. Townsfolk lined the street and cheered the return of their loved ones and the soldiers and elves who had come to their aid. Those that had remained in Serna now all wore militia livery–when they had departed, not even all of the militia that marched into the wood had livery.

Somehow, the column made its way onto town green, stacked all of its equipment in orderly lines, and the officers dismissed their soldiers for the day. Large casks of wine and kegs of brandy and beer were already being rolled out by townsfolk under the direction of Beren Enkr'ail, the merchant-turned quartermaster. The tenleaders and foremen of the town, barely able to contain their young men and women, bade them farewell for the day.

Julian walked his horse, Pine, to the stable at the Moradran Inn, which had also undergone some changes. Julian took them in. The smell of ashes was gone, uncovering the familiar smell from the outdoor soup counter built onto the inn's side. A cluster of tents and hastily-built shacks occupied the space where some of the buildings had burnt down. Other lots had the constructions of new buildings of wood and stone well underway, with lumber and block piled by the sites. Idle work tools left about told Julian that the workers had joined the festivities.

A small addition on the stage-side of the Moradran, complete with its own door, designated a dedicated space for the quartermaster's office, according to the sign that hung over the door. Julian was not a lettered man, but he surmised it was the quartermaster's office by the sign depicting a key, a chest, and a few paintings of food, coin, and horses. Julian recalled that Master Enkr'ail had taken over the common room of the Moradran when they left and had wondered how long Mistress Moradran would tolerate the practice.

The stable had also been enlarged. Before, it could hold five or six horses. A second shelter had been erected which would hold another ten horses, and many of the stalls were full. Julian led Pine into a stall, unsaddled her, and rubbed her down with a brush from the saddle bag. He made sure that there was water in the stall barrel to drink, and scooped out some grains from a barrel at the end of the stable into a bag, then dumped the oats onto a feeding bucket in the corner of Pine's stall. Julian glumly scratched Pine behind the ear before closing the stall door on his way out.

Julian walked away from the stables and crossed the road while weaving through revelers. He ducked into an alley and sheepishly squeezed around a couple that had just discovered each other and waded further past a stack of work tools and an overturned barrel that was leaking something. He emerged on the other side of the row of buildings. This is where the workshops started, and the smell said that the workers had been very busy in the last two months. The tannery was ripe with the smells of drying and curing skins, ash and sawdust mixed in the air by the smith, the wagonwright, and the carpenter.

It looked like they were building a second smith, judging by the piles of stone, sacrificing the space from a candle-making shop. *Where were they getting all of the people for this work?* It seemed that the shops were abandoned for revelry, aside from a few revelers or people on their way to the center of town. Tools and materials were left out in haste, forges left with one or two unfortunate shophands stuck with minding the fire until it cooled. Julian dragged himself past the tannery and passed to the first row of workmens' houses. He approached the second one on the right. He had only been here a few times. As most of the houses were built, strong timbers made the frame and were filled in with a mixture of mud and sticks under a tiled roof. He knocked at the door.

From further back in the house, he heard a musical, "Come in! Just a minute." Julian entered and looked around bleakly. This was the common room and kitchen in the same room. From what Julian remembered, there had been only two other rooms in this house: one meant for children that had not yet been conceived was used for odds and ends; the other was Terah's bedroom. This kitchen had also been turned into a seamstress parlor. Terah had brought her work home and was probably part of the reason that everyone had livery now.

She popped out from around the corner of the door to her room. She wore a pink dress with no sleeves and lacing on the front of the bodice over a white shirt. A red-and-white checked shawl draped over her shoulders, tied in the front and was partially covered by tresses of auburn hair falling past her shoulders. *This is her best dress*... he thought bleakly.

Her face was alight for an instant, then surprised. "Julian! It's great to see you. I'm so glad you're back." Julian said nothing. He was unable to meet her gaze, turning his face to the side. "Where's Ervan? You're taking me to him, right?"

Julian's throat constricted, but he forced out what he could. "Terah. Would you please come to the farm with me? There's something I need to tell everyone." Spots of water appeared on the floor between Julian's feet.

"Julian, where's Ervan?"

***

The guard gave Mkaela a surly look as he handed her the rope. Mkaela was fairly sure that the source of his mood was because he was one of the unlucky few with camp duty while all of his fellows were off reveling and carousing. His particular duty involved guarding the only two orc women they had taken prisoner from the enemy commander. Mkaela was sure that he, like everyone else in the camp, knew that she was the only reason they were taken prisoner instead of executed. The other prisoners, numbering a few hundred orcs, were mostly women and children. The cluster of them squatted and huddled a few dozen paces off under the watch of other sour-faced guards.

Mkaela had received a mixed interaction on the month's march back. Some placed their hands on their heart, a gesture normally reserved for elders and other clergy of Orneth. Some made hex signs of crossed fingers to ward her off, which is what she expected for being a witch. Some spat at her or called her 'orc-lover,' which she was not surprised about either. Most, however, generally got on with whatever they were doing and gave her a friendly smile when she spoke with them. She was not sure where this guard fell, but she knew that she was the reason that he was not off having a good time right then. She took the rope and thanked him.

He left quickly, his duties completed, to doff his armor and make for the celebration. She stared at the rope awkwardly and followed its connection to improvised rope collars about the necks of the two prisoners. She suddenly felt very wrong about the whole situation. The two orc women looked at the ground ambivalently. Mkaela got the sense that this was far from the first time their ownership had changed, but she resolved to make this the last. She dropped the rope, pulled her belt knife, and approached them. The two of them reacted abruptly, collapsing to their hands and knees, words erupting from their mouths. Mkaela did not know what they were saying, but from their tone it seemed like they were begging to live.

Mkaela backed away, left hand open and trying to seem unthreatening, right hand putting the knife away. "Merik, could you please find one of the elves that speak Orcish so I can tell them that they're not about to die?"

"No, My Lady. I cannot leave you here at their mercy. It is too dangerous," said Merik.

"Ugh." Mkaela sighed vexedly. "Then will you stay with them while *I* go get one?"

"Yes, My Lady," he said.

Mkaela set out in search of one of the elves that she knew spoke Orcish. It was no small task, trying to find anyone in the cheering throng. She passed over bothering Tyrnimar; she did not feel up to translating what Tyrnimar said to her. Looking around and moving from place to place, she bumped into someone. It was Taram.

"What are you doing?"

"What?" she said. The noise from the crowd made it difficult for her to hear anything above the din.

"I said, what are you doing?" he called to her.

"I'm looking for someone to speak Orcish," she called back.

"What?" he said. She grimaced in annoyance and waved him over, out of the edge of the crowd so they could speak.

"I'm looking for someone that speaks Orcish so I can talk to the two prisoners."

"Oh," he said. "I think I can help with that."

251

She was looking over the crowd, questing for telltale ears and shining hair when he said that. She whipped her head around and looked at him in surprise. "You speak Orcish?"

He shuffled and looked away uncomfortably. "It's been a long time." He looked like he regretted saying that he could assist her. "Ah, look, maybe I'll help you get help. I probably can't remember any of it."

"No, please," she said, "I'd like you to help if you can."

He shifted again, looking away, running a hand through his long scraggly hair. "Alright," he said, "but, please, uh, don't tell anyone. I probably shouldn't've said anything."

"Alright, I won't say, but why?" she said.

"Uh…" He hesitated. "It'll go places I don't want to be. Listen, I don't really want to get into it. Let's just go see your two ladies." Mkaela nodded and led Taram back to the two prisoners. They rounded a tent and Mkaela froze as she felt Taram go stiff and the air tense. She looked back at him. He stood still, gaze fixed. She followed his gaze and saw that Merik was still standing there with the two prisoners looking curiously at Taram.

"I didn't know he could speak Orcish. Really that anyone besides the elves…" Merik wavered as Mkaela minutely shook her head.

"We won't say anything," she assured Taram. Taram moved forward again but seemed wary.

"Alright, so what do you want to ask them?" Taram asked.

"I want to know what they want to do," she said.

Taram paused, looking off to the side before speaking again. "Mkaela, there are some things about the life they led that you've got to understand."

"Like what?" she asked.

"Like they've been slaves their whole life. They've never been allowed to want anything, so they're not going to know what you mean. It's never entered their minds," he said.

"What!?" Mkaela accused angrily. "How would you know?"

Taram sighed. "Fine, I'll ask them." Taram turned and

spoke a few words at them. They looked up at them, their noses flared a bit and brows furrowed momentarily, and the one on the left said something back.

"What did they say?" Mkaela asked impatiently.

Taram turned slowly. "They want to know if I'm their new owner or Merik is."

"What's that supposed to mean? Didn't you ask them what I told you?" Mkaela accused again.

"Yes, I did." Taram let out a sigh. "Look, Mkaela, I'm trying to help, but don't get angry at me because I'm trying to teach you something. That's the problem with you people, you know? Goin' around thinking you know everything no matter how young or old you are."

Mkaela looked at him, taken aback a little. She had never seen Taram express frustration before. "Fine, then." She took a breath. "Tell them that neither you or he are their new owner and then tell me some things so I can understand this."

Taram turned and spoke to them in a few more Orcish words and then turned back to Mkaela. "So, whaddya want to know?" Mkaela noted his odd Eklendan accent. She had hardly ever heard it before and guessed that it was slipping out in his irritation. It was not like the other Eklendan accents in Serna. In Serna, there was an even split of people who grew up speaking Eklendan and then learned Marin, while others grew up speaking Marin and then learned Eklendan. It was common for someone to have an accent speaking one when they grew up on the other, but they were both speaking Eklendan right now and his words were different. Mkaela had heard Taram speak like this before, but very rarely. She never really marked it before, but it suddenly seemed obvious.

"I want to know why they think someone owns them," she said.

"Because that's how most orc tribes are. The men own the women. Not all men own women, but every woman is owned by a man."

Mkaela was stunned to silence for a moment. "The women are *owned*?" she said in disgust.

"Most of the time, yes," he said. "There are some times

when it's different, but usually it's because they got away from their tribe and did something else."

"So only the men are free?" she said.

"Well, no, the men aren't really free either. The tribe leader or the… clan leader, I guess, they're really the only ones that are sort of free. They can do whatever they want to the men in their tribe. Tell them to hunt, kill, kill each other, he can kill them, but only in a fight." Taram shrugged, as if to say he was helpless against her disgust. "The tribe leader can do pretty much any of that except take stuff from the men in his tribe, including women. Except when he kills a man in a fight—then he can take all of the dead orc's stuff." Taram took a breath and continued. "But even the tribe leader always has to look over his shoulder. Leadership of the tribe is considered a possession, and any orc can challenge him and take it, and there's no way to retire from being the tribe leader."

Mkaela was silent and thought about that. "Tell them that I want them to be free like men, then."

After Taram exchanged words with them. "They asked me if this one," he translated, pointing to the one on the right, "owns the other one."

"What? No. Tell them that they are to be free like men, but they will never own another person. Tell them that they can be free and live their lives and be happy as long as they don't go back and help the other side."

Merik gave Mkaela unvarnished wide-eyed skepticism. Taram looked at Mkaela. "I can tell them some of that, but I can't tell them anything about being happy."

"Why not?" she asked.

"Because, for one, the words do not exist in their language. At least, not in the dialects I know. These are ideas that orcs, generally, do not get a chance to live or think about." He grimaced, glancing at the orc women. "For them, happiness would be survival, conquest, owning a lot of stuff and slaves, and having a lot of little green kids. For these two in particular, they usually get owned and are part of producing the kids, but they don't really get to enjoy any of that."

"Just tell them, then, that they can be free like men, stay

with us, not own any slaves, and work here," she said, growing tired of the barriers.

Taram spoke to them more. There was a lot more back and forth before Taram looked back at Mkaela. "So, they understand, but they don't understand. They know now that they're free like men, but they don't know what that means or what to do."

Mkaela sighed again. "They can stay with me, then. There's room in the bakery. I'll set up some pallets there until I can get some more proper things in order."

"Uh–" Merik began.

"I'll have to teach them to speak one of the languages here. Taram, which one do you think would be easier for them to learn?" Mkaela grew up speaking a mix of both languages and was not sure which one was harder or easier.

"Uh, My Lady," Merik began again.

"Yes?" Mkaela rounded on Merik with a hint of impatience. "Sir Merik?"

"My Lady, you will not be staying here to take care of them," he said.

"Oh, no?" she challenged. "What am I going to be doing then, Merik?"

Merik grimaced. "My Lady, you know this is just the beginning of a war. There is going to be more and worse of what we just saw." Mkaela looked at him, despairing that he was right, but said nothing. "There is no way that the Prince is going to leave you, the only healer known since Kostray himself wrote his chapters," Merik continued, "unless you believe the legends about the Church Wars and those such tales… no way that he is going to leave you here." Merik paused. "And, no way that you would let all those people suffer and die of wounds when you know you can help."

Mkaela knew he was right. She could not bear the thought of all those soldiers fighting to defend these people and places, places like Serna and people like… like herself, like Taram, like… like Bonwyn and Baryn Kevr'ail. Mkaela was suddenly nervous.

She could tell that her ability to heal was significantly weaker after Kostray's ghost had left her. She had treated the lesser injuries on the march back with much less effect, and quickly exhausted herself. She had turned to learning about more herbs and splints and other remedies from the prince's surgeon and her assistants. Mkaela had some knowledge from her apprenticeship just a few months ago, but it had been something on the side and she had not really focused on it. She had not told anyone that her ability was weaker, but she also believed what Kostray told her: that she would grow stronger with practice.

"Taram, can you tell them to not worry about the knife? We're just cutting the ropes around their neck. Tell them that they can live with me and learn the language. Ask them what their names are," she said to Taram.

"They don't have names," he said to Mkaela.

"What do you mean 'they don't have names'?" she said.

"I mean that only their tribe leader has a name and it's the name of the tribe. Everyone else is just in the tribe. So, if you ask 'em, they'd say 'I am of' whichever tribe they're in," Taram said.

"Then tell them to think about it and they can pick their own names," she said. "Tell them they will need their own names to live with humans." The two green-skinned women watched nervously through the corners of their eyes as Mkaela cut the rope around their necks.

"Give them time to think about that, alright?" said Taram. "Thatta be a big change for 'em."

"That's fair. Can you help me get them to the bakery?" Mkaela said. Merik watched the scene quietly.

"Surely," Taram said, then hesitated. "Uh, we might want to cover them."

"Why?" Mkaela said until she understood. "Oh." The sight of orcs walking freely in town for most people would be cause for fear, anger, and likely bloodshed. "You're right. I'll fetch something. Can you explain it to them?" Taram nodded and Mkaela left to find a cloak or blanket.

Finding anything spare in the town, anything at all in the town for that matter, during the celebration proved to be fruitless. She quickly gave up and made for the bakery to fetch a spare cloak and a blanket. Weaving through the throng and the alleys, she got to the bakery relatively quickly, fetched what she came for, and was locking up to make for the regiment's camp.

"Mkaela?" said a small voice.

Mkaela looked around and spotted a pair of eyes peering at her from an alley. "Yeah? Who is it?"

The person stepped out from around the corner. A large, young blonde woman with a strangely gaunt face, in a ragged brown dress with holes torn in it. Mkaela was struggling to recognize this person. She was too large to be... *no...* "Aphra?"

"Can you help us?" Aphra said.

"Aphra? That's you?" Mkaela said in disbelief. "Yeah, what's wrong?" Mkaela approached Aphra, but Aphra shrank back into the alley a bit. As Mkaela drew closer, she could see bruises on Aphra's face.

"Yeah, can... can you help us? We have nowhere to go," Aphra said. Mkaela spotted another large person lying in the alley.

"Is that Marlar?" Mkaela asked. Aphra nodded. "Marlar?" Mkaela nudged Marlar, but she was not awake. Marlar's breathing was ragged. Mkaela felt her forehead. "She's burning up. Can you help me get her inside?" Mkaela looked at Aphra. Aphra was having trouble walking. *They're both with orc child,* Mkaela realized. "You have nowhere to go, do you?" Mkaela asked. Aphra shook her head. *Shunned by her own kin.*

"They said we were carrying Pitspawn and turned us out," Aphra said. Mkaela strained to get Marlar upright to drag her inside. Mkaela paused and shuffled, managing the weight awkwardly as she felt around in her pocket for her keys. Finding them, she tossed them to Aphra. Aphra opened the door and Mkaela dragged Marlar in, Aphra shuffling after her. The place was dusty and the oven had been cold for three months. She was sure that everything she kept in the larder was no good.

Mkaela sighed, thinking of everything she had to do for these two in addition to her two new green-skinned wards. "Aphra, listen, uh," Mkaela began as she set up a pallet for Marlar. "I'm going to be bringing some people back here. I have to leave and go get them once you and Marlar are set here."

"Oh?" Aphra said weakly.

"Yeah, uh, a church knight, Taram, and…" Mkaela braced for it, "a couple of women."

"Women?" Aphra asked, curious but still weak.

"Orc women," Mkaela said.

"Orc women!?" Aphra's alarm came through her fatigue.

"Listen, Aphra, they were slaves and we freed them… sort of. They won't hurt anyone," Mkaela said.

"But they're orcs!" Aphra protested.

"Listen, Aphra, I was trying to get some blankets to sneak them into town. They've got nowhere else to go." The two went back and forth a few more times before Aphra relented, utterly fatigued. Mkaela found a couple of spare light cloaks for warmer weather and went back to Merik, Taram, and the orc women.

"What took so long?" Taram asked.

"You remember Aphra and Marlar Lin'ail?" Mkaela asked. Taram was quiet. He knew. Merik was confused, but his face turned glum as Taram explained the situation on the way to Mkaela's bakery.

Chapter 21

The town green of Serna, Yvel Principality.
By the Human Calendar, Weddingday, second week of Aiz, 794.
The next morning.

"**Y**ou shall submit to this inquisition!" Authority rang in the shout from the older, long-bearded man. The Blue-Eyed Man approached from a distance. He could see the older man accompanied by a group of people; soldiers, from the glint of sunlight on steel. They were marching through the town from the north, calling out what townsfolk and militia were nearby.

Judging from his red and purple vestments, the older man was an abbot. The thread-of-gold cord draped from the right side of his collar lacked the knots denoting years, which meant that he had been promoted to abbot within the past year. The new arrivals stopped at the edge of the town green, which had largely been turned into a supply yard for rebuilding and fortifying the town but was currently littered with empty bottles and kegs strewn about.

There was a crowd of onlookers–the few people that had been awake roused others to watch. Judging from how people were looking at him, he was probably Serna's priest of Orneth who had been conspicuously absent the last two months. Koval and a few others had told the Blue-Eyed Man of this man—probably this man. Dum'ail was the name the Blue-Eyed Man remembered being told by them, and had taken issue with the town's acceptance of witches.

The Blue-Eyed Man spotted Koval and Judane behind himself. He waved them back from intervening. The older man had brought an entourage of fifteen church knights of various orders and a sizable baggage train. From what the others had told the man, Dum'ail was only the elder for this town's chapel, but this level of support represented significantly more status. Either he was more important than it seemed, or he had made some kind of deal about the situation and owed some political favors. Also possible was that the church bureaucrats had gotten overly excited at the prospect of a witch hunt. There had not been a full inquisition since... he would have to ask Nicholas, but it must have been a good sixty years since the Reformed Church of Orneth had an inquisition. He would have to ask Nicholas for a dossier on this Dum'ail, too.

"And so, you come to look after the everlasting salvation of these people now, after abandoning them in their time of need for months on end?" the Blue-Eyed Man said.

"This is a Church matter and none of your concern. Now stand aside," said Dum'ail.

"You watch how you speak to me. You know who I am," the Blue-Eyed Man warned.

"You are newly minted and eager to prove, but your predecessor was wise enough to acquiesce to the Church," Dum'ail said dismissively.

The Blue-Eyed Man quietly stepped close, so close so no one else could hear. When he spoke, his face was expressionless. "Never speak of my predecessor again. You are unworthy in every way." His core was tense with rage, but he kept his anger controlled. "He turns in his eternal sleep at your worthless filth. He never had problems like these. But when there were problems, he weighed all of his options and the risk, and made prudent decisions."

The Blue-Eyed Man shifted his weight to the other hip and towered over Dum'ail silently glaring up at him. "What you and your fellows bring is self-interest when these people and their Prince could greatly use the *vast* resources of the Reformed Church." The Blue-Eyed Man stepped even closer and whispered, "Listen, you shining jar of hot piss, I am someone, and you are nothing and no one. End this, tuck your tail in, scamper off where you will never be seen, heard, or smelled, and I will let you live if you do so quickly enough."

"How dare you–" Dum'ail began to blurt out.

"I can handle this for you, sir," interrupted a voice behind the Blue-Eyed Man. The Blue-Eyed Man looked over his shoulder and saw Merik and Mkaela, the Healer witch.

Right on time. This might really pay off. It'll be a real hassle to manage too many schemes at once, so I have to pace myself. Really have to think of a different term besides 'witch.' Too much stigma, the Blue-Eyed Man pondered. They approached. "Sir, with the greatest respect for everything you have made possible, I beg your leave to deal with this in the best interest of these people," Merik said. Merik wore his order colors of silver and purple on a surcoat over his mail and plates all over, but carried his helmet. Mkaela wore her gambeson and carried her spear. The crowd had parted for them, murmuring nervously in their wake. The Blue-Eyed Man broadly gestured, stepping aside as Merik and Mkaela approached.

Merik began. "I declare this inquisition void."

The church knights had their helms on, visors down, but they all were surprised by Merik's bold statement. The man could see them tense and straighten. "On what grounds!?" demanded Dum'ail.

"An inquisition seeks to find and deal with heretics. There is no practice that I have seen here that has not been in defense or aid of the common people here or as written in the Five Holy Books," said Merik.

"You're one given over to them! A heretic yourself!" Dum'ail cried, calling over his shoulder. "Is there some kind of cult inside the Order of Kostray?"

"*No!*" came three protests in unison.

"'Watch for the pure of heart in the one who can undo the shedding of blood.'" Merik intoned. "Book three, Kostray: chapter five, verse thirty."

"You say she can undo the shedding of blood!?" accused one of the knights. The man could not quite tell which.

"I am," Merik said, removing a gauntlet and tucking it into his belt. He drew his dirk and opened a line of skin across his palm. It blossomed red as he held it high for Dum'ail and the knights to see. He looked at Mkaela and they exchanged words that the man could not make out. She took his hand in both of hers and she looked at it very intently.

A moment passed and the Blue-Eyed Man found himself a touch nervous. *Did she burn out? Was it overwork? Was it fleeting to begin with?* Then, at last, a small light shone. The man had watched Mkaela work a few times and saw the golden light shine brightly. This time, the light was much more dim, but after a moment, Merik withdrew his hand, wiped away some blood and held it high, showing the cut to have closed and mostly healed.

"Mark this," Merik cried, his hand held in front for Dum'ail and his pawns to see.

"Have sense, Brother Merik. You are clearly bewitched," one of the church knights said. The Blue-Eyed Man guessed that it was one of the three that were wearing the same order colors as Merik; probably the same three that protested earlier. They probably knew Merik personally, and likely did not know many of the others.

"It is *you* who are bewitched! Bewitched by this farcical glory and gain spun by this one," Merik pointed at Dum'ail. "Have sense, Brothers and Sisters. These are the things that are written about, that we study, that we are sworn to uphold and protect and advocate! And yet, when it appears in front of us, we deny it?" Merik said, speaking to an audience.

"Have sense, brother knight, cast off the spell. You cannot turn back from this later," said another.

"*You* cast off the spell!" Merik rebuked. "How easy would it be for me to ignore this, purge this and others here as witches when they have just saved the lives of dozens of their own–and mine? How easy would it be to do that, mark this down as an interesting day, go back to my estate, drink blackberry wine and be with my wife?" Merik swept his hand across all of them. "You lead me into the temptation of the easy path. 'The measure of each man's and woman's belief is whether or not they choose it over comfort and fortune.' What will you choose, fellow knights? Your beliefs or your comforts?"

Two armored figures moved forward past Dum'ail. "See?" Dum'ail jeered. "Your lies cannot move them."

"You will be tried by combat, brother," said a woman's voice from under one helmet, "as a measure of your belief." She carried an axe on a long handle and wore the colors of red and silver, signifying she was of the Order of Saint Acrist the Judge. The other wore a darker red and silver with a long-handled sword. *Might be a new surcoat, or the other one might be the Graffin Order*.

"My faith will bear me through," said Merik before donning his helmet.

The Blue-Eyed Man noticed Mkaela's concern, but motioned to wave her back and winked reassuringly. She nodded skeptically but backed into the crowd. Merik drew his own arming sword and held it low with an even stance to keep both opponents in view. They tried to circle around him to place him in between them, but he weaved around, trading a few clangs, placing one of them between him and the other.

"To the left!" the Knight of Acrist said. She was getting flustered and angry. The Blue-Eyed Man watched on appreciatively. Merik was shrewd in his way. He must have known that one of them would grow impatient with zeal to strike justice, and he was deliberately frustrating them. Finally, Merik allowed himself to be circled with the woman knight's long axe of judgment on one side and the man knight's sword to defend the weak on the other. They both sprung for Merik at the same time.

Merik fluidly moved, having anticipated the dual strike. The sound of steel plates shifting and grinding on one another and feet shuffling in the dirt were the dominant sounds for an instant. Merik slid towards the long-handled axe, well inside its reach. The swordbearer moved closer towards Merik as Merik moved away. Merik stepped around the axe-wielder to his right, avoiding the lateral swing of the axe. The axe head met the swordbearer with a loud, ringing clang as it bounced off of the swordbearer's helmet.

The swordbearer dropped and the wielder of the axe made a vexed sound. She recovered her axe and made for another lateral strike, but Merik stepped in and firmly pushed her with his offhand, sending her stumbling backwards. She recovered and brought the axe high for an overhand strike. Merik sidestepped the axe, batting it aside with his arming sword. He brought his left foot up and jammed down on the axe haft at her hands, knocking it from her grip and punched her in the side of the helmet with the pommel of his sword. She fell to a knee, clutching her helmeted head with both gauntleted hands.

Merik walked past them, panting slightly. "My faith has carried me through this trial. I have bested my accusers–while leaving them instruments of the Church, I add–and beaten the charge. I say this again. This inquisition is void. I declare it so."

"Heretic! The witch aids you with spells and tricks!"
Dum'ail pointed.

"Here now–" Merik began.

"Merik!" Mkaela cried, suddenly. Merik's head whipped
around as the axe-wielder fell upon him from behind. She jammed a
dagger into his armpit, over the rim of his breastplate, breaking steel
links of mail.

"No one escapes judgment, heretic!" she hissed.

Now's the time to intervene. "That violates the code of trial
by arms," the Blue-Eyed Man said, walking towards the combatants
in the center of the green. Merik shrank away from the Knight of
Acrist with the dagger. He slid off the dagger and crumpled onto the
ground.

"I told you to stay out of this," Dum'ail warned as the
Acristian knight held the dagger towards him threateningly.

The Blue-Eyed Man, who had been enjoying the peace of
the sleepy town in the early morning, wore grey breeches, a long-
sleeved blue tunic with embroidered scroll-work about the collar,
and a white cape to keep the chill off. He was hardly dressed for
this occasion, only having an arming sword himself. The sword
whipped out of the scabbard, severing two fingers from the knight's
hand at the second knuckle and sent the dagger flying ten paces or
so. She clutched her hand by the wrist in shock. She did not notice
the Blue-Eyed Man's approach until he, like Merik, punched her in
the helm with the pommel of his sword, sending her sprawling. He
stepped on the wrist of her good hand and planted his sword point
into the ground through it. She screamed in pain.

"There now, I think we've settled that," the Blue-Eyed
Man said and then looked up at Dum'ail.

"I cannot ignore this!" Dum'ail yelled.

"Nor can I," the Blue-Eyed Man interrupted calmly.
"You said this is an internal Church affair. And yet, you come
here demanding the death of this woman," he pointed at Mkaela,
"a lay-person: not a member of the clergy, nor a sister knight.
A lay citizen of this village–the *Prince's* citizen in the *Prince's*
village!" The Blue-Eyed Man threw his arm wide to take in all

of the gathered onlookers. "She helped the other people of this village—the *Prince's* village! The *Prince's* people! Where were you? Helping these people when they needed you, or off making yourself important? Does not your entire scripture devote itself to describing the importance of helping people in need?" The Blue-Eyed Man stepped toward Dum'ail, pulling his blade from the axe-wielder's hand, drawing a pained moan.

While the Blue-Eyed Man and Dum'ail spoke, Mkaela had moved to Merik, unbuckled his breastplate, and lifted his mail and torn gambeson. She placed her hand over the puncture. Her hand softly glowed purple as Merik relaxed with the waning of his pain. He sagged and laid down, passing out.

"That is not—" Dum'ail began.

"Shut your mouth," Mkaela said calmly, but the words cut through the air. The crowd was tensely still. She was kneeling down with the unconscious swordbearer, removing his helmet. She looked down at him. "All you ever did was whine about how important you are. Can you be bothered with anything else?" She held the swordbearer's head. A soft purple glow emanated from her hands. He coughed some blood, but then breathed easily. She moved on to the axe-wielder, who recoiled from her at first.

"It is time for you to depart," the Blue-Eyed Man said to Dum'ail.

"Quit being a baby," Mkaela scolded the axebearer. She took the hand missing two fingers.

"I demand judgment!" Dum'ail called. Mkaela knelt on the stomach of the axe-wielder's breastplate, clutching her hand and healing the stumps shut to stop the bleeding.

"Judgment has been made," said one of the knights behind Dum'ail. He turned, but the three knights bearing the red and white colors of Kostray strode past him. "Our brother passed the trial and the eager judge violated the code," said the knight.

Another knight spoke in a woman's voice. "From Acrist's own writings, 'It is the hasty judge that divides and destroys us,'" she intoned. The three stood with the Blue-Eyed Man, blocking Dum'ail's view of Merik and the other two wounded knights.

"Get away from me!" the axe-wielder shrieked. She

scrambled away from Mkaela and past the other knights. "I'll not be touched by your filth, heretic!"

"Fine," Mkaela said plainly, gesturing towards Dum'ail. "Go be touched by his scatty speech, then."

"Perhaps this whole town needs the attention of the Church," Dum'ail said. There was a stillness for an instant. The crowd moved slowly, but it moved, second by second. A spear appeared, a bow was strung, a sword drawn, and axe fetched. Bit by bit over the course of a tense moment, the town bore arms against the interlopers.

"We will see about this," Dum'ail hissed. He turned to leave town, flanked by the remaining church knights. The crowd watched them mount their horses and make off on the north road, a cheer chasing them out of town. The man glanced at the three Knights of Kostray that were talking with Mkaela and Merik. The swordbearer still lay on the ground, but was blearily coming to. *Good. That was a bit of a risk, but it is proceeding quite as I had hoped.* As the crowd dispersed, the Blue-Eyed Man wove through it until he found Koval, keeping half of an eye and an ear on the swordbearer.

"Sir Merik," the swordbearer called weakly. "Lady of Grace?"

"By Kostray! Don't call me anything like that, do you hear?"

"Yes, Your Grace–" the swordbearer continued.

"Stop that!" Mkaela interjected.

"Y–yes, uh, My Lady, uh… well, Sir Merik bested me. Both of us, I suppose. That means he was right about you," said the knight.

"Just by those means? Just fight over it and that's it?" Mkaela asked incredulously.

"My Lady, I, Sir Jo'Kaul of the Order of Saint Graffin will…" The Blue-Eyed Man lost Sir Jo'Kaul's voice in the crowd as he made his way to Koval.

"Ah, there you are Koval," he said over the throng.

"Yes, sir?" Koval said.

"Listen, I know that there are a lot of things still going on, but there are a lot of things that need to happen in the city," said the man.

"Of course, sir, I understand, you are very busy with–" Koval said.

"I mean that you and a good number of yours should come to the city," the man interrupted.

"Sir?" Koval said uncertainly.

"The Prince must present the people in the city with a parade for their brave soldiers, and there's a coronation to be had," the man said. "And a funeral," he added glumly.

"Of course, sir, but I cannot leave the town defenseless. I appreciate the sappers that have been helping build back the town and fortify it while we've been gone, but they'll all leave. I need most of the militia here."

"Yes, yes, Koval," the Blue-Eyed Man assured, "most of them will be here. I just want some of your people to represent everything this fine town has weathered and accomplished. To enjoy some appreciation. There are some things that the Prince would like to talk to you about on the way and things that the Prince needs you to do."

Koval hesitated. "Of course, sir."

Figure 9: Map of the City of Yvel and surround area

The City of Yvel

N

to Merman

to Borly

Baldinet
"New Marka"

Martin Quarter

Mid's Hill

Old Town

New Town

Roomtown

Palace

Fene Abbey

Danbet Hill

Trukan

Ferney Way

River Gath

Barkton

To Garber and Serna
(road forks in 20 miles)

Chapter 22

A prison, somewhere in the Yvel Principality.
By the Human Calendar, Restday, first week of Aiz, 794.
A late spring morning, cloudy and brisk.

The clang of the lock startled Jak. "Get up, greenskin," said the jailer, "you're bein' moved." Jak obeyed and rose as the jailer entered the cell. Jak was significantly taller than the jailer... just as he was significantly taller than everyone he ever met. Two guards waited in the corridor. The jailer stood aside and motioned for him to move out.

Jak shuffled out of the cell into the corridor. "Listen up. I'm puttin' this bag on yer head so you's don't see what's goin' on. We're movin' ya and some others." Jak saw the rim of the bag come over his head and cover his eyes, his scraggly beard grating against the bag. He felt a nudge from the jailer and a hand on his left shoulder roughly guiding him, and moved blindly along the corridor, occasionally grazing the wall. The jailer's hand guided him through the jail, the smell of outside air getting stronger. While he stumbled and shuffled, he heard others being roused from their cells and given similar instructions.

"Where're we goin'?" Jak asked through the bag.

"I dunno, some mines or some such place where no one sees ya ever again," said one of the guards. *They don't know*, Jak decided, but did not care for a while as he felt sunlight and smelled outside air. He still smelled refuse and mold, of course, but the outside air cut through so much. He had forgotten the smell of fresh air after inhaling only moldy air, rife with vomit, piss, and excrement from living in and around it for... however long.

The hand pulled him to a stop and released his shoulder. "Put yer green hands in front. Ya feel a wagon. Get in," the jailer said.

Jak awkwardly felt the wagon in front of him and climbed in. He was not alone.

"Keep the bag on," the jailer ordered.

One by one, more prisoners were prodded into the wagon behind him. He overheard others being prodded into more wagons nearby. The space grew tighter as it was packed full, people's arms and legs dangling out the sides. Jak heard a few words between the guards from the prison and the wagon drivers, and they were off with a rumble. He kept the hood on, not really for fear of consequences, but rather because the light outside was too bright after having lived in the prison for so long.

"Hey," said one of the other prisoners.

"What?" said Jak.

"Where're we goin'?" he asked.

"Dunno," Jak said, and let himself drift off to a nap.

He was jolted awake when the wagon stopped. The sun was setting, he guessed. Some voices. Footsteps, approaching the wagon; the steps were light. He could not make out her words, but they were said in a woman's voice. The wagon vibrated with the movement of people getting onto the wagon, *or getting off?* Heavier footsteps were moving away from the wagon. The drivers changed. After a moment, the transport lurched back into motion. Jak kept the hood on, to keep the cold wind off of his skin.

***

Palace Library, Palace of Yvel City, Yvel Principality.
By the Human Calendar, Morningday, third week of Aiz, 794.
The morning of the return of the prince's party.

The Blue-Eyed Man pushed the broad doors open and briskly

strode into the library. A team of servants were putting the finishing touches on a display of pastries, desserts, hot mulled wine, and coffee. He motioned to one and spoke. "Please excuse us. We have private matters to discuss." The servant bowed and quietly reported to the others, who quickly finished their tasks before departing.

"Oh," called the Blue-Eyed Man, "please also have Mistress Koziathin brew another pitcher of coffee, but this time in goat's milk. My thanks." The last servant out wordlessly bowed and departed.

The Blue-Eyed Man turned towards the chief librarian. Nicholas sat at his desk, draped in his dark grey robes, with a coat worn over the top. Books, both open and closed, spread across his desk amidst ledgers and maps. He was looking at the Blue-Eyed Man with concern on his face, but had otherwise not moved. "I'm–" he began.

"How far along is the plan?" the Blue-Eyed Man asked abruptly.

"Right down to it, then?" Nicholas said in disbelief. "No–"

"No. There's no time for it," the Blue-Eyed Man affirmed flatly. "So. How goes the plan?" He plunked himself down in a chair by the spread of sweets, poured himself some coffee, grabbed a dull knife and cut a piece of sugared bread. He dipped it into a cup of whipped cream and bit off a piece, sighing deeply after the first bite and a sip of coffee, and seemed to relax for the first time in several weeks.

Nicholas sighed in a combination of concern and disapproval. "The prison warden gave my people custody over two months ago. If I understand the reports from the messengers, it was when you were on the march out of the hills."

"How long until they are ready to begin?" the man asked.

"They're already organized into their teams, for better or worse. Another month before we have them in proper position with equipment."

"Any direct contacts?" the Blue-Eyed Man asked.

"Please," Nicholas said in mock offense, "many layers of separation. These are my people, mind you."

"Ah yes," the Blue-Eyed Man said, conceding. "Well, then, it turns out that the Prince will be thankful. Be careful what you ask for, though, I suppose," he said wryly.

"Are you sure–" Nicholas began again.

"Yes, yes," the Blue-Eyed Man snapped, then sighed. "Alright, the Prince was loved by all. Even the Prince–the new Prince–is greatly affected. But he must, in this time of need, put on the best face and do what must be done." The Blue-Eyed Man firmly set his coffee cup down, its clatter echoing in the room. Leaning forward, he pointed with his finger to accentuate his words. "This plan is especially fortuitous. It is a great risk in different ways than envisioned, but it is quite necessary at this point."

"Different how?" asked Nicholas.

"Soldiers, supplies, time, land to move armies around. Yvel will be swallowed if it fights alone."

"That brings up something else," Nicholas said.

"Oh?"

"What is this nonsense about witches?" Nicholas asked pointedly.

The Blue-Eyed Man flinched, startled. *Of course! No one would have believed any rumors*. "Sense, actually."

"I beg your pardon?" Nicholas said dubiously.

"Granted, friend," the Blue-Eyed Man said mockingly, before speaking earnestly. "Truly–we would all likely be dead if not for the witches of Serna," he said, "at least, that's the Prince's opinion." Nicholas skeptically half-smiled. "Truly," the Blue-Eyed Man insisted. "They had numbers, and they had cunning."

"I'm sure you had cunning, too," said Nicholas. His skepticism was still strong and quite evident.

"But not the numbers," the Blue-Eyed Man said. "Not like that. Nor could we see as well as they at night. You were right about all of that, you'll be pleased to know." He finished his sugared bread.

"Indeed." Nicholas still seemed suspicious. "So, tell me of them."

"Right," the Blue-Eyed Man began. "Well, there's a girl that shoots fire from her hands, and another that controls the winds. They're sisters, I think. And there's a Healer witch. The Order of Kostray crony is convinced that she's some kind of sign from the scripture."

"And where would he get that idea?" Nicholas chided.

"Ah, you wound!" The Blue-Eyed Man mockingly clutched both hands over his heart. "Anyways, the Firecaster is the only one that seems to not be able to control her powers. Oh, and there's one more. Not sure if he's a witch or just... odd."

"What do you mean?"

"He doesn't seem to have any powers, except that he doesn't get old," the Blue-Eyed Man resumed sipping his coffee and started on a pastry.

Nicholas's head shot up from eyeing the pastries. "The Ageless Man!?"

The Blue-Eyed Man was surprised. "That's what interests you? Not the girl that closes bleeding wounds with her hands, or the other one burns foes to ash and cinder? A man that doesn't get old? You say it like it's a specific person."

"It is." Instantly, Nicholas was on his feet behind the desk and leaned forward intently. His hand nudged a book off of the table, but in his intense focus he ignored it. "There's a history of this man, if it's the same one. He's quite a legend in my field. Some say he's a myth, but… may I meet him?"

"You dropped… sorry, meet him? I… don't see why not. I'll arrange–" the Blue-Eyed Man eyed the book on the floor.

"It cannot be obvious," Nicholas broke in.

The Blue-Eyed Man regarded Nicholas, having moved on to a hard biscuit half dipped in molten chocolate before cooling to a chewy casing. He took a bite and regarded Nicholas to the point that Nicholas looked sheepish. "Never seen you so excited about something, through all the plans."

"It's widely believed that he does not exist; that he's just a story to scare the younger ones."

"Funny that you're widely believed to be a simple chief librarian," said the Blue-Eyed Man. "I'm sure a discreet arrangement can be made that will seem innocuous at first." He frowned and gestured with his empty hand. "I imagine the Prince will have to throw some kind of ball to celebrate our glorious return after announcing the big expansion. And there is this little coronation thing that is supposed to happen. All are fine reasons to fabricate the opportunity."

"Big expansion?" Nicholas said.

"Oh, right, that one didn't get sent," the Blue-Eyed Man said. He plucked another pastry, a honey cake, and paused as a servant entered with another pitcher of steaming coffee. He poured a cup, inhaling its steam and relishing the creamy taste while the servant departed. "Gunst will be the adjutant for Yvel's Army."

"I heard," Nicholas said.

"He won't have his battalion. Those two battalions will be combined and filled out into a regiment led by House Covendran."

"Covendran! Really?" Nicholas said in surprise.

"Yes, they were quite dependable, apparently." He took a bite of the honey cake, savoring the sweetness before continuing. "You remember how persuasive the Lady Mariss was in laying out her argument. Well, her husband, son, and daughter are no less effective leading and fighting." *Wouldn't mind seeing the daughter more up close, either*, the Blue-Eyed Man mused. *Now, how would a prince look upon it? How would the Prince be looked upon if...* "It will be difficult for them to pick which one stays to watch Yvel being fortified, but they'll have their hands full with that regiment. Gunst will recontract every soldier under Covendran and then begin levies across all of Yvel, as well as mercenary contracts. There is no lack of need for more battalions and regiments. What's needed, as well, is people to lead them and pay to arm them."

"That is a trick. The coffers can only take so much," agreed Nicholas.

"Yes, and that's why the plan is now necessary, not a leisure project," said the Blue-Eyed Man.

"Yes, I suppose," Nicholas agreed. "So, what of these witches, then?"

"Well, for one, there needs to be a better name than 'witches.' The people are still a largely superstitious lot and excitable. We need something that sounds more... dignified," the Blue-Eyed Man said.

"Wizards? Sorcerers?" Nicholas suggested. "I pluck these titles from stories."

"Sorcerers. Hm. Needs something that says that they're ours," the Blue-Eyed Man said.

"Crown Sorcerers, then? Like the Crown Guard," said Nicholas.

"There it is, then!" the Blue-Eyed Man said with a grin, proffering another pastry. This one was a circle of dough folded in half over fruit and a sugar sauce, with a row of small slashes through the middle for steam to escape during the baking. He bit some off–blackberries–and washed it down with some coffee.

"I anticipated you would want a selection when you returned, but I didn't think you were going to eat everything,"

Nicholas said.

"Oh, some more time in the practice yard and it will be fine. Three months on the march takes me out of good habits," the Blue-Eyed Man said.

"Like this one?" asked Nicholas.

"Oh, mind you like a mother," the Blue-Eyed Man retorted before gesturing to himself. "A foot in the world of books, and a foot in the world of war. Things are well sorted."

"Fine, then. So, what about with the witches–sorcerers, I mean." Nicholas slowly sat back down.

"They'll need a training ground. Maybe an academy later. For the time being, a place where they can practice without hurting anyone," the Blue-Eyed Man said.

"Hurting anyone?" Nicholas said curiously.

The man gave Nicholas a very direct look. "Oh, yes, we all may be alive because of them, but they definitely burnt a few good soldiers up because they couldn't control themselves. It's a wonder they didn't burn their whole village down sooner if the orcs hadn't done it for them."

"I thought you said it was just the one that couldn't control it."

"Yes, but the other one is untried, really. The wind was helpful, but only to move the fire away from us and towards the orcs. They will need to train together to be more useful. The only one that we can use now is the Healer," the Blue-Eyed Man explained.

"The Healer. How… what does she do?" Nicholas asked.

"Not sure. She puts her hands on people, and their wounds close," the man said, his brow furrowing pensively. "Though it seems like it changed in the hills. At first, it had a golden light to it, but it's usually purple now. That and the healing isn't as strong." He shrugged. "Still, she saved a lot of people and put them back into fighting shape sooner than eight months of rest and care."

"How many?" asked Nicholas.

"Not sure. And in more ways than one. She's the only reason that we took prisoners. The soldiers were going to kill them all," the Blue-Eyed Man said.

"Prisoners?" Nicholas said.

"Yes, a few hundred. Mostly women and children, but the adults are still quite strong looking." The Blue-Eyed Man took another bite of the honeycake and chewed. "There were a very small amount of little blue things that we are told are goblins. Their full-grown size is about half of ours, more or less. Have to put together someone to run them around and get work done hauling stone and timber for building." He finished the honeycake and washed it down with coffee. "Two orc women, in particular, though. They were the concubines of the enemy commander, who, incidentally, was not an orc," the Blue-Eyed Man said.

"Concubines? 'Not an orc'? You're leaving out quite a bit, my friend," Nicholas stopped pacing behind his desk.

"Yes, well, there's a lot to tell." The Blue-Eyed Man's gaze followed as Nicholas began to pace anxiously. He sipped his coffee and crossed a leg on his knee. "So, where were we? Right. First, the witches–the Healer, uh, Mkaela, I think. She knew a couple of women the orcs had first captured. Well, now they're with child. Half-orc."

"Half-orc children?" Nicholas said with trepidation. "Graffin protect us."

"The Healer brought them here with her."

"Why would she bring them here?"

"Fresh start, maybe. Imagine being in their shoes? Carrying the enemy's baby in your belly. How's everyone looking at you? Friends and family look at you like you're one of them." The Blue-Eyed Man shrugged.

"I suppose. Maybe we should trade places and you could be the spymaster," said Nicholas.

"You don't want this job and all that comes with it… and…" the Blue-Eyed Man chuckled.

"Yes, yes. Well, go on. You were about to be on about something else."

"She has taken charge of some of the prisoners. They've been released into her care. Two of them," he said.

"Why would she take them?" Nicholas sat back down.

"She seemed to have a problem with killing defenseless people," the Blue-Eyed Man said.

"But the Prince needed her here, and she brought them with her, too."

"What!?" Nicholas asked incredulously.

"Oh, yes, and her entourage grew when she returned to Serna. They're all covered up, of course. The orc women, I mean. She's right that they'd be killed on sight by most people. Gunst and the Covendrans had to give orders. There were a few unfortunate scenes, with the other prisoners, too.

"Huh. Right out of scripture," Nicholas said.

"Isn't it?" The Blue-Eyed Man raised his eyebrows sardonically before finishing the cup of coffee from the second pitcher brewed with milk. He picked up the cup from the first pitcher, brewed in water.

"I wager," Nicholas said. He looked amused for a moment. "A bit of an aside, but how were they?"

"Who?" the man asked.

"The orc women. You said before you left that all that breeding didn't sound so bad," Nicholas said.

"Ah, that did get said. You know, they're not bad. Not bad

at all. A bit tall and burly, but rather exotic, with the green skin and all… and the burliness. There's a different appeal, but… it would be enjoyable. Some of them have green hair, you know?" the Blue-Eyed Man said.

"And did you?" Nicholas asked.

"Oh, I can't imagine an opportunity. Not anytime now or in the future," the Blue-Eyed Man said with a sigh. "I mean, there's propriety to be observed. We're not the Easterners with their harp-playing harems. How would the Prince–"

"Alright, alright. I was just asking," Nicholas said. "Maybe asking for a simple librarian's sake," he muttered under his breath.

"Well, you've brought up the subject. It's on the mind," the Blue-Eyed Man continued.

"Oh?"

"You should have seen the elf women." The man leaned back in his chair and put his feet up on another chair and took a deep breath. "It's true what they say, that they can break a man's heart just by the sight of them."

"Is it really that bad?" Nicholas asked wryly. "You're being a bit of a poor poet."

"Ah, you wound again!" the Blue-Eyed Man mocked. "They were something–the hair, and they smelled like flowers. A couple of them had skin the color of snow." He sighed wistfully. "But you could still take them out to the yard and they'd turn you over with the practice swords."

Nicholas shook his head. "Only you would find it interesting to get poked by a woman with something stiff."

The Blue-Eyed Man chuckled. "Ah, well, you'll see them at the Prince's Ball, for sure."

"So how were they?" Nicholas asked, rummaging through his books and documents. "For practical matters, that is, not for your raging, undirected lust for a wife to settle you a bit."

"They were quite reliable and helpful. For the most part, I would say that they are genuinely well-intentioned," the man said.

"But?" Nicholas prodded.

"But they're hiding something. They don't travel for joy–or, if they do, it is an abysmal fortune they've struck upon, wandering into this mess." The Blue-Eyed Man looked up and squinted towards the top shelf of one of the book cases as he mused. "Certainly, they saved Serna in the near term until Gunst and Arladran could get there with the Prince, and they certainly helped afterwards."

"I wager they did," Nicholas said quietly. "This is quite a mess. Are you sure–"

The Blue-Eyed Man knew where Nicholas was going. "Yes, I'm fine. The Prince is fine. We're all fine. Prince Gerald was widely loved, but Prince Gerald is dead."

Nicholas looked at his friend for a moment with concern. "Long live the Prince," he said at last.

"Here, here," replied the Blue-Eyed man, finishing the other cup of coffee and starting on the mulled wine. "Long live the Prince."

"How do you do that?" Nicholas said.

"Do what?" the Blue-Eyed Man said.

"Have coffee and then wine and eighteen different things from that bakery all stuffed in your mouth at once. It's a wonder you didn't grow so big that they have to build a new castle to fit your huge clothes," Nicholas said.

"Ah, mind you, the practice yard is the answer to all problems." He talked gesturing with his wine glass. "Can't sleep? Practice yard. Can't concentrate to read? Practice yard. Eating too much? Practice yard. Can't get a woman? Don't want to preside over court? Tired of annoying ministers?" The Blue-Eyed Man gave a teasing tone to that last: "practice, practice, practice."

"All that practice adds up. The day would have to be longer to fit it all," said Nicholas.

"Hm. Maybe forty hours in a day for practice," the Blue-Eyed Man winked. "By the way, I haven't had a straight answer from anyone, and I meant to ask right away: how did it go for Gundr'ail, up at Borly?" the Blue-Eyed Man asked.

"You didn't get the messenger?" Nicholas asked.

The Blue-Eyed Man looked at him and took his feet down to lean forward. "No." He looked at Nicholas expectantly.

Nicholas pursed his lips, seeming to consider his words, "Gundr'ail's here on his death bed. Lucky as you were around Serna, there were no witches or elves to save the day in Borly."

"So, what's the situation now?"

"They're holding on. Barely. I'm sure there are a great many people who will turn in their ashes and dirt for what I'm about to say, but we have to thank our neighbors in Heath, Versinth, and Versingit for being such deplorable creatures over the last hundred years with their border raids. If they hadn't been so detestable, then Borly would never have built a stone wall."

"So, they hold?" the Blue-Eyed Man said intently.

"They do, but by a finger." Nicholas hesitated, finding the ledger he was seeking. "Here's the last report of supplies, soldiers, and casualties. We sent the other battalion, the Kersis, up there two weeks ago." He grimaced uncertainly. "They should be there now, but no messages since."

The Blue-Eyed Man exhaled sharply, burying his forehead in one hand and taking the ledger in the other, his wine forgotten on the sweet-laden table. *Of course, with no one here with the authority to make decisions, it's left to the spymaster under the guise of a lowly librarian to convince people to do the needed things and that they won't get in trouble for it. All the meanwhile, there are no trained soldiers in the ACTUAL CITY unless we count constabulary trained to beat drunks!* the Blue-Eyed Man thought bitterly. "Don't mind. Not angry at you, just the situation."

"I understand," Nicholas said.

The Blue-Eyed Man scolded himself. *No Berin the Great would be this much at ease, gorging on sweets and coffee, leering at the servant girls and country maidens when he has soldiers out getting rained upon and slaughtered.*

"So, what will you do?" Nicholas asked.

"The Prince. Must. Act," the Blue-Eyed Man said. "We'll have to fetch Gunst and Dorrels, the Covendrans, the Healer, others. There's a lot to do."

"I'll see to it they come immediately," Nicholas said, rising. "You have those close around you, too."

"Yes, good," the Blue-Eyed Man said. "Gunst has a lot to do for administering. Dorrels can turn tonight's welcome home feast into the ball, he'll have to move the coronation to this afternoon instead of next week, the Covendrans have to ride to relieve Borly–without their witches." He felt very tired, as though he had underestimated the weight of a burden he was already carrying. "Mkaela has to pull Gundr'ail off of death's doorstep so the Prince can make him Marshal of the Crown. Mkaela also needs to foot off with the Covendrans." The Blue-Eyed Man's eyes searched for questions and answers. "Someone needs to set aside empty land for the witches–sorcerers, I mean. Someone else needs to grab up these prisoners and bring them... somewhere. And do something useful with them."

"Yes, sir," Nicholas was moving to the door to fetch a servant.

"There's more to tell, friend. I haven't told you about the hobgoblins, yet. The schism we've instigated in the Reformed Church–this rubbing from a ruin in the hill."

"Of course, friend, at the end of the ball?" Nicholas said, wide-eyed at the mention of a schism.

"That'll have to do."

***

Elsewhere in the palace.

"This way, I think, My Lady," Merik said.

He had told Mkaela that he had been through the palace in Yvel a few times. Mkaela was not filled with confidence that her chaperone knew exactly where they were, or how to get to their destination, but she was trying her best to be patient. The message, 'General Gundr'ail is on his death bed,' had sounded pretty dramatic, but apparently he had been on his death bed for three days.

She looked at Merik again. His arming sword was at his hip, belted over a plain white doublet with silvery-threaded bands embroidered about the cuffs and collar, and light red breeches tucked into his brown riding boots. He seemed a bit distracted. The face he wore seemed like the one that Mkaela herself displayed when she imagined winning arguments in her head.

"Something bothering you, Merik?" she asked.

"Yes, deeply," he said. Mkaela was surprised again at how direct he was. She liked that about him. She had felt more comfortable knowing that he was married, and had decided that once he calmed down, he would be a good friend. Every now and again, she felt a pang of guilt at how rude she had been to him, but he never brought it up. He did not elaborate on what was bothering him, though.

"Do you want to talk about it?" she asked as they briskly turned a corner and started up some stairs.

"No," he said, his gaze casting about as he tried to remember which hallway was the correct one.

"Well, maybe I can help," she suggested.

He sighed sharply. "You already have."

"What's that supposed to mean?" she said defensively.

He looked at her in surprise. "What? Oh," he sighed more calmly, "listen… My Lady, a lot is about to change in the Church."

"I understand," she said.

"I'm sorry, but you don't," he said.

She hesitated for a moment. "Can you tell me then?"

He took them on a left turn, jostling her by accident, apologizing as he righted himself and walked a bit further away. "Really, I have to thank you. We all do. Even Sister Knight Olavy."

"Who's that?"

"The knightess who lost her fingers and you partially healed."

Mkaela was uncertain of his meaning. "Why would she thank me…?"

"It's what I had said before in the town green. Before the trial by arms."

They walked for a bit, and took a right turn. "We're almost there."

"You didn't answer my question," she prodded.

"Oh. What I meant was what I said before. It would be simple for me to take the easy path. Before I met you–and you saved my life–I was on the easy path. My worries were mostly about managing my estate on behalf of the Church, and trivial bureaucratic matters."

"Alright…?" Her tone made it clear that she still did not understand his full point.

"So, we were all on the easy path. We are all on the easy path," he said.

"What's wrong with that, if there are no problems? I mean, none of you knew about this whole mess, before we met. There wasn't a mess to be worried about."

"There's always a mess to be worried about," he said bitterly.

"What do you mean?"

"Sorry." He paused. "I mean that being a Knight of the Church is not supposed to be an easy path. Each order has its focus, its ideals, that each is supposed to labor for. We exist to help people in various ways. Each order has its own way." He shook his head. "The knights that you saw on that town green weren't there to help people. They were there to help themselves–to protect their own self-interests–and before we met, I was the same."

Mkaela looked at him with concern, but said nothing. After a moment, he made another vexed sound. "And so, that means we have lost our sense of purpose and instead chosen to labor at vanity and trivialities. Lost sight of why we exist as an order. As a Knighthood. As a Church!"

Mkaela was silent for a moment before she answered. "I'm no person of the cloth, but it seems like many would take that as heretic talk."

"Surely, they do," he said bitterly, "but, truly, I–we–have to thank you. If not for this situation, we would still be regaling back at our estates, fretting about horse breeding and tablecloths."

"So, what about your wife? Will she agree?" Mkaela asked.

"My wife? Oh, no. She'll be right cross with me on this. I can't even make the words to describe it. It was good of Julian to take the message."

"Julian's a fast rider," Mkaela said. "Besides. He doesn't

have much anymore."

"Because of his cousin?"

"Yeah. The whole family blames him. He was the older cousin and he was supposed to make sure that Ervan was fine in the end."

"I've seen that kind of thing before. Been a while, though."

Another left turn, past some stone-arched windows with the glass panes pulled shut to keep the autumn wind out. The windows looked down into a practice yard set with sparring and archery dummies, heavy stones the size of a person's head, practice swords and javelins, and other odd implements. *I wonder how many people use all that. It's an awful lot of space. I figured a palace would have a garden or something in the courtyard, like in all the storybooks.* She ran her fingers over the smooth window pane as they walked down the hall, blurring the figures below that labored and tortured themselves in the practice yard.

"Well, if he's gander for it, I'll hire him on as a squire," Merik said abruptly.

"A squire?" Mkaela was surprised.

"If he's willing," Merik said. "I sent three letters with him explaining the situation to my wife, my head squire, and my head servant. I imagine that some of them won't agree with my decision and I'll lose some, most, maybe all of my staff and squires." He looked down as they walked. "Already lost the two squires that I brought with me to the Prince's Crown Guard." His expression looked bleak for a moment. "Might even lose my wife."

"I didn't know that church knights had squires. I thought they all were, I don't know, monks first," she said.

"Same thing, really," he said. "It's one of the paths to become a Knight of the Church." He threw his hand out derisively. "See? There it is again."

Mkaela looked around. "What is?"

"Sorry. I mean the bureaucracy. It used to be that the knighthood, at its very beginning, was made up of those who would work and fight for the ideals of the Church. Protect the weak, help people to be strong, teach them self-sufficiency." Merik grimaced while shaking his head in denial. "Now it's more about careers, wealth, prestige, factions, and politics. We've lost our way while paying lip service to it."

Mkaela was quiet for a while. She was about to reply when he spoke again. "And then there's the matter with my brothers and sisters. There has not been a violent conflict among the church knights since the division and reformation."

"That was… a long time ago?" Mkaela had not always paid the closest attention to her religious studies. It seemed that many people did not.

"Yes, some eight hundred years ago," he said. "I am hopeful that my brother and sister knights, Arami and Kozain, are in time to warn the rest of the Order." They rounded a corner to a set of arched double doors. "Here we are," Merik said, pulling one of them open.

Inside was a dimly lit room, sunlight slipping through partially closed shutters. Glass window panes held back the wind. The light was supplemented by candelabras spaced throughout the room, casting light over tables with books laid out, pages open to reveal diagrams of the human body. The stone walls, like those of the rest of the palace, were punctuated with arched windows. Above, stout beams supported wooden timbers.

They were not alone in the room. At the center, near the wall with the windows, lay an older man, pale in the light and sleeping. He appeared to be a bit older than Koval, maybe in his fifties, lying on a raised bed and covered up to his shoulders in blankets. Steaming bowls of boiled herbs were placed on a table at the head of the bed. The covers draped over him laid flat where there should have been a right leg. Leaning over him on either side were a young man and an older woman, clearly two physicians, with a few additional assistants loitering behind them. When Mkaela and Merik entered, the two physicians looked up from the patient, presumably General Gundr'ail.

Mkaela knew the man: Master Danfreys. Danfreys was the surgeon that had been on the march with the prince. His manner was crisp, clean, and unfriendly. They had helped each other with the care of all of the wounded soldiers. At first, he had been skeptical of her talents, but after a few demonstrations, accepted them without comment. She had to credit him—he accepted things that worked.

The older woman, definitely older than Koval and their patient, had iron-grey hair kept in a tight bun and wore a grey dress smeared with the stains of her work. Lines of care and labor were etched into her face. Danfreys looked at the older physician, clearly gauging her reaction to Mkaela and Merik's entry.

The senior physician looked from Mkaela, back to Danfreys, then back to Mkaela. "Fine! Why not!" She threw up her hands, stormed to the other side of the room and sat down before irritably beckoning one of her aides for tea. Mkaela looked at her anxiously as she approached the patient's bed, Merik on her other side.

"Don't mind," Danfreys said in a low voice. "She's frustrated and she's known the general for a long time." He licked his lips. *He's also nervous. They talked about me before I got here. I suppose they already argued about trying this... He's stuck his neck out on this*, she realized.

"I'll do what I can," Mkaela said. She pursed her lips. She had actually learned quite a bit from Danfreys and his staff, borrowing some of the techniques for her own applications. For instance, it helped her healing magic—*is it magic? I suppose there's no better word*—very much to know what was the matter with the person before trying to heal their malady. So far, it had been fairly obvious. The person had a stab wound from a spear; close the wound. The person had a cut from a sword; close the cut. Other times, with older wounds, dirt or some filth had worked its way in, complicating treatment. And sometimes knowing which kind of weapon caused the injury meant that it might be deeper than it appeared, and closing the wound's opening would only do so much.

She had been able to figure out some kind of probing technique, which had been critically helpful for breaking Aphra's and Marlar's fevers. *That's something else to deal with.* Mkaela had brought the two orc women along with Aphra and Marlar. The sisters shunned the orc women; meanwhile, the two orc women had nowhere to go and no company. She frequently requested Taram's aid in order to communicate with them beyond hand gestures, and even with his help, the translation was not always smooth.

Reminding herself of the task at hand, she chided herself and returned to the present. "I'm guessing the missing leg is recent. How long has that been?"

"A month and a half or so," Danfreys said. Mkaela puffed her cheeks, exhaling. *That's a long time.*

"Anything else?" she asked.

"Several deep cuts on the body, probably from spears or sword thrusts," Danfreys said. *How did he live through all of that!?* Mkaela could not keep the surprise from her face, but quickly brought it under control.

"Let's start with the leg," she said. They peeled back the blanket. Mkaela's gut turned. She had seen worse wounds, but they were all fresher. This one. The two surgeons had clearly worked on it before. Extra skin had been flapped over the cut and stitched it closed. The skin around the stitches was a mottled mixture of pale white and angry purple. Crusted around it was a red and yellow surface. Purple veins etched away from the wound, up the leg. Mkaela had never smelled anything like it as she wrestled to control her stomach.

She placed both of her hands around the leg and concentrated. A soft green glow emanated; that was the glow from her probing technique. She could feel things, clumps of things, that were not supposed to be there. Her hands traced above the stump and over the knee. "I can get the problem out of the leg, but this part of the leg is dead. I think you'll need to take more off."

"I'll need your help to make sure he doesn't die from

bleeding. Let me know when you're ready to begin," Danfreys said.

"Let me look at the other wounds, first," she said.

The older surgeon, Mistress Kerzin as Mkaela would come to know her, lingered in the corner with a scowl fixed upon her face.

***

In the royal apartments, the Palace of Yvel.

The doors to the apartment opened. Praxia looked up from dabbing tears away from her ten-year-old brother, Larz's cheek, who she was holding tightly on the couch. She brushed aside a silky lock of black hair. Pantaria, her twin sister, sobbed loudly in the next room. Dark rings around Pantaria's eyes, already ever-present from complications with her health, were further exaggerated by her grief. Velthuria, the third eldest, drank her tea in silence, her expression bleak. Normally tall and proud with her red hair free, now she brooded, dark eyes staring far off, and her red hair braided neatly. Beside her, Aered stared at the tabletop.

Despite being the youngest in the room, Larz was not the one taking the news the hardest. Pantaria was usually the one to cry first and hardest. Today, of all days, was no exception. Praxia and Pantaria were the next youngest. They were both sickly pale in their complexion and frail in their health and had their mother's lustrous black hair and dark eyes. Larz, by contrast, had their father's sandy brown hair–or at least, Praxia remembered her oldest brother saying, it used to be brown. Larz sniffled and squeezed Praxia's arm, prompting her to squeeze him back. Above them in age came Aered and Velthuria, with Velthuria being the oldest here.

At least, Velthuria was the oldest present until the door opened. The guards stepped aside and Praxia's two eldest brothers, Arnold and Oswald, walked in. Both were tall, with their father's brown hair and blue eyes. Their faces were grim. Arnold nodded to

Oswald, who ducked into the next room to fetch Pantaria.

When they returned, Arnold spoke grimly. "The people need us. All of us. There is something for each of us to do."

***

A small room in the lower levels of the keep, Palace of Yvel.
Less than one hour later.

"Would you mind?" the Blue-Eyed Man said to the guard.

"Of course, sir." The guard stepped out.

The Blue-Eyed Man turned to the stone table. The late Prince Gerald laid upon the table, his eyes sunken. He had been dead for over a month. The smell of decay was overpowering and the Blue-Eyed Man knew the guard appreciated the chance to take a rest from it. Though the smell had been much worse on the march, the wind had dissipated its potency. Now, in this enclosed space, it concentrated upon the Blue-Eyed Man's nose.

The late prince was dressed in his plate armor with an extra high collared arming jacket underneath the breastplate and gorget, but the Blue-Eyed Man saw the pulled and ripped skin. The skin was taut and tearing from where Danfreys had done his best to stitch the late prince's head back onto his body.

The Blue-Eyed Man sank to his knees beside the altar and laid his hand over a cold gauntlet covering desiccated flesh. He hung his head, staring at where the base of the altar met the stone floor. His shoulders began to shake, then his whole body tensed to cramping as he tried to hold it in.

"We will make them pay, Your Grace. I... why... we will get them, and we will make them pay."

Chapter 23

The Great Hall, Palace of Yvel City, Yvel Principality.
By the Elven Calendar, eighty-first day of Spring, 18030.
By the Human Calendar, Morningday, third week of Aiz, 794.
Afternoon.

" . . . And with this crown, may your thoughts always be clear, Your Grace."

The old man in purple and white ceremonial robes placed the crown upon the prince's head. He bowed and backed away. A collection of assembled nobles and dignitaries clapped. For most, it was a polite clap, but for the few that had been accompanying the prince for the past few months, their clapping was deeper and more energetic, expressing feelings of solidarity and hope.

"You're still skeptical?" Trinien asked in Elvish.

"In his aura persists a strangeness," Tyrnimar replied. Someone to their side shushed them and glared. The two minded themselves for a moment as the newly crowned prince spoke to the assemblage.

The two watched from a platform on the side of the hall, which was raised by two steps and separated from the floor by a railing. It was the area designated for minor nobles, staff, and retainers of nobles important enough to be seated, but not important enough themselves to have earned a seat. The Covendrans certainly were there, less Lady Mariss, who was supervising the continued fortification of Serna. Some of their fellow travelers were also in attendance; besides Trinien and Tyrnimar, Irduin, Holbrin, and Parendien were also present.

"Where is the place for the three young ones?" Tyrnimar whispered to Trinien. "Their viewing of this could help in the choice of theirs, for the choosing of order would be important in my thinking."

"Holbrin has them on something else. Not sure what," Trinien answered quietly, but motioned that Tyrnimar should listen.

They watched the prince take a step forward on the stone dais.

Prince Arnold was a young man, even by human standards. Tyrnimar estimated him to be between twenty-two and twenty-six summers old. The newly-coronated prince wore a clean cape with his house colors, the grey chevron on the red background, over a white doublet, and blue breeches tucked into riding boots with the tops turned down. He had a narrow nose and fair skin like many Marins, but his great height strongly implied an Eklendan heritage. Tall–even for an Eklendan–taller than most of the elves, too. His brown hair and blue eyes could be an indication of either background.

He clasped his hands as he grimaced at the floor for a moment. He seemed to be collecting his thoughts. Tyrnimar concentrated and the colors of his aura appeared. Tyrnimar grimaced. He had studied the now-prince's aura several times and there were many colors of which Tyrnimar did not know the meaning. *Quite perplexing are the qualities here.*

"It is a tragic thing," he began, "that we are gathered for this occasion so soon. A surprise to many of us." He cast his gaze about the room, seeming to engage each and every one in the audience, even in the gallery where Tyrnimar was seated. "We do not have the time to pause and mourn, wish that we could. There are a great many things that we must do. We are beset from the east by things–by monsters!–that many of us never knew existed, thinking that they were creatures of story and legend. The Prince–" Tyrnimar produced a notebook, a tiny vial of ink, and a pen, scribbling a quick note here and there. *Why as if the Prince is another person not there does this prince speak?* "–has made some plans with the various able minds around here, and there will be some necessary changes in this time of need."

Prince Arnold shifted his weight to one hip and held a raised finger to emphasize his words. "First, to fight this great new threat, our army must become large and great. We will form a host of regiments to turn back this tide of green sweeping down upon us." He gestured with his other hand to a man who looked simultaneously at home being a bureaucrat and exhausted of its burdens. "Lord Gunst Ver'ail will hold the office of adjutant, ensuring the administration and provisioning of this army. The soldiers he and the heroic, late Lord Dorvin of Arladran brought to battle are re-contracting as we speak to form the first of these new regiments." Trinien spared an annoyed glance at Tyrnimar's pen scratching on his notebook.

Pointing out Koval Covendran and his able Judane and Dareum. "These will be combined with the militia of Serna, and led by Lord Koval of Covendran to finish this first regiment." Some heads turned to follow the prince's gesture, looking at the Covendrans; some with curiosity, others with distaste. "There will also be a position for a marshal of the army to ensure good orders to fighting units so that they are in the right place, at the right time. What is needed is more soldiers and more leadership." He shifted his weight to the other hip and cast his hand over the assembled nobles and dignitaries. "Your Prince extends this offer: should you have the desire to fight and lead, Your Prince is granting commissions for fighting units."

This brought a scattered murmur from the audience, but quieted as he continued. "This all will bring a greater need, not only for soldiers, but for laborers and crafters of all types; for what army can run without supplies? What army does not need to eat? Move supplies without wagons? What wagons are not made of wood and iron? What general can plan without maps, paper, and ink? What army needs no clothing?" His voice rose over as he listed the various needs of the endeavor. Anxious whispers and glances rose from the crowd.

He waved his hand horizontally to quiet the nervous whispers in the crowd before continuing more calmly. "The list extends on, but this brings about the second change. We will release criminals who are willing to work. This is not only necessary for addressing the matters at hand, but a tradition of goodwill in our proud land, common to many occasions such as this. They will fill any task needed, according to their capability." Tynimar's quick pen noted the release of the prisoners. "We will not release anyone that could threaten this plan, or our overall livelihood. This second change will be on a larger scale than what we have seen in the past when a new prince rises."

Tynimar noted that the prince seemed to brace himself for something. *Opposition, perhaps*. "We call upon cooperation from our friends in the Merchant Council to not only accept these new workers, but expand their industries and to be generous and forgiving in these troubled times." He could see rustling in the crowd. Trinien whispered that those were the members of the Merchant Council, judging by their dress and their lack of house insignia. They had earned seats in the hall, but, knowing merchants, they were unlikely to be generous or forgiving of debts or late payments.

"That brings us to our third and largest change." Prince Arnold paused to take a breath again. Tyrnimar suspected that the new prince was daunted by what came next. "Friends, the third change is the most exciting and the most terrible at the same time. There are certain stories and legends that I must tell you now, without a doubt, that are true to their fantastical nature." Tyrnimar knew what the prince was about to say and could feel Holbrin and Trinien groan internally next to him.

"We have in our very midst, sorcerers–users of magic–" That sent a murmur through the crowd with a few chuckles. "It's true, Your *Prince* tells you!" he emphasized. "Many of you know of the near complete disaster at Borly. One of these sorcerers–a maiden of holy description, I add!–has restored health and ability to General Mot Gundr'ail." Whispers of surprise, skepticism, and anxiety etched through the crowd. "She has done this already, and the good general is resting. Well he should, for he will be the marshal of our new army." Prince Arnold's voice rose over skeptical noises and murmuring from the audience. "Your Prince tells you, friends, if not for these sorcerers, many of our fighting men and women would not have survived the past two months, for lack of their aiding magic. We shall, therefore, have a training grounds for the safe practice of their arts to hone them into effective instruments of war and peace."

The speech went on, but Tyrnimar was still puzzled at the prince's speech pattern and asked Trinien about it. "You did not notice the first time we passed through here?" responded Trinien. When Tyrnimar waved his hand, indicating he had not, Trinien continued. "It is a fashion among some, particular to Yvel and some of the other Gershan cities, to speak about oneself as if oneself was another." Tyrnimar nodded in thought.

After a moment, with the prince continuing his speech in the background to their quiet conversation, he heard Trinien mumble. "Coincidental on their choice of the word 'sorcerer.'" Tyrnimar turned in surprise. Though they spoke in Elvish, the topic was largely forbidden by Holbrin to be discussed near humans. 'Sorcerer' was the word that the elves used to describe practitioners of this particular type of magic–sorcery, or blood magic; the type of magic that was intuitive to a person from their own direct use of magic energies. This was in contrast to wizardry, also known as book magic, being a use of the latent magical energies in the world.

Tyrnimar had tried explaining the difference to others in the past, but had failed to produce suitable analogies. The closest he could come was by explaining the difference between lifting a rock oneself, versus using a lever to lift it, but still, the analogy was lacking. One could only lift a rock by themselves with so much power, whereas the magic of sorcery was stronger than that of wizardry. Lifting a rock with a lever harnessed more power, but was very specific. The rock could only be lifted in certain ways–but book magic, though weaker, was much more versatile and flexible.

Then there were the other forms of magic, such as that through summoning. Sometimes that was called witchcraft, though there were supposedly forms of prayer that had the same effect. Tyrnimar understood Holbrin's reluctance to expose any of the subject to humans, as their ignorance led them to refer to the whole set of practices collectively as 'witchcraft.' And *that* was a whole different matter altogether. *Witchcraft*–

Tyrnimar's internal ponderings were interrupted by Trinien tapping him. Tyrnimar looked up from the floor, where the weight of his thoughts had drawn him. People were filing out of the room whispering in a mixture of excited and skeptical tones about magic, or the gloomy drone of merchants and their impending lost profits.

He joined Trinien outside in the hall. "Where was Eevarel?" he asked.

"That is oddly direct for you." Trinien smirked.

"For her, seeing and hearing this occasion would be wanted by her," Tyrnimar said. "That would be my thought."

"You remember the fire at Serna?" Trinien said. Tyrnimar

nodded. "Well, Eevarel lost a lot of her belongings in that fire, including the two dresses that she had for occasions like these. Same reason she will not be at the banquet this evening."

***

Later in the afternoon.

Tyrnimar hurriedly exited one of the large gates to Yvel. His horse carried him quickly, but he had lost much time getting the precious information that he needed and lost even more time navigating the crowds of the city. Exiting the gate, he urged his horse, Urasen, to a canter, finding the first edge of the forest about three or four miles away. Slowing to a walk, they entered the tree line. It was not long before Tyrnimar had to dismount and lead Urasen by the reins.

He was glad for all the riding and fighting practice that Eevarel had overseen, though he was glad that they had not spent time practicing fighting from horseback. Aside from the difficulty, they would not be able to use their full-length bows, and it would not have been incredibly useful over the past two months. There had only been limited use of cavalry at the last engagement, in what some had come to call the Battle of Serna. Tyrnimar had only studied history in passing, but knew enough that he suspected a more accurate name to be the *First* Battle of Serna.

Reaching an area far enough into the woods with the fading light, he searched until he found the appropriate kinds of plants; ivy and ferns amidst trees of middling age, between forty and eighty summers. Some leaves were not fully out of their buds, and a number of trees were still covered in spring blossoms instead of summer leaves. Glimpsing around one last time to make sure he was not watched or followed, he produced a book from Urasen's saddlebag while uttering an incantation to give a minimal amount of light by which to read.

Turning to the appropriate page, he began tracing runes in the air and whispering. Tyrnimar had not done this before, but quickly contrived of how it *could* be done as soon as he understood the need. The vines leapt to obey his command. He did not tear

298

them from the ground, nor from the branches they gripped. Rather, the vines and fern leaves agreeably let go of where they had been, and joined together to become something wholly different. Weaving the ivy leaves and ferns into a tight fabric, binding them together and separating enough moisture so that they would last, he sealed the new fabric before cutting it into shaped segments.

Joining the segments seamlessly, he finished the first piece. He used the fern stems and ivy vine to form two supplementary pieces; one, a verdant green, using colors from the vines that resisted the change of seasons longer; the other, using browns from a different vine. Tyrnimar was careful to include a cleaning clause in the incantation to remove the dirt, noting that it was a root vine.

Having finished the first piece, he moved on to the second. Casting a withering charm to turn leaves to the colors of autumn more than a season early, he repeated the same process, but recycled some of the moisture removed from the first garment, to reinforce this fabric. If left dry, it would crumble, and crumbling would not do. Once he had sealed it, he began to repeat the same process, but stopped. It would not do to have the same thing simply in a different color. Something had to be different. He considered adjustments, made the necessary changes, and finished the second piece in colors of dark orange, brown, and red, with a third vine accessory piece.

Now was the last part. On his way out, he had hastily bought a copper cup and two leather bags in the market. He knew that he had overpaid, but time was of the essence, and he never had the patience for this so-called 'haggling,' which seemed an entirely unnecessary step. He took one more furtive glance around him before clearing a patch of dirt. It would not do to set the forest aflame. Holbrin would give him no end of grief. As it was, Holbrin would be none too pleased with this, anyways, but no need to do something conspicuous. Really conspicuous. There was no way Holbrin would see this and not know what it was, but it was innocuous enough that it could be passed off as mundane to humans.

He heated the copper cup until it crumpled under its own weight and it hovered in the air, one large globe of liquid metal shining in the faint light. Tyrnimar could feel the heat of it. He drew out two droplets, and formed them into ten thin rings slightly smaller than the diameter of his hand's width. He sharply drew the heat out of them, and then gave some back before dispersing the remaining heat in the air and taking the ten rings to put in his pocket. His whispering continued, drawing the remaining molten metal into mostly equally-sized droplets, with one about twice the size, and one last drop of copper held off to the side. He flattened the droplets into discs, and towards the edge of each formed a hole.

Rethinking his plan, he destroyed two of the smaller discs before forming them into two ends that married together. He used one last piece of vine, turning it into a supple cord, and completed another part of the project. Tucking the last bit of copper into his pocket and folding the other pieces into Urasen's saddlebag, he drew out the leather bags. Reciting a new incantation, he disassembled the leather, recut the leather into new segments, and formed two objects, then traced them with the copper.

Time was running out. He doused his light and made back for the city in a hurry. The sun was completely down now. He raced back to the gate. The guards let him in, but made it clear that, had he dallied longer, they would have shut the gate with him on the outside. Pigeons fluttered out of his way as he made for the palace along cobbled avenues.

Not all of the streets in Yvel were paved in stone, but the main ones, ones that led from the gates to the market or the palace, were. The previous time he had been here, he had been fascinated by the architecture and its vague resemblance to Dwarven architecture, using stone in a very blocky, straightforward kind of way. Most of the buildings along the main avenues were stone, or at least stone on the first floor or two, with clay and wooden timbers finishing the upper floors. Clearly, there had been no attempt to reach an agreement with the stone, and it was all held in place with mortar, clay, and timbers.

Some of the buildings were up to five or even six floors tall. A few were taller. The same tiled roofs from Serna were here. Or rather, the same tiled roofs here, were also in Serna. Tyrnimar navigated the crowd with waning patience. There really was not much time, but at last, he reached the palace, handed Urasen to the helpful stablehands, and carried the saddlebag to the apartments in which the elves had been generously quartered, one for the men and one for the women. Each had their own bedrooms, with a few to spare. The rooms were well-furnished, though most elves found human carpentry to be crude, resorting to nails and glues, though Tyrnimar admitted that there was an incredible skill with its own nuances involved when one did not have the benefit of magic.

He knocked upon a door and was greeted by Bierien. She stared blankly at him standing awkwardly in the hallway.

"May entry be made by me?" he said.

"What are you about?" she asked him.

"That… there are things that must be delivered in order for the appropriate events of the banquet to be made by me," he said.

"Delivered to whom?" she asked.

"To Eevarel," he said, somewhat breathlessly. She gazed at him for a moment longer and stood aside, wordlessly permitting entry.

Bierien indicated towards the hall with the bedrooms, most of which had open doors. Tyrnimar found Eevarel's and knocked. She looked up from oiling her sword. "Tyrnimar! Is it time for tea already? Or did you come for it early since you will be at the banquet?"

"It is imagined by me that yourself will be found at the banquet by you," he said.

"Me? No," she said. "I lost most of my fine clothing in the fire. Remember? You almost lost your books in that, too."

Tyrnimar remembered, but there was nothing for that now. He did not want his friend to be sad. He placed the saddlebags down and opened one and pulled out the first project. The ferns and ivy leaves had formed the fabric of a deep green dress with a long skirt, one panel in the front and two for either side and the back. The bodice was composed of four panels, one for the front and back, and one on each side, with a neckline swooping just under the collarbone. The sleeves were fitted to the elbow and billowing to the wrist. The skirt and bodice were separated by a belt of fine, leafless ivy vines woven together. He produced the first accessory, a circlet and hair bindings of green ivy vines and laid them out on her bed. The supple fabric lay as any fine linen, with a faint shine from the oils trapped in the leaves.

Eevarel's eyes were large in surprise, one hand pressed on the top of her chest, the other covering her mouth. Tyrnimar continued, producing the second piece. Another dress, again with a long skirt. The second dress had an underskirt. The outer skirt was deep orange, the color of the later autumn leaves, and had three panels: one in the back, and two for the sides and front. The underskirt was of similar construction, but of brown. The bodice matched the brown of the underskirt, but had only three panels, one for either side and the back. The front was open with cord made from root vines to lace it closed over an underdress or undershirt. The sleeves were the red of autumn leaves and tight to the wrists, only flaring at the cuffs. This dress had a brown vine cord as a circlet and hair bindings.

Tyrnimar reached into his pocket and pulled out the ten thin copper bracelets, five for each wrist, that would just fit over her hands if she scrunched them, and the necklace of copper discs with a large central disc on a brown vine cord. Lastly, he drew out of the saddlebags two slippers of sturdy brown leather sculpted to the shape of her feet, chased with delicate copper scrollwork.

"Th-this is… for it to be worn by you tonight, so that the banquet may be attended by you. A-and this is… for if a need is had by you in the next season…" Tyrnimar said hesitantly.

Tyrnimar felt nervous for some reason of which he was not sure, but he knew that Eevarel would have liked to see the coronation and the banquet. He hoped that she would at least be able to see the latter. "How did you…. what is this?" she asked after a moment of dead silence. He turned back to look at her and started to repeat himself. He had been strangely nervous to look at her for some odd reason, so he had not. He tried to speak, but before could, Eevarel seized his head in both hands and pressed her face onto his. Lips met lips. The world ceased to exist for Tyrnimar outside of what was immediately happening. For the first time that he could ever remember, he stopped thinking.

"What. Is. This?" Another voice jarred him out of his reverie. Tyrnimar was not sure if it had been seconds or hours. Days even. He was out of breath for some reason.

Never before, he thought. He trembled slightly. "Uh," he tried to explain, but no words came to mind. Eevarel seemed sheepish, something that Tyrnimar had never seen before. *Though, anyone being kissed by her has never before been seen by me, either.* "Uh," Eevarel echoed.

"Splendid," said Bierien. "Tyrnimar, I think you need to get yourself to the men's quartering, do you not agree?" Bierien's tone communicated that she was informing Tyrnimar that he had already agreed.

"Right." He sheepishly trudged out of Eevarel's room. Irduin clapped him on the shoulder on his way out. No, not congratulatory. Her hand stayed on his shoulder. She was escorting him out. The world was a bit of a blur for Tyrnimar right at that moment. He was not sure his feet were even touching the ground with how light he felt. He barely noticed as Irduin marched him into the men's quartering and found Trinien and whispered in his ear. Trinien's eyebrows arched in surprise.

"Tyrnimar... what are you doing?" Trinien asked.

He hesitated. "That is not known."

Irduin began. "But surely it is understood by you what that means."

"It is..." Tyrnimar said.

"But your path is known," Irduin said firmly.

"It is." Tyrnimar was feeling incredibly foolish, but wildly uncertain as to what exactly he had done. He was simply trying to help a friend in a way that he thought she would appreciate. Was he not? It was not he that had... that had... Tyrnimar was having a very difficult time thinking. Was he *actually* trying to...?

Back in Eevarel's room, she stood by her bed, staring down at the two dresses of intricate beauty. She did not notice Bierien peering around the corner. *Ah, Tyrnimar, my good man,* Bierien thought, *ever the instant virtuoso with whatever whim crosses your mind. What could you do with a piece of steel and a forge? What riddle can you answer with that?*

***

At the Elven women's apartment, Palace of Yvel.

"A moment," Holbrin said, "if you please."

"Yes, Holbrin," Eevarel said, not meeting his scrutiny.

"You know the customs."

"I do."

"You know what happens when we return," Holbrin said.

"I do."

"Then what are you doing with him? You know where he comes from. You know what his family expects of him. You know what his order expects of him. *And* what *yours* expects of *you*."

"I do."

"Then what are you doing with him, I ask you?" he said.

"I do not know."

"You should stop. Crush him as it would now, all the more it would when we return."

"I cannot," she said.

"Why?" he asked plaintively.

"I do not know," she said. "I cannot seem to resist him."

"Resist *him!?*" Holbrin's tone was mild to the casual observer, even another elf, but to those who knew him, this was a statement said in shock and perplexity. *He certainly cannot resist you. He never made tea for anyone else or spent so much time in the company of others and then this! I have known Tyrnimar there and again for seventy years and he always preferred the company of his books. Never... never anything like this! Not even remotely like this. And yet, it is you that cannot resist him!?*

Holbrin slowly let out his breath before straightening. *I suppose I cannot change the mind of this young one. It seems that is the way of youth. They wish to learn the hard way.* "Do not come to anyone as if you have not been warned. You really should stop this now. You have only been encouraging him up to this point. But today," Holbrin paused with as close to exasperation as he was willing to express, "I cannot even begin. Do not say that you have not been counseled when we stare at reality in our return home."

Holbrin left the room and met Irduin in the hall. She pursed her lips in thought for a moment. "Have you–"

"Yes, I just spoke to her. She said that she cannot resist him," Holbrin said.

"Resisting *him* cannot be done by *her*!?" Irduin said incredulously, slipping into her native dialect pattern, like Tyrnimar's. Holbrin knew Irduin well enough to clock her surprise, though to most others, her tone seemed as mild as if she was discussing what would be for breakfast.

"I do not pretend to understand. I simply laid out the parade of awaiting consequences. I will try again, but… she seemed rather fixed on it, to my surprise."

"May they be spoken to by myself, as well?" she asked.

"Please do," he said.

***

The Great Hall, Palace of Yvel.
That evening.

The normal court benches had been cleared away to make space for lords and ladies dancing in the center, urged on by fiddlers or recorders. Tables were lined with seating and heaped with feasting of all types: a full hog, roasted Markian-style, stuffed with roasted apricots and tomatoes; catfish from upstream in the River Guth, baked and crusted with herbs; bowls of caramelized turnips, even some dark breads baked in the Berk style. No doubts, those last ones came as a contribution from the Bishop's staff. The din of conversation was overbearing in most parts, and the music filled in the rest.

Turin wove his way through the crowd in the Great Hall of the Yvelian Palace. He was familiar with working in these kinds of events, but it had been quite a while since he had seen one this grand; maybe even be the grandest he had attended. Certainly, with the presence of the Elven contingency, the most exotic.

He spied quite a few of them. They all looked quite regal

and dignified in a strange sort of way. Perhaps it was the elegant, scrolling embroidery of leaves and vines ornamenting their dresses and tunics. Some acted like they were too good to have fun, but others seemed quite comfortable enjoying themselves with everyone else. He spotted a pair, one wearing a peculiar green dress that seemed to have the most detailed print of leaves ever made, with a copper necklace and thin copper bracelets that jingled together every time she moved. Turin's eyes lingered on her for a moment. The dress and the copper went very well with her auburn hair, though it was odd seeing those pointed ears poking out of her hair.

Turin had seen very few elves, and never an ugly one, but this one was proving to be too much of a distraction. She was with another elf, a man. The man looked uncomfortable enough to crawl out of his own skin. He seemed more the type to skip an event like this to stay in his bedroom reading a book. He was even taller than she was–probably one of the tallest people he had ever seen, almost as tall as the prince–the new prince, that is. He had silver hair and wore a tunic of the deepest blue he had ever seen with white–or was it silver?–embroidery at the cuffs. They were rising from their table. The man was looking back longingly at his seat as she pulled him towards the dance floor. Turin let himself linger just a few more seconds on the elf women, but he had things that he needed to accomplish.

He meandered his way past feasters and dancers, into the gallery. This was the other exotic aspect of this particular feast. Commoners. Some of the commoners had been invited to this feast for their brave fighting to the south. In fact, one of them was of particular interest to Turin. He made his way up the stairs to the second floor of the gallery that looked down on the festivities. Smaller tables lined the railing along the gallery on both floors for the rest of the attendees: staff for some of the nobles and lesser retainers, but now soldiers and even common militia.

Here is where Turin found his quarry. Tucked in the back corner of the upper gallery were the people who were uncomfortable in crowds. He saw a few humans, dressed in their holiday best, and, surprisingly, another elf woman. She sat with a human man, both nursing some drinks and picking at their food.

She wore a tunic of red with brown embroidery of vines, but every now and again an embroidered sword or arrow would cross the vines. Some of the elf women downstairs wore tunics and some wore dresses. It seemed to be based on preference.

Past those two were a third and a fourth person: humans, a female and a male. The male looked in his fifties with scraggly, unkempt hair. He spotted Turin right away and moved off, brushing past him. The woman looked a bit younger than him, coming into her forties. Her demeanor was that of someone accustomed to a life spent outdoors in the rain and the cold, though her olive skin was losing its tan with the season. Wrinkles had formed around her eyes, likely from squinting at the elements. One of her locks of hair was turning white, probably from the events of the last three months. Her hair was otherwise black, but glossy, like a raven, and she had a very intense gaze with her dark eyes. She seemed to mimic the elf women that wore tunics, as the vast majority of human women were wearing dresses for this occasion. That, or maybe she did not have a dress and this was all she could scrape up or borrow. He approached, but she had regarded him before he did, sensing his intent. *She's well accustomed to being both the hunter and the prey, it seems.*

"May I join you?"

She looked at him up and down skeptically. "I'm a fair bit older than you, so what are you about?"

There was that gaze again. "I represent a small office in the Prince's government that has need of your specialized skills, Madam Korane."

"My specialized skills?" she said with a sardonic smile. "I think I'm a bit old and lowborn for the Prince."

"Nothing like that." *The first meetings were always the most awkward.* "I understand that you are the master of scouts for the Serna Militia."

"What's your name, young man?" she said, half-patronizing, half-suspicious.

"My name is Garrick," said Turin, and Turin fell to work for the next few hours.

***

Nicholas had watched his own quarry evade Turin. It was not Turin's fault–he had his own task and quarry. Besides, tracking quarry of his own, the man with scraggly hair, was much more recreational, and likely to amount to nothing. His official capacity was supervising his recruiters and agents at this function. Turin did not even know Nicholas, and Nicholas only knew of Turin by his dossier and reports, and glimpses of his work at functions like this. He glanced back to see Turin seated with his target before following his own. Nicholas artfully glided through the crowd, well familiar with fleeting pleasantries to a great many that knew of the chief librarian and extended courtesies fitting to such a minor dignitary.

His quarry navigated the crowd similarly, but in a way that evaded notice, rather than Nicholas' approach of hiding in plain sight and minimizing friction. Most everyone knew of the chief librarian or, at least, imagined that there would be a library and someone in charge of managing it. Most did not notice him, let alone pay him any regard, which was perfectly suitable to both Nicholas' profession and preferences.

His own prey made for the opposite end of the gallery on the lower floor, surrounding himself with more noise and crowd as a blanket, but still on the fringe. It was a fine technique if one was not aware of being prey, yet when Nicholas parted through the last screen of the crowd, the man with scraggly hair waited patiently and looked at Nicholas completely unsurprised. He sat in a chair at a table for two with one ankle crossed over the other knee. He was sipping a glass of wine; plum by the look of it, probably Eklendan, from what Nicholas knew of the prince's cellar.

"May I–" Nicholas began, but the man's hand had beckoned to the other chair, anticipating what Nicholas would say. *Well, let us see about this, then.* "Bellarden," Nicholas said. His company at the table paused. *He was not expecting that.* Nicholas said another name. "Joriss."

"I am not interested," the other man said.

"Master Taram, please, just a bit of your time," Nicholas said with insistence. Taram reluctantly stayed seated as Nicholas continued. "There are many who do not believe you even exist. To think at my excitement when I heard of a man that does not age."

"Look, I left the life behind. I credit you for catching me unawares, but I am but a nameless soldier and I *greatly* prefer it that way. Good evening, sir." Taram rose and departed. Nicholas turned looking after him.

It was enough. *I met the legend. He will not say anything. He can figure at my profession, at least a portion of it, if not the full scope, just by my knowing of him and finding him in the crowd. But he will say nothing. For him to say something would draw questions about how he knows. And he knows that I know that.*

Nicholas passed the rest of the evening enjoyably. He noticed an empty wineglass with an apple core next to it at Turin's table. That was his signal for successful recruitment. Good. It would be very helpful to have an independent scout. In time, her skills and uses would expand with the appropriate handling. He spotted several other signals from his other agents, reporting successes and some failures. From a servant, Nicholas also receives an unhappy note from the prince, directing him to assemble a war council tonight after the ball. *He really should have Dorrels do this instead of relying on the chief librarian*, Nicholas thought irritably. *He is the chamberlain, after all.*

He sighed internally. *Well, better start finding the cats and putting them in the bag.* Nicholas rose to find the people that he knew would need to be there, starting with Gunst.

Chapter 24

The Council Room, Palace of Yvel City, Yvel Principality.
By the Elven Calendar, eighty-first day of Spring, 18030.
By the Human Calendar, Morningday, third week of Aiz, 794.
Late in the evening, after the ball.

P rince Arnold motioned for the guard to close the door as the last of the attendees entered the council chamber, a room that was normally reserved for interactions between the Merchant and Guild Council and the prince. But this occasion was different.

Most of the prince's family was there. Judane recognized them from the ball, though she had not met any of them. Most of the Merchant and Guild Council members were present, but so too were a collection of other nobles and staff, including Lord Gunst in his new position as adjutant of the army, and, for whatever reason, the Prince's Librarian. Judane looked across the faces. All were still in their formal dress from the celebration, many with tired eyes from already having eaten and drank too much, and the hour being late.

She had met Kovarre, the widow of the late Lord Dorvin Arladran, who had died in the hills with so many others. Kovarre was younger than Dorvin by maybe ten years, Judane guessed; probably in her early thirties. Also present was Dorrels Joledran, the aging chamberlain of the prince, and Melz Belifar, the Bishop of Yvel. Melz was an older man, balding on top, wrapped in robes of purple and white. Erest Ben'ail, one of the merchants on the council, joined them. She had a stern face that seemed accustomed to brokering hard deals; Judane recalled that she had said she dealt mainly in building materials.

Judane's own father and brother were also there, as were most of the elves. She happened to glance at Kovarre and was surprised to see poorly contained contempt and malice straining against her mask of decorum. She followed Kovarre's line of gaze and saw a young man, about Judane's age, maybe a little older, lurking in the background amidst the prince's retinue of Crown

Guard. *Jof*, she thought. *Jof Toliodran*. Judane remembered him from the march. He was one of the company leaders in the Arladran Battalion. She remembered that they had taken very bad losses.

The room would have been amply spacious for a smaller gathering. It was high in the palace, in a large, circular room with a domed ceiling. Large windows with small baskets of herbs on the sills, placed there for scent, overlooked the city and the rest of the palace, but were currently shut and covered by tapestries to keep out the cold wind. The walls were stone, arched in the openings of the windows and doorways. On the far side of the room was a large fireplace, which was welcome with the breeze evading the tapestries and passing through the windows. The floor was polished wood, but was visually dominated by two long tables placed in the center of the room, with a gap between the two to allow one person to be in the center and address all. Six chairs lined each of the two tables, one for each of the guilders and merchants. The prince had his own table and chair at one end of the long tables, with room for an advisor on either side and set back in the space so that one could pass around the prince's table and in between the council members' tables. More seats lined the walls in two additional rows. While all of the chairs were uniformly formed of finely carved wood, the prince's chair alone had a considerably higher back.

No one sat in the chairs, not even the prince, for there were too many people in the room, and to sit would be to miss the event. Someone had laid out a map of Yvel's territory on one of the long council tables. Judane looked it over before the doors closed. It showed Yvel near the center with Borly to the north, and Serna and Keppa to the south, close to the border of Soorin, the bordering Gershan principality. Mernan and Ralang, two more of Yvel's vassal towns were safely tucked to the northwest, towards the Lake Tald. North of Borly was the border of Versingit, another Gershan principality. The map marked a road coming out of Yvel City, streaming to the west towards Vidara, the Gershan principality to the west, with more of Yvel's towns, Garber, Bervale, and Krogen, dotting the road.

"Good of you to all make it, with the late hour and all," the prince began, "but there is much to be done. Many of you know one another, but not all." Prince Arnold began to walk among the crowd and introduced the twelve council members and the various nobles assembled. Judane followed most of the names, but it was late and she was eager for the handsome, tall prince to get to the point. Her skin had started itching and she wanted to go to sleep so that she could be about the 'much to do' the next day.

"As you heard earlier, Lord Gunst is now the adjutant of our growing army. He was absent from this evening's feast because of his new duties. He has re-contracted most of the soldiers in his own battalion and the battalion from House Arladran to our army instead of their original livery. The Prince hereby appoints Lord Koval of House Covendran to be the lead of this new regiment, with no petition necessary." He smiled as he passed through a clique, forcing them to part as he meandered.

"As you may remember, this regiment has four battalions. Two are already at Borly from the start of this. Lord Gunst and his staff are already working on recruiting an additional two battalions for the Yvel Regiment to replace the two at Borly. The battalions at Borly will stay there and form the basis of the Borly Regiment." He stopped by the map and pointed at Yvel City. "Lord Gunst is also working on another battalion, perhaps more than one, that is specifically assigned to defend Yvel, so that the Yvel Regiment may campaign as a whole. In time, the Yvel Regiment will have companies of cavalry and archers and detachments of scouts, as will all regiments." The prince turned towards the cluster of elves with Holbrin at the front and nodded to them. "We have had the benefit of the treasure of knowledge from our Elven friends and from history to better our decisions in constructing this new army."

There were some whispers in the crowd, but not many, as some of these rumors had already traveled amongst them previously. "There are six points on this. First, the Prince would like Lord Koval to choose his own internal leadership, though I anticipate that it would largely come from his wife and children." Judane saw her father shift on his feet uncomfortably as the prince continued. "The second matter is that Borly desperately needs relief, and the Prince directs this regiment to ride for that purpose, accompanied by the Prince, the Crown Guard, our newly acquired healer, and a few other groups and people."

"The third matter is that the Prince will waive the

customary commission donation for any persons wishing to be company and battalion leaders. The Prince shall appoint regiment leaders and assign battalions to them." This brought at first a hush and then a burst of whispers. "Please, good people, please." The prince called for silence. "Though it may seem kind, the Prince shall bear you truth." He sighed plaintively. "As most can see, we do not possess a grand army. The funds you would normally give as a donation for consideration of appointment, you will need to raise your own companies and battalions. Cloth them, arm them, feed them. Your Prince urges each and every one of you to raise fighting men and women and prepare to defend everything that we have."

"And what of our neighbors, Your Grace?" asked someone in the crowd. Judane saw the speaker, a younger man in his twenties. He was short and pudgy, with blond hair and the narrow Markian nose. Judane remembered that he was from the Der'ail family, but could not remember his given name. "What shall they do for this?"

Prince Arnold smiled as he examined the floor before looking up to answer. "A most pertinent question, Lord Bers. Even before our two fine battalions returned from fighting in the south, we had already sent messengers with requests for assistance. However, Your Prince must inform you that they will not help."

"And why is that, Your Grace?" said Bers of House Der'ail.

"Because they would rather see their rival–that would be us–spend itself entirely on an unknown enemy. Their thinking is that, ideally, this new green and blue enemy will exhaust itself in destroying us, so that they can easily defeat it and then annex Yvel." Prince Arnold spread his hands credulously, to show that this should be plain to all. "No doubt they feel that way with our neighbors to the north and south, as well, as we have information that they are all under attack." The prince paused. "And rightfully, if they were to commit their armies to our defense, they would have no means of protecting themselves should the invaders triumph, nor would they be able to defend themselves from the Berks in the north or the Tamarks in the west."

"What of the dwarves to the east, Your Grace?" Bers pressed.

"What of them?" the prince asked. "Do you mean did we ask them for help, or do you mean what are they doing?"

"Either one, Your Grace," said Bers.

"Well, we have no reliable relations with any of the Dwarven crowns, so Your Prince and his advisors cannot say for sure what they are doing, or even have a clear idea of whom to ask. However, since this new threat is coming from–or through–their territory, it is our belief that the dwarves are unable to control it, and may have suffered some of their own defeats." The prince glanced at the map pensively. Just for a moment, Judane felt that he was not acting, and that he was genuinely clueless, hesitant, and curious about the dwarves' situation. Whatever his thoughts were, he shook them off and spoke on. "We also have some information that our neighbors to the north and south are not faring as well as we have in recent days." The prince looked around. "Any other questions?"

"Your Grace," another speaker began. The prince and other council attendees turned to the speaker. Judane flushed as she continued to speak while all eyes turned on her. "You speak of raising a large army to defend ourselves at every corner. How will we feed this army with most people in arms instead of working fields and mills?"

The prince beamed at her for a moment. "You have a very sharp mind, Lady Judane. Supplying an army is absolutely essential to its use and I appreciate you bringing up my fourth point." The prince turned towards the clustered crowd of merchants. "The people of Yvel shall be quite reliant on the charity of the merchants and guilders for their stocks of grain, crops, meats, breads, and all that such, along with the rest of the long list of varied, many things that armies need. *Your Prince*," he emphasized, "extends a great amount of gratitude in advance for your near or complete charity in this matter. The treasury here will soon be exhausted, as will the granaries." The prince paused pensively.

Judane glanced at the merchants and guilders, most of them resentfully scowling. *Misers*, she mentally growled at them. "One more thing on this. Not part of the Prince's original list of things to discuss tonight, but important to know as early as possible. This will toll very heavily on food stores just as we move into harvesting season." His eyes were solemn as they met each reluctant guilder and comfortable noble from the west. "Plan for how many people you leave to harvest and how many you recruit into arms. This winter will be difficult, but the Prince does not believe that this will be over by planting season, and will make the next winter very, very difficult."

Judane detected skepticism in the whispers in the crowd. She started in surprise as her gaze cast about the crowd and stopped on the prince's brother, Prince-Heir Oswald. Oswald wore a smirk and she realized that he had been looking at her since she spoke. As tall as his brother, he gazed at her with deep blue eyes that she could feel across the room and over the crowd.

"Make no mistake," the prince continued, drawing Judane's attention back, "lords and ladies, this will continue through the cold of winter. Your Prince has seen this enemy with his own eyes and they are a hardy bunch, marching down from the mountains that are frozen this time of year."

Hearing the whispers hushing after this admonishment, the prince continued. "My fifth point is that General Mot of Gundr'ail is alive and well, albeit less a leg." This brought about more anxious murmuring in the audience. Judane had heard that General Mot was badly wounded at Borly a month or so ago and was expected to die of his wounds, only for the prince to announce at the ball that Mkaela had saved his life. "He," the prince continued, "will fill the office of Marshal of the Crown. He, along with Lord Ver'ail, will be among the Prince's chief advisors on matters of the army, and will make decisions about the use of the army, particularly deployments and allocations for soldiers, while the Prince is unavailable."

"The sixth point is that the Prince will use one of his own estates as a location for the Crown Sorcerers to train."

"You mean 'witches.'" Bers broke in. The prince turned and gazed at him silently and impassively. Bers began to wilt under the attention as the whole crowd looked on. "… Your Grace," Bers added after an awkward moment.

"Your Prince said 'Crown Sorcerers' and that is what *Your Prince* meant." Prince Arnold rose to his full height and loomed over Bers from across the room. "The Prince understands that there are many beliefs and suspicions of people with abilities like we have not seen in centuries, not since storied times. If we believe those stories, that is, that these people bring evil and misfortune upon all of those around, then we–must–change. The Prince can tell you truly that, if not for these sorcerers, all of House Covendran collected here, their town, the battalions, our Elven friends, the Crown Guard, your *new* Prince, and his beloved brother would all be dead."

"And so, ideally, we can remove the dark cloud that dwells over these people and view their abilities as a blessing instead of a curse." Bers still looked skeptical, and the prince continued. "Of course, some of you have heard that these abilities are still dangerous, and the Prince believes that training will help them sharpen their control over their powers to make them safer and more effective."

The prince finished his announcements, and there was a tense silence in the room as he looked around. "The Prince will listen to your questions but otherwise invites you to see Lord Gunst with your petitions to raise and lead companies and battalions. One more consideration is that we eschew the traditional soldier of Yvel as being only armed with a spear and shield. Our good friends here," the prince said, gesturing to Holbrin and some of the other elves, "have advised us to vary our armaments. Your Prince commends you to seek out their advice in these matters."

Judane spent the next hour, maybe more, watching the pretty prince and Gunst wade through the various lords and ladies that were offering to raise companies and battalions, angling for positions and jockeying for additional incentives. The prince's clerk, Stanis, was madly scribbling in a ledger. Erion, the prince's squire, Sir Aleksan, Sir Garn, and a few other members of the Crown Guard lurked in the background. The whole time, Judane was aware of Oswald's frequent, if not constant glances in her direction.

The prince made very few concessions, but there was one for which she and her family were waiting. It was not until most of the others had left and the prince was rubbing an eye through a yawn. Gunst looked very tired. The Covendrans were not alone; Holbrin and some of the elves also lingered.

The prince gave a quiet smile. "You linger yet, friends. For what purpose?"

Holbrin spoke first. "With your permission, Your Grace, many of us are scholars and are fascinated by your acceptance and use of sorcerers. We would like to study them while they train, if you please."

The prince regarded them, and, for an instant, he seemed much less tired. "The Prince agrees, but would request additional assistance in such a capacity that only one of yours would be allocated to study them at a time."

"That is acceptable, sir. We are glad to lend continued assistance."

"Good. First, please avail yourselves to the various lords and ladies as they raise their own companies. We have spoken several times and I am very interested to see fighting units with the Markian tall bow over the Eklendan shortbow most of us know, in addition to more variations of infantry." The prince nodded hopefully. "As time and opportunity allowed, I remember reading in Berin the Great's writings about the wrath of Elven mounted archers. Presuming that such a thing was practicable, that would also be very helpful to build within this soon-to-be grand-enough army."

"That will not be a problem, Your Grace."

"Second, your assistance will be greatly appreciated in training translators to speak and read Orcish and as many other of those filthy languages, particularly to aid in interrogations… but also to accept their eventual surrender."

Holbrin paused an instant before agreeing. This was the most surprise Judane had seen him express. "I would further recommend sparing a few to learn a few dialects of Goblin, sir."

"Third," the prince continued, "the Prince understands you have a master of metal in your troupe. Her assistance will be invaluable to our smith guild in their soon-to-come mandate to expand production."

"Yes, Your Grace."

"Last, for now, the Prince respectfully requests two of your number to accompany the Crown Guard on its various tours to advise, fight, and train."

"We agree, Your Grace, and we are glad to do so," Holbrin

318

said with a small, but strangely warm smile. *It's almost like he's getting comfortable*, Judane noted.

"Most excellent, friend. Please see to the details with the marshal and the adjutant." The prince turned to Judane, Koval, and Dareum. "Well, friends, what can the Prince do for you?"

"Your Grace," Judane's father began, "we cannot join the Serna Militia Company with the first regiment."

"Oh? Why is that?"

"The militia will not sign contracts to fight away from Serna if they think their home is still at risk," Koval said.

"The Prince and his marshal will see to it that Serna is safe," said the prince. *Still handsome when tired,* thought Judane. She cast a furtive glance at Oswald. *Him, too.*

"Like it was before!?" Dareum broke in. Judane suddenly felt angry with the prince for being so dismissive of their troubles.

"The threat remains and it *will* return," Judane's father said quietly. Judane fought her own fear of more orcs and hobgoblins pouring out of the woods over Serna. They could be doing so even now. Her skin itched hard, but she schooled herself to calm. *How could the Prince be so careless? And how did I not notice that mole on his neck?*

The prince looked taken aback. He blinked at them and adjusted his crown. He looked at Judane. "Lady Judane, surely–"

"Begging your patience, sir, but the concerns stand," she said coldly. For the briefest instant, he looked annoyed and stood up straighter.

"Now look," the prince began in an altogether different tone, "the Prince understands your concern, but that regiment needs leadership."

"Then I will go, Your Grace," said Koval, "but Serna needs that company and it needs leadership, too."

"Fine, then, but it comes at a price," said the prince.

"And that is?" Koval said, an edge to his tone. The prince stared at him in silence until Koval lowered his eyes a bit and added, "Your Grace." *It's very unlikely that the orcs would recover from such a defeat so quickly*, Judane thought suddenly, reasoning herself out of the momentary fear.

"Raise a whole new regiment, two if you can, to guard Serna and Keppa, if need be," said the prince.

"Two!?" Koval said bewilderedly. "What of the Keppans? Both of their thumbs turning brown from being sat on?"

"Two," the prince said flatly, "if you can. No need to be so crass. The Prince is leaning just as hard on the Toliodrans to stand up three regiments, hoping they can scrape together one. Eventually, we need to turn the favor against the enemy and start attacking them if we want to survive with what's ours."

"We don't have those kinds of funds," Koval said, searching the floor for answers.

"In this case, friend, the Crown will provide some funds as it can. Serna has already given much, and served as a warning to the others. The Prince shall also send an additional detachment of sappers."

"I am very appreciative, Your Grace," Koval said, the tension draining from him. Judane saw that Dareum was calming down, as well. Tyrnimar had taken to scribbling notes now, of all times, as Koval and the prince spoke of more details. *I suppose I like the mole, especially right there*, Judane decided as they were about to leave.

***

Later that night.

The Blue-Eyed Man parted the doors to the library. The hour was very late after everyone had left the war council.

"Thanks for waiting, friend," he said to Nicholas.

"It's alright, friend. I had the staff bring up some coffee." Nicholas pointed to a table heaped with books and a steaming pitcher with a waiting cup next to it.

The Blue-Eyed Man poured himself a cup and slouched into an arm chair, crossing his ankles. He smelled the rich flavor of the roasted coffee berries brewed in goat milk before taking a sip.

"Ah," he sighed contentedly. "Now, what's first? The plan. How soon can the groups be ready?"

"A little more than a month," said Nicholas.

"They have the special weapons we discussed?" the Blue-Eyed Man asked.

"Yes, some," Nicholas said. "That is part of the delay. I sent some men back to the battlefield to get some more. We may have to make copies, but it will be a quality job."

"Excellent. Vidara is the first foreign target, as we discussed," the man said.

"And internal?" Nicholas asked.

"Hmm," the Blue-Eyed Man pondered into his coffee, "no specific target. Make it indiscriminate to develop the situation, then we'll use security as an apple."

"I see," said Nicholas. "Does that settle that?"

"I believe it does. How did the recruiting go?" the Blue-Eyed Man asked.

"Well. We have several new assets. A particularly promising one from Serna for deeper scouting."

"Good. I think I know the one you're talking about. That'll work out fine," the Blue-Eyed Man said. *It's coming along nicely. There's still a long way to go and a great deal of risk, but it's coming along nicely.*

"That was a nice speech the Prince made this afternoon," Nicholas said. "All the right signs that he can deny."

"Wasn't it?" the Blue-Eyed Man smirked. "Tonight at the council, Bers did his job well."

"Bers is reliable," Nicholas agreed. "Not always the brightest, but he has no problem being the odd man in a crowd."

"Have you ever spoken with him at all?" the Blue-Eyed Man asked.

"Talk with an asset? No, no, no, don't be ridiculous. That would be very unwise," Nicholas said. He thought for a moment. "Though, I did break my own rule this evening."

The Blue-Eyed Man took note of that. *Oh?* He sat up from

his slouch and looked at Nicholas flatly. Nicholas looked sheepish suddenly. "The ageless man. He's a legend, you know. I had to talk to him."

Are you serious? "Do you realize what you just put in jeopardy...?"

"Worry not, worry not," Nicholas waved dismissively. "He will not say anything because he cannot."

"Because he would reveal his own past?" the Blue-Eyed Man said skeptically.

"Precisely," Nicholas said.

The Blue-Eyed Man gave a wry smile. "It would be best to not take risks that are not needed. We have enough left to uncertainty." The man sipped his coffee for a few moments. "Speaking of uncertainty, the Prince is almost certain that..."

"That what?" asked Nicholas after the Blue-Eyed Man trailed off.

"How does the Bishop's blessing go at coronation?"

"Uh..." Nicholas was perplexed by the odd question. "Let me see." He walked over to one of the tall, packed bookcases and perused the shelves. He passed to the next case, perused more books, then circled back to the second. Finally, after three more passes, he produced a book and paged through it while walking back. "Ah, here it is. 'With this crown, may your thoughts always be clear.'"

"Give it here." the Blue-Eyed Man waited and took the book Nicholas handed to him. "Thanks," he offered, paging through it in silence for a time before snapping it shut. "Do we have Deweter's Chronicle?"

Nicholas hastily paged through a catalog before pointing in the right direction. "Ninth row, fifth shelf."

The Blue-Eyed Man stalked to the case and returned to his cooling coffee with the second volume of *Deweter's Chronicle of the Broken Lands*, albeit a translation from the original Old Paetic. *Have to get around to learning that. Oh, right.* The Blue-Eyed Man produced a piece of paper with a relief of letters rubbing in charcoal. "Here, find out what this means."

Nicholas took the paper. "Old Paetic."

The Blue-Eyed Man sat down and paged through Deweter, reading a paragraph here, skimming a page, skipping ahead a dozen pages. This went on for several minutes before jamming his finger onto a page. "Aha!"

"What do you have?" Nicholas asked, coming over to look. The Blue-Eyed Man showed him where he was pointing and Nicholas scanned it quickly. "You really think so?" The Blue-Eyed Man nodded. "Well, then," Nicholas said appraisingly.

"The Prince will have to get the stone set on a chain," the Blue-Eyed Man said.

"You really, truly think so," Nicholas said.

"Oh, yes. In fact, we may have two or even three more witches on our hands," the Blue-Eyed Man said.

"Who?" Nicholas asked intently.

"The Covendrans, the ones here. Two, or even all three. The Prince was under the impression that Koval and, what's his name, Dareum, tried to influence the Prince." The Blue-Eyed Man tapped the page in Deweter's chronicle.

"Huh," Nicholas said pensively.

"It would also explain, if there's any pattern to it, how easily the Lady Mariss was able to gain support from the Prince–the previous Prince, that is–to such a level," the Blue-Eyed Man said.

"It is a possibility…" Nicholas said. "You don't think all three?"

"Hard to say," the man said. "The two men made an impression on the Prince. Judane seemed uncomfortable the whole time for some reason."

"What do you think about the elves?" Nicholas asked.

"What, with wanting to monitor the sorcerer training? Oh, they're hiding something. It is quite possible that they know much more than they let on. Possibly… hm… they take the whole witches and magic thing with no superstition at all. Why would that be?" The Blue-Eyed Man said.

"I can think of a couple of reasons," Nicholas said.

"Go on," said the Blue-Eyed Man.

"Either, they already knew it was going to happen, or they have the ability themselves. Maybe both," Nicholas said.

"Maybe so. Watch them," the Blue-Eyed Man said.

"I'll put someone on it," Nicholas said and then sighed. "I'll need to recruit again soon, at this rate."

"As much as you need. Now, since there are a few hours before the Prince and company ride to Borly, let's talk about the hobgoblins."

"You also said something about a schism in the Church…
"

Chapter 25

The Great Hall at the Stone of Rykooth, high in the shelter of the Kaskev Mountains.
By the Goblin Calendar, twenty-third day of the Sixth Moon Cycle, 3114.
By the Human Calendar, Weddingday, third week of Aiz, 794.
Sometime in the middle of the night.

"We were able to take some new slaves, Great One," the Borys-Karang said. They stood at the map table in the Great Hall, the firepit, scones, and braziers shedding plenty of light, but also casting severe shadows.

"Any dwarves?" Oygariyet asked. They spoke in Oygariyet's dialect of Goblin.

"No, Great One. They burned all of their manuals and killed themselves while we were storming the fortress. Same as the dwarf settlement here," said the Borys-Karang. He pointed to a drawing showing the Ardaran fortress with several underlevels, a mine, and a Dwarven trading post, deep underground. It was similar in several ways to the Stone of Rykooth, where Oygariyet stood now. "At first sign of us, they started melting everything down and destroyed their equipment. Their laborers jumped to death in a deep hole, and their warriors fought to the last."

Oygariyet sighed. *If only we had a few more like that. I definitely cannot get that from this green filth. Still, they fill a role and better to spend their lives than those of my own.* "What state is the Stone of Ardara in, then?"

"It is mostly intact," the Borys-Karang said. "The Drell did their job well and were able to climb over most of the fortifications and we avoided a long siege. We stormed the core of the fortress after fifteen nights."

Only fifteen nights? I will have to make sure they cannot do this back to us. Oygariyet had an idea. "Bring their tribe leader to me. I wish to honor the Drell with a gift." Oygariyet had another idea. "How many slaves did you take?"

"Almost eight thousand," the Borys-Karang answered.

"Keep half to do with as you see fit. Have your pick. I suggest that you use at least half of them for labor. The rest come here to me." Shifting at the edge of Oygariyet's vision drew his attention for half of a breath. The Borys-Karang had brought an entourage that were waiting obediently at the edge of the room. Like all orcs: tall, strong, armed like warriors, and stupid. Or so it seemed. Oygariyet noted that some in the Borys-Karang's retainers seemed to understand this Goblin dialect. *I must be careful not to underestimate them, as apparently some beyond just this one take the time to learn things.*

"You are generous, Great One," the Borys-Karang said, with just a hint of mockery in his tone. Oygariyet was aware that they both knew that they were just using each other, and could easily turn on each other if it served their needs. But Oygariyet also knew that he was the Borys-Karang's best chance at serving his own interests, just as it was to Oygariyet's own interests to use the Borys-Karang's influence over the other orcs on this side of the Mountains–just as Oygariyet was using the tribes of goblins, orcs, bugbears, and gnolls further away along both sides of the Mountains.

However, the uneasy alliance could only be played so far. Each of the peoples had their own legends, but common to all of them was that long ago, they dwelled in the lowlands, where the winters were less harsh, and hunting and farming easier. It was a time of plenty until they were forced into the Mountains. All of their legends held this in common, though with different heroes and villains. The villains were often humans, elves, and dwarves, but the heroes were always from the people of the legend's origin. More elves were cast as villains in the legends from the tribes on the Invader Side of the Mountains than here. Here, on the Liberator Side of the Mountains, humans were often the enemies, just as dwarves were most often the enemies of the tribes beneath the surface. The leaders of each of these peoples, especially Oygariyet, knew that this could only continue for so long before they turned on one another, for each people had other folktales of the strongest or most clever one of their own people outsmarting all of their neighbors.

"Let us continue," he said to the Borys-Karang. "When will you be ready to take the Place-called-Versingit?"

"The siege begins before the next bright moon. The Borys-Karang is present with your Muydiyet, with her entire host of wolf riders. The Borys-Karang also has a warband of the goblin Talz, the entire host of the Venjeer, the hordes of the Donbat-Karang, and the Ahng-Gorah."

"Good," said Oygariyet, though he worried that the Ahng-Gorah might be too soft for the task. He motioned to another hobgoblin standing along the wall patiently. "This is Maglaban."

Maglaban was tall–taller even than Oygariyet–with the purple-tinged skin of a hobgoblin from the Invader Side of the Mountains. He wore a motley assemblage of overlapping plates on his upper body, ending in a skirt of plates the length of his waist to his thighs. Underneath were thick leather trousers and mail-covered boots. In his hand, he held a helmet decorated with plumes of dark feathers and hair too fine to be that of beast, orc, or hobgoblin–it had to be human or elf. His other hand clutched a glaive, the staff planted on the floor. "He has the Barituul, and he will return to Versingit with you."

The Borys-Karang looked at Oygariyet for a long moment before Oygariyet spoke. "You were going to oversee the siege of the Place-called-Versingit yourself, were you not?" Oygariyet made it clear in his tone what the correct answer was. For too long had the Borys-Karang avoided the blame of failure while soaking the juice of success, enjoying both by his absence. The Place-called-Versingit and the Borys-Karang would share the same fate after the disaster at the places near the Place-called-Yvel that he knew would soon be discussed. Oygariyet knew of some of the failures near the Place-called-Yvel, but wanted to hear it directly from the Borys-Karang to clarify what fault there was, and where it lay. After this, it would be victory of destruction at the Place-called-Versingit and the Borys-Karang would share that same victory or destruction.

"Yes, Great One. As you wish." The Borys-Karang's clever eyes darted to seek a distraction. "There are still some forces attacking a smaller Place-called-Borly. But on the matter of the Place-called-Versingit, the Donbat-Karang has asked to lead that siege, as they are the largest tribe there and putting the largest horde in the field." The Borys-Karang gestured to his entourage. "They have sent a gift."

His entourage parted to reveal an orc woman clad in a very small amount of tightly laced leather. A sword hilt peeked over each of her bare shoulders. Oygariyet had never known any of the orc tribes to allow women to fight or make any name for themselves, but then, the Donbat-Karang were most like hobgoblins among all of the orc tribes. He turned his focus back to his gift. She was the shortest orc that Oygariyet had ever seen, shorter even than Grotis, only rising to his shoulders in her full height, though her body rippled with powerful muscles. Her thick, black hair was bound into a loose tail down her back.

Wordlessly, she strode towards the pit of flame in the center of the hall and drew both of her swords. The blades glistened, freshly oiled. She thrust both blades into the flame and the oil ignited. The hiss of the flames was the only sound in the room. She strode to an empty space on the floor before the dais of Oygariyet's throne, commanding the attention of all, even the other slaves that were otherwise obliged to stare at the floor and was still for an instant before the blades whipped into motion.

Oygariyet had heard of the prized flame dancer slaves of the Flaming Sword, the Donbat-Karang. His eyes followed her as she leaped high into the air, her feet passing her standing height, legs splitting, swords thrust before and behind her parallel to her legs. She landed and the swords danced in graceful arcs around her as she spun. She stopped the spin abruptly, perfectly controlling motion to stillness, then sprang to the side. Blades spun in the air as her airborne body rotated sideways, feet sailing over her head before landing. The flaming blades danced further with dizzying speed before she threw one into the air, tumbling end over end. She whirled the other blade in curving arcs to this side and that before catching the flaming blade by its handle and leaping into the air, this time feet passing in front of her as her body rotated upside down. She landed in a crouch on one knee with the flaming swords spread to either side, her head bowed, tied hair dangling on the floor.

Oygariyet sighed internally. *I cannot refuse this gift. The insult would be too great to the Donbat-Karang. Of course, the Borys-Karang knew I would try to make him responsible for failure, but I have something for him, too.* "I gladly accept this very worthy gift." It *was* a worthy gift. Such a powerful dancer would add significant prestige to himself, and he did like the look of her powerful body. Clearly, she could serve as a bodyguard, though he was unsure of whether or not the Donbat-Karang had actually taught her how to fight with those swords, though the skill in handling both swords as she had would make for a very quick student.

"I have my own gifts prepared for the soon-to-be victors." The Borys-Karang looked at him with veiled suspicion as Oygariyet gestured to his Third. The eager hobgoblin on his staff made for the door to a side chamber and returned carrying a large sack that clattered and led three shivering orcs in tatters. By the looks of them, Oygariyet knew that the Borys-Karang would recognize them as Pev'Baki-Norn. This was the kind of thing that Oygariyet enjoyed: helping others to find honor and contribute, even in their failure.

"I was going to ask you for some details, but I have it from these remnants that there is nothing but failure near the Place-called-Yvel," Oygariyet said. The Borys-Karang made no sound and guarded his facial expression, but Oygariyet could tell that he had tensed. "Now, I can only be angry so far. Some of my scouts found these, and about fifteen others. Some ran off, but we have a few and they told us this much." He frowned. "That, and that the humans were helped by other humans with pointed ears, I think they mean elves. That the humans used magicks of fire and wind, and that the humans continued to fight in numbers that should have already been beaten. So, I can only be so angry that the great Borys-Karang, the All-Consuming Flame, became consumed in flame." The Borys-Karang made no motion or sound and Oygariyet continued.

"I shall help you in four ways. First, the Place-called-Yvel will be dealt with when we have more resources available, with better weapons and more allies. You will provide two hordes–not of your own–and I will provide a host of goblins, a host of hobgoblins, and I shall additionally raise other forces to deal with this threat. This is, of course, in addition to Maglaban assisting your assured victory." Oygariyet gestured with a nod of his head to Maglaban, who nodded back. Maglaban and the Borys-Karang looked across the map table at each other in silent conversation briefly as Oygariyet continued. "To be clear, I grant the honor to the Donbat-Karang, and you are there to make sure that the Donbat-Karang are victorious. Maglaban and his Barituul are there to make sure that *you* are successful," The Borys-Karang's nostrils flared slightly.

"Second, I shall take your Alone tribe, the Grotis. I have need for deeper reconnaissance and all of this will work better than attacking blindly. We have lost the surprise and will face a more determined and organized enemy. One with magicks, so I am told." Oygariyet shook off his internal anxieties. *Surely, if they do have magicks, they are not nearly as powerful as the Leriyet the Great and those gifts and blessings he has bestowed upon us. Perhaps, we are not using them well enough? Should I be taking the field myself instead of overseeing the whole effort?*

"Third, I will take the shame of the Baki-Norn from you. Those that remain of the Pev'Baki-Norn are mine, and I destroy them entirely. I alone will bear the shame of the Pev'Baki-Norn." He tapped his fist on his own chest. "Those that live are without any name at all. And fourth, are these." He gestured towards his Third holding the sack, and the three orcs on their hands and knees on the floor.

He strode towards the first orc, and spoke to it in the dialect common to most of the orcs on the Liberator Side of the Mountains. "You are weak. We cast aside our weaknesses, leaving only the strength. You will leave and never be of any tribe or clan." Oygariyet reached behind him to accept what his Third was offering by the handle: a branding iron with the word 'nameless' cast in it, already hot. He pressed it into the orc on both shoulders, the back, the chest, and the forehead. It whimpered pathetically throughout the process, though Oygariyet did not blame it. This was the best he could do in the situation. Oygariyet had to cast out weakness for others, and this one was serving in the best possible way: by being cast out. Oygariyet moved on to the next orc that was trembling in fear, anticipating the pain of branding, its face on the floor and eyes screwed shut.

Oygariyet handed the branding iron back to his Third

without looking and accepted the next tool. "You are weak," he said in the same dialect. "We eat our weak, and turn weakness into strength." Oygariyet raised his mace high and brought it down, caving in the back of the orc's head in one blow. This would be the evening feast to celebrate the departure of the Borys-Karang and the Barituul for the Place-called-Versingit.

Oygariyet moved to the last orc. "You are weak. We transform our weakness into strength by reminding ourselves of it. You will serve me as a reminder of weakness to be culled. You shall live on in servitude, with no name and no hope of glory." Oygariyet accepted the same branding iron and branded the third orc in the same places. *That is about as charitable as I can be in this situation*, he thought as he left the cowering orcs and reached into the sack.

Oygariyet produced several maces, swords, axes, and long knives from the sack. The maces used orc's skulls as heads, either cast in iron or steel, and were filled with lead or reinforced with strappings. Some used the tusks or sharpened knucklebones as spikes. The hafts of the axes and maces were made from the bones of the orcs, while the handles of the swords and knives were made from the jaws and ribs. Save for a small knife he handed to Maglaban, as he was the least risk of failure, he gave the rest to the Borys-Karang, who foisted them onto one of his entourage.

"Take one for yourself and provide the rest to the leaders of the other clans. Through casting out our weakness, eating our weakness, and remembering our weakness, we can transform what is weak into another chance for strength." He gestured towards the three forms, two cowering forms and one lifeless, then towards the weapons he had given to the Borys-Karang. In Oygariyet's own culture, that of hobgoblins, this was a show of great kindness, finding chance after chance to be strong and give to later glory. But Oygariyet knew this kind of gesture was not mirrored in Orcish culture, and only minorly so among goblins. The Borys-Karang understood Oygariyet's other message: *I am running out of patience with your failures. This is not some game to dispose of your rivals and internal threats.*

"Now, that is done," Oygariyet started, changing the subject. "Pick two hordes to begin preparing to move on from the

Place-called-Ardara. The next move after the Place-called-Versingit will be the Place-called-Soorin."

"Yes, Great One," the Borys-Karang granted.

Oygariyet dismissed the Borys-Karang and his entourage and received Murchian, a gnollish tribe leader. Murchian was an odd one, but then, Oygariyet and many others found the tall dog-people odd as an entirety. They mostly stood several heads taller than Oygariyet, with straw-colored fur and black spots, and their faces, like dogs, ended in black-nosed snouts under black eyes. As their tribes bore no name, similarly to orcs they would say they were in the tribe of their leader, but unlike the orcs, none of them considered themselves to be of the same name. Some of them took names for themselves, but Oygariyet was uncertain of the circumstances as to when one would take a name, and why another would not earn one.

As there was no pretense, Murchian and Oygariyet were a bit more comfortable with each other and, for the time being, had no maneuvering between them. Their relationship was that of a clear hierarchy. Murchian, in his own right, was a leader in his own tribe and among the others which he was able to bring in line. The gnoll briefed Oygariyet over his efforts to conquer the human lands on the Invader Side of the Mountains. For the time being, it was the lands to the right in the large human Place-called-Gilliam. They had agreed on this place, because the elves were further away, and agreed that it would be an easier target.

Murchian explained their initial success, citing one of the reasons as that the confused human defenders seemed to be not cooperating with each other for some reason. Oygariyet could understand this easily–some of his own hobgoblin tribes and their hosts did not want to cooperate at first. Some had even left the area in frustration or outrage. Oygariyet clearly saw that orc tribes would not cooperate unless a stronger tribe leader compelled a weaker one to do so, and they often had trouble enough cooperating inside their own tribe. Why would it be a surprise that humans have the same problems?

Oygariyet listened as Murchian continued to describe the other peoples their armies had encountered. Small people, looking like human children at full-grown height, but with slightly pointed ears that were similar to those of an elf, but smaller and a bit rounder. Murchian said they were called 'halflings.' Murchian described another people that lived near the sea in the lands at the rivermouths and swamps. They commonly had green skin, like orcs, with the heads of lizards. They walked upright, spoke a language of their own, used tools, and seemed otherwise like just another people to be conquered, expelled, or exterminated.

Murchian departed with glad words exchanged in anticipation of the evening's feast, which would also celebrate his departure for glory, as well as the decision about the Place-called-Versingit and the magnificent gift from the Donbat-Karang, and honoring Maglaban. Oygariyet was tired and wanted to pass some time with his slaves. *The human one is incredibly uncooperative*, he internally grumbled. *Nice to look at but more of a chore to use. It is a shame that humans had no customs to understand the honor of serving a great one. At least these particular humans do not have those customs. Perhaps others do*, he mused.

He beckoned to his First. "When the slaves arrive from the Borys-Karang–the ones from the Place-called Ardara–find any of them that speak Orcish or Goblin."

"What is your plan, Great One?" his Fourth asked. The Fourth showed some promise. Always full of questions, but not when haste was needed. She had a curious mind, but the wisdom to know when it was time to act.

"To give them a choice," he said.

"What kind of choice?" she asked.

"They can be slaves, which is otherwise their fate. Or they can fight. Some of them may serve as spies," he said.

"Spies?"

"Yes… we are starved for information about our enemies. Some may assist in other ways; opening gates during a siege, killing a guard at the right time, things of that type."

"How can you be sure they will not just flee back to their own?" she asked.

"I will think of something," he said with a twinkle in his eye. Oygariyet enjoyed challenges of compliance. Usually.

"That was a beautiful ceremony, Great One," Indariyet said.

He smiled kindly at her. "Thank you. I hoped you would all enjoy it. It is refreshing to see weakness drain away and be made anew into strength and potential." There was a cheer from his Second, and the fists of his First and Third cheerfully pounded the table. Oygariyet took joy in helping those who had failed to realize new potential. But then, if there were enough failures, even among the orcs, he would run out of orcs to send, and he would be forced to send more hobgoblins, who were much more limited in number. A similar threat was that once they realized too much success in the lowlands, the alliance would fail. Each tribe would turn on one another and attempt to take as much for themselves as they could. The greatest threat was from the orcs, particularly the Borys-Karang. If there was one thing that an orc would fight before a human or hobgoblin, or even an elf, it was orcs from another clan, and there was one place where he could get a lot more.

"Has anyone been to the Place-called-Ikria?" he asked.

"I have, Great One," Maglaban answered.

"I will need their numbers," he said.

"Then you will have to go and get them," Maglaban replied. Oygariyet looked up from the map at which he found himself staring, but there was no disrespect conveyed in Maglaban's face or stance. He was just stating what he saw as fact.

"Explain that," Oygariyet said.

"They only respond to the most perverse forms of strength, Great One. Each of the tribes there are comfortable where they are. In some ways, they have settled into activities like ourselves. They farm mushrooms and livestock, they hold games, but they do not move one finger for one another unless made to do so. They are still themselves, after all. You would have to go to each tribe there, kill their leader, and take their name. Then, they will fight for you and stay loyal, so long as you show strength."

That will take a lot of time, Oygariyet lamented. *A lot of time where my attention is needed here. But I cannot send another in my name, I must do it myself. To send another would be to invite a rival.* "Very well," Oygariyet sighed, "I suppose I shall depart in my own glory soon, as well. Indariyet."

"Yes, Great One," she answered.

"We need a warband of wolf riders," he said, "and send a few fists of goblins to help the Talz to reinforce the Borys-Karang at the smaller Place-called-Borly. You may name one of yours to oversee those green-skinned fodder. I will provide a blessing gift."

She hesitated. "As you wish, Great One." Indariyet had a very competent staff. One she was loath to lose. Oygariyet had given a number of his staff three or four times over since the Great Leriyet appeared before them. They had all gone on to lead their own hosts or green hordes that Oygariyet constituted and heap glory upon their own names, rather than on Oygariyet's own. He appreciated Indariyet's techniques of carefully selecting her staff from among the strongest warband leaders, and providing them with ample experience before setting them to meet the challenge of leading a fist or a host, but it was an approach Oygariyet could not afford. He could not be everywhere and see to everything. There were too many moving pieces. Wolves needed raising and training. Recruiting more tribes was never-ending, as was training new warriors... not to mention matters of supply.

Oygariyet gave a silent thanks to Garsiyet and Jolaban at Kogylar, and even Bindeyet and his goblin tribe there. Food and supplies would have run out some time ago without their efforts. This was not even considering the attacks of multiple areas on both sides of the Mountains. Oygariyet could not rely on the leadership of the tribes alone, particularly that of the orcs, and many times had been forced to send his own trusted representatives with their own names to ensure success. But Oygariyet was running out of options for the time being. He needed Indariyet to give up one of her precious staff for this. The staff he had now was too young for the task of leadership, and the challenges would be too great for them, as it had been for Dariyet. Even the Fourth and her inquisitive mind needed more time and experience. *At least Dariyet died well*, Oygariyet thought.

"I know it is becoming difficult. Expand as you see fit. Do not hesitate to take from the tribes that did not join."

"Yes, Great One," Indariyet said. She sat by the map table and stared in contemplation at the clan markers.

"First," Oygariyet called.

"Yes, Great One," he said eagerly.

"I need you to recruit a tribe of ogres,"

He also hesitated. "Yes, Great One."

"Do it, and you may take a name and be their great one," Oygariyet said.

The First's breath caught. "Yes, Great One!" His eyes were bright and filled with anticipation. *Great risk, great reward*, Oygariyet thought. He did not have the experience to lead, but he could talk very well and was one of the few that knew their language. Oygariyet grumbled at the limitations of his circumstances. With uncommon troops like ogres, the requirement of the language often drove who he had to pick, and Indariyet had no one that spoke Ogre of any dialect. The First had a chance of success. Fortunately, with ogres, they really needed more of a messenger than a leader and the First could handle that. The ogres would fight like the Baki-Norn, but with more strength and vigor to make up for their lack of caution or subtlety. *About as dumb, too*.

"About the Grotis tribe, Great One, how can you be sure it will not take work for the humans?" the Fourth asked again.

"For the humans!?" he said incredulously. "What human would even speak to an orc right now?"

***

Nearby, in the harem chamber at the Stone of Rykooth.

She awoke to a clatter, but she did not open her eyes. Either it was the food tray being taken away, or a new one being left. If there was a threat, she would know by the sound of the cage door unlatching. She could see the glare of sunlight through her eyelids and knew that if she opened her eyes, she would see everything that she knew would be there and did not want to see, or she would see someone that was a threat and that she did not want to see.

She hated them. Hated them all. There was the blue-skinned man that seemed to own everything here, as well as an assortment of other blue-skinned people, mostly about the height of other people. Some were the height of children but seemed fully grown in their bodies, both men and women. Some carried even smaller, tiny, blue- or purple-skinned babies, impossibly small, yet still hideous to her.

She had never seen the likes of any of this. They all had strange hair. Black, brown, grey, and tawny were the most familiar looking, but they also had bizarre shades of red, orange, purple, and blue. Many of them had earrings or rings pierced through their nose or eyebrow… or elsewhere. Some had drawings on their body in ink that never washed away. There was a red-skinned woman that usually had a sour expression on her face. *Maybe she hates it here, too.* The red-skin got rings pierced on her yesterday and not in the ears.

There were others, more blue- or purple-skinned men or women that did not share his bed, and the occasional hulking greenskin ones, like those that took her from the mundane life for which she now pined. Every now and again she would hear monstrous barking nearby, like that of giant dogs.

If she opened her eyes, she might see one of any of those that made the tin plate clatter. If she opened her eyes, she would see the stone floor, walls, and ceiling of her cell that adjoined some kind of large bed chamber. Her cage and a few others were against the wall. The room was strewn with large pillows and cushions where most of the other women lounged and laughed. She could smell the place well enough to know what was happening. When the owner was away, the other women would eat, rub tallow on their skin to make it soft, draw designs on each other, or use strange paints on their nails.

She would watch the one that owned everything enter the room, retiring for the day or taking leisure time with blue- and purple-skinned women. At least once a day, they would try to force her to participate. It was a ritual they went through, at this point. She would kick and scream as they pulled her out of the cage. She would resist and slap and kick and bite and spit, and she would do the same thing the next day. The other women would sometimes try to talk to her in their own filthy language. She could tell by their tone they did not like her and were all too happy to see her get beaten.

"What is your name?" She heard a voice. She almost missed the words, thinking it must have been a dream, but she realized that she had actually heard words aloud. She had not seen, let alone heard the human man that she was brought here with in months. The words were in Eklendan, though uttered with a noticeably strange accent. Her eyes fluttered open. She was only a bit surprised. It was a greenskin wearing hardened leathers reinforced with studs of steel. He had a long knife at his belt and an unstrung hunting bow. She looked at it–him, she supposed–unsure of what to say.

"Is this the wrong language?" it–he asked.

"No. I know it," she said. It had been... a long time since she had spoken. At least, since she had said anything in a conversation. She had screamed curses and insults until she ran out of breath before she realized it made her too tired to resist.

"Then what is your name?" he asked. She... she had to think for a long moment, trying to remember her name.

"Selonikah," she said.

"You are from the Place-called-Serna," he said.

"Yes," said Selonikah.

"I am curious," he said, "why do you do the same thing every day?"

"What choice do I have?" she accused, suddenly angry.

"You have every choice," he said matter-of-factly.

"What are you talking about?" she said.

"Do you want to stay here?" he asked.

"Of course not! I hate this place and every one of you in it," she spat.

"Fine," he said, sighing in annoyance at her hostility. "Then, why do you not do something about it?"

She gestured angrily. "Because I'm in a cage!"

"So? You could try to learn the language so you can hear what they say and gather information. You could use the times that they take you out to learn about the place. If you cooperate with

338

them a bit, you can volunteer to be a bodyguard and learn to fight. You can make choices. You could even choose to stay and enjoy the honor that they try to bestow you, if you wanted."

"What!?" she said, shocked. The other things made sense, but choosing to stay? That was a revolting thought.

"All I say to you is that you have choices. You have answered my question, though," he said.

"I did?" She was surprised.

"Yes. You do the same thing because you did not know you could choose to do differently. I am curious still, but will come back later."

"Why?"

"I told you. Because I am curious," he said. "You do not listen well." He turned to go.

"Wait! Can… Can I ask you? I was brought here with another man, a human, from my town. Have you seen him? Is he… alive?" Selonikah asked.

He half turned to her. "He is with Indariyet. He is her favorite, but that may or may not be a good thing for him. Do you know his name?"

"N–No. I never got a look at him, so I don't know who was taken with me," she said.

He shrugged and turned again to walk toward the door.

"What's your name?" she called after him.

He was already at the door. "Grotis."

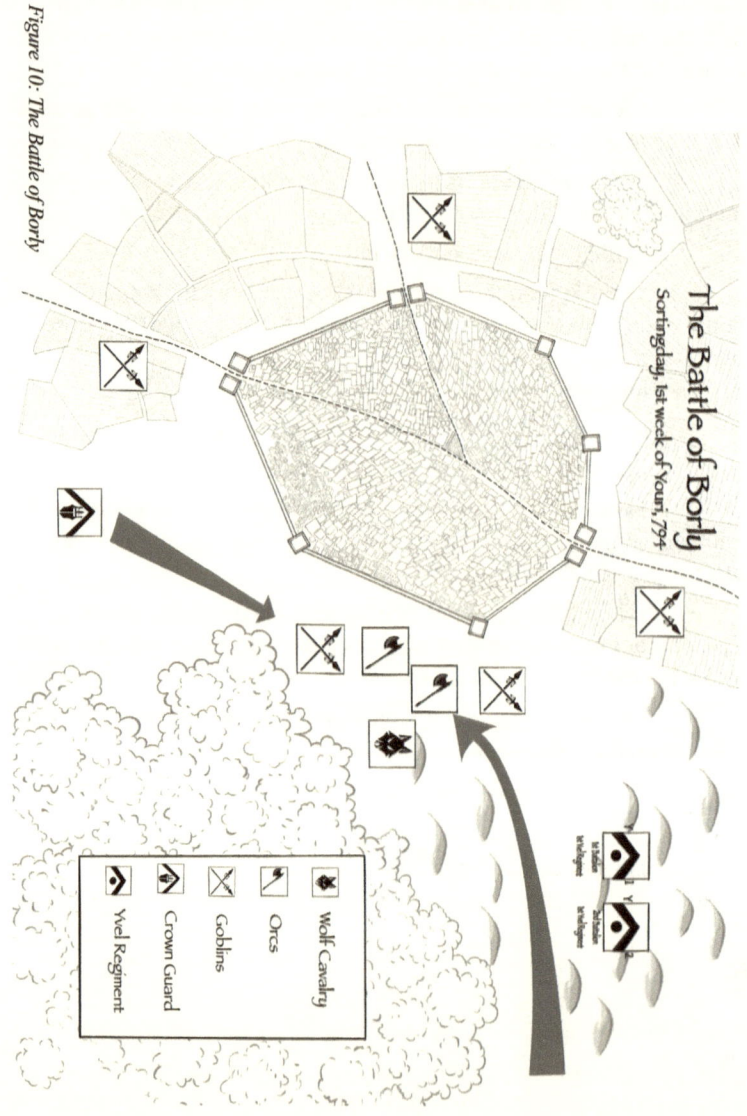

Figure 10: The Battle of Borly

Chapter 26

Near Borly, Yvel Principality.
By the Elven Calendar, sixth day of Summer, 18031.
By the Goblin Calendar, early in the Seventh Moon Cycle, 3114.
By the Human Calendar, Sortingday, first week of Youri (fourth month of
the year), 794.
An early summer afternoon, raining.
Almost two weeks later.

"The scouts report the enemy in two hours' march, sir. They're besieging Borly, but Borly stands," said Koval.

"What engines do they have? What's their composition?" Prince Arnold demanded.

"Three stone throwers and two siege crossbows. It looks like they are building more. The enemy has about three hundred orcs and six hundred blueskins," Koval said, "but the blueskins are about half the size. The scouts say they're 'goblins.' The siege is from the east with pockets of enemy surrounding the town. Borly has three gates: the southeast, east, and northwest."

"Goblins? Instead of hobgoblins? Any cavalry?"

"A little. Looks to be about a hundred wolf riders. They're not in use right now."

The prince was quiet for a moment. "That's a good scout you brought with you. Would the Prince be too forward to hire him away from you? What's his name?"

"Most of them are from the regiment, sir, except for one militia and one of the elves," Koval said. "I'm sure the regimentals would be honored to sign on as the Prince's personal scouts. This particular militiaman and elf seem inseparable."

"Indeed," the prince mused. "Well, fine, they all deserve a commendation after this one."

"Very good, sir," Koval said, running a hand through his salt-and-pepper hair.

"Right, then, gather the battalion and company leaders,"

Prince Arnold said to Koval before calling to Sir Harl. "Harl! Draw a map of the area around Borly. Talk to Koval for details."

Over the next half hour, Koval, Sir Harl, and his squires–two women, Chariss and Yander, and a man, Deni–fussed with Erion, the Prince's own squire, Sir Aleksan, and Stanis, over a cleared off patch of dirt. Together they sketched a crude estimation of Borly and the surrounding fields of the enemy from a birdseye view. The regimental leadership assembled on the prince's red banner with a grey chevron, the Yvel Regiment's red banner with the same chevron and a single grey dot underneath it, denoting the First Regiment of Yvel's new army, and Koval's own banner of House Covendran, a blue and white checkered banner. The banners marked the prince's location where Koval, Harl, the squires and the prince's staff toiled in the mud.

"Make sure to add the hills there and the woods," the prince said, cajoling Sir Harl and his squire as they labored over the creation of an annoyingly accurate 'approximation' of the terrain.

"Is this suitable, sir?" Sir Harl asked, containing his irritation at being lorded over while drawing pictures in dirt.

"It'll do, Harl. Your Prince thanks you," said the prince.

"Very good, sir," grumbled Harl.

"Right, then," began the prince. "Koval, take the regiment around to the east behind them; use this route through the wood to conceal yourself."

"That will take five hours' march, sir, and the soldiers are good right exhausted from being on the march for the last three weeks," Koval said.

"Don't forget the rain over the last two days," the prince added with an exasperatingly cheerful smile.

"And the rain, sir, with the wind, has really taken a toll on the soldiers," Koval continued.

"Right, that's why you have until sunset to do it. And thank the rain for keeping the dust from announcing our arrival," the prince said matter-of-factly.

Koval stared in disbelief. "That's barely two hours away."

"Yes, and you will do it," said the prince.

"Sir, we can't just keep pushing–" Koval began.

"Yes, we can. And we must, so we will," the prince forcefully replied.

"Now look here, these soldiers are going to drop dead from exhaustion just laying sight on the enemy," Koval began. Harl felt the hair on the back of his neck rise at the alarmed tone of Koval's words. Harl had met Koval only three months before, but knew enough to recognize that if Koval was concerned, then everyone should be scared.

But the prince simply gave him a mildly amused smile. "Sunset will be the signal for the Prince and his Crown Guard to charge the siege works from the south. We shall scatter them into chaos with surprise. Just as they begin to mount a coherent defense and counterattack, you will be bringing the regiment over the hill here," he said, pointing to the western most hill on the dirt sketch, "and fall upon their flank. This will bring the most forces to bear upon the enemy at roughly the same time."

Koval glowered at the prince and Harl's level of anxiety dropped. He took a surprising amount of comfort in the prince's explanation of the plan, and decided that the dirt sketch had been helpful.

"We will be quickly outnumbered, Your Grace, once they figure out that there are more of them than us," Koval said quietly.

"Fear not, good man," the prince said with mocking drama. "Surprise and fear are on our side." He cast his hand before him in exaggerated dramatics. "Once we break the main siege camp, mop up the perimeter siege parties by breaking into two battalions, one to the north and one to the south. The Prince and the Crown Guard will pursue any coherent units in retreat and then turn on to mop up individuals." The prince had pointed to the various parts of the dirt sketch describing his own actions during his explanation, and finished in a dismissive wave. Actions that Harl would be part of.

"I would like to move with the spears, brother," Princess-Heir Velthuria said to Prince Arnold. Harl realized that it was a request.

"Can you keep up?" the prince asked.

"That I can," she said and he nodded in approval. "You are

not the only one out for vengeance."

Arnold looked at her grimly. "Indeed. Fight well, sister."

Koval departed and made to hurriedly prepare his own units. Harl could hear the arguments between Koval and his companies and battalion leaders. Harl knew a few of them. They had all been hastily picked by Koval and Gunst, though Koval hardly knew any of them. *That's the way it is with country nobles, though. They don't know any of the right people when they need them. On the other hand, being country nobles, they don't have to put up with the wrong people that stay in the city.*

The rain picked up again. Not heavy, but precipitous enough to remind everyone that they were miserably cold despite the season and sick of being rained on. Thankfully, it would be enough to muffle the sounds of Koval's regiment until it was too late for the enemy.

Harl and his squires prepared to ride with the prince. Harl had brought three squires, Deni Oilaravan, Chariss Ordavan, and Yander Reskladran. All young and promising, all well-bred from Gershan-Eklendan families in southern Yvel and Soorin. Yet, Harl could tell that this was nothing that they or their families had bargained for. This was supposed to be a political move for each of them, and no more dangerous than a competition or the occasional border dispute with a neighboring prince or princess; not a war for survival. *Not that it'd be much safer if they were back with their families*, Harl observed.

Harl had heard from a messenger a few days ago that Ardara had fallen to the orcs and some other vermin, and the invaders were now moving into eastern Soorin. Harl had several cousins and siblings by marriage in Eklenda, and guessed that this invasion didn't follow the neat lines that happened to be borders for humans. He grumbled a bit that the orcs could not even follow civilized rules like informing someone you were going to attack them before doing so, and imagined that they did not really even understand the idea of borders.

Yander strapped Harl's Daearan warsword to Harl's saddle. Chariss held his lance nearby. Harl hated lances, but it was necessary for what they were about to do. Harl thanked her with a pat on the shoulder and wordlessly gestured for her to prepare her own kit. The squires would earn their own sets of plate upon reaching knighthood. Each being more Eklendan-blooded than any other and having no relations in Daeara like Harl did himself, they favored the Eklendan disposition of compromising moderation between armor and mobility.

Like the other two squires, Chariss had a suit of fine mail, a lance, and a bevy of axes, maces, and swords. She had taken to using a hunting bow from the saddle and had been practicing with it, citing her readings of the Mardalons of the east fighting in that manner. Harl had been absently looking at the bow when he saw the four elves riding with them in the background making their own preparations. He looked on to their preparations. He thought he recognized Irduin, but was not sure of the names of the other three. They were all wearing very light armor of reinforced leather and gambesons under shirts of mail. Their bows unstrung and stored, they each armed themselves with shields and an arming sword or riding spear.

Harl had been told by one of the other elves–Holbrin or Trinien, or maybe it was Irduin?–he could not remember; they all sounded the same with their calm voices of a frozen stream–that these three were very young, for elves, that is, and had not yet, as they put it, 'chosen the path of their life.' They all looked the same, at least in terms of age. Irduin had a demeanor that gave the impression that she had been a professional soldier for a very long time, but there was nothing in her appearance that made her seem older or the others seem any younger. *Awful problem to have*, Harl grumbled. *No aches or pains, either, I wager. How can they really enjoy life without any of that, hm?* He wondered what they really thought of all of this. *They act like nothing bothers them. Was that really so? If it was, then why were they helping?*

Harl shook himself and reminded himself that he still had other duties. He left his squires to finish their preparations and he moved around the rest of the Crown Guard and others that had attached themselves to the prince's retinue, whether tethered by loyalty or other motive.

Harl's thoughts were interrupted by a shadow abruptly casting on him. He looked around to see the prince astride his mount, trailed by Sir Aleksan, Erion, and a pair of additional squires he had picked up in Yvel…though one of those was not exactly a squire, but was one of company leaders from Dorvin Arladran's battalion before it was remade into Koval's regiment. Jof was his name, Harl thought. Jof of the Toliodran clan. Harl recognized one of the prince's younger brothers, Aered, as the other squire. The prince looked at Harl with an expectant expression. Harl did not say anything immediately, turning to face them.

Jof spoke first. "The Prince wishes to be underway now. It is nearly sunset." He spoke snappishly, like he was wearing the prince's rank a bit.

"Right, then, sir," Harl said, turning.

"Do not speak to Your Prince in this way," Jof snapped. Harl had a feeling of where Jof was. His unit was mostly destroyed and then he himself was taken from his post. He was looking for a new purpose and was eager to prove. Harl could tell Prince Arnold understood the same from the prince lifting a hand to ease hostilities.

"At once, Your Grace," Harl said. Harl turned and stalked the ranks of the Crown Guard, "Alright you slugs, time to move!" He moved about, cajoling everyone onto their saddles before placing himself on his own a minute later. Chariss handed him his lance, which he raised while motioning the Crown Guard and its Elven companions forward at a trot before moving into a canter. They moved in silence in the fading light, muted through the cloud casting light rain on them, alternating between a trot and canter depending on the slope of the road.

Cresting a small rise at a trot, Harl could see Borly in the distance and the main siege camp a few hundred paces off. He had been to Borly several times and knew the walls to be of stout stone, but only the height of two men. The orc's siege engines were hurling stones and great spears of bolts from the siege crossbows towards the short walls of Borly. While the wall's height was more than enough to keep out bandits and ambitious petty nobles from Versingit with their small raiding parties, it was not up to the task of repelling a protracted siege. *Thank Orneth and Saint Graffin they even lasted this long*. In the distance, he could make out where the wall was crumbling, the gap filled by rubble, loose stone, overturned wagons and carts. He could see skirmishers creeping around wreckage and the remains of the buildings outside the walls to shoot arrows at the defenders. The mass of besiegers lay before him in those few hundred paces. Green and taller or blue and shorter, for the most part. Wolves were loitering in the rear of the siege camp, away from Borly.

And it was time.

He raised his lance again and the Crown Guard quickened from a trot to a canter to a gallop, hurling mud in their wake. Harl was nervous about this part. While each knight in the Crown Guard could fight with a lance, even himself, although he detested it, they had hardly ever trained to charge as a unit. They had been a relatively small assemblage, tacitly accepting new members and temporary members such as the squires and Elven riders, with whom they had never trained, bringing their number from forty-eight just a few months ago to a hundred and thirty-six. *No time to worry about that now!*

The ground thundered beneath the horses and the air echoed with the shouts of their riders urging them on. Rain had concealed their arrival from the besiegers up to this point, and their sudden arrival achieved what Harl thought was the prince's intended effect–fear, panic, and chaos erupted as the Crown Guard poured down the gentle hill. Short, blue-skinned besiegers in hardened leather armor and the taller orcs abandoned siege crossbows and stone hurlers to flee in all directions. The charge broke through a thin line of skirmishers that had been moving up for another spar with the defenders and were caught in the middle by the charge.

Harl caught one orc through the eye slot of his steel helmet. His lancetip embedded wetly and then broke a few handwidths away from the tip. *Stupid lance.* This was why he hated lances. You could not rely on them past the charge. Throwing the broken shaft aside, he drew his hand axe. The charge broke up and waded through the blue and green mass of panic, amidst rudimentary tentage and cookfires. Harl rode down three orcs, his squires keeping with him, but missed the swings on two of them as he rode by. He swung by a short blueskin and missed again, hissing in irritation. He found another blueskin and rode it down, but missed that one. *This is stupid.* He kicked his horse to canter over towards a mass of panicked blue flesh and dismounted roughly, snatching his Daearan warsword from the scabbard on the saddle, the horse stumbling over his shift in weight with his heavy Daearan plate.

This was where Harl preferred to fight. He hefted and swung his sword in both hands cleaving through fleeing blueskins. He chuckled lightly. A group of six of them turned on him. They seemed to think they could bring him down. Maybe they were right, maybe not. Two were down in one swing as they foolishly rushed him, after which the remaining four were more cautious. They circled him.

Harl grinned. The other three closed in on him from the sides and behind as he rushed the fourth. It backpedaled and stumbled, screeching as Harl brought his blade down to the sounds of snapping and breaking bones. He did not see the other three rushing behind him so much as he knew they would. Twisting his body and grip, he wrested the blade free of the cracking ribs on the ground and swung it blindly before feeling it connect with one of them. He rounded on the other three. They were surprised by his seeming to be able to see behind him. Harl's face started to ache from grinning, but he did not care. He swung at one and missed as it backed up. They exchanged glances and began to run.

Harl lurched two steps forward and brought down another blue-skinned besieger as the other two fled. They did not get far before Deni's mount trampled one under foot and he gouged the other with his spear until it stumbled and stopped moving. Deni needed more training before he could charge with a lance, so he had trailed behind the first mounted wall of steel lance and spear tips, instead riding up to opponents and spearing them, either as they fought or fled. From the blood spatters on his mount and the bits of gore that were draped from the contours of his spearhead, he was proficient in that. Harl made a mental note that Deni was ready for more lance training. *If we ever have time, at this rate.*

There! Amidst the growing tide of fleeing short, blue-skinned enemies, Harl spotted what he yearned to see: tall, green-skinned orcs standing and fighting. He lumbered in their direction as they attempted to form a line, spears forming a fence to defend against mounted attackers. Harl dropped his grin to concentrate as he cleared aside their spears with his Daearan warsword, brushing them aside, breaking the shafts and tangling them with nearby greenskins. He advanced further and began breaking their line with swing after swing. Sweat streamed into his eyes from the exertion. His heart pounded and breath tore through his lungs and throat as strokes and swings ripped their defense to pieces.

Here and there he would hear or feel a ping as his plate deflected the attacks of spears and swords, sometimes pivoting towards the annoying noisemaker and striking it down. Behind him, other cavalry poked the line measuring attacker and defender spear and lance lengths against each other, while other cavalry pursued the fleeing besiegers. They were almost breaking when the enemy reinforcements arrived, wolves ridden by short blueskins, to plug the hole that they had made in their line.

No, with them there was one tall blueskin in heavier armor with black-painted plates, mail, and leather, a cape of fur trailing behind him. All the same. Harl was now behind the orc line of defense. If they decided they did not need to worry about his fellows breaking through, Harl would be quite surrounded. He charged forward, sword raised to meet the first rider. It dodged past him and his blade missed. He was knocked to the ground by the next. That was trouble. Daearan heavy plate protected from all but the mightiest of blows, but it lived up to the potential of its name. Once one fell, one was very hard pressed to arise quickly and without help.

Harl's momentary fretting was interrupted when a wolf's open maw came into view through his helmet's eye slit. The jaws closed around his helmet and began to gnaw and twist. Its teeth screeched against the steel as his helmet bowed and creaked, but it held under the strain. The bigger problem was that the wolf might break Harl's neck from jerking his head around. His sword had already been torn from his hand. With both hands, he reached up and felt around the wolf's head to stabilize the movement on his head and neck as it shook him. He felt around the reins of the harness on the wolf's neck and gripped them with one gauntleted hand and balled the other gauntleted hand into a fist and punched the wolf hard in the eye. It yelped and lurched, falling over. Harl rode the wolf's momentum, pulling himself to his feet and stumbling forward.

The goblin rider was too surprised to dismount, his right leg crushed under the squirming wolf as it pawed its eye. The rider's right arm was trapped underneath him, probably broken. Harl grinned again and chuckled as he plucked the small axe from the defenseless goblin's hand and split its head open before doing the same to the wolf. It took three strikes before the wolf's head came open. Casting his eyes about his surroundings for a moment, Harl heard shouting as he searched for his blade. There. He recovered it and turned to the sound of yelling.

He was vaguely aware of Prince Arnold's voice shouting behind him and the sound of the defenders collapsing. Another green-skinned defender shouted a challenge at him. Harl could not understand its words, but all warriors intuitively understood the tone and stance of a challenge. Cries of anger and the wounded sounded in a chorus surrounding him as Harl advanced on the tall orc with overlapping coats of mail and a long axe. The orc held its axe, thick shaft guarding across its chest, blade high and ready to use its weight to strike him. Harl trailed his blade low behind him and to his right. He had sparred with the prince–before he became the prince–and Arnold favored this approach. Harl became convinced after losing to Arnold a few times. The stance invited the opponent to strike first but gave the opportunity for a strong reply.

The other defenders and attackers rained blows on each other around the two combatants, both still for an instance before they both lunged towards each other. Harl hopped back a pace and a half as the axe whistled by him. Heavy plate or no, the bulging arms and chest of his opponent joined with the long axe might be just the thing that Harl did not want to experience for himself. Bringing the sword to a high guard with the point leveled at the orc's face and neck, Harl pressed forward and thrust. His counterattack yielded the gratifying pressure as the tip of the blade parted the mail links and leather before plunging through its throat. At the same time, the orc had used the momentum of his axe swing with the tension of its arms and brought the axe back for another diagonal strike from the opposite direction. The axe crashed into Harl's right arm below the pauldron. He also felt his shoulder move out of place and his whole arm dropped.

Harl had never broken his arm before, but he imagined that

this is probably what it felt like. It was excruciating. Harl glimpsed a spray of blood from the direction of his opponent while he was falling backwards. He hit the ground painfully hard, aggravated further by his broken arm. He rolled to the side to take pressure off of it. Still chuckling, he passed out.

***

Irduin hacked her way through the line. Koval Covendran's infantry would be close by now. Should be. She leaned in the saddle, plunging the tip of her slightly curved sword into an orc's flesh, where the shoulder and neck met. The blade was sharpened to an edge finer than thread, parting thick leather, gliding around steel studs of reinforcement, and breaking links of mail like small spring berries. The blade rested there for an instant. The fading light of the overcast sky briefly reflected the runes on her blade before she pulled it out in a spray of bright blood, the orc's face still twisting in surprise as the life left its eyes.

She was surrounded, as was all of the other cavalry. Their young prince had charged in. Again. Had made a plan with significant risk. Again. Irduin guided the mount with her knees and a pull of the reins, facing the steed to receive a handful of orcs and goblins on her strong side. They were probably rushing to fill the gap in the line that the cavalry had poured through. Really, there was no reason to fill the gap because there was nothing behind the cavalry. Koval's infantry would be coming from the east.

Irduin cast her eye to the east but saw none of the Yvel infantry coming down the hill. Irduin patiently worked through the handful. Two of the goblins decided that the hole could stay unfilled as their fellows lay on the ground. Irduin noted that the orcs were significantly better equipped than the ones they had fought two months earlier in the forests and hills east of Serna. Most wore armor made of hardened leather, reinforced with iron or steel studs and bands, and some even wore mail pieces or even a few plates, though none had a full suit.

Harl Oleandran had been the first to charge through. Irduin spotted him lying on the ground. *Maybe he lives. It seems he bested the Garad'dai, at least.* Irduin again cast about her gaze, spotting the young prince playing games with five wolf riders. Perhaps he had earned the right to charge alone. He would come back with dents in his plate, but so far, he always came back. Irduin internally hissed in annoyance at his apparent recklessness. Everyone followed his example through the gap–and he would be dead if they did not–but it was an awful risk to commit the cavalry like this on the assumption that the slow-moving infantry would move such a distance and arrive on time.

Though there was a line of orcs that formed against the cavalry, much of Yvel's horse was still moving within the camp, pursuing and harassing the mostly scattering goblins. In fact, there were goblins scattering everywhere inside the line, too. *There!* Irduin spotted a tall wolf rider: that would likely be their commander, if the battle east of Serna had been an accurate guide. *This is a perfect bow shot, if only I had a horse bow. It has been over a hundred summers since I had one, though.*

Irduin abruptly pitched forward and to the left. The horse had stumbled over a small crowd of goblins fleeing from a band of jeering squires poking them with spears. Irduin had been looking at the hobgoblin, and the goblins were looking at the squires, when they ran under Irduin's horse. With a practiced hand and leg, Irduin vaulted off of the saddle and landed in a crouch, but she heard the horse's leg snap and it whinnied in pain. Irduin was becoming quite annoyed.

A goblin crawled away from her flailing horse towards her. She flicked her wrist twice, rapping it on the temple and crushing its throat with her fist. Rising, she strode towards the hobgoblin as it battled the other cavalry. She could tell it was trying to get to the young prince, who was conspicuously acting as the leader. Irduin quickly but patiently dealt with momentary interruptions, dispatching orcs and a goblin or two that challenged her. Another rider–a fellow elf–intercepted the hobgoblin, and their mounts pranced around each other as they traded blows.

She glanced back towards the main melee and could see that the enemy would soon overwhelm Yvel's horse. Plenty of wounded and dead lay on the ground and while there were quite a few more enemy casualties, they still had considerably more numbers. The wolf rider blocked the elf's sword with its own and grabbed the elf's sword hand with its off hand. It pulled the elf close and smashed its helmeted head into the elf's. The elf rocked backwards, dropping her sword. She quickly drew a shorter sword, a backup, as the wolf crowded her mount. The wolf rider stopped her downward slash by catching her weapon hand in its own. It twisted the hand, pointing the blade toward the elf and forced it in. *That infantry would be very helpful right now,* Irduin grumbled internally before chiding herself. *The task at hand.* The horse panicked as the elf reeled back and fell from the saddle.

"It is done, but I will give you a good death," she called in the dialect of Goblin that she knew. There were plenty of other dialects, but she hoped that this one would be close enough that it would understand her meaning. The wolf rider looked over and broke away, approaching Irduin on wolfback.

A feminine voice answered from beneath the mask of the helmet. The accent was very heavy and some of the words were different, but Irduin believed she said 'we shall see." The wolf toothily grinned at her as the rider approached Irduin with her strong side, her blade raised in what Irduin knew to be a hobgoblin's salute of respect. Irduin returned one of her own.

The wolf loped forward suddenly, the hobgoblin's blade swinging behind to deliver a sweeping underhand strike. Irduin's downward answering strike cleaved through the mail sleeve the hobgoblin wore and severed the forearm at halfway. Irduin's blade darted, curving around and away from her opponent before slashing diagonally upward, cutting deeply into the rider's torso at the armpit. Irduin ripped her blade away and speared the snarling wolf through the eye. The rider crumpled towards her and fell from the saddle as the wolf staggered to the ground and twitched.

Irduin looked up at the sounds of cries and cheers. The infantry was finally arriving, advancing down the hill. She spotted Koval Covendran and Velthuria Torg'ail mounted and wading into the fray. Irduin could tell they were exhausted from the hours of forced march through the muddy forest for this flank attack, but it still presented another surprise to the enemy and they were routing.

Irduin moved a few paces to her fallen opponent and crouched. She took off her opponent's helmet. A female hobgoblin.

Blue-skinned, like the other goblins here and the hobgoblins from
two months ago. She had lean, angular features, large eyes, and
large, sharply pointed ears jutting to the sides; similar to her own,
though elf ears were more backswept. With her helmet off, her ears
stuck out more to the side. She had yellow eyes and thick black hair.
"Pretty," Irduin said to her.

"Pretty," her opponent repeated, as blood rushed out of her
mouth.

***

"Let's move onto the next one," Mkaela said, picking up her bag.
She had taken to carrying a bag of tools, thread, needles, and
bandages. She had learned much from the Prince's Surgeon, Master
Danfreys, and his assistants. It was necessary now. There were too
many wounded for her to do her best with all of them, especially
since the main part of the fighting was over. She provided enough
healing to save their lives, if she could, and used more conventional
methods to speed their recovery. That took too much out of her,
too. The healing magic was becoming much more familiar with
the amount of practice she was getting, but she was far from being
very good. Walking along, she held her bag open, squinting in the
last shreds of twilight through the clouds, checking to make sure
everything was there and whether she needed restocking. Satisfied,
she closed the bag. "I'll need some more thread soon, Merik." She
looked around, "Merik? Merik!"

"Right, My Lady." Merik was fussing over someone that
had not survived.

"Come on! The living!" she insisted.

"Alright." He came away dismayed, hustling towards her,
his strides clanking from the sound of the plates over his legs and
his mail shirt. He beckoned their two orderlies along. In truth, they
were the Orcish women that Mkaela had saved from execution.
To everyone else, they were large humans that hardly ever spoke.
They had still not chosen names for themselves, but they had started
to pick up a few words of Marin and Eklendan, though to the two
Orcish women, it was all one language and they would try to form

sentences with words from both.

Merik had left his helmet and other plates and all but his arming sword at the hastily built camp for the Crown Guard erected from within Borly's tired walls. The regiment had moved into Borly, as well. Mkaela and Merik were out of the walls, tending the wounded with a small escort of regimentals. They reached the area in the field before Borly where the orcs had made a line against the cavalry. All around, wounded stirred amidst the dead in a field strewn with hundreds of bodies. The light rain continued, muffling their moans of pain and diluting the bloody mud. Humans, orcs, and goblins were strewn across the field.

"Can we get to Sir Harl first, My Lady?" He pointed to what had to be Sir Harl laying on the ground in the rain. He was still helmeted, but his armor was distinctive; smooth steel with a rippling pattern, and looked very heavy. Mkaela had heard that it was a style of craft unique to Daeara. Merik had said it was called 'Daearan water steel' and it came from forging things from different pieces of steel forced together. She had also been told that Daeara was a land to the south of Eklenda, but she had neither been there, nor seen it on a map, nor even heard of it. *World's pretty small when you're a baker*, she thought. *Gets a lot bigger when you have something people need.*

Mkaela approached the might-be Sir Harl and gently peeled off his helmet. It was Harl. He was asleep, which was for the best as his arm was bent the wrong way. She went to remove the bent plate on his armor, but Merik interjected. "Please, My Lady, let me. Harl will fuss over it if the straps are hard to replace and if you take it off a certain way, it will wake him.

Mkaela sighed and put her hands up. "After you, Sir Knight." Merik cut away the straps with a dagger and carefully removed the bent plates. Harl lay on his back and there were a number of sizable dents about the belly and chest of his front plate. His helmet had a few dents and creases from slashing and axe strikes. Mkaela placed her hands on Sir Harl's upper arm and above his shoulder and concentrated.

After a moment, green light emanated from Sir Harl's skin under her hands. She had figured out this technique to 'feel' inside wounds. She could 'feel' Sir Harl's upper arm pulled away from where it 'felt' like it was supposed to be, and a lot of fleshy strings and ropes were stretched or ripped. His arm was broken, too. She nodded to Merik, who firmly held Sir Harl in place. The green glow changed to a purple as she moved the arm back into place and attempted to mend the strings around it enough to heal further. The bone would heal on its own. Harl's eyes popped open and he yelped in pain. "Easy, Sir Harl," Merik said, "you've been through a bit."

"I got him?" Harl asked, sweat from pain freshly beading on his forehead.

"Yes," Merik said. Mkaela got up to move on. "Sir Harl, about Yander... " she heard Merik say. She did not know a Yander, did not know what Merik knew about Yander, and did not have time. Some other regimentals and folk from Borly were picking around amongst the dead. No. Not just picking around, they were finishing off the wounded.

"Can you stop?" She demanded.

The soldiers and Borly militia looked up. One of them called back. "What for? Does one of them owe you money?" The others chuckled.

"Because–" Mkaela began hotly.

"Because they are prisoners," broke in a calm and clear voice. They all turned to see the new arrival. Mkaela recognized Irduin being trailed by Lazura and Erensed. She had never heard the two younger elves speak much. She was told the latter two were younger, Mkaela could not remember by whom, though all three looked to be in their mid-twenties. Supposedly, Irduin was really, really old, but Mkaela was skeptical. That anyone could even *be* that old. Besides just dying of old or sick, Mkaela was skeptical that old people would not get bored or tired of the world, get tired of people making them change, having the same arguments, all kinds of things, without going crazy.

"So?" the joker called back.

"So, prisoners are useful. You learn their language. You question them to learn about the enemy. You make them fix the walls. You put them to work."

The joker hesitated. One of the militia spoke up. "Yeah, but these are all dyin.'"

"What do you think the Healer is here for?" Irduin said, gesturing matter-of-factly to Mkaela. "Now," she said, "I imagine you have duties to be about that are more important than beating someone that is about to die anyways. Off with you–no, even better, stay here and help your Healer."

They hesitated. "Why should we help a green-loving witch?" another one called.

"I am sure you would enjoy discussing the issue with Sir Merik," replied Irduin, nodding to the approaching armored man.

That seemed to solve the argument. Irduin shooed them off and Mkaela brought her two orderlies with her. "Can you check for ones that still live?" she asked her orderlies.

"Yas," they said in clumsy unison. They knew a few words and were learning more. The aspect that surprised Mkaela most about these orcs was that they seemed very human in many ways. They definitely were not dumb the way it was told in storybooks. Story and legends painted orcs and goblins as villains, and much of the time the orcs were dumb cowards and the goblins were sneaky, weak cowards. Mkaela had not met any goblins–so far–but the orcs were different–at least *these* orcs–from what she expected. They picked about the lines of blue and green bodies, finding a few still alive.

"Thanks, Lady Irduin," Mkaela said.

"You are welcome," she said, calm as a still morning breeze.

Mkaela hesitated. "What are you doing out here, Lady Irduin?"

"Just Irduin, please," she said. Mkaela almost felt like it was an expression of familiarity, but she was not sure. Irduin continued. "Building a funeral fire."

"A funeral fire?" Mkaela said absently before catching herself. "Oh, I'm–"

"It is fine. Lierialuth is in the next eternity. This is our custom when we are away from our homeland."

Mkaela was awkwardly silent as Irduin moved on with the two younger elves. Mkaela could see their youth now. They could not mask their grief as well. She could see it in their faces.

Merik arrived and nodded grimly when Mkaela told him what Irduin had said. He readily set the soldiers and militia to work searching for survivors of any type and calling over Mkaela. Mkaela would have really appreciated Master Danfreys and his assistants, but Prince Arnold had sent them to help the wounded inside Borly who had been without any proper medicine for months. Mkaela knew she would be helping there after she and Merik finished out here.

Lierialuth's funeral fire blazed brightly at the top of the hill. Mkaela healing those that needed it, if she could, as far as they needed it to live and recover. She and her orderlies worked for hours in torchlight and silence, broken by the shuffling of dragged bodies, living and dead. The orderlies were becoming quite helpful. They had quickly learned how to press and stitch wounds. They were strong and could lift bodies and their Marin-Eklendan mixed dialect was becoming slowly more coherent. The three of them bandaged, splinted and braced those who did not need healing and those who were healed enough to live. More of the soldiers were set to guard the growing number of prisoners who would live, many of whom could walk. They huddled nervously, goblins and orcs alike in one growing cluster of blue and green with the occasional red-skinned goblin.

Hours later, Irduin approached from the darkness. "Mkaela, may I have your help?"

Mkaela sighed aloud before realizing that she did not want to be rude to Irduin. "Sorry, yes." Irduin led her away in the darkness with only Irduin's torch. Mkaela could see Merik and the others by their torches. She stumbled through the tufts of grass, branches, and tree roots while Irduin walked with a sure step, though slow enough for Mkaela to keep up. Irduin stopped abruptly and Mkaela could hear hoarse, thick, labored breathing. Mkaela strained to see until Irduin moved her torch to shed better light. "A wolf!?" she asked incredulously.

"A wolf *steed*," Irduin emphasized. "There are no spare horses and mine died."

Mkaela glanced at the giant wolf, four paces long. It had passed out but would probably not last the night. "Are you sure?"

Mkaela asked. Irduin glanced at her, "I mean–"

"It is fine. Yes, I am sure," Irduin said calmly.

"Very well." Mkaela began to work on the wolf. The soft glow of green and then purple rivaled the torchlight. "It'll probably be a fine steed for you."

"It was a fine horse," Irduin said abruptly. "I enjoyed that horse. And I enjoyed Lierialuth. She was very young." Mkaela looked over her shoulder at Irduin standing behind her, "The least they could do is provide me with a new mount." Irduin tossed something that landed in front of the wolf. It landed wetly. *Meat*, Mkaela realized. Mkaela was not sure what kind of meat that was and decided that she did not want to know.

"Are you fine here, uh, Irduin?" Mkaela asked.

"Yes," she said, "thank you." She had planted the torch on the ground with the bottom of the handle wedged in the mud to keep the flame aloft. The wolf was coming to, but Irduin seemed completely at ease. Mkaela was getting very tired. She grabbed a stick and wrapped it in rags torn from a nearby body's garments and lit her own torch. It would not burn long, but it would be enough to get her back to the others. She shambled off in the direction of the other torches when the wolf looked up and began to growl. Irduin slapped it hard across the snout, grabbed it by the ear forcing its head to the mud and glared directly into its eyes. *She seems to know how to go about it*, Mkaela thought as she began what would seem to be hours of her walking, tripping, crawling, and stumbling back to the other torches. She lost her torch to the drizzle and the mud, but it was enough for her to go off of the ones in the distance. She arrived at the gathering of the others and spared a moment for one heaving breath before getting back to work.

It had drizzled all night and the morning twilight was beginning. They were exhausted. Mkaela had her orderlies tell the orc prisoners that could walk to build litters and carry those who could not. Irduin managed to get the goblins to do the same, though it took longer, explaining that they spoke a different dialect than what she knew. Mkaela was surprised at first, but then decided it made sense. After all, humans spoke plenty of different languages. Why would goblins or orcs all speak the same 'Goblin' or 'Orcish' language? The militia walked the prisoners into town, Mkaela and her small entourage trailing them alongside Irduin and her two elves.

Borly looked very similar to Serna; a town with a main road and a mountain stream passing through it. One- and two-storied buildings made up most of the place, with shops and houses and workshops off of the main road, and two three-storied buildings that were probably inns. Most of the buildings were log-walled with mud and clay filling the gaps and, like Serna, had a mixture of thatch and tile roofs. The main differences were first, that Borly had a stone wall about five or six paces tall, though it had taken a lot of abuse over the past few months of siege, and second, that it had a very modest stone keep rather than a manor house.

Mkaela leaned to one of the militia. "Good thing you had those walls. Otherwise, they would have tried burning you down."

"Huh?" said the militiaman. He was older, Mkaela guessed in his late thirties, with hands used to work, and early greying in his once-trimmed beard. He scrunched his face. "Come to think of it, I never saw them try anything like that at all. Not once in the three months. Just little cookfires."

"Really…" Mkaela said. "Huh." They passed through the town and came to what had used to be the town green, and was now transformed into a camp and supply dump. Mkaela was lost in thought, or maybe too tired to think, when she realized she stopped. *Why did I stop?*

She stopped because Merik stopped. *Why did Merik stop?* Merik had stopped to speak with Koval and the prince. Koval still wore his mail and plate, but had left his helmet somewhere. The prince was dressed down to his mail shirt and trousers, with his grey and red cape and an arming sword at his hip.

"–And they will gather in Yvel," Merik was saying.

"But you're not there," the prince said.

"Yes, y–uh, sir, they will probably send a few to find me, probably here to Borly unless we go elsewhere and send word to Yvel. The rest will muster there. I left instructions to help with whatever preparations General Gundr'ail needed," Merik said.

"Very good," said the prince.

Irduin strode up. She almost looked excited–nothing in

her facial expression, but she had a quickness to her step. "Your Grace, Lord Koval," she greeted, "I have learned that some of the goblin prisoners are siege engineers and should be able to assist in repairing the walls."

"Ah! Very good, then!" The prince clapped his fist into his open hand and hurried off with Irduin, leaving the three of them.

Koval spoke first. "Mkaela, *the Prince,*" he bit his tongue with irritation, "has asked that you help Master Danfreys and deemed it unnecessary to tell you so himself."

"Uh, yes, My Lord… where…?" With lazy, tired irritation, Koval waved towards one of the inns, saying it was being used as an infirmary.

Mkaela sighed and trudged in its direction. The inn had been converted entirely to an infirmary. Once inside, she saw Danfreys and his staff. They all had blood spatters on their arms and tunics from their work. The common room was where the fresh wounded were brought, as well as the freshly dead who had not long survived their surgery. A row of bodies lay to the right under blankets waiting for burial or burning. The tables held those being treated by Danfreys and his team; seven of them at the moment. Mkaela guessed that all of the guest rooms on the second and third floors were holding others healing from wounds and surgeries.

She fell to work in a daze for hours and abruptly woke up sitting at one of the tables with her face in her folded arms on the table. The table had been cleared of its patient and the sun was down. Someone had draped a blanket over her. The bodies had been taken elsewhere. The patients all had been moved from the common room. Her two orderlies were sleeping at some of the other tables. Mkaela would ask them what they had been doing in a moment. Just a moment.

A wooden thunk jolted Mkaela's eyes open. It was bright. Sunlight blazed into the room through the windows. One of Danfreys' staff had entered the infirmary.

"My Lady, why don't you get some breakfast?" she said.

"Huh. That's a good idea," Mkaela replied blearily. She hoisted herself to her feet and roused her two orderlies. The three of them stumbled out of the infirmary and eyed the other inn across the town center and shambled in that direction. The air was brisk with the season. A gust of wind rattled some leaves. The town-turned-camp was bustling with activity, but there was a renewed sense of purpose to it. When she arrived in town last night–or was it the night before?–there had been a pall of bleakness to everything that was just beginning to fade. Now, for the first time in two months, people had hope. They went about their work with a little more energy, though there were fewer about. She guessed that many were asleep for the first dedicated rest in a long time.

The place still smelled awful. All of the farmers that had been able to reach the town brought the livestock they could, which had helped the town survive. But cattle dung and chicken scat littered the streets, and yesterday's rain renewed its scent mingling with the mud. Soldiers and workers moved throughout, having collectively heaved a sigh of relief, shooing chickens away, moving supplies, and mustering for drill. Mkaela and her two orderlies entered the other inn.

Garven and Arynn were seated at one of the tables. Irduin was further off in a corner, carving a shaft of wood a bit more than a pace long and half-eating a plate of food. *It's like she never sleeps*, Mkaela thought. Garven, facing the doorway, saw them and waved them over. Arynn turned in her seat to see who he was motioning to and watched them sit. They both were finishing up a bowl of firm-boiled eggs and cups of fresh milk. Mkaela was suddenly reminded that she had not eaten in a long time and that she had not had fresh food like this in over a month.

"You're still here. I thought you would have left by now," Mkaela said. *Orneth! I want to eat!*

"We're leaving just now after helping out here a bit," Garven said.

"Both of you, right? That's a long road down to Serna on foot," she said.

"Oh, we are riding," Arynn said.

"I'm surprised there's a horse to spare," Mkaela said.

"No, he's riding with me," Arynn said. Garven looked away.

Mkaela hesitated. "Are you going to finish that?"

Epilogue

At a farm, west of Yvel City: the Crown Sorcerers' Proving Grounds.
By the Elven Calendar, seventh day of Summer, 18031.
By the Human Calendar, Laborday (seventh day of the week), first week of
Youri, 794.
A cool, early summer evening.

The pen made scratching sounds as it tore grooves into the paper, leaving a trail of ink. Sinuous, graceful arcs of the pen soared across the page leaving a scrawl. Fingers gripped the pen with an ease that left an odd mixture of urgency at the subject and the familiarity bordering on nonchalance as the hand moved the pen in response to what the eyes saw. The muscles around the eyes strained and were tortured by squinting in the hopes that by straining just a bit harder, a new aspect of the aura would be revealed.

"It's hard to concentrate when you're staring that hard, Tyrnimar," said Ayza.

The pen came to an abrupt stop. "Uh…" Tyrnimar fumbled. "Sorry. There is great interest to me in what is strived after by both of you."

"Uh," Ayza began. "Right…"

"Have your feelings during the power use of yours been explained to your sister by you?" Tyrnimar asked Kora.

"*Yes*, Tyrnimar. Three times in the last hour and you were–right–here–when I explained it. I'm tired and I'm not going through it again today," Ayza huffed. "Don't you have somewhere to be?"

What else needs to be observed in which greater importance exists? "No," Tyrnimar said.

Tyrnimar counted himself incredibly fortunate that Holbrin allowed him to watch the progress at the sorcery grounds. Prince Arnold had set aside some of his own fields that had finished harvest early and designated them as the 'Crown Sorcerers' Proving Grounds.' Tyrnimar was surprised that Prince Arnold was so eager to give up such a large farm for this purpose; a farm of this size gave Kora and Ayza miles of space to practice that could otherwise produce enough food to feed Yvel City for half of a winter. Still, it must be worth it to the prince.

Tyrnimar considered a second factor: this was probably the prince's closest estate to Yvel City that was not located in a very populated area. They had arrived over a month ago, with a small detachment of the prince's household to move the farmers out. The farmers and their families were moved to another one of the prince's estates, save for a few that agreed to stay on as servants and grounds staff for the sorcerers. Another uncomfortable thing about war, Tyrnimar noted. The needs of a ruler in protecting a whole people sometimes outweighed the needs of some of the people in need of protection.

And it was that time. The sunlight was giving way to twilight, and Kora and Ayza were both exhausted from the day's attempts and practice. Kora was close, but she had some kind of block. Tyrnimar knew that most every creature had some kind of sorcerous potential in their blood, but it required a large dose of danger, fear, and emotion for the abilities to manifest, so much so that most people usually died from the strain before their powers unlocked. Most elves, like any other creature, died before the power opened. The majority of elves that practiced magic did so through book magic. Tyrnimar was no different, though he was twice rare because he had unlocked his power, his blood magic, as well as being exceptionally accomplished at book magic.

Tyrnimar was a Seer. His power, aura reading, had manifested during his examinations for his position in the Order without him fully realizing what was happening. In some ways, Tyrnimar had an unfair advantage. He could see some of the auras of magical energies latent in the world, which he would then evoke in his spells. This had earned him a few jealous enemies in the first years, though he was able to make amends with most of them once they had made their own accomplishments, and he had been sure to congratulate them and cite their works in his own research. This was a kind of esteem one scholar gave to another, though one could not do it too often without coming across as disingenuous.

But his ability was giving him only hints of the problem

the sisters were facing. He could see Kora's and Ayza's auras and they both looked quite formidable. Ayza had clearly been using her powers before the orc raid four months ago. "Ayza?"

"Yes?" she said. They were eating a dinner of pheasant stewed with parsnips. Tyrnimar was finding it awfully bland and was annoyed at the prohibition from using magic to cook and flavor the meal. Still, he did not have to cook it himself, and the farmers that stayed worked hard to maintain the house for them to live without worry of anything but training.

"How long have your powers been used?" he asked.

She paused before taking another spoon of the stew. She hesitated for a long moment. Long enough that Kora stopped eating and looked at her. "A few years."

"*Years!?*" Kora and Tyrnimar erupted in unison. Ayza looked away sheepishly.

It was Tyrnimar's turn to speak first while Kora hesitated, staring agape. "What was being done by you?" he finally asked.

"I..." She searched for words. "I... used the winds to protect crops and the town from storms," she said.

"All at once?" he asked.

"What do you mean?" Ayza asked.

"Was protection given by you for the whole town and fields all at once?" he said.

"Oh, no, I've never been that strong," she said.

Tyrnimar cupped his chin in his hand as he furrowed his brow in thought. *A matter of time*, he thought.

"What do you mean 'a matter of time'?" she asked.

"What?" he said, surprised at her reading his thoughts.

"You said 'a matter of time'," she accused.

"Uh," *Was that actually said out loud!?* He stumbled. "What was meant... was that... so much progress has been made by you up until now. Only a matter of time before your skill is developed more."

Ayza eyed him suspiciously and there was an awkward silence for a while. Kora spoke abruptly. "Tyrnimar."

"Yes?" he answered.

"Why do you talk like that?" she asked.

He was perplexed. "Like what?"

"The way you do," she said.

"What is meant by you?" he asked.

"See? That's it," she pointed.

He was still confused. "It is what?"

Ayza huffed in annoyance. "The way you speak; you say things like someone else is doing them."

"Is that done by me? It is believed by me that each statement is clearly given by me that someone has done something when it occurs," he said, muddled by their words.

"That's exactly it," she said. "We say 'I did this' and you say 'this was done by me.'"

"Is there a difference…?" he asked. Ayza huffed again and threw her hands up. She took her stew and went to the other room and sat alone.

After Ayza left, Kora continued the conversation. "Why do you say it differently?"

"Supposed by me, it is the way Elvish was learned by me. It is the dialect spoken by many people where I am from," he explained.

"A dialect of Elvish," she said to confirm.

"Yes," he said.

"But we're not speaking Elvish. We're speaking Marin," Kora said.

"Yes," he said in exasperation, "it is known by me which language is spoken by us at this time. The habit of how the language is spoken by me is carried over to other languages."

"So, you speak all languages like this?" she asked.

"Yes," he answered.

They ate in silence, finishing their stew.

"Why don't you try speaking the other way?" Kora asked.

"Why?" he asked back.

"So, it's easier to understand you," she said.

"It is difficult for me to be understood by you?" He was slightly bewildered. "No idea of any misunderstandings was had by me. This problem was not had by anyone else. Hm."

"Will you try?" she asked.

Tyrnimar was quiet for a while. He poured two cups of his daily floral tea, lost in thought for a while.

"Tyrnimar?" she asked again after a while.

Tyrnimar jumped in his chair. He looked around and saw the other cup of tea untouched. *Oh, right. In another place, others are being helped by her.* He poured the tea from the second cup back into his copper-lined gourd bottle and wiped out both cups before putting them away.

"*Well?*" she asked exasperatedly.

"Well, what?" he asked quizzically. Kora looked at him with a look that Eevarel never gave him.

"I don't know what to say. Nevermind," Kora said.

Tyrnimar retired to his room and paged through some of the books that he had brought. He could not credit the coincidence to forethought. It was merely happenstance that he had packed the particular book through which he was paging. Though, he chided himself that he should have thought of this as an obvious choice given the purpose of the travel that had commenced nearly six moons ago when Eevarel had plucked him from his quiet, studious life to answer the Guardian Council's summons.

He paged through Arranel's *Essays and Descriptions of Natural and Unnatural Sorcerous Awakenings*. It was a fine work with an exhaustive study of relatively recent natural awakenings and records of the induced awakenings. The induced awakenings were one of the main driving factors behind the only war among elves recorded in history, the War of the People, which had resulted in the schism in the People. It was very long ago, about three thousand summers ago. There were a few elves that remembered it, but Holbrin was the only one that Tyrnimar had ever actually met. *Holbrin...*

"I could tell you about it." Tyrnimar spun in surprise to see

Eevarel. "But you have something plainly in front of you."

"You! You… are… are you not elsewhere?" Tyrnimar said. Eevarel stepped aside, unblocking the window. Blazing sunlight streamed in and bombarded Tyrnimar. Squinting, he shielded his eyes. *It is the morning??* He was on the bed in his room at the Proving Grounds. Eevarel was gone. *Or not there to begin with? A dream? A dream…*

Tyrnimar looked down to see Arranel's book of essays open on his stomach. He picked it up to see a diagram. His eyes widened slowly.

The next hour was a blur of breakfast, morning greetings, hustling Kora and Ayza out to the proving grounds, and a very tortured explanation of an idea, at the end of which, Ayza said "Yes! That's what I've been trying to explain!"

Tyrnimar coaxed her calmly. "Now, let it just be tried by you." Kora skeptically glanced at Tyrnimar before extending her hands and breathing evenly. The three of them were silent. Kora breathed. Nothing happened. Tyrnimar noticed a bead of sweat beginning to form.

"It cannot be forced by you," he said. She shrugged and relaxed her shoulders and took another deep breath. Moments passed. The glow began suddenly and then sputtered as sparks spat out of Kora's fingertips.

"Aha!" she laughed. The sparks died as she jumped with glee.

"Tyrnimar," Ayza laughed, "how did you think of that?"

"Yes, how *did* you think of that?"

The three of them spun at the sound of the fourth speaker's voice. A human woman was behind them, dressed in a dress with a red bodice and skirt with watery blue sleeves. She looked to be in her twenties, with dark brown hair in waves reaching past her shoulders, held from her face by a leather band. She had a narrow jaw, but fair skin with many freckles. Tyrnimar had read a few books on human blood heritages west of the Kaskevs before the beginning of the journey. While her jaw marked her as Eklendan, the fair skin would mark her as Marin, which was a common combination in this area. Even Prince Arnold was a mix. The freckles were something he had not seen yet, though if he had to guess, they marked her as having the blood of a Tamark. She was leaning on a cattle fence ten paces away between them and the farm house.

"Uh," Tyrnimar stammered in surprise.

"Who are you?" Ayza broke in.

"Oh, forgive me." She smiled. "My name is Zaya. I study history and I was able to convince one of those bureaucrats in Yvel to let me watch you and record your work." She smiled with excitement. "I never thought I would get to see history being made."

"Right…" Ayza said. "Who did you say gave you permission?"

"Oh, I don't remember. One of those fuddies in the palace." She waved a hand dismissively. "Don't mind me, dear, you won't even know that I'm here. I brought a very small staff."

"*A staff!?*" Ayza and Tyrnimar both said in exasperation.

Kora made excellent progress after that day. Within six days, she could sputter sparks at will, and by nine days later she could shoot a narrow stream of flame eight paces. Ayza was making steady progress, as well. Her obstacle was being comfortable using her powers in front of others. Her command of the wind became more refined. She could shape Kora's flames; project them, disperse them. She could also form the winds into a stronger shield than the one that she used at the Battle of Serna Hills. By the end of the tenday where Kora could shoot narrow flames, Ayza could create a shield of wind in a curved shape. Those were the enjoyable things for Tyrnimar and he had to send for more parchment and ink for the notes he was taking.

Everything else that month was decidedly not enjoyable for any of them, but especially Tyrnimar. Blood magic sapped considerable energy from its wielder. Kora was incredibly hostile and moody. She ate voraciously, which was consistent with Tyrnimar's historical accounts. This was not incredibly surprising, but it was still not enjoyable. Ayza ate more, as well, but seemed more accustomed to it and was more even-tempered.

What was both surprising and very decidedly unenjoyable

was the presence of this Zaya Yand'ail, as she later introduced herself. She came from a noble house of very modest holdings west of Krogen but had grown up in Yvel. She claimed to have studied history all of her life and read of the old legends of magic. She had managed to cajole someone into giving up the location of the Proving Grounds and invited herself to observe. *What manner of cajoling was done by her…* Tyrnimar internally groaned.

But who she was or where she came from were not the particularly annoying aspects. What was annoying, to say the least, was that she was either eyeing Kora and Ayza like a bird eyes worms, or turning the same gaze on Tyrnimar. She found Tyrnimar anytime he was trying to think in quiet. She would not stop talking to him, pestering him for answers, washing him with compliments about his profession, his knowledge, his looks, and found odd excuses to 'accidentally' brush against him. Tyrnimar was very, very certain that this was frowned upon in most cultures west of the Kaskevs, save for the true Berks and, maybe, the Tamarks, but he had only read on the Tamarks and not seen very many true Berks. She would also try to peer into his notebooks and once, he had caught her going through his books when he came to change notebooks.

That was too much. He weighed his decision with labor, but ultimately decided that he could not afford the risk. He packed up all of his library and took a day to bring it to Trinien at Prince Arnold's palace, leaving word with Trinien to pass along to Holbrin about the potential espionage attempt.

The warmth came into its fullness as the summer progressed. One windy and rainy unpleasant day, he and Kora were out in the Proving Grounds. The wind had proven to be too much for Zaya, *thankfully*. Ayza had discretely created a bubble of wind around her to keep the rain off of her, but that prevented her from being near Kora for risk of capturing her sister's flame and self-immolating. Kora was burning a bare patch on the ground through the rain. Steam, mist, and smoke rolled off of her and mixed with one another.

Tyrnimar shrugged off a shiver to write clearly in the shelter and comparative cool of Ayza's bubble. He kept only one working notebook with him and blank spares. Every five days or so, he made a trip to Yvel to give another notebook to Trinien. This was especially frustrating because Tyrnimar knew a variety of wards that could defeat this kind of security threat with very minimal effort. *But nooo… magic just could be used for fear that its knowledge would be learned by the prying humans.*

But here and now, he was with Kora, and her powers were developing quite nicely. She was learning to shape her flames into fans and arcs, which would adjust her range, and she could shoot the same narrow beam of flame twenty paces now. But now, she stopped abruptly. "So what about Eevarel?"

"Huh?" Tyrnimar was stunned by the question. *Why would Eevarel also be thought of by her at this time?* "What about Eevarel?" he asked dumbly.

Kora made a vexed sound. "So you're just going to drop her and go around with this Zaya harlot?"

"That, uh, harlot? is not being gone anywhere with by me," he protested, fumbling around the new word.

"So, you're still with Eevarel?" she pressed.

He hesitated. "There are many obstacles that would have to be overcome by both Eevarel and myself. It is wondered by me if we even could."

"So, you're just *playing* with her!?" she accused.

"No, I–" Tyrnimar broke off as she shot a spout of flame at him.

Tyrnimar reflexively brushed it aside. The beam deflected off of his hastily constructed protective spell and hit a fence post. The post flashed brightly for an instant, leaving a charred crumbling mass of ash. *Wait–I–*

He had. He had used a shielding ward. Kora was standing there wide-eyed, agape and speechless.

"You–" he began.

"By Orneth! Tyrnimar! I'm so sorry! I didn't–I didn't mean to–" The words tumbled from her.

"It is alright. I am fine. Please. *Please*, no one can be told by you. *Please!* No one." he begged.

"O-Oh, alright. I'm so sorry. I didn't mean–" she

continued, dropping to the ground. She began to sob. "It's just like before!" She whimpered and shook with the sobs.

Flummoxed, Tyrnimar awkwardly crept forward. "It is alright," he said, "but, really, please, it cannot be said enough times by me. *No one can know*." He hissed the last sentence. On an impulse he scrutinized her aura, and then he understood.

From the window of her lodging, Zaya wore a small, satisfied smile, recording this latest development for inclusion in the upcoming tenday's report.

***

North of Yvel City, Yvel Principality.
By the Goblin Calendar, early in the Seventh Moon Cycle, 3114.
By the Human Calendar, Fryday, first week of Youri, 794.
In concurrence.

"Here you are then," said the man.

Kolus did not know this man, but Kolus was told to meet him here, north of Yvel City. Kolus had not been told in person, as he never was in this profession. No one was told to do anything face to face, as that would compromise the security of his handler. He would be passed notes, written in blocky script to conceal the hand and usually signaled in some mundane way–a spilled wine goblet, or a crushed biscuit on a particular table. This time, it had been an odd dessert served with lunch from the prince's guest kitchen.

The unusual dessert was never the same, but it was always an odd one. There would be a note with blocky writing under a bucket of herbs along the wall in the dining hall, kept there for their scent rather than for cooking. Today's unusual dessert was something called 'licorice,' which Kolus tried and immediately loathed beyond description. He pocketed a few for later use.

The note instructed him to meet this man north of the city. He was not the only one to get such an instruction. This was also odd. Odd enough that he felt nervous. Kolus was rarely nervous, but when he was it was on a task, not when receiving a task, which made him even more nervous. Kolus did his best to conceal it, though.

The other person, a third human besides this man, was a woman. She had the hair of a raven, save for one lock of white, and stared intensely with her dark eyes. She looked like a country bumpkin, baring her hunting knives openly on her belt with a bow slung over her back. The man turned to her. "You have your instructions?"

"Yeah."

"Here you go, then," the man said as he shoved a little blue man at her, wrists bound with rope. Those were the other things here, the non-humans. Goblins, he was told, that's what they were. Kolus was a little surprised. When you see the enemy, you expect to see a monster. This creature literally looked like a little man, maybe waist height or a little taller, with sharp teeth, blue skin, large, pointy ears sticking out to the sides, very large eyes, and a nose that somehow fit in the middle. It looked different, but it still mostly looked like a man. Or was it a woman? It had black hair that was rough-cut and coarse. It eyed all of them suspiciously.

"Let's go, you little piece of scat," she spat. It just stood there, eyeing all of them.

"It doesn't understand you," the man said.

"You mean it doesn't speak our tongue!?" she said incredulously.

"*No*," the man said. He was annoyed at the question. The answer seemed obvious to the man, Kolus supposed.

"So, what am I supposed to do with it? I was told–" she broke off from digging into him when he interrupted.

"You're supposed to figure it out. That's what's needed. That's what we all do. What's also needed is that you don't tell anyone what you were told. You're supposed to know that. Did you *just* join? No. Don't answer that. Just take him and go," the man said.

She glowered at the man, but silently took her new unwilling companion with kicks and nudges. Kolus and the man both watched her go. "Firebrand, that one," Kolus said.

"Yeah, if looks could kill, she would've skinned me

alive," the man agreed.

"I don't have instructions," Kolus said.

"I know. Here." He gave Kolus a sealed envelope. It would have instructions in those blocky letters.

"Mind if I read them?" Kolus asked the man.

"You have to, actually. I'll turn. Let me know when you're done," the man said.

Kolus opened the envelope, scanning them and the map that accompanied. "This is pr–" Kolus began.

"Don't," the man interrupted. "Don't tell me. I only have *my* instructions."

"Fine. But I can't do this alone," Kolus said matter-of-factly.

"Well, I don't know about that, but that's probably why you need this," the man nudged his head towards the covered wagon behind him. It was a long, four-wheeled wagon pulled by two mules. It was enclosed with wooden sides and a wooden roof. Separate from the mules, there was a horse tethered to the wagon. There was a covered seat for the driver and a small area to sleep immediately behind it. Strapped to the side was a long bag cinched shut with a leather strap and buckle.

"What's that?" Kolus asked.

"A bunch of shovels, sledges, picks and other tools," he said.

"Oh. And the users…" Kolus said. He did not like what he was pretty sure he was about to be told.

"I don't know, but fifteen of your new best friends are inside." The man walked Kolus around the back of the wagon and opened the door. Fifteen pairs of eyes set in blue-skinned faces turned to look at the two of them. The goblins were seated and chained to the floor of the wagon. They were all dressed in crude, baggy clothing. *Oh*, Kolus thought. He could more clearly tell the men apart from the women. Some of them had grey or blue hair.

"You're not serious," Kolus said.

"I'm just completing my instructions. There's a crossbow in the front and a few other things that you'll probably find handy."

The man untethered the extra horse from the wagon and mounted it. "Safe travels," he said as he walked his mount off towards Yvel.

So this was how Kolus found himself at the destination two months later. Travel had eaten up most of the summer. He and his miserable companions were making their way deep into the hills to the east, following the signs of the map. Kolus had made good use of the time in between, and had picked up a considerable amount of their language in their time on the road. While there was the clearly defined captor-captive relationship that he had with all of them, they learned to be cordial enough; while there were plenty of misunderstandings given the language barrier and different customs, no parties were purposefully rude to one another. They were completely dependent on him for food and water, since they all knew that he could not trust them to stay put if given the chance to escape, so they stayed chained with a limited period of walking and exercise each day. Kolus had to be very diligent with that. He would need their relatively able bodies soon.

At last, they reached a grass and wildflower-covered field on the slope of a hill. On the far side was a stone ruin. He drove the wagon up the hill and sheltered it in the ruin, out of the wind. They camped there that night. On the arched wall inside one of the ruins he saw words written in Old Paetic: 'strength from knowledge, freedom from strength.'

And this would be why Kolus received this miserable task. Most of his tasks were in the city, usually dealing with one of the guilds, as that was his experience and background. But very few people could read or speak Old Paetic, and it had not been clear until this point as to why he was selected for this task. *Who picks the people for the tasks?* he wondered. *For that matter, who picks the tasks?*

Over the next month, that no longer mattered. What mattered was digging. Digging and staying fed and keeping the wolves and bears away. Jobs were normally very solitary and despite having fifteen goblins with him, he was still very alone. It became readily apparent in the first week of digging that they could not be trusted with even simple tasks like gathering firewood. Kolus had to put one down on the first day with the crossbow that had chewed through her bonds. Kolus felt bad. She was sort of cute in her weird way with her blue skin, small hands, and short legs. Still, the task at hand waited on no one.

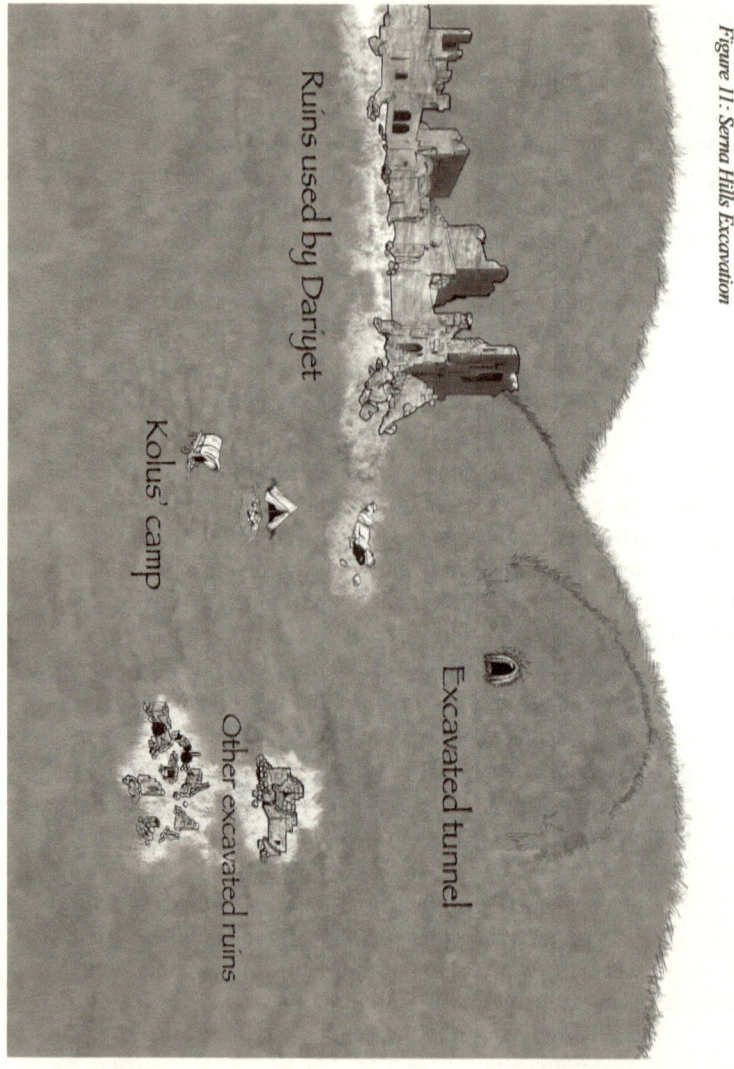

Figure 11: Serna Hills Excavation

The other fourteen ate her remains over the next three days. That was very unsettling to Kolus. They did not seem a picky lot. Kolus was not sure if this was normal for them or something they did out of desperation, but he did not really want to ask. He wondered if he would ever be reduced to that level if he was hungry enough, but he was very careful to not leave it to chance. He checked and reset his traps every morning and foraged for nuts. Generally, there was enough for each of them to have a bit after he had his share, which was always substantially bigger, and for good reasons. First, obviously, he was bigger–twice their size, as Kolus was a little taller than most humans, and needed more food to live. Secondly, it made no sense for prisoners to eat better than their jailer. Lastly, he needed them strong enough to dig, but not so strong that they could overwhelm him. He always had a knife, a shortsword, and the crossbow at hand.

The troupe worked like that for a month, digging during the days and sheltering against the rain and wind in the wagon or around a fire in the ruin at nights. Of course, they could work at night, but Kolus could not see nearly as well, and they all knew it. It would be too easy for them to make an escape attempt, so they went back in chains at night. Kolus noted that their skin turned a deeper shade of blue and their hair lightened to clearer blues and greys the more they worked in the sunlight. Some even had deep green hair.

Sunlight and cool winds blessed them on the day they finished digging, raining down comfortable warmth upon them. Even though it was well into summer, the wind coming down from the mountains still had a wintery chill, especially at night. The warmth of the sun was a blessing from Orneth herself. Given the small amount of work to do this day, he let them take longer breaking their fast. The sun rose in the warm sky and Kolus knew they were lingering longer than needed. He hustled them up and got them moving, carrying their picks and shovels. Two of them tossed a few more logs on the cookfire to keep it going while they worked.

The last month's work had cleared away the soil and rubble from the hallway, as well as the bones of the compound. It seemed that it must have been a grand enough place in its glory. Too small for a keep, yet made of a sturdy stone. The buildings cleared out well and, in some cases, they were able to dig into the cellars, though there was nothing useful. The remains of a wine cask. *Orneth! But I haven't had wine in two months!* A few skeletal remains, probably servants. There were a few other skeletons throughout that seemed to have come to a violent end–the skeletons were ripped apart or had long, jet black slivers of stone jarred through the ribs. Some were blackened and crumbling, but the bones of the others seemed well intact. Most of the remains seemed human, or at least human-sized. One of them seemed significantly larger than the others by two hands; maybe an orc? Kolus had not seen one before, but he had heard that they were about that much taller.

The arrangement of the foundations of these buildings and rooms began to give Kolus an idea of the overall layout of the compound. Kolus had been to a few palaces and well-to-do manors in his line of work and had developed a sense of how these kinds of places were built and which rooms flowed into the others. To him, the layout of the compound implied a central axis along a sort of hallway. The prize, *if there is a prize*, would be at the end of that hallway.

With the rubble cleared away, it revealed, oddly, a door: wooden, reinforced with iron strips and a latch with a pull ring. He had the goblins break the dirt away and brush it clear with pine boughs. It was in immaculate condition. Whereas everything outside that had been exposed to the elements had crumbled away with time, the door and the stonework around it were simply dirty.

"Open it," he said in Goblin to the crowd of blue-skinned workers. They hesitated until he leveled the crossbow. They shrank back, save for one of them, who sighed and lumbered down the hall. Kolus watched him as he slid the latch and pulled the ring. He slowly swung the door open, the hinges making absolutely no sound. Kolus could hear all of their breaths catch as they watched their companion.

With the door open, they could all see a faint light inside. The goblin looked back at them reassuringly and then faced the door again, taking a step forward. In a blur, his head spun off his body, spinning back towards them and splitting in two. The blurring motion lodged in the ground, another jet-black spike, like in some of the skeletons of the ruin, about the length of Kolus' elbow to his fingertips. It vibrated in the ground briefly before resting still, protruding from the ground. The lead goblin's body crumpled in place. There was a tiny screeching sound echoing from within the chambers beyond the door.

"Acrist Merciful!" Kolus exclaimed as half of the goblins shrieked and the other half quivered in fear. But nothing came. Eventually the screeching died down and everything was quiet. Kolus calmed his breathing and urged the next one forward. She refused, shaking her head violently. "I mean it, get in there," he said in Goblin. He knew his pronunciation was off, but he also knew it was close enough that she could understand.

"No!" she wailed.

He walked to her and shoved her with one hand, the other controlling the crossbow. She staggered towards the door. She gave Kolus a soulful look, but he returned her gaze with a cold stare. Her shoulders slumped for a moment before she trudged down the hallway. She stepped over the headless goblin's corpse and ventured through the door. The screeching chirped a bit, but no echo this time. She froze and it was gone. She took another step. Another. Another. Nothing.

She walked further, looked around, and called back. "It is a whole room in here. Tall." She stepped further and was engulfed in a dome of green light, a semi-sphere from the floor closing around her. It seemed to trap the sound inside, because from the outside it seemed like she had screamed for an instant before she... melted. *Graffin protect us!*

Kolus mastered his terror and uttered a silent prayer for Saint Graffin to protect them all, even the goblins. The next goblin would not go into the hole through the arch. Kolus did not want to kill him, but he had a mission, and failure was tolerated only in very extreme circumstances. And these were not extreme enough. He nudged, berated, and threatened, but in the end, he had to make the hard choice and cut the goblin's throat. The other twelve rushed him, but he sank a crossbow bolt into one, killing it, slashed another one badly with his shortsword, and fended the others back until they realized that their brief advantage of surprise had expired. He was better fed, had longer reach, and his sword was more suited to fighting than their shovels and picks. The wounded goblin groaned in pain off to the side after he restored order and bandaged the wound. *Little one probably won't make it, though*, he lamented.

"Look," he said, "we have to see what is in there. Get in there and find out what is in there, and you might live or you might die. Stay out here when I tell you to go in and you will die." One by one, they held their hands in front of them, palms facing up. As far as Kolus could tell, this was some kind of gesture that seemed to communicate deference or agreement. The next goblin went in and got up to the point where the last one disintegrated.

"I think I have something. Give me one of the picks," he called back. Kolus allowed him to return for a pick and the goblin took it back to where the last goblin had died. He struck the ground. The screeching was terrifying at first. He looked in all directions and shivered on the ground in terror. The screeching died down again after a few minutes only to be repeated with his second strike on the stone. But nothing happened again and he decided to ignore the eerie screeching echoes as he dug at the floor. "I am going to try something." Kolus watched as he tossed the pick onto the section of floor that the other died on. Nothing happened. Very tentatively, he stepped on the spot. "I think it is safe now," he called. "Safer. A little."

Kolus sent two more goblins in for a few moments before moving the rest in and following himself. The screeching was getting loud. Inside was a surprise. The passageway opened into a large room, twenty paces across and twenty paces wide. The floor was stone with a staircase on the far side of the room, against the wall. The staircase led to a balcony on the second, third, and fourth floors. Around the edges of the rooms on the upper floors were what looked to be book cases. Eerie balls of soft light strangely hung in corners and alcoves, providing a dim glow throughout the huge chamber. On the bottom floor, three long tables in a side-by-side row dominated the room. The tables were approximately two paces wide, five or six paces long, and positioned about four paces apart from one another. The outer two had a variety of books piled on top of one another and had simple, sturdy-looking wooden chairs around them. On the middle table was a skeleton bound in iron manacles with a few books lying around it, and another skeleton lying on the floor beside the table. The skeleton on the floor was garbed in brown trousers, a stained, undyed tunic, a plaid scarf, and sandals.

On the opposite walls were three doorways evenly spaced along the wall. Kolus and the goblins investigated the one on the right first. The screeching began again when they entered the first room, but its origin was from somewhere else. The first room seemed to be a sort of bedroom or lounge. It had several chairs placed in it, including an odd sort of chair with a seat long enough to lie down on. There was also a desk with a comfortable-looking chair. This room was much better lit with five of those odd, floating globes in it, one in each corner and another directly over the desk.

What struck Kolus through all of this was the untouched condition of the rooms. Everything outside had clearly been in a state of ruin for centuries, yet the door and this whole chamber were immaculate. The wood was pristine as if the furniture was only a few years old.

The iron was completely free of rust–not even discoloration where rust had been brushed away. The cushions on the bed-chair in the lounging room were simple, but still intact after all of this time, stitching and all. It was as curious as the unnatural lights dispersed throughout the place.

The second room was an even more bizarre curiosity. The room was full of rows of shelves in the walls. Again, the shelves and cases themselves were perfectly intact, but whatever used to be on the shelves was not in pristine condition. Kolus eyed the broken jars and gnarly woven baskets, mostly rotted through. Most of them had long-faded labels and piles of dried mold where they may have once been herbs. The jars had stained lines on the insides where water or some other liquid had once been, and had slowly evaporated over decades and centuries, some with an odd pile of black lumps at the bottom.

The smell was awful, yet Kolus could not place it. It was not quite like vomit or scat or rotting meat or old trash in the summer... yet not altogether *unlike* any of them. A goblin poked one of the boxes and it made an audible gaseous hissing sound, like the air slowly coming out of billows. Kolus roughly grabbed the goblin by the arm and yanked it away from the box, now emitting a reddish-brown cloud. They all watched the cloud expand warily. The hissing continued and grew louder, turning into almost a scream, like steam escaping from a hot kettle. The cloud grew bigger and pushed them out of the room. One of the other goblins closed the door, muffling the sound.

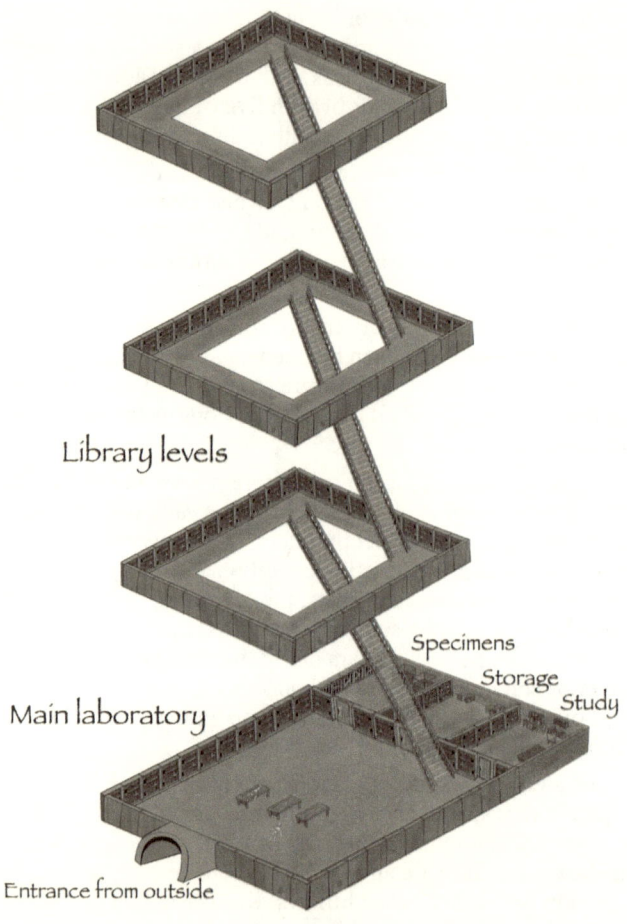

Library levels

Specimens

Storage

Study

Main laboratory

Entrance from outside

Figure 12: The Hidden Library

As they exited the room, the screeching started again. Kolus inferred that whatever was making that sound was in the third room. It bothered Kolus more because he realized that it was not just screeching, but many tiny voices screeching and squawking words. He did not know most of the words and believed there were several languages being spoken, but one of them was certainly Old Paetic.

"The Master! The Master said he would return. But a few moments he said. Master! Where is the Master?" he heard one of them say. Kolus eyed his goblins, armed with a motley assortment of shovels and picks, and nudged a few into the room before following.

The room was similarly dimly lit by four glowing orbs suspended in the upper corners of the room. A pair of glass boxes were on the far side. They were about a pace in each dimension and appeared to be full of some dark, opaque, viscous fluid. The left, right, and opposite walls each had six alcoves built into them in two rows of three with bars over them. And inside was what was making the screeching. Tiny men and women, about half of a pace tall each, with reddish skin, horns and batlike wings were railing against the bars, snarling and squeakily shouting at them.

"It is not the Master! It is not the Master!" one of them shouted.

"Who is the Master?" Kolus said to him. It had been a very long time since he had spoken Old Paetic and he knew that his words might be off. He was certain that his accent was poor. The goblins' heads whipped around in surprise that he spoke to them in a strange tongue. They stopped for a moment and regarded him before all shouting at him in Paetic.

"Who are you?" "Where is the Master?" "Valnos!"

"Someone must wake the Master!" "Whose task was that?" "Yours!" "No, yours!"

"No, yours!" "Why is the Master taking so long?"

"The Master went to the main room a long time ago, he said he would return!"

To that one, Kolus replied. "There were only the skeletons of dead men in the main room. Everything outside is destroyed."

They seemed to cheer, which was still an annoying

screech.

"The Master! The Master is dead!"

"Why? Why did no one tell us the Master was dead?"

"The Master is dead!"

"It was supposed to be us to eat him! It should have been us! I want it! I want to eat the Master's soul!"

Kolus was already nervous about his situation: being in a large, strange room, underground with glowing runes on the floor that melted people and bolts of obsidian that shot out of nowhere to skewer unwitting intruders. But, relatively speaking, Kolus was growing more nervous about the small, winged people and their cheers and demands to consume their master's soul. He backed away, motioning for the bewildered goblins to follow as the little people started to yell in one direction.

That's when Kolus spotted it. Through all of the cacophony, one of the little people was sleeping. Its cage door was open. The winged creatures called to it.

"Karas! Karas! Wake up! The Master is dead!"

Karas' eyes popped open as if he… she… it suddenly did not have eyelids. Black beads in the place of eyes surveyed the room quickly. It fell out of its upper row cage, but gracefully spread its wings, gliding by Kolus and eyeing him balefully. It easily landed on top of one of the glass boxes and pulled out a pin from a latch Kolus had not noticed. The side of the box swung down and clanged onto the floor with its iron frame.

Black liquid viscously oozed out as Karas moved on to the second box. The liquid oozed into a puddle until a tendril shot up and 'looked' at Kolus and the goblins and started moving towards them. Karas glided past and began pulling out all of the pins on the cage doors holding the other winged people inside. Oddly, through the growing chaos, Kolus noted that the pins were in plain reach of the little people through the bars. As they freed themselves, they began to swoop at Kolus and the goblins with their claws. Kolus swung at Karas with his shortsword, scoring him with a deep cut that seemed to close behind the blade. Only a tiny bit of blood emitted, spraying drops in Kolus' face and mouth along with those of some of the goblins in the room with him.

Sputtering, Kolus shoved the goblins out of the room and slammed the door shut. The little people screeched and started pounding on the door. Kolus called on the goblins to bar the door with chairs and one of the tables, but he could smell burning wood. The grey oozing creatures were burning a hole through the door with their amorphous bodies. Kolus and the others sprang back. The ooze pursued them and the little people followed through the hole, harassing the goblins. Some of them ran, pursued by the winged people. Five of the winged grabbed one of the goblins and flew him high in the chamber before dropping him to the stone floor from thirty paces. Others held two goblins down to be overtaken by the grey ooze creatures, shrieking in agony as the oozes ate and digested their bodies as they still lived. A couple of the goblins ran, but, strangely, most stayed with Kolus and fended off the winged creatures as they withdrew to the outside.

Once they got into the sunlight, the little winged people stopped pursuing Kolus and his goblins, but instead started yelling in little voices. "Free!" "Free!" "Free!" "Free!" "Free!" "Free!" They flew off into the distance.

The ooze creatures, however, still pursued them. The goblins had attempted to fight them with their shovels and picks, but the ooze bodies dissolved the iron tool heads after a few strikes and did not seem bothered. They fell back against the slow, but steady advance of the oozes. Desperately, one of the goblins grabbed a burning log from the dying cookfire and hurled it at the grey creature. It convulsed and shriveled. It was so sudden, that they all stood still for an instant in shock. Quickly, five of them grabbed smoldering or burning logs and threw them at the ooze creature, similarly killing it.

And then it was eerily quiet, except for their hoarse breathing. They collapsed in relief, panting for breath for a few moments. Kolus allowed himself a moment before getting up. "Alright," he said, "enough rest. Back in to check the place." They obeyed. Some did so timidly, some with grimness, but they obeyed.

There were no more nasty surprises, *Thank Graffin*. Kolus pulled a few books from the first shelf on the second floor. They were all written in Old Paetic. A survey of others were mostly in Paetic. Some of them were about minerals or crystals. Some were about fish or birds or animals of the land. Some were even about dragons or other creatures that did not exist… like little red-skinned, horned, clawed, winged people… but most, most were about 'magic' in, apparently, many aspects and applications.

And that *is why I was sent here.* Kolus directed the remaining goblins to load the wagon full of as many books as they could take. Two goblins had run off in fright during the fight, but he had been too busy to do much about it. This left him six of the fifteen that he had brought here, so there was a little more space.

"Well, then, the job is done. You may go," Kolus said to them.

They looked around confusedly. "Go?"

"Yes, go. You have done your part. You may go."

Still uncertain, the same one, one of the females, repeated herself. "Go where?"

"I do not know," Kolus said. "Wherever you came from."

"We cannot go back," she said.

"Why not?" Kolus asked. He was interested.

They all seemed surprised at the question. "Because we were taken as slaves at the Place-called-Borly."

"So? Why can you not go back?" Kolus asked.

"We were sent by Indariyet the Great of the Okaramine with two fists from the Talz. We cannot go back."

I'll have to find out who those people are later. Or were those places? "Yes, but *why* can you not go back?"

She hesitated. Another tried as the rest watched. "Great One, we cannot go back because our Talz were defeated. We go with the spoils."

"That does not make sense. Why can you not go back?" Kolus insisted. *Interesting.*

Another one piped in. "It is not our way, Great One. Once we are defeated in battle, we are slaves to the victor." Those words sent an unwelcome shiver down Kolus' spine. Kolus never took a slave and never would. He had grown up as a slave and loathed the practice.

"What is this 'Great One' stuff about?" he asked cautiously.

They looked confused again. "You are our Great One."

"I do not understand," Kolus said.

They looked at each other. "Are you not our leader here?" the female goblin asked.

"Well… in a way, yes," he said slowly.

"Then you are our Great One. We were taken slave and given to you as an honor gift. Was that not what happened?" she said. "Is that not how it works for your kind?"

"That is not what happened. You were taken prisoner and made to work. I simply am the one that had work needing to be done."

"Could we leave before?" the female goblin asked.

"No," he said.

"Then what is the difference?" She seemed genuinely confused about what seemed to be so plainly clear. And yet, Kolus had to admit that he struggled to find the words to explain the difference between a prisoner of war made to work and a slave. At least, in this circumstance.

Kolus spread his hands. "I cannot say. Call it as you wish, but you may go."

"We will not go," the first goblin insisted. "You will kill us if we leave or we will be killed when we return or be taken into slavery anyways. *And*," she continued, "returning after defeat and enslavement will be seen with such dishonor that we will never escape it and never make a name for ourselves. The dishonor will spread to our families." The others nodded firmly.

"Ah, so that's why," Kolus said. "Then why can you not be free in the wilderness?"

They muttered amongst themselves. "Too many uncertainties in the wilderness."

"*Too many uncertainties!?*" Kolus was dumbstruck. "What do you mean? What were you doing at the Place-called-Borly, anyways?"

"We are siege engineers," another explained. "That is what it is to be Talz."

Huh. They sure dig well. "Very well, but you can still leave."

"We will stay with you, Great One," said one of the females.

"Well, I will not!" said another one of the goblins. They all turned to the male goblin that spoke out. "I will try to be free in the wilderness. I–"

Kolus shot him through with the crossbow. He fell to the ground, his breath heaving briefly as the life poured out of him. They looked back at him.

"Sorry. It is a necessary test. I cannot afford anyone getting away with knowledge of this," Kolus said.

One of them readily said, "You are very much like our last Great One."

"I am!?" Kolus was surprised.

"Yes. You use killing to make a statement."

"We understand, Great One. You are doing what you must," said one of the goblins. "We have to do what we must, as well," she continued. "If you were not strong enough to be a great one, then we would have killed you and gotten away. We do what we must to survive. That is our way."

Indeed. "Fine, then, into the wagon for latching up. I will be back with food for the end-of-day meal." They piled in and then firmly manacled to their seats amidst piles of books. They would have to come back at least two more times to get all of the books out of here. Then, picking up the crossbow, he set off to hunt down the two goblins that ran off during the fight and drag them back or kill them. He needed to find something for them all to eat, while he was at it. The others loaded the wounded goblin that Kolus had slashed onto the wagon.

Kolus found the two wayward goblins and brought them back, totaling the party to seven goblins with Kolus leaving the ruin, including the one wounded during the revolt. The wounded goblin died the next day, leaving six.

Two days later, Kolus and one of the goblin men fell sick with a bad fever and delirium. Their skin lost most of their color, Kolus' skin turning a dark ashen grey and the goblin's skin a much darker shade of blue-grey. Their eyes rolled through the delirium, darkening noticeably. Kolus' hair began to fall out in clumps.

***

The library of Lord Risiar's Manor, overlooking the Dark Elven City of Urrissio.

Princess Erisa claimed the couch as she normally did, smiling pleasantly at the meek servant offering her a glass of mushroom wine. She sipped the wine and smirked.

"Risiar," she called musically.

"Yes, My Princess." Risiar did not look up from his study table as he read over more reports.

"Tell me, what ever happened with that little pastime with Garitan?" Erisa leaned her head upside down to look at him and then rolled over onto her elbows, the predatory gaze of her all-white eyes fixed upon him.

"My Princess, I do not understand how you derive amusement by feigning ignorance of a major component of our plan. I do, however, know how you derive amusement at my expense when my wife questions me about your tone towards me," Risiar said.

"Oh, your wife, Risiar," she mocked.

"Yes, My Princess, she knows of everything that happens in this house with listening and viewing charms. I really would prefer to not have so many of those conversations." Risiar turned a page in the report he was reading, his own glass of mushroom wine resting on the table, half-finished and forgotten.

"Oh, you are just as much fun as Seros. Boring Seros. Boring Risiar." Erisa gave him an exaggerated frown and sipped her wine.

Turning another page, Risiar spoke while his eyes scanned

the text. "I save the fun for my wife, My Princess."

"Risiar!" Erisa sat up in mock surprise and outrage.

"But to answer your question, My Princess, Drenia's invasion has stumbled and lost its vigor. Seems that Aedon, Medria, and Dranomar became aware of Drenia's mobilization. After Drenia invaded Medria, Aedon attacked Drenia and laid siege directly to their capital, Grednir." Risiar glanced up. Erisa listened with interest, no jest in her pose of face, so he continued. "The Drenians crushed the siege and are marching towards Kandaneria right now."

"Do they do too well?" Erisa asked.

"It may seem so right now, My Princess, but Drenia is smaller than its neighbors and lost too many of its boons. They will tire themselves against their three neighbors. But it will still serve the purpose, My Princess," Risiar said, putting the report down and absently reaching for another one on a short stack.

"Tell me, Risiar," Erisa began but then stopped.

"Yes, My Princess." Risiar opened the next report.

"How did you meet your wife?" she asked.

Risiar suppressed an eye roll. "Indeed."

End of Book 1. The Witches of Serna.

Appendix I. Glossary of Terms

age of selection: Period of time where a young elf reaches adulthood and they embark upon journeys and apprenticeships to select and petition for a vocation or occupation within one of the orders of elven society. See Appendix XI: Elves.

Aiz (*iez*): Third month of the Human Calendar, and the third month of spring. See Table 1: Comparison of Yearly Calendars Between the Races of Paeta.

Anz (ahnz): Second month of the Human Calendar, and the second month of spring. See Table 1.

Arinochis (a-*rin-oe*-chiss): Tenth month of the Human Calendar, and the first month of winter. See Table 1.

Banreni (bahn-*ren*-ee): Seventh month of the Human Calendar, and the first month of autumn. See Table 1.

battalion: Among western human armies, a military organization consisting of two or more companies, usually three, totalling to generally be three hundred soldiers and led by a battalion leader. See Appendix X: Humans: Organization for War.

Berenk (*behr-enk*): Sixth month of the Human Calendar, and the third month of summer. See Table 1.

Black Order: See Order of Trade.

Blue Order: See Order of the Book.

blueskin: Derogatory term used to refer to goblins and hobgoblins, stemming from the fact that western goblinkind are predominantly blueskinned.

Breathday (*breth-dae*): Fifth day of the human week. See Appendix VI.

cast-out: Term for the peoples driven out of the lowlands and into the unforgiving climes of the Kaskev Mountains. Most often it refers to orcs, goblinkind, gnolls, and similar groups, but has broadened to include other mountain-dwelling peoples such as ogres, who have rarely had positive relations with humans and elves.

Charmer: Sorcerer who imposes their will on others through an influence that appears benevolent. See Appendix IX: Magic: Blood Magic.

Chosen: From Ornethian scripture, an individual selected by the saints or by Orneth herself to receive a blessing or a special task.

Church of Orneth (*oer*-neth): Primary religion of humans on the continent of Paeta, founded over a millennia ago by a woman of the same name. Its primary tenets of belief are mercy, justice, peace, humility, and hard work. Nearly eight centuries ago, the Church of Orneth split into an Eastern and Western Church.

company: Among western human armies, a military organization consisting of approximately one hundred soldiers, organized into groups of ten (called 'tens'), led by a company leader. See Appendix X: Organization for War.

Darri (*dar-ee*): Fifth month of the Human Calendar, and the second month of summer. See Table 1.

Elder (title): Relatively senior clergy rank for a member of a clerical order of the Church of Orneth.

Ers (ers): First month of the Human Calendar, and the first month of spring. See Table 1.

Fearmonger: Sorcerer who imposes fear on others. See Appendix IX: Blood Magic.

Firebrand: Sorcerer who controls the flow of heat, usually expressed by the ability to create and control fire. See Appendix IX: Blood Magic.

Firecaster: See Firebrand.

First: Highest-ranking subordinate to the great one of a hobgoblin tribe. See Appendix XIII: Hobgoblins: Cultural Attributes, Tribal and Clan Construct.

fist: Among hobgoblin, and goblin militaries, a military organization. Generally, four to six hundred hobgoblin soldiers or two hundred to one thousand goblin fighters. See Appendix XIII: Organization for War.

foot: Using the benchmark of the average of a foot of an adult Vostindin male human, roughly analogous to twelve inches or 30.5 centimeters in the real world. See Appendix VII: Units of Measurement and Navigation.

Fourth: Most junior-ranked member of a great one's staff of a tribe of hobgoblins. See Appendix XIII: Cultural Attributes, Tribal and Clan Construct.

Fryday: Eighth day of the human week. See Appendix VI.

Garad'Dai (*gar*-ad *die*): Term among orcs that loosely translates to 'subleader,' and is awarded to orcs that have proven loyalty (most importantly) and strength or skill to their Great One. A great one may appoint any number of Garad'Dai for any number of tasks. Garad'Dai may even be appointed over other Garad'Dai. Appointments may be either temporary or permanent, though most temporary appointments end in death through some form of betrayal or assignment of an impossible task. Such situations are sometimes used as clever ways for a great one to eliminate political threats within their tribe.

Great One: Title for the leader of a tribe of orcs, goblins, or hobgoblins, though the actual word and nuance will differ between the Orc and Goblin languages. See Appendix XII: Orcs: Culture and Tribal Construct; Appendix XIII: Culture and Tribal Construct; Appendix XV: Goblins: Culture and Tribal Construct.

Green Order: See Order of the Harvest.

greenskin: Derogatory term used to refer to orcs, stemming from their green skin.

Guardian Council: One of the governing bodies of the Elven people. See Appendix XI: Elves: Governing Bodies and Societal Organization.

Halinochis (hall-i-*noe*-chiss): Eleventh month of the Human Calendar, and the second month of winter. See Table 1.

hand: Informal measurement, which is simply the spread of a person's hand, thumb-tip to pinky-tip. It is highly subjective. See Appendix VII.

headman: Lowborn community leader based on seniority among western human societies.

Healer: Sorcerer whose power is to heal wounds on and within a person's body. This is a rare type of sorcerer. See Appendix IX: Blood Magic.

Invader: Term for the sun used by goblinkind, orcs, and other races that live on the slopes or heights of the Kaskev Mountains.

Invisible Hand: Sorcerer who can control objects and master invisible forces with their thoughts. See Appendix IX: Blood Magic.

Iron Crown: Crown to the title of the king of the Dwarven realm of Drenia.

Laborday: Seventh day of the human week. See Appendix VI.

lay lord: Non-clerical nobles that are part of the flock of the Church of Orneth.

Liberator: Term for the moon used by goblinkind, orcs, and other races that live on the slopes or heights of the Kaskev Mountains.

Longnight (*long-nite*): Holy day among Goblinkind (goblins, hobgoblins, and bugbears) and orcs. See Appendix VI and Appendix XV.

magus (may-*gus*): Trained and sanctioned user of book magic among the elves of the Blue Order.

Marshal of the Crown: Title among several human militaries for the senior military official in service to a ruler.

Merchant Council of Yvel (*wie*-vel): One of the governing bodies of the Principality of Yvel which represents the interests of laborers, craftspeople, and so forth, represented in the prince's court. In practice, it functions as a council of oligarchs.

mile: Measurement of length which is two thousand paces (280 feet shorter than a mile in the real world). See Appendix VII.

Ministry of Information: Cabinet-level organization within the government of Yvel that collects, researches, and reports information to the Crown to aid in decision-making and governance.

Morningday: First day of the human week. See Appendix VI.

Nansima (nan-*see*-ma): Ninth month of the Human Calendar, and the third month of autumn. See Table 1.

Old Paetic (*pae*-tik): Ancient, now-dead language dating back to the days of the Ornethian Empire.

Ongkanir (ong-kha-*neer*): Eighth month of the Human Calendar, and the second month of autumn. See Table 1.

Order: 1. Division of Elven society by practice, such as agriculture, knowledge, martial studies, and so forth. See Appendix XI: The Orders.

2. Organization, either clerical or militant, of clergy of the Church of Orneth.

Order of the Book: Order of Elven society devoted to scholastic pursuits, primarily focused on magic. Also known as the Blue Order. See Appendix XI: The Orders.

Order of the Harvest: Order of Elven society focusing on agriculture. Also known as the Green Order. See Appendix XI: The Orders.

Order of Peace: Order of Elven society comprised of diplomats and ambassadors, often informing the decisions made by members of other orders. Also known as the White Order. See Appendix XI: The Orders.

Order of the People: Order of the governing bodies of the elves. Membership is based upon appointments, nominations, and petitions and is reserved for those most esteemed within their previous order. Also known as the Order of the People's Will, the Order of the Will, the Will, and the Purple Order. See Appendix XI: The Orders.

Order of the People's Will: See Order of the People.

Order of the Sword: Militaristic-based order of Elven society. As well as providing soldiers, generals, and weapon masters, members are also often scouts, spies, or logisticians. Also known as the Order of the Sword or the Red Order. See Appendix XI: The Orders.

Order of the Sun and Moon: Order of Elven society comprised of artists and craftspeople. See Appendix XI: The Orders.

Order of War: See Order of the Sword.

Order of the Will: See Order of the People.

Order of Trade: Order of Elven society concerned with mercantilism, trade, travel, and commerce. Also known as the Black Order. See Appendix XI: The Orders.

pace: Measurement term for the average stride of the same one hundred adult Vostindin males, which is two and a half feet. See Appendix VII.

Place: Definite article used for locations in the Goblin language, adopted into Orcish (e.g., *Place-called-Kogylar*).

Playday: Ninth day of the human week. See Appendix VI.

Primarch: Senior official of the Church of Orneth. There is a Primarch of the Western Church of Orneth, as well as the Eastern Church of Orneth.

principality: Realm governed by a prince or princess.

Purple Order: See Order of the People.

Red Order: See Order of War.

regiment: Among western human militaries, a collection of two or more battalions, usually three, generally comprising roughly a thousand soldiers and commanded by a regimental leader. See Appendix X: Organization for War.

Restday: Tenth day of the human week. See Appendix VI.

ridin (*rih*-din): Liquor made from mashed, fermented, and distilled roots or tubers.

sapper: Soldier trained in siege warfare, specializing in the construction of fortifications, siege engines, and related works.

Second: Second-highest ranking subordinate to the great one of a hobgoblin tribe. See Appendix XIII: Cultural Attributes, Tribal and Clan Construct.

Seer: Sorcerer capable of perceiving phenomena beyond the ordinary ability to perceive reality and surroundings. One such manifestation is to see the auras of people. See Appendix IX: Blood Magic.

Seer Council: One of the governing bodies of the Elven people. See Appendix XI: Governing Bodies and Societal Organization.

Sister Knight: Address between knights of the Orders Militant of the Church of Orneth.

Sortingday: The sixth day of the human week. See Appendix VI.

Soulblade: 1. Enchanted weapon, usually a sword, which draws power from a living soul that has been sacrificed and imbued into the weapon.

2. In goblinkind legend, a weapon in which the respective gods of goblinkind imbue the soul of one of their own into a weapon and gift the weapon to a chosen champion.

spawner: Goblins of breeding age in a clan that participate in breeding. See Appendix XV: Family, Fertility, and Property.

Stone: Definite article for locations in goblin languages that are particular to castles, fortresses, and fortifications that stand apart from towns or cities (e.g., *Stone of Rykooth*).

Stormbearer: Sorcerer capable of controlling the air around them and, to some extent, the weather. Colloquially termed 'Stormwitch' by some. See Appendix IX: Blood Magic.

Stormwitch: See Stormbearer.

Talinochis (*tah*-li-noe-chiss): Twelfth and last month of the Human Calendar, and the third month of winter. See Table 1.

ten: Among western human militaries, the basic fighting unit of ten soldiers, led by a tenleader (included in the ten). See Appendix X: Organization for War.

tenday: Term referencing the week of ten days, by the Human Calendar. See Appendix VI.

397

tenleader: Title for a supervisor of ten soldiers (including the tenleader). The title is prevalent in most human armies west of the Kaskev Mountains. Colloquially, the term 'tenman' is often used. See Appendix X: Organization for War.

tenman: See tenleader.

Third: Second-most junior member of a great one's staff in a tribe of hobgoblins. See Appendix XIII: Culture and Tribal Construct.

Thirstday (*thurst-dae*): Fourth day of the human week. See Appendix VI.

Traveler: Elf that is abroad from the Elven Lands to experience non-elven lands, peoples, and cultures, and collect information on behalf of the ruling bodies of the Elven Lands. See Appendix XI: Governing Bodies and Societal Organization.

Twosday (*tooz-dae*): Second day of the human week. Folklore amongst humans links this day to meeting a person that one will eventually marry. See Appendix VI.

Unbreakable: Sorcerer who can grow a very hard layer of outer skin, often metallic, that protects them, while remaining as flexible to their movements and actions as their own skin. See Appendix IX: Blood Magic.

Under-Provost: Rank of seniority within the Order of the Book.

underworld: Realm beneath the sunlit lands, home to cities, communities, and various livelihoods.

Warmonger: Sorcerer who can induce strong feelings of anger in others. See Appendix IX: Blood Magic.

The Ways: Religion of the Elven people. See Appendix XI: Culture and Economy.

Weddingday (*wed*-ing-*dae*): Third day of the human week. Folklore links it to a fortunate day to marry. See Appendix VI.

White Order: See Order of Peace.

The Will: See Order of the People.

Woodwarper: Vocation among elves to magically shape wood, not only for furniture, tools, and art, but also for dwellings, including those shaped from the interior of living trees.

Youri (*yoe*-ree): Fourth month of the Human Calendar, and the first month of summer. See Table 1.

Appendix II. Index of Characters

Abiah Zug'ail (ah-*by*-uh *zug*-ai-yil): Female ethnic-Marin human. Townswoman from Serna.

Aered Torg'ail (*ae*-red *torg*-ai-yil): Male mixed-ethnic Marin-Eklendan human. Prince-Heir to the throne of Yvel. Son of Gerald; third eldest sibling of Arnold, Larz, Oswald, Pantaria, Praxia, and Velthuria. See also Torg'ail, House of.

Akriun Ydren (ak-*ri*-un *ee*-dren): Male High Elf. Has red hair and a long face, often wearing an expression of impatience. Member of the Order of Peace. Councilor of the Guardian Council.

Aleksan Odr'ail (a-*lek*-sun *ode*-drai-yil): Male ethnic-Marin human. Knight in the Crown Guard.

Alis Benidran (*al-iss ben*-e-dran): Female ethnic-Eklendan human, from the town of Serna. Works at the local tannery.

Allana Hunr'ail (al-*an*-a *hun*-rai-yil): Female Marin human. Carpenter from the town of Serna.

Amryst Veradran (*am*-rist *ver*-a-dran): Female mixed-ethnic Marin-Eklendan human from the town of Serna.

Anrior: See Lierialuth Anrior.

Aphra Lin'ail (*af*-ra *lin*-ai-yil): Female ethnic-Marin human from the town of Serna. Brown hair, blue eyes, with a deferential demeanor. Twin sister of Marlar.

Arami (ah-*ram*-ee): Male ethnic-Berk human. Reverend Knight of the Order of Saint Kostray the Pure.

Arbera Rollodran (*ar*-ber-uh *roe*-loe-dran): Female ethnic-Eklendan human, from the town of Serna. Tends towards superstition. Married to a miller; relation of Danick.

Arkiban the Great (*ark*-a-ban): Male purpleskinned (Eastern) hobgoblin. Great One of the Okaramine tribe until losing a duel to Oygariyet the Great of the Zirn. Died during the Sixth Moon Cycle, 3113 by the Hobgoblin Calendar (Aiz, 792, by the Western Church of Orneth calendar).

Arladran, House of (*ar*-la-dran): A clan of nobility, loyal to the Crown of Yvel. The banner is eight vertical stripes, alternating between red and white. See Dorvin Arladran, Kovarre Arladran.

Arnold Torg'ail (*ar*-nold *torg*-ai-yil): Male mixed-ethnic Marin-Eklendan human. Particularly tall for a Marin, with icy blue eyes, a narrow nose, backswept brown hair, and a distinctive mole on his neck. Clever and hard-working. Prince-Heir of Yvel. Son of Prince Gerald; eldest sibling to Aered, Larz, Oswald, Praxia, Pantaria, and Velthuria. See also Torg'ail, House of.

Arozrien: See Holbrin Arozrien.

Arvr'ail: See Jaro Arvr'ail, Sora Arvr'ail.

Arynn (*ah*-rin): Female High Elf of the Order of the Sword. Exceptionally skilled at tracking, as well as possessing staunch emotional self control. Reserved and dutiful, even by Elven standards. One of the travelers appointed by the Guardian Council.

Aselifar: See Merik Aselifar, Risit Aselifar.

Autumnleaf: See Lazura Autumnleaf.

Ayza Orint'ail (*ai*-za or-*in*-tai-yil): Female ethnic-Marin woman with black hair, blue eyes, and pale skin, and a medium build and height. She is level-headed and protective of her sister, Kora. Apprentice glassier in her family's workshop in the town of Serna.

Baryn Kevr'ail (*baer*-in *kev*-rai-yil): Male ethnic-Marin human, from the town of Serna.

Baswyn Gerndran (bass-*win gern-dran*): Female ethnic-Eklendan human, from the town of Serna.

Baydran: See Garen Baydran, Jorn Baydran.

Belifar: See Melz Belifar.

Ben'ail: See Erest Ben'ail.

Benidran: See Alis Benidran.

Beren Enkr'ail (*beh*-ren *en*-krai-yil): Male ethnic-Eklendan human. Reserved, meticulous, and pragmatic, but carries a pot belly with him. Traveling merchant based in Serna.

Bers Der'ail (*burz der*-ai-yil): Male ethnic-Marin human; short and pudgy of stature with blond hair. Bold and opportunistic public speaker, though not often convincing. Yvelian nobleman.

Bierien (bi-*ehr*-i-en): Female High Elf of the Order of Industry. Wavy brown hair and green eyes. Almost always wears belted trousers with a tucked shirt, frequently also wears the leather apron of a smith. Empathetic and perfectionist, and a skilled blacksmith. One of the travelers appointed by the Guardian Council.

Bindeyet (bind-*ie*-yet): Blueskinned (Western) goblin leading multiple tribes of goblins operating in Kogylar.

Blar'ail: See Orn Blar'ail.

Bonwyn Kevr'ail (*bon*-win *kev*-rai-yil): Female ethnic-Marin human. Wife of Baryn Kevr'ail.

Buin (*boo*-win): Male ethnic-Eklendan human child from the town of Serna.

Cavalry Leader, the: Female blueskinned (Western) hobgoblin. Subleader of cavalry from the Wiridil tribe. Dark eyes and deep black hair reaching mid-back tied into a tight tail and tucked inside her helmet. Uses berries when available to stain her hair purple.

Chariss Ordavan (*char*-iss *oer*-da-van): Female ethnic-Eklendan human, squire to Sir Harl.

Clay: Male ethnic-Marin human. Barkeep at the Valley Spring Inn in Serna.

Conwyn Extardran (*con*-win ex-*tar*-dran): Male ethnic-Eklendan human, from the town of Serna.

Covendran, House of (*kov*-en-dran): A small noble family in the principality of Yvel that holds lordship over the town of Serna. The banner of House Covendran is checkered blue and white. See also Dareum Covendran, Judane Covendran, Koval Covendran, Mariss Covendran.

Creasan (*cree*-sen): Dareum Covendran's horse.

Damarus Olid'ail (dam-ar-*us* o-*lid*-ai-yil): Male ethnic-Marin human from Serna. Stablehand at the Valley Spring Inn.

Damerwyn Perndran (*dam*-mer-win *pern*-dran): Male ethnic-Eklendan human from the town of Serna.

Dandran: See Garn Dandran.

Danfreys (*dan*-frees): Male ethnic-Marin human. A surgeon in service of the Crown of Yvel.

Danick Isrdran (*dan-ik* is-*er*-dran): Male ethnic-Eklendan human. Townsman from Serna.

Dareum Covendran (*daer*-ree-um *kov*-en-dran): Male ethnic-Eklendan human; red-haired with a temper to match. Tends towards idealism and fast action. Nobleman and son of Koval and Mariss; brother to Judane. Known by his family as 'Darups.' See also Covendran, House of.

Dariyet (*dar*-ie-yet): Male blueskinned (Western) hobgoblin of the Zirn. Aquamarine-eyed and muscular, with two gold earrings and a cape made of human faces. Raised from numbered status by Oygariyet to command a portion of the Borys-Karang orcs in the forest and hills east of Serna.

Deni Oilaravan (*den*-nee oy-*lar*-uh-van): Male ethnic-Eklendan human, squire to Sir Harl.

Der'ail: See Bers Der'ail.

Dorrels Joledran (*do*-rels *jol*-a-dran): Male ethnic-Eklendan human. Chamberlain under the Prince of Yvel.

Dorvin Arladran (*dor*-vin *ar*-la-dran): Male ethnic-Eklendan human. Nobleman and head of House Arladran. Battalion Leader in the Crown Army of Yvel. Husband of Kovarre. See also Arladran, House of.

Dryalos: See Erensed Dryalos.

Dum'ail: See Ereman Dum'ail.

Dyram Torin'ail (*die*-rum tor-*in*-ai-yil): Male ethnic-Marin human, from the town of Serna. Blond and blue-eyed, with an expression that invites challenge and a propensity to act and speak brashly. Relation of Sedra and Seedar.

Eevarel Mazurnine (*ee*-var-el *maz*-ur-nine): Female Wood Elf with green eyes, auburn hair, a fair complexion, and a slender but muscular physique. Partially descended from High Elf lineage. Notably independent and enjoys playfully teasing those of whom she is fond. Prefers modest, practical garments and coiffing. Member of the Order of the Sword. One of the travelers appointed by the Guardian Council.

Enardran: See Iblar Enardran.

Enkr'ail: See Beren Enkr'ail.

Ereman Dum'ail (*ehr*-e-man *doom*-ai-yil): Male ethnic-Marin human. White-haired and long-bearded. Elder Reverend in the Church of Orneth, Order of Saint Kostray the Pure. Sole and senior religious figure in the town of Serna. Presides over religious services from the chapel in Serna.

Erensed Dryalos (*eh*-ren-sed *drie*-a-los): Male High Elf at the age of selection. Blond hair and green eyes. One of the Travelers appointed by the Guardian Council. Under the tutelage of Irduin Usrani.

Erest Ben'ail (eh-*rist ben*-ai-yil): Female ethnic-Marin human. Has a face that has made many hard bargains. Member of the Merchant Council of Yvel.

Erion Feradran (*eh*-ri-on *fer*-a-dran): Male ethnic-Eklendan human. Squire to Arnold Torg'ail.

Erisa of Urrissio (*eh*-riss-a, *er*-iss-ee-oe): Female Dark Elf. Very black skin, like charcoal, with white hair. Beautiful, playful eyes, and a mischievous smile. Graceful in her movements. Princess of the subterranean Dark Elven city of Urrissio.

Ervan Panr'ail (*ur*-van pan-*rai*-yil): Male ethnic-Marin human. Known to be jovial and bold, bordering on foolhardy. Livestock farmer from near the town of Serna. Younger cousin of Julian Panr'ail. Engaged to Terah Miykodran.

Evren Jundran (*ev*-ren *joon*-dran): Male ethnic-Eklendan human from the town of Serna.

Extardran: See Conwyn Extardan.

Feradran: See Erion Feradran.

Garen Baydran (*gehr*-en *bay*-dran): Male ethnic-Eklendan human. Farmer in the Serna township. Son of Jorn Baydran.

Garitan of Drenia (*gaer*-a-tan, *dren*-ee-a): Male dwarf of the deep clans. Emissary of King Nerim of Drenia to the city of Urrissio.

Garn Dandran (*garn dan*-dran), Male mixed-ethnic Marin-Eklendan human. Knight of the Crown Guard of Yvel.

Garrick (ga-*rik*): See Turin.

Garsiyet (*gar*-see-yet): A blueskinned (Western) hobgoblin overseeing logistics at Kogylar.

Garven (*gar*-ven): Male ethnic-Marin human. Medium height and scruffy, with shaggy brown hair and brown eyes. Curious and perceptive with an easy manner. Huntsman from the town of Serna, apprenticed to Korane Lowdran.

Gerald Torg'ail (*jer*-ald *torg*-ai-yil): Male mixed-ethnic Marin-Eklendan human. Tall and handsome, with grey (formerly brown) hair and blue eyes. Crown Prince of Yvel. Father to Arnold, Aered, Larz, Oswald, Pantaria, Praxia, and Velthuria. See also Torg'ail, House of.

Gerndran: See Baswyn Gerndran.

Grotis the Loner (*gro*-tiss): Male orcish mercenary from the hills of the Western Kaskevs; literally translated to "alone." Atypically short for an orc (standing roughly the same height as a tall human male), with closely cut black hair. Wears reinforced leather armor dotted with a myriad of pouches, pockets, knives, and other tools. Characterized by an unusually curious and scholastic nature.

Gundr'ail: See Mot Gundr'ail.

Gunst Ver'ail (*gunzt* ver-*ai*-yil): Male ethnic-Marin human. Aged in his forties, with a careworn face and receding hairline. Nobleman and head of House Ver'ail, and battalion leader in the Crown Army of Yvel. See also Ver'ail, House of.

Harl Oleandran (*harl* oe-*lee*-an-*dran*): Male ethnic-Eklendan human. Knight and co-leader of the Yvelian Crown Guard and Baron of Borly.

Hifen (*hih*-fen): Male ethnic-Marin human. Apprentice smith from Serna.

Holbrin Arozrien (*hoel*-brin *uh*-roz-*ree*-en): Icy-eyed, brown-haired male High Elf of the Order of the Sword. Known by his placid demeanor and unshakeable self-possession. Holder of a wing-engraved blade. Appointed as lead traveler by the Guardian Council.

Hunr'ail: See Allana Hunr'ail.

Iblar Enardran (ib-*lar* e-*nar*-dran): Male ethnic-Eklendan human farmer from the town of Serna.

Indariyet the Great (in-*dar*-ee-yet): Female purpleskinned (Eastern) hobgoblin. Keeps her black hair tied into a tail. Often wears a gambeson or brigandine with a curved cavalry sword at her belt. Meticulous, shrewd, and impatient. Raised from second status and named by Oygariyet the Great to be the Great One of Okaramine tribe after Oygariyet's duel with Arkiban. Manages planning and logistics of the war on behalf of Oygariyet.

Iquarren: See Tyrnimar Iquarren.

Irduin Usrani (*ir*-doo-in *us*-rhan-ee): Female Grey Elf of the Order of the Sword and holder of a wing-engraved blade. Snow-white skin, silver hair, and violet eyes. Author of several books regarding swordcraft and military history. One of the Travelers appointed by the Guardian Council. Mentor to Lazura, Lierialuth Anrior, and Erensed Dryalos.

Iriaden Olari (ir-ee-a-*den* oe-*lar*-ee): Female Grey Elf with light blue hair and a pleasant and easy smile. Member of the Order of the Book. Councilor of the Guardian Council.

Isrdran: See Danick Isrdran.

Isriaden Kasriel (is-ree-a-*den kas*-ree-el): Female Grey Elf. Under-Provost of the
Tower of Ebariel.

Ja'Kend (jah-*kend*): Female ethnic-Berk human. Dame Reverend Knight of the
Order of Saint Kostray the Pure.

Jak "Greenskin": Male half-human, half-orc, and taller than most humans. Has a
scraggly and unkempt beard. Released prisoner from a jail somewhere in
Yvel Principality; originally from the Yvelian town of Keppa.

Jaro Arvr'ail (*jah*-ro arv-*rai*-yil): Male ethnic-Marin human. Knight of the Crown
Guard of Yvel. Husband to Sora.

Jof Toliodran (*jof to*-le-oe-dran): Male ethnic-Eklendan human. Tall, slender, blond,
blue-eyed, and dashing. Young member of House Toliodran of Keppa.

Jo'Kaul (*jo*-kawl): Male ethnic-Berk human. Reverend Knight of the Order of Saint
Graffid the Defender.

Jolaban (*joe*-la-ban): A purple-skinned (Eastern) hobgoblin overseeing logistics at
Kogylar.

Joledran: See Dorrels Joledran.

Jorn Baydran (*jorn bae*-dran): Male ethnic-Eklendan human. Farmer in the Serna
township. Father of Garen Baydran.

Jovaela Varion (jo-*vale*-uh va-*rie*-un): Black-haired, black-eyed female High Elf of
the Order of the Sword. Wears her hair in a single thick braid. Adheres
strictly to rules, instructions, and social normatives. One of the Travelers
appointed by the Guardian Council.

Judane Covendran (joo-*dane kov*-en-dran): Female ethnic-Eklendan human. Dark
of hair and eyes, with an angular, narrow jaw. Eager to prove that she can
fight. Noblewoman and daughter of Koval and Mariss; sister to Dareum.
See also Covendran, House of.

Julian Panr'ail (*joo*-lee-an pan-*rai*-yil): Male ethnic-Marin human. Lanky and lithe
livestock farmer with a mop of sandy brown hair from outside the town
of Serna. Defined by his reliability and stoicism. Elder cousin of Ervan
Panr'ail.

Jundran: See Evran Jundran.

Jutzdran: See Yamis Jutzdran.

Karas (*ka*-ras): A minor demon kept in captivity by Valnos the wizard.

Karidran: See Taram Karidran.

Kasriel: See Isriaden Kasriel.

Kersis, House of: Ethnic-Vostindin house of nobles that sided with the west during
the Great Shattering and settled into the lands around Yvel.

Kerzin (*ker*-zin): Female ethnic-Eklendan human. Chief Surgeon in the service to the Crown of Yvel.

Kevr'ail: See Baryn Kevr'ail, Bonwyn Kev'rail.

Kolus (*ko*-luss): Male ethnic-Eklendan human. Ruthless and practical. An operative of Lord Nicholas on behalf of the Ministry of Information.

Korane Lowdran (kor-*ain loe*-dran): Middle-aged female mixed-ethnic Marin-Eklendan human from Serna. Jet black hair, save for a silver lock in the front that appeared after the attacks on the town of Serna. Tends towards brooding and vindictive behavior.

Kora Orint'ail (*kor*-a or-int-*ai*-yil): Red-haired, brown-eyed ethnic-Marin female human of medium build and height. Immature, and prone to feeling strong emotions. Often acts out of anger or panic. Apprentice glazier at her family's workshop in the town of Serna. Sister of Ayza.

Koval Covendran (*koe*-vahl *koe*-ven-dran): Male ethnic-Eklendan middle-aged human. Black hair with silver wings, and a trimmed salt and pepper beard. Proud, and does not like his authority or competence questioned. Quick to rely on intimidation in order to get his way. Lord of the town of Serna and surrounding villages and farms. Father of Dareum and Judane, husband to Mariss. See also Covendran, House of.

Kovarre Arladran (*kov*-air ar-la-dran): Female ethnic-Eklendan human in her mid-thirties. Pale olive skin, black hair, and dark, brooding eyes. Bitter, coldly vengeful, and committed to defeating orcs and goblinkind. Noblewoman and wife of Dorvin, head of House Arladran. See also Arladran, House of.

Kozain (*ko*-zaen): Female ethnic-Berk human. Reverend Knight of the Order of Saint Kostray the Pure.

Koziathin (koe-*zie*-a-thin): Female ethnic-Berk human. A cook in the Palace of Yvel's kitchens treasured for her skill in brewing coffee.

Larz Torg'ail (*larz* torg-*ai*-yil): Male mixed-ethnic Marin-Eklendan human. Sandy brown hair and blue eyes. Prince-Heir to the throne of Yvel. Son of Gerald; sixth oldest sibling of Aered, Arnold, Oswald, Pantaria, Praxia, and Velthuria. See also Torg'ail, House of.

Lazura (*la*-zur-a) Autumnleaf: Female Sylvan Elf at the age of selection. Blond hair and blue eyes. One of the Travelers appointed by the Guardian Council. Under the tutelage of Irduin Usrani.

Lena Pardran (*len*-uh *par*-dran): Female ethnic-Eklendan human, from the town of Serna.

Lierialuth Anrior (leer-*ie*-a-*looth ahn*-ree-or): Female High Elf at the age of selection. One of the Travelers appointed by the Guardian Council. Under the tutelage of Irduin Usrani.

Lin'ail: See Aphra Lin'ail, Marlar Lin'ail.

Liri Venodran (*lee*-ree *ven*-oe-dran): Female ethnic-Eklendan human from the town of Serna.

Lowdran: See Korane Lowdran.

Machidran: See Nicholas Machidran.

Maglaban (*mag*-la-ban): Male purpleskinned (Eastern) hobgoblin. Shaven bald with a grim face. Wears armor for all occasions, and carries a glaive used to direct people as much as it is used in combat. Practical, honor-bound, and loyal, with no patience for petty conflicts, selfishness, or cowardice. Great One of the Barituul, hailing from the hobgoblin city of Golardeg.

Mariss Covendran (*ma*-riss *kov*-en-dran): Female ethnic-Eklendan human. Dark hair and dark eyes. Introverted, sweet, and exceedingly persuasive. Lady of the town of Serna. Wife of Koval, mother of Dareum and Judane. See also Covendran, House of.

Marlar Lin'ail (*mar-lar lin*-ai-yil): Female ethnic-Marin human from Serna. Has brown hair, blue eyes, and an argumentative streak. Twin sister of Aphra.

Marsen Fris'ail (*mar*-sin friz-*ai*-yil): Female ethnic-Marin human from Serna.

Mazurnine: See Eevarel Mazurnine.

Melz Belifar (*melz bel*-i-far): Male ethnic-Berk human. Elderly, bald, and slow-moving. Ornethian Bishop of Yvel.

Merik Aselifar (*mer*-ik *ae*-sel-i-far): Male ethnic-Berk human. In his mid-thirties; taller (and broader) than average, with a muscular build. Has brown hair and hazel eyes. Is loyal and idealistic. Reverend Knight of the Military Order of Saint Graffid the Defender.

Miykodran: See Terah Miykodran, Ziek Miykodran.

Mkaela Ran'ail (*mik*-ae-la ran-*ai*-yil): Female ethnic-Marin human. Wavy brown hair and brown eyes; petite with a soft build. Kind and humble, but often blunt of manner. Baker and apprentice apothecary of the town of Serna.

Mot Gundr'ail (*mot* gund-*rai*-yil): Male ethnic-Marin human. Heavy set, with a large, hard belly hanging over his belt. Clean-shaven and mostly bald with wisps of white hair combed over. General of the Crown Army of Yvel.

Murchian (*merch*-ee-yan): Male gnoll. Tribal leader on the Slopes of the Invader (Eastern) of the Kaskev Mountains. Part of Oygariyet's coalition.

Nerim of Drenia (*nehr*-im, *dren*-ee-a): Male dwarf of the deep clans and King of Drenia.

Nicholas Machidran (*nik*-oe-las *mah*-chi-dran): Male ethnic-Marin human. Sports neatly-combed black hair and an intelligent expression. Is studious, thorough, and urbane. Guarded to most, friendly to a selected few. Chief Librarian and Minister of Information in service of the Crown of Yvel.

Odr'ail: See Aleksan Odr'ail.

Oilaravan: See Deni Oilaravan.

Olari: See Iriaden Olari.

Olavy (oe-*lah*-vee): Female ethnic-Berk human. Dame Reverend Knight of the Order of Saint Acrist the Judge.

Oleandran: See Harl Oleandran.

Olid'ail: See Damarus Olid'ail.

Ordavan: See Chariss Ordavan.

Orint'ail: See Ayza Orint'ail, Kora Orint'ail.

Orn Blar'ail (*orn* blar-*ai*-yil): Male ethnic-Marin human. Shingler and thatcher from the town of Serna.

Orsir, Trinien: See Trinien Orsir.

Oswald Torg'ail (*oz*-wald tor-*gai*-yil): Male mixed-ethnic Marin-Eklendan human. Similar in appearance to his older brother, Arnold. Prince-Heir to the throne of Yvel. Clever, laconic, often with an amused expression. See also Torg'ail, House of.

Oygariyet the Great (*oi*-gar-ee-*yet*): Male blueskinned (Western) hobgoblin. Bald, muscular, and agile; prefers to fight with a sword and mace. Ruthless yet kind; visionary and bold; clever and scheming. Respectful of his possessions. Great One of the Zirn tribe. Oygariyet forged an alliance between most of the hobgoblin and goblin tribes of the mountains.

Panr'ail: See Ervan Panr'ail, Julian Panr'ail.

Pantaria Torg'ail (pan-*tar*-ee-a *torg*-ai-yil): Female mixed-ethnic Marin-Eklendan human with black hair, blue eyes, and a sickly constitution. Princess-Heir to the throne of Yvel. Daughter of Gerald, fifth eldest sibling of Aered, Arnold, Larz, Oswald, Praxia (her older twin), and Velthuria. See also Torg'ail, House of.

Pardran: See Lena Pardran.

Parendien (pa-*ren*-dee-en): Male High Elf of the Order of Peace. One of the Travelers appointed by the Guardian Council. Has black hair and blue eyes. Enjoys trying different alcohols.

Perndran: See Damerwyn Perndran.

Pine: Julian Panr'ail's horse.

Praxia Torg'ail (*prax*-ee-a *torg*-ai-yil): Female mixed-ethnic Marin-Eklendan human with black hair, blue eyes, and a sickly constitution. Princess-Heir to the throne of Yvel. Daughter of Gerald; fourth eldest sibling of Aered, Arnold, Larz, Oswald, Pantaria (her younger twin), and Velthuria. See also Torg'ail, House of.

Ran'ail: See Mkaela Ran'ail.

Reskladran: See Yander Reskladran.

Rielan Yidr'ail (*ree*-lun yih-*drai*-yil): Male ethnic-Eklendan human. Townsman from the town of Serna.

Risiar of Urrissio (*riss*-ee-ar, *er*-iss-ee-oe): Male Dark Elf. Dashing and handsome, with white hair and black eyes. Eloquent, diplomatic, quietly charismatic. Nobleman of Urrissio. Friend and ally of Princess Erisa.

Rollodran, Arbera: See Arbera Rollodran, Danick Rollodran.

Seedar Torin'ail (*see*-dar tor-in-*ai*-yil): Female ethnic-Marin human from Serna. Cousin to Dyram Torin'ail.

Selonikah (*sel*-on-*ik*-ah): Female ethnic-Eklendan human. Is blonde with brown eyes, and a little plump. Barmaid and housekeep at the Valley Spring Inn in the town of Serna.

Seros of Urrissio (*ser*-roes, *er*-iss-ee-oe): Male Dark Elf. Is nearly always dressed in laboratory clothes, showing the stains of alchemical agents or other materials. Keeps his white hair cut short. Lean, but not muscular. Is cautious, methodical, and mercenary. Under contract as a magus to Princess Erisa and Lord Risiar of Urrissio, to perform various types of magic and alchemy, as well as the crafting of drugs and poisons.

Sieraean (see-*rae*-en): Female High Elf of the Order of the Sword. Wears her black hair in a thick waist-length braid; highly proficient with the shortbow. One of the Travelers appointed by the Guardian Council.

Sora Arvr'ail (*soe*-ra arv-*rai*-yil): Female ethnic-Marin human. Knight of the Crown Guard of Yvel. Wife of Jaro.

Stanis Tw'ail (*stan*-is *twai*-yil): Male ethnic-Marin human. Clerk on the Prince of Yvel's staff.

Taram Karidran (tar-*am kar*-i-dran): Male mixed-ethnic Eklendan-Daearan human; elder resident of the town of Serna. Aged but virile appearance, with scraggly, greyed hair and deep wrinkles offset by well-defined musculature and posture.

Terah Miykodran (*ter*-ah *meek*-oe-dran): Female ethnic-Eklendan human. Has a medium complexion, auburn hair, and dark brown eyes. Seamstress from the town of Serna. Engaged to Ervan Panr'ail.

Toliodran: See Jof Toliodran.

Torg'ail, House of: The ruling family of Yvel Principality. The House of Torg'ail banner has a red, upward-pointing chevron on a gray background. See Aered Torg'ail, Arnold Torg'ail, Gerald Torg'ail, Lars Torg'ail, Oswald Torg'ail, Pantaria Torg'ail, Praxia Torg'ail, Velthuria Torg'ail.

Torin'ail: See Dyram Torin'ail, Sedra Torin'ail, Seedar Torin'ail.

Trinien Orsir (*trin*-ee-an or-*seer*): Male High Elf of the Order of Peace. Wears an amused expression and, when circumstances allow, pink hair (though it is naturally blond, and worn as such in the presence of humans). One of the travelers appointed by the Guardian Council.

Turaean (tur-*ae*-an): Male Wood Elf of the Order of the Sword. One of the Travelers appointed by the Guardian Council.

Turin (*turr*-in): Male ethnic-Marin human. One of Lord Nicholas' operatives in the

Ministry of Information. Also known as Garrick (*Gar*-ik).

Tw'ail: See Stanis Tw'ail.

Tyrnimar Iquarren (*teer*-ni-mar *ik*-war-en): Silver-haired, violet-eyed male Grey Elf of the Order of the Book (the Blue Order). Very tall and thin, with an air of uncomfortability about him. One of the Travelers appointed by the Guardian Council.

Urasen (*ur*-a-sen): Tyrnimar Iquarren's horse.

Usrani: See Irduin Usrani.

Varion: See Jovaela Varion.

Velthuria Torg'ail (vel-*thur*-ee-a *torg*-ai-yil): Female mixed-ethnic Marin-Eklendan human. Tall, like her older brothers, with red hair and dark eyes. Is eager, daring, and calculating. Princess-Heir to the throne of Yvel. Daughter of Gerald; second eldest sibling of Aered, Arnold, Larz, Oswald, Pantaria, and Praxia. See also Torg'ail, House of.

Venodran: See Liri Venodran.

Veradran: See Amryst, Veradran.

Ver'ail, House of: Noble house in the Principality of Yvel. Banner is blue and gold in a checkered pattern. See Gunst Ver'ail.

Virek (*vir*-ek): Male ethnic-Marin human. Knight and co-leader of the Yvelian Crown Guard.

Yamis Jutzdran (*ya*-mis *juts*-dran): Male ethnic-Eklendan human. Townsman from Serna.

Yand'ail: See Zaya, Yand'ail.

Yander Reskladran (*yan*-der *resk*-la-dran): Female ethnic-Eklendan human. Squire to Sir Harl.

Ydren: See Akriun, Ydren.

Yidr'ail: See Rielan Yidr'ail.

Zaya Yand'ail (*zai*-ya yan-*dai*-yil): Female mixed-ethnic Marin-Tamark human. Has wavy dark hair, a narrow jaw, and a fair, freckled complexion. Talkative, enthusiastic, and determined. One of Lord Nicholas' operatives within the Ministry of Information.

Ziek Miykodran (zee-*ek mik*-oe-dran): Young male ethnic-Eklendan human. Has olive skin, medium brown hair, and is prone to finding himself in troublesome situations despite his best intentions. Resident of the town of Serna.

Zug'ail: See Abiah Zug'ail.

Appendix III. Index of Tribes and Peoples

Ablar (*a*-blar): Hobgoblin vassal tribe to the Zirn.

Ahng-Gorah (*aun-go*-rah): Tribe of orcs from the eastern slopes of the Kaskevs. They favor swords with forward-curving blades, as is more common on the eastern side of the mountains. The Ahng-Gorah falls under the broader umbrella of tribes that are vassals to the Borys-Karang.

Baki-Norn (*ba-ki norn*): Orcish vassal tribe to the Borys-Karang; literally translated to "The Thrill of Blood."

Barituul (*bar*-i-*tool*): Tribe of purpleskinned (Eastern) hobgoblins from the Hobgoblin city of Golardeg. Led by Maglaban the Great.

Berk (*burk*): Human ethnicity predominantly populating Berkmar and northwestern Gersh; majority representation of clergy in the Western Reformed Church of Orneth. Physically tend towards lighter complexions and stocky builds. See Appendix X: Humans; fig. 13: Humans by Ethnicity: Berks and Tamarks.

Borys-Karang (bo-*reez ka*-rang): Orcish tribe; literally translated, "The All-Consuming Flame." Vassal tribes include the Ahktakan, the Bren-Derz, the Derz, the Gardek, the Gezierad, the Talz, and the Tiralk, among others.

Bren-Derz (*bren-durz*): Orcish tribe. Literally translates to "the Crushing Fist of Very, Very Hard Stone."

bugbear: Physically largest race of goblinkind.

Daearan (day-*ar*-an): Ethnicity of humans predominantly from the Kingdom of Daeara.

Dark Elf: Elves that were banished from the surface long ago after a conflict between the Elven peoples. See Appendix XI: Elves: Physiology, Appearance, and Ethnicity.

demon: Creature from the Pit.

Derz (*durs*): Orcish vassal tribe to the Borys-Karang. Literally translates to, "the Fist Made of Hard Stone."

Donbat-Karang (*don*-bat ka-*rang*): Orcish vassal tribe to the Borys-Karang. Literally translates to, "Flaming Sword."

Drell: Tribe of kobolds.

dryad (*dri*-ad): Race of tree fairy with minor powers.

dwarf: Short, stocky humanoid, standing halfway between a goblin and a short human. Dwarves primarily live in subterranean environs.

Eklendan (ek-*len*-den): Ethnicity of humans that are the predominant population of the Kingdom of Eklenda and southern Gersh. Compared to most western humans, they tend to be tall and slender, with narrow jaws, olive complexions, dark eyes, and black, brown, or red hair. See Appendix X: Humans: Physiology, Appearance, and Ethnicity; fig. 14: Humans: Eklendans and Marins.

elf: Tall and graceful sentient humanoid, blessed with beauty and long life. Elves are roughly the height of medium to tall humans, but more agile, and slighter in frame. See Appendix XI: Elves; fig. 15: Elves and Humans.

Gezierad (gez-*eer*-ad): Orcish tribe. Despite being powerful in their own right, they are reportedly deferential to the Borys-Karang.

gnoll (*noel*): Odd mix of a bipedal creature and a canine with spotted fur, as tall as orcs.

gnome (*noem*): Diminutive humanoid with proportions between that of a human and a dwarf, but scaled small enough for two or three to comfortably stand on the palm of a human hand.

goblin: Smallest of goblinkind. See Appendix XV: Goblins; fig. 20: Goblins Arguing with a Human.

goblinkind: Collective term for humanoid creatures comprising goblins, hobgoblins, and bugbears.

Grey Elf: Ethnic minority of elves, largely concentrated around the city of Ebariel. See Appendix XI: Physiology, Appearance, and Ethnicity.

halfling: Humanoid race resembling that of humans, but reaching full height at approximately one pace, or half of a human's average height.

High Elf: Majority ethnic group of elves, primarily centered in Elven cities. See Appendix XI: Physiology, Appearance, and Ethnicity.

hobgoblin: Middle-sized race of goblinkind, standing the same height as a tall human. See Appendix XIII: Hobgoblins; fig. 18: Hobgoblins Planning an Attack.

human: Most populous people of Paeta, but fractured across many ethnicities, cultures, and realms. See Appendix X; fig. 13, 14.

Kilindiban (kil-*in*-di-ban): Hobgoblin vassal tribe to the Zirn.

kobold (*ko*-boeld): Race of small, bipedal horned lizards, roughly half the height of humans (similar in stature to goblins, halflings, and dwarves). Typically dwell in caves and mountainous climes.

Marin (*mah*-rin): Ethnicity of humans, predominantly from the Kingdom of Markia. Marins tend to be short in stature with light complexions, narrow noses, blue or brown eyes, and blond to medium brown hair. See Appendix X: Physiology, Appearance, and Ethnicity; fig. 14.

lizardfolk: Race of bipedal lizards; unlike kobolds, are taller than humans (on par with hobgoblins) and lacking horns. Prefer warm, humid regions, generally along the southern Paetan coast east of the Kaskevs.

Okaramine (oe-*kar*-a-*meen*): Hobgoblin tribe. Led by the Great One Indariyet.

orc: Race of tall, greenskinned physically powerful people. See Appendix XII: Orcs; fig. 16: Portraits of Orcs; fig. 17: Orc Warrior and Orc Slave.

Peradek (*per*-a-dek): Goblin tribe, literally translated to "the Stone-Breakers."

Surent (sur-*ent*): Hobgoblin vassal tribe to the Zirn.

Sylvan Elf: See Wood Elf.

Talz (*talz*): Tribe of goblins renowned for their engineering and technical prowess. They have a wide scattering of clans between Kogylar and Berkasliriyig.

Talz (*talz*): Tribe of orcs that is resentful about being mistaken for the tribe of goblins of the same name. The Talz are a vassal tribe of the Borys-Karang.

Tamark (*ta*-mark): Ethnicity of humans primarily from Tamark and western Gersh. See Appendix X: Physiology, Appearance, and Ethnicity; fig. 13.

Tiralk (*teer*-alk): Orcish tribe, literally translated to "the Smell of Foot Treads in the Night."

Venjeer (ven-*jeer*): Goblin tribe from the city of Kogylar.

Vostindin (voe-*stind*-in): Ethnicity of humans that populate the human realm of Vostind, east of the Kaskev Mountains.

Wiridil (*whir*-i-dil): Hobgoblin tribe. Led by the Great One Muydiyet.

Wood Elf: Reference to an ethnicity of Elves, though over the centuries, the term has also come to include non-ethnic Wood Elves who opt for a rugged lifestyle or path. See Appendix XI: Physiology, Appearance, and Ethnicity.

Zirn (*zern*): Hobgoblin tribe. Led by the Great One Oygariyet. Its vassals include the Hobgoblin tribes of Ablar, Kilindiban, Okaramine, Surent, Barituul, Wiridil, and others.

413

Appendix IV: Gazetteer

Aedon (*ae-don*): One of four large dwarven kingdoms beneath the Kaskev Mountains, alongside Dranomar, Drenia, and Medria. Some of its major cities include Adyrnaarn, Ashgar-Isriol, Ezkaarn, Kandaneria, Verenaz, and Zol. The dwarves of Aedon are called Aedons.

Aezel (*ae*-zel): Island northwest of Tamarkand, across from the Boznin Sea. See fig. 1: Map of Paeta.

Agnesia (ag-*nee*-see-a): Island off of the southwest coast of Eklenda, in the Agnesian Sea. See fig. 1.

Agnesian Sea (ag-*nee*-see-un): Sea off of the southern coast of Eklenda. See fig. 1.

Ardara (ar-*dar*-ah): One of the princely cities of the Gershan Lands. Nestled at the foot of the central-western Kaskev Mountains, Ardara is a major exporter of ores and minerals to eastern Gersh and northern Eklenda. Ardarans are primarily a mix of Eklendan and Daearan humans. See fig. 2: Map of Yvel Principality and Nearby Vassal Towns.

Atlayan Mountains (at-*lae*-un): North-south range of mountains that separates Vostind and Gilliam from Mardalon. See fig. 1.

Baan (*bahn*): City further north of Kogylar and Rykooth, primarily populated by orcs and located in the mountains.

Ballic Marshes (*bahl*-ick): Wetlands formed by the River Ballic entering Lake Tald. See fig. 2.

Balta (*bahl*-tuh): Capital city of Gilliam, sitting on the southern coast. See fig. 1.

Berkmar (*burk*-mar): Kingdom of humans northwest of the Gershan Lands, west of Markia, and northeast of Tamarkand, populated almost exclusively by ethnic-Berk humans. Berkmar has a territorial dispute with Markia, holding the view that Markia has taken Berk lands. Berks from Berkmar and northwest Gersh comprise the vast majority of the clergy, both clerical and militant orders. See fig. 1.

Bervale (ber-*vale*): Vassal town of Yvel Principality, on the road between Yvel City and Vidara; west of the town of Garber. See fig. 2.

Bissen (*bis*-in): Capital city of Eklenda, sitting on the southern coast. See fig. 1.

Boaz (*boez*): Princely city in the Gershan Lands on the western shore of Lake Tald. Populated by ethnic Berk and Tamark humans. See fig. 2.

Borly (*bor*-lee): Walled vassal town of Yvel Principality, sitting between Yvel City and Versingit. See fig. 2.

Boznin Sea (*boz*-nin): Sea off the coast of northern Tamarkand, northwest Gersh, and west Berkmar. Transitions into the Korozian Ocean. See fig. 1.

Clovis (*kloe*-viss): One of the princely cities of the Gershan Lands, chiefly populated by ethnic-Berk humans. Clovis is the location of the Cathedral-Palace of the Western Reformed Church of Orneth and seat of the Primarch of the Western Reformed Church of Orneth. The Prince of Clovis has nominal power and is largely (and unofficially) subordinate to the Primarch. See fig. 1.

Cogril (cog-*rill*): Vassal town of Soorin on the road between Keppa and Soorin. See fig. 2.

Daeara (*dae*-ar-a): Human realm at the southern tip of the Kaskev Mountains, nestled in a large valley at the southern end of the Kaskev Mountains where the range splits. Inhabitants of Daeara are called Daearans (dae-*ar*-ans). See fig. 1.

Dotinhinin (*doet*-in-hin-*in*): Capital city of Daeara. See fig. 1.

Dranomar (*dran*-oe-mar): One of four large dwarven kingdoms beneath the surface of the Kaskev Mountains, alongside Aedon, Drenia, and Medria. Dranomar is roughly the depth of the Kingdom of Drenia and deeper than most of Aedon and Medria. Like Aedon and Medria, Dranomar profited from Drenia's decline through a combination of border skirmishes, mining, and industry where Drenia only saw loss. The dwarves of Dranomar are called Dranomars.

Drenia (*dren*-ee-a): One of four large dwarven kingdoms deep beneath the Kaskev Mountains, alongside Aedon, Dranomar, and Medria. Roughly the same depth as the realm of Dranomar. Drenia fell into decline over the past century, having lost territory to wars against its neighbors, as well as to underground flooding which made several very productive mines untenable and forced the Drenians to abandon the cities of Mezar-Rin and Rael Dol-Buen. Other major cities include its capital, Grednir, as well as, Veres-Dyra, Korolus, Goroboln, and Toen-Kosh. The dwarves of Drenia are called Drenians.

Ebariel (ee-*bar*-ee-el): Elven city in the western Elven Lands, in the low mountains on the eastern side of the middle of the Kaskev Range.

Eklenda (ek-*len*-da): Human realm on the western side of the Kaskev Mountains, towards the southern end of the range; west of Daeara and south of the Gershan Lands. See fig. 1.

Elven Lands: Homeland of all Elven peoples on Paeta. A rich land of fertile fields and vibrant forests in the center and the east and the foothills of the Kaskev Mountains in the west. Lakes and rivers divide the landscape and a small number of cities concentrate a portion of the population, mainly Juin, the capital city, and Ebariel in the west. The Elven Lands are ruled by a series of councils of experts, notably the Guardian Council and the Seer Council. Only elves are permitted in the Elven Lands. No humans, orcs, or any other kind has successfully entered the Elven Lands in recent memory. See fig. 1.

Garber (*gar*-ber): Vassal town of Yvel Principality, between Yvel City and Vidara; east of Bervale. See fig. 2.

Gavant (*guh*-vant) Vassal town of Versingit. Sits on the shore of the River Ballic, near the entrance of the marshes. See fig. 2.

Gersh (*gursh*): Region in western Paeta, landlocked between the Kaskev Mountains in the east, Eklenda to the south, Tamarkand in the west, and Berkmar and Markia to the north. Gersh is populated largely by a mixture of the Eklendan, Tamark, Berk, and Marin ethnicities of humans, with a small population of Daearan humans in the south. Gershan terrain is plains, forests, rolling hills and river valleys. Several rivers drain from the mountains and cross Gersh in a generally westward current. Lake Tald is the dominant terrain feature in Gersh, where several rivers meet and other rivers begin their flow out to the western seas. People from Gersh are collectively called Gershans, though there is no particular unity between Gershans. The Gershan Lands are a collection of thirteen city-states ruled by princes or princesses, which include Ardara, Boaz, Clovis, Heath, Ivria, Kangad, Keata, Kotara, Soorin, Versingit, Versinth, Vidara, and Yvel. See fig. 1.

Gilliam (*gil*-ee-um): Human realm east of the Kaskev Mountains, on the southern end of the range. Daeara and the southern Kaskev Mountains are to the west, the Kingdom of Vostind is to the northeast, and the Koroz Ocean to the south. See fig. 1.

Ginrisian Sea (*gin*-riss-*ee*-un): Sea off of the northern Markian coast on the northern end of the Kaskev range. See fig. 1.

Golardeg (*goe-lar-deg*): City of hobgoblins on the eastern slopes of the Kaskev Mountains; home to Maglaban and the Barituul tribe of hobgoblins.

Grednir (*gred*-neer): Capital city of the Dwarven realm of Drenia.

Gulf of Atlan (*at*-lan): Deep inlet at the southern end of the Atlayan Mountains. See fig. 1.

Gulf of Kuzore (koo-*zor*-eh): Body of water linked to the Korozian Ocean that separates Eklenda and Tamarkand. Provides the only seafaring port (Ivria) among the Gershan Lands. See fig. 1.

Gulf of Tazaria (ta-*zahr*-ee-a): Body of water forming an inlet between southeastern Eklenda, Daeara, and southwestern Gilliam. See fig. 1.

Heath (*heeth*): One of the princely cities in the Gershan Lands. The city overlooks the northern shore of Lake Tald. Roven is one of its vassal towns. Populated by ethnic Marin and Berk humans.

Ikkal (ik-*kal*): Island on the far side of the Sea of Szolobad, southeast of Mardalon. See fig. 1.

Ikria (*ik*-ree-ah): Dwarven-built city; former territory of the Kingdom of Drenia. Currently occupied by orcs.

Invader Side of the Mountains: Eastern slopes of the Kaskev Mountains and the lands that lie further to the east. The peoples of the Kaskev Mountains view the mountains as the center of the world and directions are given in reference to the mountains. See Glossary of Terms: Invader.

Juin (*joo*-in): Capital city of the Elven Lands, situated on the River Beros in the eastern portion of the Elven Lands. See fig. 1.

Kaitur (*kie*-tur): Capital of Berkmar, situated on the northwestern coast. See fig. 1.

Kandaneria (*kan*-dan-*ehr*-ee-a): Underground city in the Dwarven realm of Aedon.

Kangad (*kan*-gahd): Princely city on the border of the Gershan Lands across from the Kingdom of Markia. The northern forests of Markia stretch down into Kangad's lands. Kangad is an agrarian-based territory.

Kaskev Mountains (*kass*-kev *mown*-tens): Long, generally north-south mountain chain that bifurcates the continent of Paeta. See fig. 1, fig. 2.

Keppa (*kep*-ah): Vassal town of Yvel City, located between Yvel and Soorin on the River Pelik. South of Serna, the town serves as an access point to several mines and quarries vital to industry and construction for Yvel Principality and elsewhere. Notable districts are Old Town, New Town, and South Village. See fig. 2.

Kogylar (*kog*-il-ar): Goblin city in the central western slopes of the Kaskev Mountains, built into the walls and floor of a vast sinkhole. Kogylar is a major trade hub for the various peoples of the mountains, with markets on every level of this vertical city offering goods from food and crafts to industry and slavery. The city also supports agriculture through diverted mountain streams and underground rivers to provide running water, sewage, and irrigation to the city and surrounding area. While predominantly goblin, its population also includes hobgoblins, orcs, kobolds, and various half-breeds. Many of the goblin tribes of Kogylar answered Oygariyet the Great's call to muster.

Koroz Ocean (koe-*roez*): Ocean south of the continent of Paeta. Named from a Gill-culture folktale after a sailor, Koroz, who explored the southern coast of Paeta. The same explorer appears in Tamark-culture tales, associated instead with the Korozian Ocean. See fig. 1.

Korozian Ocean (koe-*roez*-ee-an): Ocean east of the continent of Paeta. Named from a Tamark-culture folktale after a sailor, Korozi, who explored the western coast of Paeta. The same explorer appears in Gill-culture tales, associated instead with the Koroz Ocean. See fig. 1.

Koult (*koolt*): Island off of the eastern coast of Thabia. See fig. 1.

Krogen (*kro*-ghen): Vassal town of Yvel City, sitting on the road between Yvel and Vidara, west of Garber and Bervale. See fig. 2.

Ladern (la-*dern*): Vassal town of Yvel Principality, sitting on the northeastern shore of Lake Tald on the mouth of the Ballic River and at the edge of the Ballic Marshes. Ladern is a fishing town that also has transloading docks for transferring cargo between river boats, lake ships, and road transportation. See fig. 2.

Lake Tald (*tahld*): Large lake in the Gershan region on the western side of the Kaskev Mountains. See fig. 2.

Left Side of the Mountains: Region of the Kaskev Mountains, named from the perspective of those who live there and view the range as the center of the world (the cast-out races). On the eastern slopes it refers to the northern end of the mountains (or further north along the eastern slopes); on the western slopes it refers to the southern end (or further south along the western slopes).

Liberator Side of the Mountains: Western slopes of the Kaskev Mountains and the lands that lie further to the west. The peoples of the (Kaskev) Mountains view the Mountains as the center of the world and directions are given in reference to the mountains. See Glossary of Terms: Liberator.

Mardalon (*mar*-da-*lon*): Human realm at the eastern end of Paeta, beyond the wall of the Atlayan Mountains. See fig. 1.

Markia (mar-*kee*-a): Human realm at the northern tip of the Paetan land mass, west of the Kaskev Mountains and north of Berkmar. See fig. 1.

Mastania (mahs-*tan*-ee-a): Continent to the east of Paeta, across the Red Ocean.

Medria (*med*-ree-a): Dwarven kingdom beneath the surface of the Kaskev Mountains, bordering Aedon and Drenia. Medria is at a higher depth than Drenia or Dranomar, and roughly at the same depth as Aedon, even possessing some cities, outposts, strongholds, or other settlements with surface contact. Like Aedon and Dranomar, Medria profited from Drenia's decline by creating opportunities where Drenia saw loss.

Mernan (*mer*-nan): Vassal town to Yvel Principality, deeper within Yvel's territory. See fig. 2.

Nustavian Sea (noo-*stav*-ee-an): Sea off of the Thabian coast, on the northern end of the Kaskev Mountains. See fig. 1.

Paeta (*pae*-ta): A large continent, centrally divided by the Kaskev Mountains. Predominantly inhabited by humans, though many other races live on Paeta. See fig. 1.

Ralang (rah-*lang*): Vassal town of Yvel City that sits on the eastern shores of Tald Lake. Ralang is predominantly a fishing town with a transloading dock for transferring cargo between lake-faring vessels, river barges from the River Guth, and wagons. See fig. 2.

Red Ocean: Ocean to the east of the continent of Paeta. See fig. 1.

Right Side of the Mountains: Region of the Kaskev Mountains, named from the perspective of those who live there and view the range as the center of the world (the cast-out races). On the eastern slopes it refers to the southern end of the mountains (or further north along the eastern slopes); on the western slopes it refers to the northern end (or further south along the western slopes).

River Ballic (*bahl*-ik): River which serves as the border between the principalities of Yvel and Versingit, originating in the foothills of the Kaskev Mountains. See fig. 2.

River Beros (*beh*-ros): River that runs off of the eastern slopes of the Kaskev Mountains, flowing through the Elven Lands, past the city of Juin before joining a larger network of rivers and lakes.

River Chessa (*cheh*-sa): River that runs from its source in the Kaskev Mountains to the Gulf of Kuzore in the west. Joined by the River Eron and the River Pelik at the city of Soorin. See fig. 2.

River Eron (*eh*-ron): River that originates deep in the Kaskev Mountains, joining the River Chessa and the River Pelik at the Gershan city of Soorin. The River Eron terminates at its joining with the River Chessa. See fig. 2.

River Guth *(guth)*: River that originates in the Kaskev Mountains and splits with the River Pelik. The River Guth flows by the princely city of Yvel and empties into Lake Tald. See fig. 2.

River Pelik (*pel*-ik): River originating in the Kaskev Mountains. It flows generally westward, splitting with the River Guth and joining the River Eron and the River Chessa at the city of Soorin, where it terminates. See fig. 2.

Samzik Mountains (*sam*-zik): Small range of mountains that separate Tamarkand from the Gershan Lands. See fig. 1.

Sea of Polonikin (poe-*lohn*-ik-in): Sea east of the Thabian coast and north of the Atlayan Mountains. See fig. 1.

Sea of Szolobad (*zoel*-uh-bad): Sea south of the Mardalon coast. See fig. 1.

Serna (*ser*-na): Vassal town of Yvel City, sitting on the road between Yvel and Soorin. Places of note include the Valley Spring Inn, Moradran Inn and Soup Shop, Mkaela's bakery, and Covendran Manor. See fig. 2; fig. 3: Map of Serna; fig. 4: Map of Serna, After the Fire.

Soorin (*soo*-rin): One of the princely cities of the Gershan Lands. Soorin controls the intersection of a major north-south road intersection with the River Pelik, the River Chessa, and the River Eron, and boasts a robust network of bridges. Soorin is an important Gershan city in trading and transloading ore from mines and quarries in the Kaskev foothills, as well as other cargo and curbing the historical threat of the Eklendans to the south. Sooriners are primarily ethnic Eklendan humans, though despite this, possess a historical animosity towards the Eklendans of Eklenda. See fig. 2.

Srkyavna (sir-*kyav*-na): Continent west of Paeta, across the Korozian Ocean.

Stone of Rykooth (*rie*-kooth): Dwarven-built fortress high in the Kaskev Mountains. Oygariyet the Great conquered Rykooth years prior to embarking upon his endeavor to reclaim the lowlands.

Tamarkand (tam-ar-*kand*): Human realm at the western tip of the Paetan land mass. See fig. 1.

Tawruk (taw-*ruk*): Capital of Tamarkand, sitting at the inner reaches of the Gulf of Kuzore. See fig. 1.

Thabia (*thay*-bee-a): Human realm at the northeastern tip of Paeta. Thabia lies east of the Kaskev Mountains and north of the Elven Lands, Vostind, and Mardalon. See fig. 1.

Thabian Channel (*thay*-bee-an): Body of water separating Thabia from Koult; joins the Nustavian Sea and the Sea of Polonikin. See fig. 1.

Thabian Mountains (*thay*-bee-an): Mountain range extending east from the Kaskev Mountains into Thabia. See fig. 1.

Thafanmir (*thaf*-an-meer): Capital of Vostind and former capital of the ancient Ornethian Empire. See fig. 1.

Ungat (*oon*-gaht): Continent south of Paeta, across the Korozian Ocean.

Urrissio (*er*-iss-ee-oe): City of Dark Elves. Urrissio is built far beneath the surface at the depth of the dwarven kingdoms.

Verdunsk (vur-*dunsk*): Capital of the Kingdom of Markia, the northern-most realm of the western human lands of Paeta. See fig. 1.

Versingit (ver-*sing*-et): One of the princely cities of the Gershan Lands. Controlling the intersection of a major north-south road intersection with the River Ballic, Versingit trades ore and stone that come from mines and quarries in the foothills of the Kaskev Mountains, transloading them from barge to river boats out to the Lake Tald or on to land transports. Versingiters are primarily ethnic-Marin humans. See fig. 2.

Versinth (ver-*sinth*): One of the princely cities of the Gershan Lands, located between Gersh and the Kingdom of Markia. Its territory spans hills, forests, plains, and rivershore, with roads connecting south and west to the rest of Gersh. Versinth serves as a gateway for Markia and eastern regions coming through the northern passes of the Kaskev Mountains.

Vidara (vih-*dar*-a): One of the princely cities of the Gershan Lands. The city overlooks the southern shore of Lake Tald. Populated by ethnic Eklendans and Tamark humans. See fig. 2.

Vostind (voe-*stind*): Largest human kingdom in the eastern lands and largest remnant of the Ornethian Empire. Vostind is populated by ethnic-Vostindin humans. See fig. 1.

Yvel City (*wie*-vel): Capital of the Yvel Principality in eastern Gersh. Districts and landmarks of note include Baldinet ("New Markia"), Banik Square, Barkton, the Marin Quarter, Mikal's Hill, the Palace of Yvel, Roentown, Trent Abbey, and Trukan. See fig. 1, fig. 2.

Yvel Principality (*wie*-vel): One of the thirteen city-states of the Gershan Lands, Yvel is located in Eastern Gersh, between the foothills of the central Kaskev Mountains and the Tald Lake. Yvel has the following vassal towns: Borly, Serna, Keppa, Garber, Bervale, Krogen, Ralang, Ladern, and Mernan. See fig. 2.

Appendix V: Index of Figures, Artifacts, and Events of Lore and History

Achadar (*ak*-a-dar): First ruler of Eklenda.

Arranel (*ar*-run-el): Elven author and member of the Blue Order, known for writings on blood magic awakenings among primarily elves, both recent and historic.

Beren the Great: See Berin the Great.

Beres Wars (*beh*-ris): Series of minor conflicts over the past three centuries between Gilliam and its neighbors, with shifting alliances across the different wars.

Berin the Great (*beh*-ren): General in the Eastern Ornethian Empire in the late imperial period, who fought to preserve the cohesion of the empire and attempted to conquer the Elven Lands. Widely renowned as an effective leader and tactician. In the west, he is referred to as Beren the Great.

Book of Graffin (*graf*-in): Sacred text within the Book of Orneth, extolling the virtues of mercy and protection of the weak.

Book of Kostray: See Five Holy Books.

Book of Orneth: Holy scripture and authoritative record of the teachings of Orneth.

Church of Orneth: See Appendix I: Glossary of Terms: Church of Orneth.

Deweter's Chronicle of the Broken Lands (*doo*-ett-ur): Multi-volumed history books regarding the formation of Gersh and its neighbors after their secession from the Ornethian Empire.

Five Holy Books: Sacred portion of Ornethian scripture, also called the Book of Kostray, teaching the purities of spirit, intent, and purpose.

God of Stuff: See Jirmishik.

Great Shattering: See Western Secession Wars.

Imperial Secession Wars: Series of conflicts, fought eight centuries past, in which the western territories of the Ornethian Empire sought independence.

Jirmishik (*jur*-mish-ik): Formal name of the chief deity in the Orcish pantheon, presiding over material possessions; commonly referred to as the God of Stuff.

Lady of Grace: Formal title for a holy person; colloquially, a saint walking in the flesh.

Lady of Seven: Fairy from a folktale, said to have seven eyes, seven arms, and seven very skinny legs. Tales describe rituals to summon her, such as uttering 'seven' seven times, seven minutes after sunset. She is often depicted wearing a long skirt, seated on a lilypad, and drinking tea.

Leriyet (lehr-*ee*-yet): Legendary hobgoblin who briefly united all hobgoblins under one banner and authored the Holy Rules.

Ornethian Empire (*oer*-neth-ee-an): Human-ruled empire that controlled all lands on Paeta except for Mardalon and the severe climes of the Kaskev Mountains and surrounding ranges. Dominance ended with the Imperial Secession Wars eight centuries ago, followed by gradual collapse over the next five centuries.

Pit: Religious concept predating Ornethian belief, denoting a place in the afterlife for evil souls.

Saint Acrist the Judge (*ak*-rist): Disciple of Orneth during life, embodying justice, law, and mercy. Patron saint of victims, constables, jailers, executioners, convicted and released criminals, as well as repentance, redemption, and forgiveness.

Saint Andren the Builder (*an*-dren): Patron saint of carpenters, masons, coopers, wagonwrights, drivers, and architects. Writer and exemplar of construction, community, and productivity.

Saint Graffin the Defender (*graf*-in): Patron saint of the weak and oppressed.

Saint Kostray the Pure (*kos*-trae): Patron saint of causes, purity of intention, innocence, kindness, self-sacrifice, and martyrs.

Valnos (*val*-noes): A long dead male ethnic-Daearan human wizard. His studies were specialized on the barrier between life and death.

Western Secession Wars: Conflict preceding the Imperial Secession Wars during which the newly seceded Western Ornethian Empire disintegrated. Also called the Western Shattering or the Great Shattering.

Western Shattering: See Western Secession Wars.

Appendix VI: Calendar Systems of Paeta

Within this world, upon which the continent of Paeta and the other nearby continents (Srkyavna, Mastania, and Ungat) exist, the solar day is twenty-four hours, the solar year is 360 days, and the lunar cycle is thirty days.

For humans, the year is divided into twelve months of thirty days, each organized into three ten-day weeks. The days, in order, are the following:

1) Morningday	6) Sortingday
2) Twosday	7) Laborday
3) Weddingday	8) Fryday
4) Thirstday	9) Playday
5) Breathday	10) Restday

The Western Human calendar treats the year 0 as the break between the East and West Churches of Orneth. The humans east of the Kaskev Mountains have an older date of their calendar's origin, 2634 years ahead of the western counterpart.

The human new year begins in the first month that plants noticeably bud, according to where the calendar was originally set. They celebrate the seasons placing a large emphasis on the new year in the spring.

Coincidentally, dwarves begin the new year on the same day, on average, as it is when the thaw on the surface has flooded the underground waterways the greatest, coinciding with the spring season's thaw and rains on the surface. Their calendar, developed over centuries, marked the most frequent day (measured by the amount of surface days, which they had to send an expedition to measure) when the floods began as the first day of the year and measured the number of days, on average, until the next first flood. The whole year is considered one 360-day month. The idea of 'days,' a different concept to most dwarves, came from trade with surface dwellers and the very few dwarves that ventured to the surface or Dwarven settlements that have surface exposure. To most dwarves, it is simply a measurement of time on their mechanical clocks that coincides with their preferences for sleeping and waking. Few know or understand that it has to do with the passing of the sun and moon.

Goblins, hobgoblins, and bugbears mark the new year by the winter solstice and celebrate the occasion which they call Longnight, the longest night of the year. Longnight celebrations take place on the winter solstice, the longest night of the year. It symbolizes a time of greatest safety and advantage against their historical enemies, the humans and elves as well as the mark of a new year. Customs differ by region, race, and tribe, but there is generally some sort of celebration involved.

Elves organize their calendar by the season, each of which is ninety days of the season. The end of the year is marked by summer's end. Elves have no set work or rest days, assuming that each elf will make the best choice for their livelihood and the needs of the many when work is needed.

Orcs, with their shorter and (generally) more violent lives, tend to have little use for marking the years. As orcs reach adulthood quicker than the other races (thirteen years is a mature adult orc analogous to a human of twenty years). They mark the time of day by the position of the moon or sun, and the time of the lunar cycle by the phase of the moon. City-dwelling orcs, whether in an orc city or another race's city, usually goblins or hobgoblins, usually use the calendar system utilized by the rest of the city. This is generally the Goblin Calendar, though there are cases where orcs use the Dwarven Calendar, such as the orcs that conquered the Dwarven city of Ikria.

Table 1: Comparison of Yearly Calendars Between the Races of Paeta				
Season	Human Month	Goblin/ Hobgoblin Lunar Cycle	Elven Season	Dwarven Calendar
Spring	Ers (New Year)	Fourth Moon	Spring	New year begins with spring, when underground rivers flood. Dwarves mark 360 days individually until the next flood
Spring	Anz	Fifth Moon	Spring	New year begins with spring, when underground rivers flood. Dwarves mark 360 days individually until the next flood
Spring	Aiz	Sixth Moon	Spring	New year begins with spring, when underground rivers flood. Dwarves mark 360 days individually until the next flood
Summer	Youri	Seventh Moon	Summer (New Year)	New year begins with spring, when underground rivers flood. Dwarves mark 360 days individually until the next flood
Summer	Darri	Eighth Moon	Summer (New Year)	New year begins with spring, when underground rivers flood. Dwarves mark 360 days individually until the next flood
Summer	Berenk	Ninth Moon	Summer (New Year)	New year begins with spring, when underground rivers flood. Dwarves mark 360 days individually until the next flood
Autumn	Banreni	Tenth Moon	Autumn	New year begins with spring, when underground rivers flood. Dwarves mark 360 days individually until the next flood
Autumn	Ongkanir	Eleventh Moon	Autumn	New year begins with spring, when underground rivers flood. Dwarves mark 360 days individually until the next flood
Autumn	Nansima	Twelfth Moon	Autumn	New year begins with spring, when underground rivers flood. Dwarves mark 360 days individually until the next flood
Winter	Arinochis	First Moon (New Year)	Winter	New year begins with spring, when underground rivers flood. Dwarves mark 360 days individually until the next flood
Winter	Halinochis	Second Moon	Winter	New year begins with spring, when underground rivers flood. Dwarves mark 360 days individually until the next flood
Winter	Talinochis	Third Moon	Winter	New year begins with spring, when underground rivers flood. Dwarves mark 360 days individually until the next flood

Table 2: Formulae for Calculating Year Differentials by Calendar	
Western Human Year (benchmark)	Western Human Year + 0.
Eastern Human Year	Western Human Year + 2634.
Dwarven Year	Western Human Year + 9690.
Elven Year (spring)	Western Human Year + 17236.
Elven Year (summer, autumn, and winter)	Western Human Year + 17237.
Goblin Year (spring, summer, and autumn)	Western Human Year + 2320.
Goblin Year (winter)	Western Human Year + 2321.

Appendix VII: Units of Measurement and Navigation

Of all that shapes the conception of the world around us, some of the most subtle influences are the words, measurements, and benchmarks which we use to describe it to one another. Below are a few units of measurement, mostly from the western human lands of Paeta, along with a brief note on how the peoples of the mountains perceive the world around them.

- **Foot:** The benchmark of the average foot of an adult Vostindin male human, shod in winter boots, with a sample of one hundred adult Vostindin males. This is roughly analogous to twelve inches or 30.5 centimeters in the real world.

- **Hand:** An informal measurement, which is simply the spread of a person's hand, age of thumb-tip to pinky-tip. It is highly subjective.

- **Mile:** One mile is two thousand paces, which is 280 feet shorter than a mile in our world.

- **Pace**: The average of the measured stride of the same one hundred adult Vostindin males, which is two and a half feet.

- **Stone:** A weight of measurement widely used by many cultures, but often inconsistent between realms. While a stone is probably the same between neighboring realms (or the differences are known and accounted for in habitual trading relationships), for example, between Yvel and Heath or Eklenda and Soorin, it would likely be different between Tamarkand and Gilliam, and certainly between any human realm and those of the dwarves or goblins. The difference comes from how heavy the benchmark stone is. Goblins from the city of Kogylar use a benchmark stone equivalent to four pounds (1.8kg) in our world, while the Eklendan humans may use a benchmark stone equivalent to five pounds (2.26kg).

Note: Orcs, goblinkind, and the other outcast races mostly live in the Kaskev Mountains; therefore, the mountains are the center of the world to them. Pervasive iron deposits make magnetic compasses dance, so their navigation is based on an outward view from the mountains. The eastern slopes are the 'Invader's Side,' meaning the east - the side from which the sun first invades the safety of darkness. Hobgoblins, for example, standing on the eastern slopes would refer to the Left of the Mountains (north), the Right of the Mountains (south), Further from the Mountains (east), and Closer to the Mountains/Deeper into the Mountains (west). The western slopes are referred to as the 'Liberator's Side,' which references the moon chasing off the sun and restoring the safety of darkness and limiting the activity of humans and elves. The directions are reversed. The same hobgoblin standing on the Liberator's side would refer to the Left of the mountains (south), the Right of the mountains (north), Further from the Mountains (west) and Closer to the Mountains/Deeper into the Mountains (east).

> Note: The sun and the moon are respectively termed the 'invader' and 'liberator,' as the moon and darkness of night give the cast-out races the advantage of their heatsight, enabling them to see in darkness (see Appendix XII, XIII, and XV for more information). When the sun 'invades,' it removes that advantage from orcs and goblinkind. This is the primary reason that orcs and goblinkind view the night as a safer time, whereas the humans and elves view daytime as the safer time of day.

Appendix VIII: Currency

The metal, size, weight, shape, and print of coins varies throughout the wide array of realms across Paeta, but most people use coins as their main currency. While barter economies exist, they are not the mainstay for any people.

Humans on the west side of the Kaskev Mountains use tin, light copper (a copper-nickel alloy of a yellow tone), copper, brass, silver, and gold in minting their coins. The Principality of Yvel mints the following coins:

- **Tin pennies:** Tin; castle on one side, farm on the other.

- **Wheat/oak penny:** Light copper; wheat sheafs on one side, oak tree on the other.

- **Boar/stag:** Copper; boar on one side, stag on the other.

- **Brass sword:** Brass; crossed swords on both sides.

- **Crown or silver crown:** Silver; crown on one side.

- **Double crown or gold crown:** Gold; crown on one side, the reigning prince or princess at the time of minting on the other.

Of all of the cast out races of the mountains, the goblins and hobgoblins have the most consistent currency, at least in terms of the metals used. Each of the cities of the mountains, like a state unto themselves, mints their own currencies. When conducting trade between cities, the gross weight of coins is measured for exchange rates. Coins are often minted with a stamp of a symbol denoting their value on one side and a symbol of their city or the face of its ruler on the other. Below are the coins minted by the Goblin city of Kogylar.

- **Tinhead:** Tin; mushroom on one side.

- **Hog:** Light copper; hog on one side.

- **Pine:** Copper; pine tree on one side.

- **Black mountain, black stone, or simply mountain or stone:** Bronze, mountain on one side.

- **Spear:** Oblong brass; spear on one side.

- **Wolf:** Silver; wolf on one side.

- **Crown:** Gold; crown on one side, the ruler of Kogylar or the owner of the mint on the other.

Appendix IX: Magic

Magic is based on a set of natural laws and uses those laws to convert those energies to other purposes or forms. There are three main types of magic: book magic, blood magic, and borrowed magic.

Book Magic

Book magic is like wizardry, in which the rules and laws of magic are learned through study. This is a weaker form of magic than others, but is able to accomplish intricate and nuanced tasks. It is much more versatile than blood magic, capable of clever designs and subtlety, and has the most utility in improving life and work. Great skill on the part of the book mage is required to approach matching power for power with a neophyte blood mage, though such a skilled book mage would also have more efficient and indirect ways of defeating a blood mage.

Book magic had been widely used by many peoples, but a series of historical events has led magic to be lost and forgotten by most. Only the elves and the dwarves retain the ability to practice book magic, and both protect its secrets for different reasons. The elves remember the horrible wars waged with magic, and are actively preventing others from regaining access to it. The dwarves guard it as a trade secret, just as any other special crafting technique. Humans, goblins, orcs, hobgoblins, halflings, and other races have collectively lost the knowledge of book magic.

Different cultures had different uses and applications for book magic. Just as technology develops to make work and life easier, so too did magic develop for these utilities first. Examples can be seen in those who still practice book magic. For the elves that know some spells, they weave it through their daily lives; they clean or cook with it, stitch garments, heat forges, and light paths on dark nights. For the dwarves, they primarily use book magic to further perfect their craftsmanship, making materials stronger and measurements more precise. The goblin magi of old would, among other things, inscribe and enchant runes on various objects to impart qualities to the object or enhance existing qualities, such as making a musical instrument louder, clearer in sound, or more enjoyable to play.

As the innovation of magic bent to the demands of life and industry for various peoples, so too did that innovation bend to the winds of war. Various peoples of the land wrought great destruction upon one another and sometimes themselves, in the name of conquest, self-defense, rebellion, and loyalty. Over time, the human magi mostly killed one another off in a series of wars. Those that survived went into hiding for the rest of their days. The elves convinced the halflings to stop practicing magic. Living in peaceful lands and desiring peaceful lives, the halflings agreed.

But other problems did not solve themselves as neatly. The elves spent significant and costly efforts in terms of time, blood, and treasure to eliminate the book mages among the goblins, hobgoblins and even the orcs and bugbears.

The only other users of book magic known to the elves and dwarves would be dragons.

Blood Magic

Blood magic is also called blood sorcery, a more powerful form of magic used to directly harness and move the energies of the world. In most cases, this is a much more powerful, but much clumsier form of magic. Its raw power is best suited to warfare.

It was in the preludes to war when the rulers of lands took more interest in blood magic despite its dangers. Especially for smaller and weaker realms, the deployment of blood mages were seen as a way to neutralize the large armies of their more powerful and aggressive neighbors.

Each person has the potential to wield blood magic, but it is locked behind a biological barrier. The barrier can be opened, but it requires a person to undergo a highly traumatic physical, emotional, or psychological event that typically results in death. As such, blood sorcerers are exceedingly rare.

Everyone's gift is a bit different. This is genetic. In some cases, depending on the nature of their power, it may be inconspicuous, so much so that the blood sorcerer him or herself does not realize what they're doing and may simply consider themselves lucky about some things.

In time, the discovery was made that there was a way to extract the blood magic gift from one person and give it to another. The process was fatal for the donor, as it amounted to removing a part of their being. The practice was used as a reward to faithful noble families during the reign of the Paetic Empire and, separately, led to the War Among the Elven Peoples.

Wielders of blood magic may include the following:

- Charmer: a sorcerer who imposes their will on others through an influence that appears benevolent. Those affected may find themselves revealing secrets which they intended to keep, openly answering unwelcome questions, or acting on suggestions despite their misgivings.

- Fearmonger: a sorcerer who imposes fear on others. The Fearmonger can vary the intensity from unease to hysteria, dependent on their skill. Typically, the subjects of this magic feel fear towards its wielder, but skilled Fearmongers may also control what the source of fear is perceived to be, and may even drive others to perform specific tasks or adhere to directions through this emotional manipulation.

- Firebrand: A sorcerer who controls the flow of heat, usually expressed by the ability to create and control fire. As the heat follows the sorcerer's magic, it leaves the absence of heat (coldness). Also called Firecaster.

- **Healer:** A sorcerer whose power is to heal wounds on and within a person's body. This is a rare type of sorcerer.

- **Invisible Hand:** A sorcerer who can control objects and master invisible forces with their thoughts.

- **Seer:** A sorcerer capable of perceiving phenomena beyond the ordinary ability to perceive reality and surroundings. One such manifestation is to see the auras of people.

- **Stormbearer:** A sorcerer capable of controlling the air around them and, to some extent, the weather. Skilled Stormbearers can create solid volumes or layers of air and generate enough static electricity to produce lightning. Colloquially termed 'Stormwitch' by some.

- **Unbreakable:** A sorcerer who can grow a very hard layer of outer skin, often metallic, that protects them, while remaining as flexible to their movements and actions as their own skin.

- **Warmonger:** A sorcerer who can induce strong feelings of anger in others. The expression of this power may be linked to a suggestion towards action, or the cause of that anger. Highly skilled Warmongers can induce rage in others towards a third party without outwardly expressing anger themselves.

Borrowed Magic

Borrowed magic occurs when a spirit or some other supernatural entity grants a magic user a portion of the spirit's power. This can be done through prayer, contract, summoning, binding, invoking fey laws, and so forth, depending on the entity granting the power. There is a wide variety of entities that can grant powers this way. Additionally, the spirits can, in some cases, unlock the blood magic barrier of a potential user.

Figure 13: Western Humans by ethnicity

Appendix X: Humans

Overview

Humans are the most abundant and dominant of the sentient races of the land. They balance many qualities that other sentient races take to the extreme, at least within their cultures. Their ethnicities are widely varied throughout Paeta and the other continents.

Physiology, Appearance, and Ethnicity

Humans have diverse ethnicities but, more or less, look like humans as we know them. There are, of course, subtle differences between the ethnicities. The following are the ethnicities in Western Paeta, but this is not representative of all the ethnicities of Paeta or the other continents. Especially in Gersh, ethnic interbreeding has been commonplace for centuries. In the cases of mixed bloodlines, the traits intermingle and blend.

Marins, from Markia and Northern Gersh, tend to have light frames and are shorter in stature than most westerners. Their skin is fair to pale, with blue or brown eyes and brown or blond hair, though there are exceptions to these norms. They tend to have narrow noses. Their spoken language is Marin and the common suffix for their surname is '-ail'.

Berks are from Berkmar and northwestern Gersh. They have fair or ruddy skin and may have facial freckles. Some will have whole-body freckles, but this is uncommon. Berks tend to have blue, hazel or green eyes with blond, brown, or red hair. Their builds tend to be heavier, with broader shoulders, hips, and jaws than most, but there are plenty of moderate frames among the Berks. They speak Berk and mark their surnames with the suffix '-ifar.'

Tamarks are from Tamarkand and western Gersh. They generally have florid, ruddy complexions with blue or green eyes and blond, brown, or red hair. Their frames are often of a medium build, but many also have a barrel-chested, thicker build, and can appear similar to those of Berk descent; unlike Berks, however, Tamarks have a very high occurrence of facial and whole-body freckles and tend to be narrower in the shoulder. They speak Tamark, which has a separate alphabet from the other western languages.

Eklendans, from Eklenda and southern Gersh, tend to have medium to light olive skin. Most commonly, they have medium to thin builds, narrow jaws, tend on the taller side for Westerners. Their hair is brown, black, or red hair with light or dark brown eyes. Eklendan is their spoken language. The common Eklendan surname suffix in Gersh is '-dran,' with uncommon instances of '-avan.' The latter suffix is more common within the Kingdom of Eklenda.

The old Paetic language from the days of the Paetic Empire had a different alphabet based on its eastern influences and looks largely different from western alphabets, though there was some influence on the western alphabets during imperial rule.

Culture and Economy

The Gershan peoples are unlike their ethnic counterparts in the coastal realms. There are divisions and distrust between the various ethnicities, but within Gersh, it is more a character of city against city, rather than people against people. Because the Gershan Lands are a confluence of different ethnic groups centered around princely cities, Eklendans and Marins from Yvel are more likely to get along with each other than their ethnic cousins from the cities of Soorin or Versingit, let alone from Eklenda or Markia.

Marin humans, especially ones from Markia, are used to long and cold winters. They have a practical and pragmatic way of life that reflects living with one eye always fixed on the coming of the next cold season. They tend towards the more stoic side and can come across to others as callous. Marins generally do not pronounce vendettas or engage in theatrics (though there are exceptions to every rule), but they do hold grudges, have no appetite for waste, and do not give up on anything lightly.

Berks, ironically, are the closest to the Western Church of Orneth, but are also the closest of all the western Paetan traditions that predate imperial rule. They still commonly decide legal disputes through trial by combat, which largely died out in other regions. Physical strength is considered respectable and attractive among Berks and they have many sports for the display of it, especially among commonfolk. Berks also respect their elders (both in terms of age and seniority) and will defer to older members of their own group, such as a family, a group of merchants, or a religious order.

Tamarks tend to be a kind and warm people. They very much believe that the nobility of their lands and the laws they make are there to protect the common people. This is a belief held by both the commonfolk and the nobility, who will use this belief to explain away and dismiss situations or justify actions. Tamarks are a prosperous people that benefit from trade, both overseas and inland, through land and river trade routes. They greet one another with warm smiles and hugs, and easily share meals with strangers.

Eklendans have a strong respect for custom and decorum, and can be sticklers for propriety and tradition. As such, they have a polite set of manners and smiles for the sake of courtesy. Behind the smile may be genuine benevolence, tired courtesy, or an ulterior motive. Eklendan upper society can be socially ruthless, especially for those not aligned to a powerful figure. Non-Eklendans know some Eklendans (particularly those from Eklenda) as cunning, subversive, and occasionally greedy. Eklenda has a history of producing notorious and storied spies.

The vast majority of humans worship Orneth and her Saints, and consistently attend religious services. In Western Paeta, the majority of clergy members are ethnic Berks from Clovis or southern Berkmar. Clergy members are the most educated members of society, at least in terms of formal education. There are no other universities in Western Paeta besides the Holy University at Clovis. Some

436

humans may spend significant time in self-study, but it is not formal education and will be viewed as such by graduates of the university.

A point worth noting is that not all graduates of the university are clergy members. Wealthy noble families often send their youth to Clovis for a few years of education. For most other folk, most nobles know how to read, write, and arithmetic while commoners have a much lower instance of being fully literate. Most commoners will know enough arithmetic for trade and to manage their occupation.

West of Kaskevs, most common folk are born free, though slavery is practiced in most realms west of the Kaskevs with varying levels of societal attitudes towards it. Common folk, for the most part, are free to take on any trade or enterprise and own property, if they have the means to do so. Farming and livestock raising and related or supporting activities are, by far, the most common vocations among humans anywhere, followed by various industries, fishing, hunting and trapping, mining, transportation/trade, and military occupations. Sex is not a discriminator to occupation or station in western Paeta. Men and women equally hold office, own property, fight under banners, crew ships, suffer punishments, and so forth.

Every town, village, hamlet or farmstead falls within the domain of one noble or another, whether or not their manor is nearby. These nobles may tax and levy commoners (and even other nobles operating enterprises within their domain) at their discretion.

In most of Gersh, trade and travel are by road, either on foot, horseback, or drawn cart. Rivers do support trade and transportation into the larger lakes and outward to the seaports in the coastal realms where cargo is transloaded for shipment over the sea. Rivers closer to the Kaskevs quickly become too shallow for ships. Barges and rafts are used, where feasible, but they quickly become either obstacles for travel or sources of water, fishing, and some minerals.

Fashion

Most humans prefer to wear varied colors, unless their occupation calls for otherwise. Dyes are common enough from local fauna. Most towns of sufficient size weave their own fabrics and make their own dyes from a variety of sources, be they berries, wood, leaves, local minerals, vermin (bugs or snails), and other organic materials. Some colors are limited (or available in abundance) by the availability of certain materials.

The clothing itself is largely based on local materials. For the most part, southern Paeta clothes itself largely in cottons and linens, saving wool for winter clothing and blankets, and leather for work clothes. Northern Paetans favor wool clothing for larger portions of the year, wearing scarves for much of it, and donning furs or fur-lined clothing for the winter.

Jewelry is largely limited, due to societal norms, to pairs of matching earrings on women or men, generally no more than one earring per ear, and some rings. The most common ring is a wedding ring, worn on the third finger of the left hand. Tattooing is fairly common in Paeta.

Shoes and boots are commonly worn and usually made of leather. In colder areas, they are lined with wool or fur. In warmer areas, such as the coffee or rice fields of southern Paeta, leather or wooden sandals are worn as often as shoes or boots.

Music

Musical tastes and instruments vary by ethnicity and social station, but popular instruments among many human cultures are the fiddle (particularly amongst the commoners), recorder (or flute), and various forms of drums and guitars. Guitars, frequently accompanied singing by the guitarist or another singer, are more popular in southern areas of Paeta, believed to either be developed there or brought by traders from the far-off land of Ungat. Drums, fiddles, and singing are more popular in the northern areas of Paeta. Harps are more common on the eastern side of the Kaskev Mountains (moreso closer to Mardalon), and very rare in the west.

Food and Drink

While examples of common foods by ethnicity and realm are listed here, this is far from an all-inclusive list. Excepting coffee (see note below), foods are indicative of the crops and livestock grown in each climate.

- **Markia and Marin Gersh**

    ○ Beverages:

        ▪ Coffee brewed in goat's milk (in southern areas, like the town of Serna, it is brewed in sheep's milk)

        ▪ Marin dark wine (dark red grapes)

    ○ Foods:

        ▪ Turnip soup

        ▪ Full hog, roasted and stuffed with roasted apricots and tomatoes

        ▪ Plum pie

        ▪ Peach pie

- **Berkmar**

    ○ Beverages:

        ▪ Blackberry wine

    ○ Foods

- Dark breads

- **Eklenda and Eklendan Gersh**
  - ◦ Beverages:
    - Eklendan plum wine
    - Eklendan cherry brandy
    - Coffee brewed in water
  - ◦ Foods:
    - Steamed turnips with herbs
    - Catfish baked and crusted with herbs
    - Caramelized turnips

Note:

- Although many regions have their own style of coffee, the coffee crops are grown in southern Paeta, primarily in southern Eklenda, southern Gilliam, and very small areas in the valleys of Daeara. Coffee is imported broadly throughout the rest of Paeta, though Eklenda largely controls the exports to western Paeta, due to its location.

Organization for War

This is the organization of Yvel's fighting forces, used as an example. How other cities and realms organize their forces may vary.

- **Ten:** Ten soldiers led by a tenleader or tenman/tenwoman, included in the number.

- **Company:** One hundred soldiers in ten Tens, plus a company leader, usually a minor or young noble or an experienced tenleader that has been promoted in time of need; battery for siege engines.

- **Battalion:** Five hundred soldiers in five companies, plus camp followers and a battalion leader who is an appointed noble; grand battery for siege engineers.

- **Regiment:** One to two thousand soldiers in two to four battalions, in addition to a wider variety of camp followers, a company of scouts, a company or more of archers, and a quartermaster to organize and contract the camp followers on a large scale.

- **Army:** As many regiments as the task requires, additional scouts and archers, a company or battalion of sappers, cavalry organized into lance companies, a quartermaster to organize and contract the camp followers on a large scale, and a general to command the army.

- **Auxiliaries, honor guards, and special organizations:** Organization varies. The Crown Guard is an example of an honor guard, comprised of roughly one hundred medium and heavy horse-mounted cavalry.

Note: Daearan water steel is an alloy of steel cast in ingot from crucible alloying and pouring. It is called water steel because of the tiny flowing layers that spiral and whorl around each other. Daearan's display this metallurgy primarily in weapons and armor, forging suits of full plate and knightly weapons, such as the Daearan Warsword, a long-bladed, two-handed, double-edged sword that armored knights use to fight on foot. Water steel has proven stronger than alloys of other human realms over the centuries.

Figure 14: Elves arguing with a human

Appendix XI: Elves

Overview

Elves are an ancient race of stunningly beautiful people with long lifespans, and seem immune to the effects of aging. They have a love of life, nature, scholastics and the arts, but they also have a highly bureaucratic and family-based society.

Physiology, Appearance, and Ethnicity

Elves are roughly the same height as humans, albeit on the tall side, with slender frames and lean musculature. They appear as beautiful humans with pointed ears, which are backswept, holding to the head more closely than goblinkind, with their side-protruding ears. They reach physical and mental adulthood at twenty-five years old and otherwise cease to age, living a seemingly endless life. Like all other creatures, accidents and sickness happen. The most common cause of death for elves are mundane accidents such as falling down stairs or from heights, workplace mishaps, and so forth. Naturally, in times of war, fighting, injuries, and post-injury infections take the lead for the causes of death.

Elven statures tend to build wiry strength rather than bulky strength and so many elves are stronger than they look. Elves can be just as strong as any human or even dwarf, but the bulk is much smaller (though still noticeable). Their movements are graceful, and their long fingers lend themselves well to a variety of practices ranging from artistry, fine work in metallurgy, music, or dexterity with arms.

Their hearing and eyesight are both excellent; they can see detail at great distances, especially in daylight, and have superior vision at night. Their night eyesight is strong because they have more light-receptor cells in their eyes than humans do. They do not possess the heat vision (also termed 'heatsight') that orcs and goblinkind do.

Though there is much intermixing, there are three classical ethnicities of elves: High Elves, Wood Elves, and Grey Elves. Dark Elves do not typically mix with other ethnicities.

High Elves have fair or pale skin. Their hair can be straight or wavy, in blond, shades of brown, black, and (rarely) copper red. Their eyes are blue, green, or hazel.

Wood Elves are often discernable because they are more likely to have wavy or even curly hair, though many have straight hair with colors ranging from blond to red. They have a healthier-looking fair or florid complexion and the most muscular of the elven physiques. Their eyes are most commonly green.

Grey Elves have a paler complexion and fine, straight hair that they tend to grow long. Their hair is either silver or pale gold, with eyes of amber or violet.

Dark Elves are elves stained to their very soul by magical crimes they committed against other elves and nature itself. They are instantly recognizable by their sheenless black skin, dark as a moonless night, and hair as white as untouched snow in the depths of winter, though not uncommonly in silver hues as well. The color of their eyes spans the gambit of other elven ethnicities, appearing in amber, violet, hazel, or blue. Their coloration is hereditary.

Fairly commonly, some Dark Elves have further altered their appearances from rituals which they have undergone or by utilizing charms and spells, oils, or other cosmetics. Examples of these alterations could include adding luster to their hair, or changing their eye color or shape. Certain bloodlines, or those that earn other forms of favour among the Dark Elves, are afforded an opportunity to partake in a bizarre and gruesome ritual which causes their irises and pupils to disappear, leaving them with entirely white eyes.

In other ways, Dark Elves are very similar to elves in the style of their fashion, language, lifespan, view of the world, and history.

While it is common for elves to have ancestry that blends the three primary ethnicities (excepting Dark Elven lineage), there are rare examples of elves procreating with non-elves, namely with humans. These offspring are not considered elves. The child, and sometimes the parent, are not allowed in the Elven Lands. These half-elves are similar in many ways to their elven parent. Their ears will be pointed, but not as much. Their vision or hearing may be quite strong, like their elven parent, unless they inherited those senses from their human parent.

Half-elves do show some signs of aging, but at a very slow rate. They still live very long lives, as their elven parents do, but will show aging equivalent to a human in their forties (the half-elf may be two centuries old by then, though). As these half-elves live a long time among non-elves, it is common that they will have children of their own with offspring of further diluted blood.

Culture and Economy

The advantage to elves' long lives is that they have more time than any other people to work and study, learn things, and accomplish tasks for the betterment of society and all the lands. Because of this advantage, the elves clearly see not only where the other civilizations make mistakes, but also how to remedy the issues. Elves, generally, view that other races are lost in the darkness of their short lives and will benefit from their guidance and leadership.

Many elves, especially those who have traveled or performed other tasks on behalf of one of their governing councils view this as a noble obligation borne for the betterment of other peoples, and that no other race is suitable to the burden of leadership. Most elves also clearly understand that any other society will grow resentful at such treatment, so most elven actions to guide the other societies and peoples of Paeta are quite subtle and indirect.

What this implies is that elves respect age. The young respect the old, and the old understand that their experience entitles them to deference. Just as elves believe they know better (and often do) than other races, so too do older elves believe they know better than younger elves (and often do). It is uncommon, though not unheard of, for elves to go against the will of their families and superiors.

This manifests as familial and occupational elders plan the lives and careers of their children and subordinates, plotting out possible marriages and career choices for them. Elders have been living for several hundred years and often have correct perceptions of the situation. Arranged marriages and pre-planned careers are quite common among elves. The result is often harmonious, though there are occasions of disgruntlement and unhappiness.

The older an elf gets, the more they know better and the harder it is to convince them otherwise. Just as any person ages and sees a great many endeavors succeed and fail, elves develop deeper wisdom about things that will and will not work. Like any other reasonable person, elves do not want their friends, family, comrades, and partners to fail and tire of seeing it happen time after time. Older elves can become quite stubborn and argue on these points without end. Other senior elves understand that stoutly arguing has its place, but attempt to bend others to their will through great patience.

That said, it is not as if young elves have no choices at all. Elves begin their apprenticeships when they reach the earliest stages of adulthood at twenty-five years old, termed the 'age of selection.' They select a vocation from one of the Orders (see below) and apprentice with an accomplished elf in the field. If the work is to their liking, they petition to join the order. If they find they do not enjoy the work, they apprentice with a different order. While there is familial pressure to join one Order or another, it is still the young elf's decision. Apprenticeships typically last for ten years each. It is also common for elves to marry other elves from within their Order.

Elves generally marry for life. The ritual of marriage among elves is carried on from their ancient traditions and meant to be surrounded in an aura of romance. The prospective couple must kiss three times throughout the courting period. Both prospective spouses must initiate at least one kiss. After the third kiss, they must consummate their marriage and present themselves to society, their families and peers, as married. No higher authority can annul that ritual; only the couple can dissolve their marriage, and though marriages do end, it is quite rare. More commonly, one of the spouses dies. Some widows remarry, while others choose not to. Either choice is common.

Elves are considered to have reached adulthood at twenty-five years of age, when their minds and bodies have fully grown and they are ready to embark upon centuries of work and learning. Though they are adults, they are 'far less adult' then the other elves who are centuries older than they are. Most other elves do not consider the young ones to truly be adults until they are at least a century old. Although elves can marry and attempt to have children as soon as they reach adulthood, it is highly frowned upon. Twenty-five is considered too young to marry for elves. Most elves do not marry until they are at least a century old and, typically, do not seriously attempt to have children for another century after that. Elves generally do not marry other elves with more than a century of age difference, as it is considered improper.

Young or old, most elves believe they know better than the shorter-lived races, at least on some level. One thing that elves apply this belief to is magic. Elves believe very strongly that, based on what humans have shown them in their varied histories, is that the purest intentions will be corrupted and the most beautiful tools of craft will be turned into weapons of war. Elves almost universally believe that humans, orcs, hobgoblins, and goblins absolutely must not come into possession and use of magic as they would inflict great misery on themselves and their neighbors and that, eventually, elves would have to directly intervene at great cost to themselves to restore equilibrium.

Elves practice a subtle religion that they refer to simply as 'The Ways,' meaning their way of life. There is no dedicated clergy. Each elf learns the ways in their childhood. They learn respect for their wise elders and that the death of every elf threatens society. Even elves that are on poor or hostile terms with each other will deeply mourn the death of the other. As it is so difficult to expand their population, every single life is precious, and every death hurts.

As one of the two races in Paeta that possess the knowledge of magic (the other being the dwarves), elves have interwoven its uses throughout their society. While they defend their homeland with magic when they must with weapons and armors magically tempered and sharpened, much of their magic goes into the rest of their lives and livelihoods. There are charms for nearly every task from cleaning and drying clothes, cooking, growing crops, and nearly any other task that must be done as part of a profession or maintaining a household.

The application is scattered. Knowing magical charms among elves is akin to knowing how to read among humans: some do and some do not. Most know a few charms to help with some tasks. A cobbler will know a charm to polish shoes quickly. A mason will know a spell to mix mortar at the proper ratios, keep it fresher for longer periods of time, or dry it quicker to shorten the curing time. There is such a wide myriad of applications for magic that few can really be said to be mages that actively study and practice book magic.

The Orders

All elves join one of the orders and devote themselves to a lifelong pursuit of work. Below are some brief descriptions of each of the orders.

- **The Order of the Book, or the Blue Order:** This order is devoted to scholastic pursuits. Magical scholarship and advancement is their primary purview, but so too are the studies of physical sciences, nature and all of its creatures and materials, weather and season, history, the other peoples of the land, and most anything else that can be studied. Members often wear blue tunics.

- **The Order of War, also called the Order of the Sword and the Red Order:** Not only are these the soldiers, weapon masters, and generals that lead the elven armies to victory, but also the scouts, spies, and meticulous planners that keep their armies informed and synchronized. Though monikered the Order of the Sword, its soldiers often choose other weapons, such as spears, bows, axes, and the like. Weapon masters have a special marking on their mastered weapon, among which the most common is an etched, inlaid, or enameled feathered wing that spreads over much of the weapon. The Red Order does have a few select magi for deployment to battlefields. It has been centuries since they were used, the councils fearing that the use of magic against their foes, be they human, orc, goblinkind, or what have you, will reignite the idea of magic among them and induce them to seek it out on their own after the conflict. They commonly wear red tunics to honor the blood spilt in the past in defense of the elven people.

- **The Order of the Harvest, or the Green Order:** These are the farmers, shepherds, goatherders, apiarists, vintners, and every other contributor to agriculture. They produce the food materials for the rest of elven society. Members often wear green tunics or some other form of clothing.

- **The Order of the Sun and Moon:** This order is comprised of the craftsmen and artists of elven society, from sculptors and painters to masons, cobblers, and smiths of all types.

- **The Order of Trade, or the Black Order:** They are the merchants and are a critical link between the labors of the other orders. Merchants are most likely to travel outside of the Elven Lands apart from business on behalf of the Order of the People. They also manage the trading posts at the borders of the Elven Lands where humans sometimes trade with elves. Black is their chosen color because it is the most difficult to dye and maintain and, therefore, makes it the most expensive. Merchants often wear at least some piece of clothing that is black, even if not their tunics or dress, when within the Elven Lands.

- **The Order of Peace, or the White Order:** This order is comprised of the diplomats of the elves. Wearing white tunics, they mirror the Blue Order in some ways in that they spend much of their time studying the other races and realms, even the ones to whom they are hostile, gathering information and forming an understanding of how the other actor thinks and acts. The Order of Peace is a critical instrument for informing the decisions of several other orders.

- **The Order of the People, also called the Order of the People's Will, the Order of the Will, the Purple Order, or simply, the Will:** This order is the governing body of the elves. They form a variety of councils on various matters, both large and small. Their members are drawn from the other orders based on appointments, nominations, and petitions. Admittance to the Purple Order is quite prestigious as it symbolizes that an elf is among the top of their chosen field. Members of the Purple Order retain membership in their original order and wear both colors.

Governing Bodies and Societal Organization

The two most prominent councils are the Guardian Council and the Seer Council. The Guardian Council is entrusted with the protection of the Elven Lands and its people. It has the authority to mobilize fighting units, appoint leaders, and create major movements or resources to accomplish goals related to safeguarding the people.

The Seer Council is responsible for understanding the lands and peoples around the elven homeland and advising the Guardian Council and other councils on the state of current affairs in foreign lands and their anticipated trajectory. The Seer Council is limited, however, in its ability to gather new information, as its authority limits it to study, scrying, and other methods that do not involve travel outside of the homeland.

The Seer Council is reliant on the Guardian Council for gathering new information and does so through Travelers. The Seer Council identifies the need for Travelers and defines pieces of information that need to be learned or updated on the trip, but the Guardian Council validates the requirement and assembles travelers.

Language

Elves speak Elven. There are several dialects of Elven, which largely vary by settlement or vocation, though all dialects are understood by one another's speakers. The distinction of dialects is largely accent and manner of sentence construction. The most distinctly different from other dialects is the dialect of the elves of Ebariel, where Tyrnimar Iquarren and Irduin Usrani are from, in which their sentences are structured in the passive voice.

Cities and Architecture

Juin is the capital of the Elven Lands where the councils administer the rest of society. It is a city that blends the two main types of elven architecture: woodwarping and masonry. Woodwarping, also called Woodshaping or Woodsinging, is a collection of book magic spells and charms that interact with the wood itself and allow the Woodwarper to obtain agreement from the wood to reshape itself. In many cases, this is used in place of carpentry. Buildings made with woodwarping are most often great trees that grow to immense heights and thicknesses, which is part of the preparatory stages of woodwarping, before cavities are formed for stairs, rooms, chimneys, and other architectural features. Hallways and walkways are formed through the wood. Dwellings and business locations for many elves can reside in a single great tree, almost forming a village unto itself.

The other form is comparatively mundane: masonry. It is as it sounds. Elves never developed the close connection with stone that they have with wood, as they find stones too argumentative. Despite this, their stone structures are beautiful, with flowing lines that efficiently meet functional needs. Stone, brick, and mortar form graceful arches and spacious interiors for all manner of structures. Some cities and towns contain more of one type of architecture than the other; Ebariel, for instance, is mostly a masoned city. Some villages and hamlets consist of only one or two great trees with the entire village's dwellings shaped into the trees and no other structures.

Non-elves are not permitted inside the Elven Lands and will never know the beauty of these sights.

Arms and Armor

Elves favor the grace and elegance of the sword and the bow. For swords, they prefer longer, single-edged two-handed swords with slightly curving blades and flowing crossguards. Several spells and charms are used in the forging, tempering, and sharpening of these blades, making them able to defeat armors that other blades cannot. The arcs and flow of swordwork lends itself to the elven form and their general aesthetic preferences, though there are plenty of elves that choose spears, axes, or other weapons over the sword. Weaponmasters carry blades marked with an engraving, etching, inlaying, embossing, or enameling of a bird's wing spread over the length of the blade.

The longbow is preferred by most elves of the Red Order for its balance of range and power with speed. The exception is with mounted archers, whom elves will put to field, who use shortbows made of a composite of different materials laminated together.

Many of the Red Order train to fight from the mount as well as on foot. Most warriors have trained at least a bit in every aspect, given that decades are a short time to them, compared to human career soldiers whose entire fighting career might be less than three or even two decades.

Enabled by the ready hands of the Order of the Sun and Moon, elves benefit from extremely light and strong alloys of steel, also enduring several enchantments for their strength and durability. Elves will commonly wear a suit of light mail with plates over joints and some vital areas. Some elves will take the field in a full suit of plate, but this still is the lighter elven plate, stronger than most human alloys.

Figure 15: Orc Portraits

Figure 16: Orc Warrior and female orc slave

450

Appendix XII: Orcs

Orcs are large (seven feet tall is fairly common), highly aggressive, green-skinned humanoids. They are the most common of the cast out races, due to their high fertility rate. Their societies are largely based on tribal constructs and may be settled in villages or cities, be they nomadic or semi-nomadic.

Physiology, Appearance, and Ethnicity

Orcs are powerfully built humanoids with green skin, generally growing to nearly seven feet in height, give or take a half foot. Short orcs will be six feet tall or even less. The extremely tall orcs may reach eight feet in height. Their immune systems are notably robust. They have small tusks to help them tear meat, and large, powerful jaws for eating. Their eyes and ears are small, and the ears are pointed and backswept. Though their eyesight is not particularly strong, orcs have additional types of cells in their eyes that allow them to see infrared light or heat, sometimes called 'heatsight.' This vision typically takes over in the absence of normal visible light. Their hands have small claws resembling jagged fingernails to aid in climbing and similar activities. They generally do not claw in combat, preferring weapons and fists, though they may bite with their tusks or headbutt with their thick skulls.

Orcs, originally created to quickly form a mass army, grow quickly into large and powerful frames. As such, their physiology shows many characteristics of this. They have a very high metabolism, so they consume large amounts of food, stay lean, grow height and muscle mass quickly, and age rapidly. An orc reaches physical adulthood at fourteen years of age, though many see violence and attempt to heap glory upon themselves as young as ten years old.

Most commonly, orcs die a violent death, usually at the hands of another orc before they are twenty-five years old. However, should an orc not meet a violent end, their natural lifespan will have them be senior in their forties and elderly by their fifties. Orcs in their late twenties have the same kind of health problems that humans do in their mid-forties. This relation continues: orcs in their early- to mid-thirties have the health problems that humans do in their fifties and sixties. Such is the price for growing too large so quickly.

As part of rapid growth and large muscle mass, orcs of both sexes have very high natural testosterone levels, which leads to common aggressive behaviors and violent competition in most situations. Orcs, particularly males, are subject to hair fragility, balding, and full-body baldness, especially as they age into their thirties. It is not incredibly uncommon for orcs (particularly men), to go bald as they reach adulthood. Facial hair is uncommon among orcs, but some have been known to grow beards, particularly in the northern tribes. Their high metabolism can cause skin disorders, mottling, psoriasis (which they call 'itchy skin'), and excessive sweating. Orcs can become lethargic during warm weather, but need less clothing and warmth in cold weather than other races.

There is no great separation of ethnicities among orcs, like there visibly is with goblinkind. They are all green. Different shades of green are due to sun exposure, as changes with the time of year with differences in sunlight and weather.

Culture and Tribal Construct

Orcs, like the hobgoblins and elves, view themselves as a superior race over all others (and, in most cases, view men superior to women). The culture is competitive, violent, impatient to the point of instant gratification, prideful, and male-dominated almost without exception.

Their social order is based on tribes, led by a great one. The great one is the only one that has a name and it is the same name as the tribe. This differs from goblinkind, where each great one has a name different from the tribe and their deeds are recorded in the tribe's history. In this way, the great one is the tribe and the tribe is an extension of the great one. For example, the Great One of the Baki-Norn is called the Baki-Norn. All of the members of the tribe are the Baki Norn (i.e. 'we are Baki-Norn' or 'we are of the Baki-Norn,' versus the Great One of the Baki-Norn who would say 'I am the Baki-Norn'). The position of great one can be challenged by any orc, even orcs not in the tribe, though usually the incumbent wins.

Successful tribal great ones that see their tribes prosper through relative stability rule through fear of their combat prowess or can create a cult of personality based on actual or perceived competence (again, mainly martial competence). The few great ones that can transcend many of these difficulties and approach what humans would call a 'king,' a great one over several tribes, such as the Borys-Karang, would be able to not only do both, rule through fear and create a cult of personality, but also cleverly maneuver and manipulate rivals and potential rivals into eliminating one another while currying for favor. Most orcs, though, being short-sighted and craving gratification, do not have the patience required for such success.

At times when a great one needs to ensure his will is done, but has multiple commitments, he may appoint a subleader, called a Garad'Dai. Most orc great ones favor loyalty over competence, as loyalty is actually in shorter supply. Successful great ones sometimes find loyalty in orcs who are not strong or bold enough to achieve power on their own, but with the backing of their great one, can supply faithful and (relatively) effective service, though they are prone to abuse of power, however meager it may be.

The tribes are built around the adult male orcs. Each adult male's worth is weighed by the number of kills that he has and the material wealth, most conspicuously including slaves, and the number of non-adult offspring that they have. Orc women are property of orc men, almost without exception. Orcs take any race for slaves, excepting other orc men, as orc men defeated in battle would be killed and their possessions absorbed.

Once a male orc offspring reaches adulthood, he leaves the household and starts his own. Though there may be some measure of familial fondness, both father and son view each other as enemies from that point forward. Orc daughters are sold, usually in exchange for other orcs' daughters, though orcs have been known to kill each other to obtain a coming-of-age daughter.

The orcs worship, almost universally, a pantheon of four gods. They are the god of blood and strength, the god of skill, the god of fertility and prosperity, and the god of stuff. It is rare that orcs pray to these gods. They do not have clergy of any type or hold religious services, but they do swear by these gods and use these as guiding principles in how they prosecute life's problems. The gods, in many ways, serve as a map to a successful life as an orc. Through strength and violence, one attains skill. Through skill, one attains prosperity, women, and produces offspring. Through prosperity, one attains material wealth.

Despite their very high birthrate, they are far from the dominant actor in the mountains. Their need to dominate races around their tribe succumbs to their need to dominate each other within their tribe. Life is short for them: shorter yet due to their violent culture, and they have a more short- or instant-gratification fixation than other races. They are generally too busy killing one another for position and absorbing one another's material wealth to create a unified front against others.

Food and Drink

Orcs universally prefer meat over crops or even dairy products. Most orcs prefer at least some cooking, especially city-dwelling orcs, but some are indifferent and will eat their meat raw. These are usually in the nomadic tribes. Orcs do sometimes partake in cannibalism, but there is no ritual to it. In that case, meat is meat.

Most orc cooking is simple roasting or stewing, though demanding or particular tribal great ones will expect their slaves to prepare more elaborate meals ahead of time and anticipate the great one's hunger.

As with their food, orcs bend to their preference for gratification sooner rather than later with their drink. Much of the time, they drink water or fresh-squeezed juice from foraged berries and fruits. Mostly among nomadic and semi-nomadic tribes, they will also drink the blood of their hunted game or defeated foes. Orcs uncommonly prepare alcoholic drinks, due to the time required for fermentation (even if it is only a few days). Again, demanding and particular tribal great ones may be the exception and have their slaves ferment roots and berries to make various alcoholic drinks. Most alcohol that orcs drink is the boon of trade or loot.

Most any orc at war, whether city-dwelling or nomadic, will have no qualms about eating raw meat, eating their own dead, the enemy dead, the dead of their 'allies,' or drinking their blood. This is not to say they go out of their way to do it, but rather just a matter of expediency. If there is a properly supplied and ready field mess, orcs will take the cooked food (especially city-dwelling orcs).

Hygiene and Fashion

Orcs' high metabolism can cause skin conditions, the most common of which is skin sensitivity. As a result of this, orcs commonly bathe at least once every five days due to their skin discomfort. This bathing is nothing elaborate and largely consists of splashing and rubbing water on themselves, usually cold mountain stream water, and scrubbing with reeds, grass, sand, or mud (achieving an exfoliation). On the whole, orcs are generally clean.

Orcs generally prefer clothing that accentuates traits of which they are proud of. If they have a steel breastplate, they will usually wear it as part of regular clothing. If they are particularly strong, they may wear sleeveless garments. Aside from serving as a vehicle for their pride, clothing follows the barest necessities of function. If made by themselves or other orcs, the garments are generally crudely stitched. They prefer materials that require less preparation, such as furs, rather than leather or woven fiber textiles. If they have non-orc slaves, they may force them to make higher quality clothing and rush them along the way.

The exceptions, once again, are farseeing and wise great ones, such as the Borys-Karang, who understands the benefit of properly made equipment, and imposes requirements on his tribe.

Music

Orc music largely consists of singing and chanting, especially among the nomadic tribes. These songs usually come in the form of an orc boasting about his exploits and abilities. A group of orcs singing will, on a good day, be jeering one another by singing counters to one another's songs, downplaying other's virtues while embellishing their own. Drums might be employed, but are used to emphasize sung lines. When drums are used, it is by a singer. Settled orcs tend to use a few more instruments, but it is still focused on one singer-musician.

Language

Orc dialects are varied and many; however, nearby dialects can generally be understood with some gaps in vocabulary. There is more than one set of symbols for the written form of Orc. Some are phonetic, some are pictograms, and some borrow from modern Goblin or even Dwarven runes, depending on the area. While spoken Orcish could perhaps be generally understood, forms of written Orcish have a higher instance of being excluded from mutual understanding.

Cities

Orcs do build cities, but they have a strong tendency to be piecemeal with winding streets and disparate building types. Cities usually start out as the settlements of strong tribes and grow as the tribe gets stronger. Orc cities also come about as several tribes settle in the same area, neither strong enough to annihilate the other and reaching some kind of agreement, each great one thinking that they are using the other to their advantage or against a common enemy (such as humans, elves, dwarves, or goblinkind). The most prominent example of an orc-built city is the city of Ghetrak, nestled in the central Kaskevs.

Well-built orc cities are usually captured and occupied cities. Ikria is the best example, built by the dwarves of Drenia and lost to the orc hordes as the

Kingdom of Drenia waned in power and influence.

Organization for War

Orcs have a rather simplistic framework of organizing their forces for conflict with external entities.

- **Warband:** As many warriors as the local contingent of the tribe can put in the field, which varies by tribe. The warband typically travels with all of its property and noncombatants, unless it is an urban tribe or fielding a partial warband.

- **Horde:** For larger tribes, such as the Borys-Karang, as many warriors as the tribe can put in the field in aggregate. This echelon generally struggles with logistics as it is a large force for forage; internal theft and violent disputes are common.

Arms and Armor

The armament of orcs varies widely with the most common discriminator being the tribe. For example, smaller and weaker nomadic tribes, like the Baki-Norn, do not smith their own steel weaponry: they trade for it or take it as spoils, so what weapons they bring to fight varies widely, while the armor they craft is predominantly thick animal hides or no armor at all. On the other hand, a powerful tribe that is largely settled, conducts trade, and maintains a robust economy, like the Borys-Karang, forges their own steel weapons and armor and equips specialized troops to their task. For example, scouts of the Borys-Karang generally will be protected by boiled leather armor, carry shortbows (scaled to their size) constructed of laminated strips of wood, steel hand axes, round shields, and steel knives.

Common styles of weapons are long-hafted axes, commonly seen with combinations of spikes, blades, hooks or hammerheads on the back or top of the axe head and perhaps spikes on the butt end of the shaft. Orc smiths (or smiths that are slaves to the orcs) primarily forge two styles of swords. On the western slopes, orcs frequently carry square-tipped, two-handed falchions, versus the eastern style of a single-edged, forward-curving blade on a two-handed haft. Orcs also carry throwing javelins, three-pace-long spears (eight-foot shaft), clubs, maces, and so forth. Crossbows are uncommon, but bows are frequent enough among some tribes.

Figure 17: Hobgoblins Planning the invasion of eastern Gersh

Figure 18: Comparison of a horse (left) to a wolf (center) and a great wolf (right)

Appendix XIII: Hobgoblins

Overview

Hobgoblins are one of the three types of goblinkind. Taller than most humans, they tower over the goblins. While not as large and hulking as the bugbears, they are more aggressive, and more organized and disciplined by far. Their society is largely based around the tribal construct, led by a great one, but usually with no family or clan within it; rather, tribe members are organized into fighting units or supporting occupations. While highly competitive, they naturally see the sense of cooperating with each other for the betterment of the group. Like the orcs and the elves, hobgoblins see themselves as a superior race.

Physiology, Appearance, and Ethnicity

Standing slightly taller than most humans, but not so much as an orc, hobgoblins are blessed with rugged physical fortitude, rarely taking sickness, quickly recovering from injuries and strain, and having a high pain tolerance. They are also blessed with a natural agility that lends itself to the dexterity of arms, as well as many of the various vocations necessary for the equipping and maintaining an army.

Their proportions are much more human-like than the goblins or the orcs, though they also have the hallmark ears of goblinkind that protrude to the side and end in points. In scale, their ears are proportionally smaller than those of goblins.

As with other goblinkind, hobgoblins evolved a different type of cell in their eyes that allows them to see in the infrared bands of light. This allows them to see in the dark, like orcs, but with superior vision; when there is insufficient light for chromatic vision, they see infrared in greyscale where higher temperatures are brighter. This is generally only when chromatic vision fails, but their infrared vision can take over when very hot objects are in their field of view. The infrared vision also grants some advantages in metal-working.

Similar to goblins, goblin ethnicities come in four main distinctions by skin color: blue, purple, red, and gray.

Blue-skinned hobgoblins are primarily from the western slopes of the Kaskev Mountains. Their eyes vary widely in shade with violet, amber, yellow-green, aquamarine, hazel, silver, and green all being fairly common shades. They have hair ranging from black to white, with shades of gray being most common, tending to the darker side. Their hair is prone to sun-bleaching and takes well to dyeing as their hair lightens. Though uncommon, they will occasionally have green- or blue-tinged hair, which becomes more apparent through sunbleaching. Equally uncommon are shades of brown or red hair, which are largely considered unattractive among blue-skinned hobgoblins. Purple-tinged hair is rare among blue-skinned hobgoblins and considered attractive. It is therefore a common goal to dye their hair purple.

Purple-skinned hobgoblins are primarily from the eastern reaches of the Kaskev Mountains. They most commonly have black hair with shades of blue. Shades of gray are less common, especially lighter hues. Purple hair is rare. Silver or golden blond hair are exceptionally rare and factor into some folktales. Purple-skins also take to sunbleaching. Their eyes are most commonly amber, green, or yellow-green. Rarer eye colors are violet, purple, blue, and red.

Red-skinned hobgoblins hail from the northern end of the Kaskev Mountain chain on both the eastern and western slopes. Their hair is black and shades of gray with the darker shades being the most common. They are not particularly prone to sun-bleaching. Their eyes are, from most to least common colors: light gray, dark gray, silver, black, blue, violet, red, amber, and green.

Gray-skinned hobgoblins are from the southern end of the Kaskev Mountains, mostly on the eastern slopes. Their hair tends to be dark, beginning from black, with shades into blue, green, purple, brown, and gray. While sun-bleaching is a factor, their hair is thicker than most other ethnicities, so it is less of a factor than with blue-skinned or purple-skinned hobgoblins. Black is, by far, the most common eye color; however, gray-skins may also have violet, gray, purple, blue, amber, green, silver, red, or brown eyes.

Hobgoblins have an exceedingly low fertility rate: less than humans, and far less than orcs. Once life takes root in the womb, though, pregnancies are highly likely to be successful, due to the ox-like constitution of both the mother and the child. However, the problem lies in conceiving and the disruption of a long pregnancy.

Culture and Tribal Construct

Hobgoblins note their physical stature over the goblins and their predisposition for organization and discipline, especially compared to bugbears, as themselves taking the lead over goblinkind as part of the natural order. They further consider all other races to be weak in some way and therefore can only redeem themselves under the leadership of and by emulating hobgoblins.

On the whole, they have amicable relations between tribes, unless there is a clash between two great ones for dominance over a group of tribes, as was the case in the challenge between Oygariyet and Arkiban. As there are comparatively fewer hobgoblins than there are goblins or orcs, they are content to cooperate with one another to conquer and subjugate others and divide the spoils according to their contribution and success. They have a highly egalitarian view of work and station.

Tribes are led by a great one. Like the goblins, sex is no bar to the station. In most cases, the great one is the only named hobgoblin in the tribe, whose deeds and decisions will be recorded in their histories. The great one relies on their staff, usually four other hobgoblins from the tribe that have demonstrated the mental strength to plan and lead. The staff manages the affairs of the tribe on behalf of the great one and under the great one's guidance and vision. The staff positions are numbered First through Fourth and it is progressive. If, for example, the Second dies, then the Third is promoted to the Second, the Fourth promoted to the Third, and a new Fourth is selected.

The First is generally the most trusted staff and will most often be sent by the great one to act in their stead for complicated endeavors that require the great one's supervision in multiple places. The Second is usually one to manage the scouting, reconnaissance, surveillance, and spying to learn about enemy forces and the terrain for any particular endeavor. The Third plans attacks and other major endeavors. The Fourth, usually the most junior member of the staff, has the largest amount of work and learning, as they manage the logistics of the tribe. The Fourth keeps track of the number of warriors that they have ready, in training, recuperating from injury; training and materials, food supplies and production, mounts, breeding and husbandry (for tribes that put wolf cavalry in the field), infrastructure availability, condition, expansion, and planning, and all other manner of considerations.

While this is, arguably, an unrealistic level of workload, planning, and tracking, particularly for the Fourth, each of the staff has several other hobgoblins to assist them and the Fourth, though having the most to learn, benefits from the mentorship of the other staff, as they have all been a Fourth before. The great one's staff are selected from senior and successful leaders of fighting units.

An older hobgoblin tradition, one largely abandoned in most tribes and only recently being brought back into practice, is that of clans within the tribe. The leader of a clan within a tribe is named and, within the clan, may be called great one. The clan may also be named, but the practice is too uncommon in contemporary times for generalities. In the hobgoblin context, clans are somewhat analogous to fighting units, but with more status. There are no familial ties in the clans, just as there are no familial ties no true families among hobgoblins with rare, rare exceptions.

Candidates for clan leaders are the tribal great one's staff and successful unit leaders.

Depending on the tribe, the great one's staff and clan leaders, if that tribe has implemented the clan construct, are allowed to own slaves. Otherwise, only the great one is allowed to own slaves and, effectively, maintain a household.

Hobgoblins are the only goblinkind that keep their own as slaves; however, the status of slave is generally considered an honor. For a great one to defeat another tribe and take the losing great one's household into their own is considered a kindness and an honor. As such, hobgoblins have a sense of propriety on the employment, use, and display of slaves and find the practices of some other races, particularly the orcs, who abuse, humiliate, and kill their slaves, to be crass and distasteful.

An exception to the hobgoblin cultural attitude toward slavery is the use of forced labor. For example, when larger population centers are seized and the whole of another tribe is taken prisoner, they may be forced into work as labor slaves. Labor slaves and household slaves are treated somewhat differently, though there is nothing that prevents a labor slave from becoming a household slave, if selected, or a household slave from becoming a labor slave, at the discretion of the great one.

Like the goblins, hobgoblins are a no-waste culture and will utilize everything from hunted game and, whenever practical, the fallen of their enemy and their own. They employ ritual cannibalism as a method of cleansing weakness and forgiving those who failed. Unlike the goblins, the hobgoblins raise this to a level of poetry. The skin and bones of those who failed are turned into pieces of the weapons of those who will win the next victory. Hides are turned into capes, straps, shield coverings, or even parchment. Bones become grips for weapons and tools. Skulls can be the heads of maces, after casting in steel. Captives that refuse a place of honor as slaves may be (forcibly) redeemed by performing the only use left for the tribe: to be disassembled for their parts.

Family, Fertility, and Property

Hobgoblins do not have a sense of family. While they have a very difficult time finding romantic love, they form strong bonds of friendship and comradery in their fighting units and supporting vocations. Lacking the physical weakness of the goblins, they ensure their survival through conquest. As such, their view towards sex is very different. Sex is recreational and part of most relationships, especially within fighting units. They refer to sex and other recreational activities, such as strategy games, mock fighting, or full-contact fighting without weapons, collectively, as 'sport.'

Because of their extremely low fertility, there is often no consequence for sexual activity. In the uncommon instances of pregnancy, female warriors are transferred to the support vocation for birthing a child. Male warriors and unpregnant female warriors also transfer fairly regularly into such activities, as a broadening experience, if they are injured or growing too old to fight.

The young are raised and begin military training as soon as they are able. Throughout their childhood, they work in various support activities, before moving on to a fighting unit when they reach adulthood. Every hobgoblin spends at least some time, usually several years, in a fighting unit before transferring to a supporting vocation. They will spend several years in that or various vocations and then the tribal clan, fighting unit, and support leadership decide on the future career of each hobgoblin according to the needs of the tribe and their demonstrated talents.

Each tribe constitutes a whole family. Biological parents have coincidental involvement with their biological children. Otherwise, for a hobgoblin, their tribe is full of mentors to train them, siblings to fight and work alongside, and lovers to share the joy of still being alive after a battle.

Half-breed children, by the mating between hobgoblin great ones, staff, and clan leaders, their slaves and any other hobgoblins that they have allowed such access to non-hobgoblin slaves are sometimes birthed. There are also further mixes beyond half-breeds.

These mixed offspring are often in a difficult position. In the view of the hobgoblin benefactors in the tribe, it is best for them to attempt to live life as if they are a hobgoblin, yet they can never achieve the ideals of a hobgoblin because of the taints in their blood. As such, they rarely reach any position of seniority or enjoy much prosperity. Depending on the leadership in their tribe, they may be taken and given as slaves, which is otherwise abnormal, but it is sometimes viewed as the greatest of kindness (by the tribe) to give them the honorable position as a slave to a great one rather than continue their position as the perpetually lowest soldier.

Many of the mixed breed children try to escape from the tribe. Some are caught and brought back, no longer with the option of comparative household luxury as a slave, and forced into dangerous and grueling labor as a soldier or a support worker, resembling a labor slave in all but name.

Fashion

Hobgoblin fashion is primarily functional, though others may call it plain or bland. 'Fancy' clothes are simply higher quality. Hobgoblins do not wear dresses or skirts. Trousers and shirts or tunics are the mainstay. Anything heavier usually is a piece of armor or armor lining, such as a gambeson or a leather shirt that can function as an arming jacket under plate armor. Some tribes use dyes on their clothing or paint designs on their armor or shield to denote fighting units.

Music

Hobgoblin music is vaguely similar to goblin music, but it takes a different form. While they enjoy their music, sing to it, tap or dance to it, and hum it when they're alone, the music forms around its purpose: to give and keep rhythm to work. Whether marching to battle or working in the field, the music is there to invigorate and inspire, or at least break, the monotony of work. Being accessories, the drum is the central instrument to hobgoblin music with other hand instruments that can be played on the move. Their music is very percussive and steady, mimicking the footfalls of a marching soldier.

Cities

Hobgoblins are rarely nomadic or semi-nomadic, preferring the stability of fortifications for added safety and security. Tribes often construct fortified towns in the mountains using natural and constructed stone walls. They fully appreciate the protective value of stealth, and in some cases, construct their dwellings in a concealed way, if the great one believes that the best area for a dwelling is easier to hide than to overtly defend it.

Golardeg, on the eastern slopes of the Kaskev Mountains, is the largest hobgoblin city and a center for trade and exchange that rivals Kogylar. It is just as much a fortress as it is a city, though like all cities, it was built to serve a purpose other than simply to keep it. The fortifications for Golardeg or any hobgoblin settlement enhance its survivability so that it can continue the purpose for which it was built.

There is a very small contingency of hobgoblins that choose to leave their tribes, usually through escape. Many of these are mixed breed hobgoblins. Allowing capable soldiers to leave is not something great ones generally do, though there are exceptions to every rule. Some of these hobgoblins are crippled survivors of battles that cannot make their way back to their tribe and fighting unit or would be useless if they did.

These various hobgoblin fugitives, exiles, and deserters form a small diaspora. Most of them stay in the wilderness, hunting, trapping, and foraging for survival with limited trade for other goods. Others settle in towns and cities of other races, generally goblins, but sometimes orcs. Hobgoblins, especially pure-blood hobgoblins, do not allow themselves to be enslaved by non-hobgoblins. Goblins will not attempt to do this, but orcs will.

Hobgoblins, especially pure-blooded hobgoblins, that are taken as slaves by a non-hobgoblin choose to end their life nearly every time unless they envision a possibility of escape or it is an exceptional circumstance. Such a circumstance would be to serve under a very prominent great one or equivalent that they view may treat them well. They would choose to end their life rather than endure the humiliation and dishonor that would be inflicted upon them, especially by non-hobgoblins.

Food and Drink

One of the supporting activities for hobgoblins is producing foodstuffs. This comes in all of the various forms from foraging, farming, livestock raising, hunting, and processing raw materials (for example, processing milk into cheese or butter). For the most part, hobgoblin food tends to lack the passion and joy of the food that goblin cuisine has. One of the only things that hobgoblins particularly relish is alcohol. While the alcoholic drinks of other races will be interesting to them as exotic, their preference is for ridin, a strong liquor made from fermented roots (much resembling vodka, and usually made from potatoes).

While hobgoblins generally dine on a varied diet of roasted or stewed meats with vegetables, roots, berries, and the like, they do have a few delicacies. One of these delicacies is the remains of a freshly defeated enemy, usually roasted, served whole or as a dressed carcass with the edible organs prepared as side dishes. This is most often done as a celebratory or ceremonial meal.

Organization for War

Hobgoblins, built and bred to be soldiers or soldier support, have a more complex and nuanced framework for organization than orcs and differentiate troops for equipping, training, logistics, and employment.

- **Warband:** One hundred to one hundred and fifty soldiers with a leader. The leader is expected to control all of the soldiers, but commonly appoints subleaders from the experienced and dependable soldiers. Each soldier is well-equipped and well-trained, commonly capable of fighting in several roles (for example, infantry/archer, cavalry/horse archer, infantry/sapper, and so forth). Leadership titles may vary (i.e. warband leader for any infantry, versus cavalry leader for mounted troops).

- **Fist:** Four hundred to six hundred soldiers, plus a fist leader.

- **Host:** As many fists as the task requires, typically several thousand from the same tribe, generally led by the tribe's great one. The great one is assisted by his or her staff, the First, Second, Third, and Fourth, selected from successful (living) fist leaders.

Great Host: A host of hosts from multiple tribes, led by the dominant great one that has dual responsibilities for leading his or her own host. The great one tends to rely on his or her First to take over direct leadership of the host.

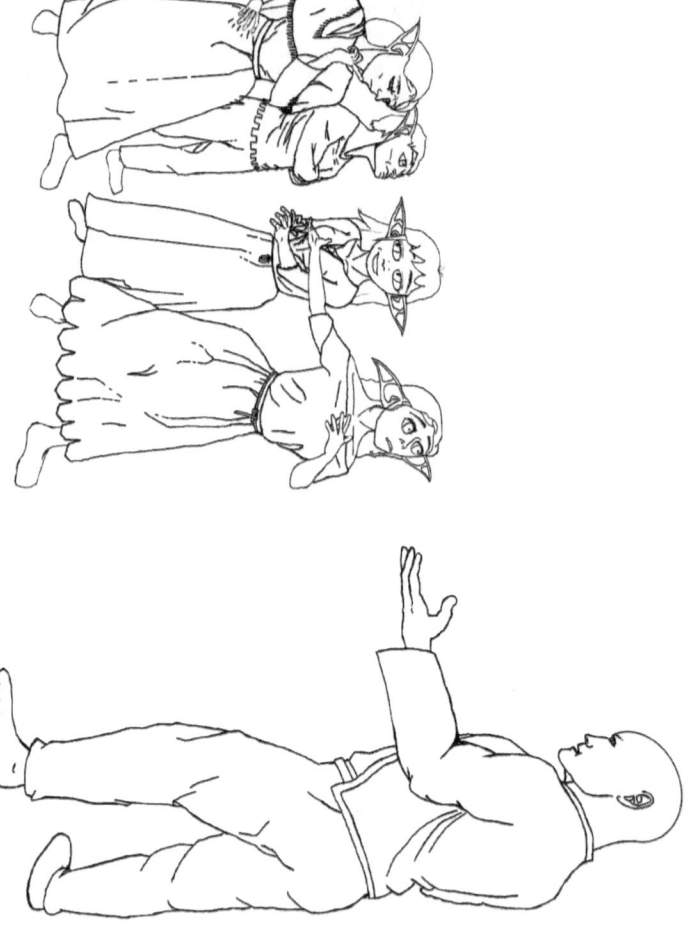

Appendix XV: Goblins

Overview

Goblins are among the 'cast-out' races and the most urbanite of three races of goblinkind. They are clannish, pragmatic, and builders in most everything they do. They have the most well-rounded view on life of all the cast out races, lacking hobgoblins' driving need to compete and dominate, and the bugbears' strong preference for solitude. Physically, they are the smallest and weakest of goblinkind and thus acutely know that what strength they have lies in cunning, subtlety, and numbers. They have a largely egalitarian, tribe- and clan-based society.

Physiology, Appearance, and Ethnicity

Goblins have a natural lifespan of approximately seventy-five years and reach physical adulthood at eighteen years of age. Depending on the tribe or clan, a goblin may be considered to reach societal adulthood and breeding age between fourteen and eighteen years. They generally fluctuate around three feet in height with common variation of a half-foot taller or shorter. There are instances of taller and shorter goblins, but they are very rare and may be a result of mixed lineage with non-goblins.

Their proportions seem like a half-sized adult human, at first glance. However, with a moment's examination, one notices that goblins have heads that are proportionally large for their bodies–shorter and wider, compared to the proportions of a human head. Their eyes are large for their already disproportionately large heads. Their ears are also quite large, protrude mostly to the side, and taper into points. They have excellent hearing through these ears, albeit heavily biased in the direction their head is facing.

Like most other cast out races, they evolved a different type of cell in their eyes that allows them to see in the infrared bands of light, sometimes called 'heatsight.' Effectively, when there is insufficient light for chromatic vision, they see infrared in greyscale where higher temperatures are brighter, allowing them to see in darkness. This is generally only when chromatic vision fails, but their infrared vision can take over when very hot objects are in their field of view. The infrared vision also grants some advantages in metal-working.

Similar to hobgoblins, goblin ethnicities come in four main distinctions by skin color: blue, purple, red, and gray.

Blue-skinned goblins are predominantly from the slopes and caverns of the Western Kaskev Mountains and built the great city of Kogylar. They have hair that is black most commonly, though shades to blue, green, purple, brown and gray are not uncommon. Sun-bleaching is a factor. Their eyes are typically black, though violet, gray, purple, blue, amber, green, silver, red, and brown-colored eyes are common enough.

465

Purple-skinned goblins hail mainly from the Eastern Kaskevs. Their hair is largely shades of gray. Black hair is also common, as are shades of dark blue (lighter shades are less common, as is purple). Sun-bleaching hair is a strong factor for purple-skinned goblins. Instances of silver or golden blond hair are recorded but not seen in recent times. Their eyes are usually amber, green, or yellow-green, with violet, purple, blue, or red being less common.

Red-skinned goblins are generally from the slopes and caverns of the Western and Northern Kaskev Mountains. The red-skins tend to be taller than the other ethnicities. Their hair is black or shades of gray, though darker shades are more common. Their eyes are light gray, dark gray, silver, black, blue, violet, or red. Amber eyes are rare, and green eyes even more so.

Gray-skinned goblins dwell in the east and south of the Kaskev Mountains. Their hair is usually black, though shades to blue, green, purple, brown and gray are not uncommon. Sun-bleaching is a factor, but less so for gray-skins because their hair tends to be thicker than the hair of other ethnicities.

Most goblins breed within the same ethnicity, but settlements with large amounts of trade or near other ethnicities' settlements do see ethnic mixing, which affects coloring. In some instances, there may be tinges of green in their coloring, which implies orcish blood in their lineage.

Goblins do not suffer the stunted fertility of the larger goblinkind. The goblin gestation period is nine months. If the coupling is mixed, then it varies.

Culture and Tribal Construct

Goblins recognize their physical and social place among goblinkind. Knowing that they are at risk for being at the mercy of those bigger than themselves and never forging friendly relations with other races of their size, such as the kobolds or dwarves, they embraced survival as a key to their culture. Much of what they do, directly or indirectly, is for the survival of their race, their tribe, their clan, and themselves.

To ensure their survival, goblins formed a society of tribes made up of clans. The clans are effectively group families or group marriages, and maintain established rules of conduct that generally govern their behavior. These rules vary from tribe to tribe, city to city, even clan to clan. Sometimes they are written in hard code, and sometimes they are known and unspoken or even such basic assumptions of their view that they do not even notice to acknowledge them.

The tribes are led by a great one, who, like other cast-out races, has distinguished themselves through some great deed. They have an egalitarian society, and the sex of a goblin is no bar to station. Unlike the other cast-out races, a great deed among goblins need not be one of war, conquest, or violence (though it is not exclusionary). Goblins have earned names among their own kind for founding and building cities or mines, inventing new technology, building bridges and dams. In ancient times, when goblins still had wizards of their own, many of them were named for the discoveries and miracles they wrought.

As with the other cast-out races, as life is usually short, and sometimes violent and cheap, names must be earned. If a goblin has not accomplished a great feat, then they are not worth remembering.

Values that are mostly commonly held by goblins are a sense of pragmatism, cunning, and farsightedness, a sense of propriety and respect for the rules that have kept them alive. What balances them most among the other goblinkind is that they seek to enjoy the lives they have. They can be mischievous and joyful, and enjoy music, food, and love.

They are not stricken with the curse of stunted fertility like the other goblinkind. Though they are not as fertile as orcs, they use the comparative advantage of fertility over their larger cousins and the advantage of their general demeanor over that of the orcs to out-populate and out-build the other cast-out races.

While most of this implies that goblins are peaceful, they have suffered a long history of abuse at the hands of many others, be they were orcs, humans, elves, other goblinoids, or even other goblin tribes competing for territory and resources. Goblins fight with great cunning and ferocity, as they believe that every conflict is a struggle for survival, or else will lead to a struggle for survival. An aspect of their pragmatism and farsight is the view that conflict is inevitable, and they prepare for it accordingly.

They have a culture of low-waste. They do not believe in infanticide, as every single body can contribute to the survival of the tribe. Every material goes to use. This is apparent with their use of the remains of livestock. After the meat is taken for eating, every other material is used. Skin for leather, fur and hairs for textiles (woven fabrics or yarn), sinews for cord and string, bones for tools or tool grips, fat for food preservation, cooking, or skin softening: everything goes to use. This is even the case for clan members. As one last contribution to the well-being of the clan, the remains of their deceased are used for all things practical.

Goblins have a fascination with their dominant cousins, the hobgoblins. They admire their strength, resolve, and ambition to the point of imitating some aspects of it. Some goblins or whole clans devote themselves to martial pursuits, but the most conspicuous imitation of hobgoblin culture is ritualistic cannibalism. After the hobgoblins' custom, cannibalism is practiced to honor a fallen family member or comrade, or to purge weakness.

Family, Fertility, and Property

Goblin families are a group marriage. Children of both sexes are raised under group parenting to adulthood (which varies between tribes and regions) and then given to other families to ensure genetic diversity. Inbreeding is strongly frowned upon and incredible care is taken to avoid breeding with cousins. The clan/family unit chooses another family within the same tribe to whom to give the young adult, based on their assessment of how well the young adult will live, and the personal relationships formed with other families during childhood. In times of hardship or in the rare cases of rural, nomadic, or semi-nomadic clans and families, survival and necessity govern

467

the decision of to which families the young adults are sent, rather than preference and personal relationships.

It is uncommon, but not rare, that tribes will exchange young adults for genetic diversity outside of the tribe. This is generally on a consensual basis, and predicated upon the two tribes having good relations and neither competing for resources nor dominance in an area (which is why it is uncommon).

Different clans and tribes of goblins differ in the nuances of these practices. For example, some clans perpetuate trades within the same families for generations and generations, continually gaining new adult members from other clans (or even tribes) and marrying off their young to other clans and tribes, maintaining genetic diversity among the clans. In a few cases of powerful urban families, they take a family name within the named clan or tribe. Other practices differ: for instance, all breeders within a family unit are generally the same age, within four to five years. Instead of continuing the same families with new breeding members, new families are often formed, most commonly when a newly-of-breeding-age young adult is three or more years younger than any member of any existing families in the clan or tribe.

Larger families are considered to be more prosperous and prestigious. This translates into tangible terms: larger families having more working adults and need larger dwellings. Most of the possessions of the clan are shared through the whole clan, with common exceptions of favorite clothes, vocation-specific tools, musical instruments and the like.

Goblins do take slaves, though not other goblins. Goblins captured during conflict with another tribe join the capturing tribe, often never seeing their original family again (save those with whom they were captured). Those joining another tribe are often at a disadvantage and have few choices as to which clans are willing to take them.

Among the adults in a clan, everyone is married to everyone, and are usually polyamorous within the clan. In cases where one goblin within a clan finds another distasteful as a romantic partner, they often adopt each other as siblings and do not breed with each other. That said, goblins joining a family must give and receive love from every breeding adult within the family. Sex tends to be playful and relatively public, within the clan's dwelling. It is common for some adults to engage in group sex while others cook, clean, work, sleep, watch, or play music. Privacy is not much of a concern within the clan.

With respect to non-clan members, goblins become very reserved. They do not display sexual activity to non-clan members, as they view it as improper behavior. Sexual activity with a non-clan member is exceptionally reviled, a transgression on the same level as murder, and often grounds for expulsion from the clan. Only in rare and extreme circumstances will the bounds of propriety allow for these rules to be bent or broken.

Slaves may be included in sexual activity amongst themselves, but goblins will not breed with slaves to the same degree that they will not engage in sexual activity outside of the clan. Any offspring from intercourse with a non-clan member or a slave would be condemned by the clan. The child may suffer poor treatment and choose (and be urged) to leave at the soonest opportunity. In many cases, these unfortunate offspring must form their own clans, which no proper goblin would wish to join, generally only being able to take other goblins in similar situations.

These honor-stained clans occupy the lowest social standing within the tribe or settlement. When there are multiple tribes within the same settlement, such as the city of Kogylar, there is generally only one or two of these clans. They often bear disproportionately heavy burdens within the tribe, taking on unprestigious jobs and vocations. In many cases, they leave the settlement altogether and join goblin enclaves in other racial settlements as part of the small goblin diaspora.

Hygiene and Fashion

Goblins routinely bathe themselves and clean their dwellings, especially in the city where there is large risk for the smell of what waste they allow themselves. They make soaps from the fats of livestock or their own deceased. Wealthier clans use fats for skin softening.

Jewelry is a common staple, especially among urban goblins. Nose rings, earrings (usually multiple in each ear) are very common. Nipple, navel, and other piercings are also common, as is tattooing, which tends to focus on floral or geometric designs.

Goblins craft garments from leather, furs, textiles from animal hairs. This includes their own hairs from their head and bodies being woven into yarn or fabric. From these, goblin clothing takes the form of trousers, long dresses, long skirts, shirts, coats, gloves, aprons, and any other needed garment. Goblins commonly knit shawls, scarfs, gloves, hats, and other garments. Men wear trousers. Women wear dresses, skirts, or trousers. Women wear trousers if they answer a muster call for war.

Plant-based fibers and fabrics are in short supply and not common among goblin clothing.

Music

Most goblin music centers around what they call a strummer (sitar), a set of prongs (marimba), and a drum or set of drums. These instruments are usually played in bands of three to five, with multiples of some instruments, especially drums. Solo strummers, prongs, or drums can also be played, but most music is enjoyed with the instruments played together. Most clans have a few players and they will routinely play during meals or love-making.

Language

There are many dialects of Goblin that generally center around the nearest city (for example, the Kogylar dialect). All dialects use the same set of symbols for phonetically written Goblin, but different dialects have varied words and accents. Goblins from relatively nearby goblin settlements, for example, the next largest goblin city, would probably be able to understand most of what a Kogylar goblin is trying to communicate, but one from far to the south, north, or deep underground, would not. Ancient Goblin was written in runes.

Hobgoblins and bugbears also speak Goblin as their own tongue, but may have their own dialects. They use the same alphabet as the Goblin language.

Cities and Architecture

Due to the restrictive nature of mountainous terrain, goblins became excellent masons, approaching a rival status with the dwarves, and built into mountains and hills. Like humans, they build up, but like dwarves, they also build down. They consider maximizing the full potential of the land to accommodate structures and functionality, and view inefficient use of the land to be distasteful and foolish. There are few orc cities, but the goblins look down upon their construction the most for its inefficiency and poor form.

They can admire human cities for their form and function, but still consider them limited. Only dwarven masonry causes them to stop and sigh, but even then, goblin and dwarf masons, if they could be on speaking terms, would have a difference of opinion. Even still, in terms of the skill with which they work stone and timber, goblins struggle to reach the level of dwarves simply by the difference in their lifespans. While goblins have a lifespan comparable to humans, dwarves have lifespans two to four times longer.

Goblins usually build cities and other settlements near surface or subsurface water sources. They dig and fill the terrain to divert and enhance water flow, providing constant recirculation. In the case of underground water sources, which is one of the very significant reasons which they build downward, they build mechanisms to carry or divert water to a higher reservoir and provide for the upper levels of the settlement.

More sophisticated cities will create water systems that provide individual domiciles with their own water intake and outtake through ducted or masoned water diversion. Generally, this takes the form of a small portion of a river or stream's flow, freely coursing through a duct or trough in the domicile.

Generally, domiciles on the lower levels of the settlement are considered more prestigious because there is more access to soil for growing roots, the soil is more fertile, the air is moist for mushroom and other fungus growth, and the low light is permissive for types of mushrooms to grow that cannot grow on higher levels. Additional assets are a closer proximity to water, and the availability to expand a domicile by building further down.

Food and Drink

Goblins grow crops and raise livestock like any other race that supports city-bound population, but they are constrained to species that survive in the austere mountains or underground caverns. They keep sheep, goats, hogs, and pigeons for livestock and grow a variety of crops, but largely roots, tubers, and mushrooms. They gather eggs from the pigeons and only use the pigeons for meat if they die, or can no longer lay or fertilize eggs. Goblins gather dairy from sheep and goats, but as they are a no-waste society, will also gather and use their own dairy within their respective clans. There is also a foraging industry for mountain herbs, surface mushrooms, berries, and bird eggs in addition to hunting and trapping.

They bake, but since they cannot grow wheat in the mountains, they use ground and dried root vegetable powder in its place. They prepare a wide variety of dishes with a stronger emphasis on soups and stews in the colder months. Some tribes also make noodles or dumplings from root vegetable flour in varying ways.

They bake bread, cakes, and pastries. They have a strong sugar industry from processing beets, one of their root vegetable crops. With a robust sugar industry, they also produce other confections, such as caramel. Caramels, in particular, are usually prepared as a special family dish.

They drink boiled water, tea from mountain herbs and flowers, and small amounts of mountain berry juices and wines. They prepare a drink from fermented birch bark or birch root, heated and mixed with honey, called birch beer. Birch beer is more common in southern goblin settlements, but the taste for it has spread to most other goblin cities and the unprocessed birch bark is among the many imports from southern settlements.

Goblins, modeling after the example of hobgoblins, also distill their own ridin from potatoes, beets, carrots, or mushrooms. Though goblins have a wide variety of drinks available, anything but boiled water and some teas are limited due to the space to grow or forage the stock for it. Less urban communities that tend to have less ready access to water immediately in their domicile and either have the space to grow and forage the stock or the lower population that will consume less tend to have wider drink varieties. Wealthier urban goblin clans tend to have wider selections of drink, as well.

As goblins have a no-waste mentality, poorly prepared food and drink is still eaten unless there is a risk to health.

Organization for War

Like hobgoblins, goblins have an egalitarian society. Men and women can answer the call for war. Goblins, being physically smaller and weaker, prefer to choose the circumstances of fighting in which they can use their cunning, large numbers, and element of surprise to their advantage.

- **Warparty:** Four to thirty soldiers from the same clan, usually led by the clan leader. Typically, the warparty is not the whole clan, as leaving some adults to care for the hearth and the young is important.

    o **Serpent**: Concept that organizes soldiers into groups of thirty soldiers or less, usually breaking a warparty into several serpents to perform a specific task, usually scouting, infiltration, or raids.

471

- **Warband:** Sixty to two hundred soldiers from various clans. So that the clans survive a defeat, warbands are led by a goblin selected by the tribe's great one or an acknowledged soldier or leader. These groups are self-sufficient and usually able to function as infantry and archers; only some tribes can provide specialized sappers.

- **Fist:** Two hundred to one thousand soldiers, led by an acknowledged soldier or leader that has also been picked by the tribe's great one.

- **Host:** Several thousand soldiers led by the tribe's great one.

Note: Goblin clans plan their pregnancies in advance and ensure that, if called upon, no more than half of the family goes to war. There are always enough females and males remaining at the hearth to care for children, raise the young, maintain the home, and provide for their welfare and prosperity.

Credits

Cover design by Sam Kipp and Morgan Spring-Glace.

All maps by Luke Bauer and Morgan Spring-Glace.

Calligraphy by Esther Wong

Illustrations

Jade Bohlsen:
– *Humans by Ethnicity: Berks and Tamarks.*
– *Humans by Ethnicity: Eklendans and Marins.*

Dale Cordes: *The Witches of Serna.*

Morgan Spring-Glace
– *Elves Arguing with a Human*
– *Portraits of Orcs*
– *Orc Warrior and Orc Slave*
– *Hobgoblins Planning an Attack*
– *Comparison of horse, wolf, and great wolf*
– *Goblins Arguing with a Human*

About the Author

Morgan Spring-Glace grew up in Massachusetts, went to college, joined the U.S. Army in 2004 and served for twenty years (and one day), and has settled in the Midwest U.S. He thinks too much and excels at losing arguments. He is a nerd and a gamer. This is his first novel and is a very fulfilling progression from when he first drew a map of the town of Serna for a future (at the time) campaign setting in 2011. For more information, updates and previews of future content, visit www.morganspringglace.com.

Note from the Author

This is the first book I ever wrote. I hope that you've enjoyed the beginning of the War of the Mountains. I hope that I've given you characters on all sides (note that I don't say 'both sides') for whom to cheer or loathe. If this has been enjoyable - or unenjoyable - please leave me a review. I read all of the reviews and am a believer that feedback is a gift. The more reviews we get, more likely it is for other readers to discover this series and the more that can share this story.

I'd appreciate your review here:
https://www.amazon.com/dp/B0DHZZQPFG

Thank you for taking this journey with me. The next book, Unseen Wrath, is waiting for you.